STONE LORD:
THE LEGEND OF KING ARTHUR

THE ERA OF STONEHENGE

BY

J.P. REEDMAN

First Published in Great Britain 2012 by Mirador Publishing

First edition: 2012

Any reference to real names and places are purely fictional and are constructs of the author. Any offence the references produce is unintentional and in no way reflects the reality of any locations or people involved.

A copy of this work is available through the British Library.

ISBN: 978-1-908200-95-2

Mirador Publishing
Mirador
Wearne Lane
Langport
Somerset
TA10 9HB

DEDICATED TO RICHARD 'KIP' CARPENTER

PART ONE — MERLIN: MOONRISE

CHAPTER ONE

The Stones demanded blood.

Blood to bathe their stony feet, to bind their cumbrous bodies to the earth.

So it had always been. The Chosen would die, the marked One touched by the spirits since birth.

In the settlement of Faraon, the child who was Chosen dwelt with his mother in a filthy lean-to that bordered the pigsty and the midden. His boy-name was Lailoq 'the Friend' — but he name was a lie. He had no friends among the people ruled by the chieftain Vhortiern.

Lailoq was an outcast, a scapegoat, along with mother, Keine of the White Streak. Children spat as he walked by, and elders made signs against evil when he went around on his daily chores, a clay pot balanced on his head and a sack of kindling bound to his scrawny back.

His mother, Keine, was to blame for his misfortune. She had been beautiful once, desirable, perhaps even a potential bedmate for Vhortiern himself. But she had a white streak in her dark hair — an ominous sign, a flaw that beckoned to interested spirits — and one night, twelve Sun-turnings before, those spirits came to claim her. She had drifted away from the Midwinter fire-feast to enter the woods, the taboo area of the Old Hunters. Three days she went missing, and the people beat ancestors' thighbones on the ground and mourned for her as one dead.

However, on the new Moon's rise, she returned, dazed and raving, telling tales of bears with the voices of men, and crows that stood tall as young saplings. They had danced with her in the forest and begged her to join them. Their leader was called Min'kammus; stag's horns crowned his head and his cloak the pelt of the spotted deer. He had led her through the dance, and wetted her lips with fire-mead, and eventually he took her away from the ring of dancing beasts and danced with her in the way of men with women. She fled at night's end, fearful of what she had done, of the dread being she had lain with in the shuddering forest, but it was too late. The horned chief, whatever he was, man or beast, god or spirit, had left her with a gift — or curse — from that solitary coupling. The seed of his unnatural loins blossomed like a dark flower in her belly, and Keine soon grew great in size to match the pregnant full Moon.

Lailoq had come squalling into the world on an eve when Tarahn the Thunderer smote the hills with his thunder-axe and sent the deer of doe-eyed Fleesh running in fright. Small and dark, with a long, black-furred head and deep, bird-like eyes, he resembled a wizened little old man rather than an innocent newborn babe. Six fingers grew on his right hand, a sure mark of the malevolent spirit-world.

So it was no surprise, some twelve years later, that he was Chosen be given to the Stones. It was not a common thing, not any more, though such sacrifices had been frequent enough in the times of the early kings of Albu — the bloody but glorious days of the tin-kings Samothos, Sarron and Longho, and before them Raven-lord Brahn and his sons Brito and Amaethan, who brought agriculture to the land.

But when Vhortiern and his men were unsuccessful in raising the final two stones of their holy circle at Din-Amnon, and the pillars tumbled down, crushing heads and smashing bones, fearful and frenzied whispers went through the tribe: "The Ancestors are angry! The Ancestors want blood and bone! Something must be done, a gift must be given!"

Chief Vhortiern had no doubt what the gift must be, and who. Axe in hand to assert his might, he went to Keine of the White Streak in her hovel, and asked for the boy. Keine shrieked and wailed and tore her hair, but he would not be moved by her torment. The boy Lailoq, sitting by the pitiful, half-dead fire, said nothing, but went quietly with the chieftain to be prepared for the act of making the stones sacred.

The time of the sacrifice was set for twilight, when the veil between the worlds of the living and dead grew thin, and barrows on the hills opened their stony wombs and released the ghosts of the Ancestors, for good or for ill. Wearing masks and painted with ash and ochre, the village folk began their procession from Faraon toward the high ground where the unfinished stone circle lay under a blood-streaked evening sky.

Even incomplete, the ring was a marvellous sight. Two massive portal stones of white quartz, twice a tall man's height, lay stretched out on the grass before empty stone-holes that yawned like waiting mouths. Behind them stood a neat oval of stunted blue-green stones, open to the East and aligned on a gap in the sunset-bloodied peaks of the Holy Mountain known as God-of-Bronze.

Vhortiern entered the circle first, as was his right as chief, followed closely by the village Shaman, the Old Woman of No Name, who had lived longer than any other in the tribe, and had blood-ties to almost all. An infant's skull hung on a loop round her neck, and a mask with a wooden nose curved like the sickle-Moon covered her shrunken face. The mask's eyes were ochred scallop shells brought from distant seashore, and masses of dung-stiffened grass hair fanned out from the rim, giving the mask a crazed, grotesque appearance.

It was the face of Death. Of She-Who-Guards.

Behind the chief and the shaman walked the important men of the tribe, harsh vertical stripes and rib-bone patterns daubed onto their torsos, their thick manes of hair plaited into fantastical knots and tails. Their wives trailed after, painted moss green from head to toe, the colour of death and Otherness. Both sexes danced as they processed into the circle, beating on skin drums and making hideous keening sounds with pipes made of perforated bone.

They surrounded the sacrifice, the fatherless boy, circling, swooping, spitting, calling on the Ancestors to take him and his evil luck away and let their stone circle stand. Lailoq walked amid them as if he feared nothing and merely looked on this as an adventure. Some folk sneered and nudged each other. "Look, he is simple," they whispered. "He does not cry, he does not know he is to die…"

Overhearing, the boy fixed them with an unnerving smile, and something about his dark, sharp face made them quail and reach inside their cowhide tunics to touch the talismans that hung there.

Lailoq had been dressed and adorned for the role of sacrifice — the only time he had ever worn other than scraps of skins. A pale linen robe tumbled to his calves, and his long black hair had been greased back with pig-fat and twined with the feathers of hawks. His face was painted a livid blue, the colour of a corpse, to show that he was already dead to the tribe, already half in the Otherworld.

Vhortiern gazed at him uneasily. He wanted this night to be over. He was not squeamish about breaking the boy's head and letting out his spirit, for he thought the brat should have been exposed at birth — but there was a depth, a darkness, in those glittering and somehow ancient black eyes that almost unmanned him.

Unconsciously, he stroked the worn, gold-pinned head of his war-axe, the Good Striker, a thousand years old and made of jadeite from a half-forgotten motherland beyond the shores of Albu the White. Tonight Striker would

3

drink, and the stones would drink too, and the angry Ancestors, always demanding their due, refusing to be forgotten, would allow the Man-stone and Mother-stone to rise and stand together, framing Sun and Moon and Holy Mountain.

A sound from Lailoq made him jump, and he eyed the brat with renewed suspicion. Would this be the beginning of tears, of fighting and begging? He felt suddenly old and tired, all too aware of his own vulnerable young sons, asleep back in his hut in Faraon. He just wanted the sacrifice to be over and the stones to rise, a lasting tribute to the spirits that would make them whisper his name with pleasure and confer fruitful harvests on his folk.

He let his hard, jaded eyes travel to the scrawny, linen-clad boy, who had wandered up to the diamond-shaped Mother-stone and was staring at it if willing it to leap up from the ground and fly. Suddenly the child squatted down, staring intently into the empty stone-hole beside the menhir, making the Chief fear the brat was going to jump in and start some futile fight for existence there in the gathering gloom.

Instead, the boy kneaded the earth with his horrible six-fingered hand — like some beast's paw, Vhortiern thought with a shudder — and suddenly his eyes gleamed, glowed even, green sparks breaking their deep darkness. Vhortiern scowled, making a sign against evil behind his back. He thought of Stag-man and Bear-man and Crow-man in the woods, tumbling white-streaked Keine whom he had once desired, and getting this fey, half-animal child, and he knew it was right that Lailoq should die…

The brat was making a low, guttural noise, a self-satisfied kind of growl. He snapped his long brown fingers at the chieftain, his stance one of an equal, not of one whose life was forfeit for the good of the people. "Chief Vhortiern, you must not use Good Striker tonight!" the boy cried, his voice harsh as the shrieks of the bird of prey he resembled. Not a child's shrill voice, but that of a fell spirit, surely. "If you slay me, it will not make the stones stand. You will raise them but they will fall again, like dead men. You will bring other children to them, one by one, till the village's child-wealth is all spent and only crones and greybeards dwell in Faraon, weeping for their lost future. Never will your stones stand, and the village will become a cursed place of dust and bone."

Vhortiern's face grew white; his heavy brows bristled. "What do you know, you who are the Son of Nothing?"

Lailoq smiled slyly, his strange, fevered eyes sucking up the last of the lingering light. "I know much, much more than you think, Chieftain. In the village pigsty I listened to the grunts of the Great White Sow, dead-eater and prophecy-maker. I understood her tongue. From her, I learned how to commune with the dead in their cairns and with the hunting spirits who wander the forest. I have heard the voices of the trees and conversed with salmon in the rivers. And I hear voices calling me now, from deep beneath the earth."

"What voices are they?" Vhortiern grunted, unable to control the shivers that ran up his spine. Why did this unseelie creature disturb him so? He was just a boy. A tainted boy.

"The shrieks of Wyrms, two great serpents that battle and slash each other with their fangs!" Lailoq licked his lips almost eagerly. His tongue looked too red, too bright, to the uneasy Chief, and it was pointed like a snake's. "One is Moon-pale with eyes of flame, the other fire-red with breath of smoke. They battle for supremacy under this hill, and their shudders are what make the stones fall!"

Vhortiern felt sick. He should have guessed some evil slumbered on this hill. An old burial mound had been cleared away in order to build the circle; its bony occupants had come from another tribe and he had smashed the skulls and cast them into the offerings shafts near the village. It had been a foolish move.

The Old Woman with No Name limped forward now, removing the mask from her dried-up, toothless sack of a face. Ugly as she was, her eyes still shone a brilliant sea-blue, and they were keen and intelligent. "So, boy, if what you say about these Wyrms is true, what must be done?"

"Old Grandmother," said Lailoq, "let the men come and re-make the pits to hold the stones. They must be wider and deeper, and the women must help too by packing their bases firmly, with no gaps. The packing stones must be magic stones, red ones for the red serpent and white quartz for the pale one. Once the stones are properly laid down, they will seal the angry serpents below us, and the stones will not fall."

Vhortiern glanced at the Old Woman; he feared her, disliked her, even, but she was versed in lore and magic, and he had no choice but to ask her advice. "What is your counsel, old one?"

The Old Woman with No Name put a painted claw on Lailoq's greasy dark head; she looked almost fondly at him, and for a moment Vhortiern noticed a similarity in the thin but determined jaw, the jutting bird-beak nose. He had not noticed such a look before; the boy had seemed to him completely foreign, a changeling creature. Could the Old One have lost her edge and decided to protect this cursed boy because of some real or imagined kinship?

5

"Let us try the way he describes," she said. "He is half of the Otherworld; maybe he speaks truth. But if he fails to quiet these Serpents-Under-Earth, I myself will break his skull and add his knucklebones to my necklace."

And so, shortly before the next full Moon, the stone holes were dug anew, using the shoulder blades of oxen as shovels, and the two menhirs were tipped into them and packed firmly at their bases with skull-sized chunks of quartz and red sandstone. The Old Woman sprinkled lamb's blood on the stones, and kissed them and bowed to them, while men and women wove a spiral dance around the ring, and singing and feasting went on in the village for seven nights and days, until the full Moon crested the utmost peak of God-of-Bronze and sailed West into the Deadlands.

At last the stones stood, proud and tall — without the blood of a fatherless boy to hold them fast to the ground.

As for the Child, the Chosen One, he was no longer an object of scorn and hatred in the village. Men still feared him, but he was also revered for his wisdom in the matter of the stones. His rags were burned and offered at the circle, and the Old Woman gave him a deerskin tunic painted with magic signs. She wove bronze rings in his hair and hung a blue bead shaped like a star around his neck on a thong.

And on the Feast of the Summer-lord, when the dawn Sun made a path of gold between the massive portals of Din-Amnon, the youth stepped forward with all the tribesfolk watching, to be made a man of the people. Vhortiern gave him a bow and quiver of arrows and cut the marks of manhood on his cheeks, then rubbed them with woad that the women had ground that morning. A lock of his hair was cut and burned as an offering to the Ancestors, and the ashes scattered in the grass. So too, were his fingernails pared and then burned.

"Swear that you will serve me," said the Chief sternly, "as my magic man, from this day forward. Swear this oath, and use your wiles and wisdom to protect me and mine from the Otherworld, and you will be held higher in esteem than my best warriors!"

"I swear." Lailoq smiled his unnerving crooked smile. "I will serve you till the day you go to live among the Ancestors, great Chief Vhortiern."

Vhortiern extended his hand, thick as a club and massed with scars as pale as the white serpent now pinioned below the Man-stone at the entrance to the sacred circle. "Then let you take your place by my right hand side!

Cast off your childhood name of Lailoq, and choose you the name by which a man shall be known!"

Lailoq lifted his arms toward heaven, as if embracing the Sun, which hung like a fiery eye in the Eastern sky. He took a deep breath as he stared into the heavens, searching, seeking, summoning. A shriek sounded high above, and a winged shape suddenly darkened the face of the sun, before plunging down like a deadly dart, straight towards Lailoq.

Vhortiern shied away, grimacing, while the women watching outside the circle began to wail in terror.

They fell silent when they realised the creature did not attack. It glided gracefully onto Lailoq's upraised arm, talons carefully seizing his forearm without puncturing flesh. It flapped lustrous wings and uttered a sharp cry from its hooked beak.

It was a Merlin, a hawk, a shrewd predator who flew among the lonely hills, seeking prey.

"From now on, you will call me by the name of this beast that is my brother," said Lailoq, who was no longer Lailoq — and the hawk that was his totem-animal screamed defiance into the growing light. "From this day forth I shall be called the Merlin."

The Merlin of Din Faraon thrived in his new honoured position. Wise and canny, he advised Vhortiern in matters of commerce and war, and soon traders from far and wide traversed the green hills to reach Faraon, making white tracks across the countryside with the passage of so many feet. They traded skins and beads and weapons, all under Merlin's shrewd gaze, and soon the daggers of the men of Faraon grew longer, and they replaced their old stone axes with fine new ones of bronze.

Merlin himself continued to learn the lore of all within heaven and earth under the tutelage of the Old Woman of No Name... who, to her young pupil, was not nameless. She had whispered her secret, true name, Buan-ann, into his ear at his initiatory rites, as a sign of her trust and approval.

"I won't lie and say I wouldn't have killed you, if it had been asked of me," she cackled, when she took him into the nearby forests to gather mushrooms that would open the spirit-world, and willow-bark to soothe the villagers who had bone-bend and tooth-rot, "but I always hoped it wouldn't come to that. Man with no father... pah..." She spat on the forest floor. "I can see the Old People, the Hunters, in you, boy. Their blood's in me too,

7

probably in most of us, if truth be known. And undoubtedly something of a hunter was in your mother, too, that fateful night she vanished! Ahhheee." She laughed at her own ribald joke, slapping her thighs with gnarly hands.

The Merlin laughed too, like any young lad fascinated by talk of the secret rite between man and woman of which he had no real knowledge as yet. But he was more curious about other things Buan-ann had told him. "Who are these hunters; what is their tribe?"

"We do not know, for their tongue is like gravel falling from the hillsides! They were here before us, long before, and our fathers have been here long enough. They do not farm or build homes; they travel like the wind, eating only woodland berries and flesh of wild beasts. They are now almost gone; their life was a harsh one. Some eventually became farmers like us and hence our blood is mixed."

Merlin nodded, glad to know that his father was perhaps not a forest-demon and but a man. He would not tell any but Buan-ann that, though — a suspected otherworldly origin could aid him in his role as magic man.

Buan-ann smiled at him, all gums save for one grizzled tooth. "You secret is safe with me," she laughed "Now come, I will teach you the song that pleases old River-woman, so that she will not suck you down to her reedy bed when you go swimming!"

A year passed, and one night shortly after the Feast of Lambing, Buan-ann did not rise from her bed. The women attended her, but no potion could bring her back, and by dawn her spirit had begun the journey across the Great Plain to the Summerlands of the West.

She was carried from her hut on a plank of stout oak, held by the strongest youths of the tribe. She had been wrapped in deer hide and her hair combed and braided. Flowers wreathed her grey head and her neck was draped with amber, like golden tears on her silent breast. Beside her lay a rattle to show the gods in the Otherworld that she was a magic-woman and by her head was placed the ball of worn quartz in which she had divined the future. She was carried to a high hill with a flat top; a spirit-stone gazed out from here, pointing toward the dark slopes and rilled fangs of God-of-Bronze, which men whispered was an entrance to Ahn-un, Land-of-the-Dead.

Here she was laid out on a pyre of hazel-wood. The villagers milled round, women first, men following, singing and dancing as they circled her bier. Then, when they had whipped themselves into a frenzy of grief, they lit many torches and hurled them onto the pyre with much wailing and keening. The dry wood crackled and went up in great orange flames. Flesh hissed, and Buan-ann's skull shrivelled and blackened, bowing down toward her ball of quartz, as if summoning its power to guide her upon her final journey.

Merlin sang and howled, leaping like a young deer beneath the smoke-filled sky and pretending it was rain on his cheeks and not tears. She had been a good friend — the first ever for friendless Lailoq, and he was grieved to lose her wisdom and companionship.

When the pyre had burnt to ashes, Merlin picked through the wreckage, muttering the chant that calmed dead souls. One by one, he placed the charred and fragmented shards that had once been his mentor in a wide-brimmed urn.

He halted for a moment, breath ragged, as he spotted something shining in the heap of ash and calcined bones.

The crystal ball, bright and pure as if the fire had not touched it.

He knew then: he was meant to have it. A final gift from Buan-ann as she departed to the Undying Land. A sign for him, that he was indeed the one to take her place and commune with both man and spirit. He placed the still-hot ball to his forehead and prayed, while the sky shone with all the fires of the gods and the women carried Buan-ann's urn away to the river, to mingle her ashes with the waters that streamed out towards the flowing sea.

###

As the year grew warmer and the feast of the Longest Day and Shortest Night came and went, Merlin sought audience with Vhortiern and announced that he would be going West, to continue learning the wise-man's craft with the great high wizards who dwelt on Mhon. Grumpily, the chief granted his permission, but made Merlin swear not to stay past the autumn Equinox, the Day of Balance, when neither Light nor Dark had power over the other. "The traders come at that time," he said, "and your slick tongue soothes them better than my rough one. You owe me that tongue, boy... I mean, Merlin; it is I who saw your... greatness... and spared your life. Remember that."

So the Merlin set out for the West, carrying only his copper dagger, a bow and a shaman's hazel staff, to visit the Oak-Seers who lived in the groves of Mhon, the Mother Isle, which jutted like a spear-head into the stormy seas between Prydn and its sister isle, Ibherna. He stayed with them awhile, and they taught him of the movements of Sun and stars, and how the great spirits had made them so, and what would please those heavenly beings and keep them upon a steady and favourable path. Then, with the Oak-Seer's aid and blessing, he travelled onwards in a coracle of bark and skins, and, borne by a skirling tide, reached the shores of Ibherna itself, deep green under a red Sunset.

Trudging inward from the coast, over many days he sought out the sanctuary of the native goddess, Brygyndo, Fiery Arrow. Brygyndo was worshipped in a wooden temple in the heart of a great earthen ring; nearby were the tallest standing stones found in Ibherna, near equal in size to the great monoliths of Khor Ghor, that most famous of Temples that lay upon the Great Plain in the south of Albu.

Inside the temple precinct, an eternal flame burned before Brygyndo's Three-faced effigy, and a priestess known as Brig-ahn who was healer, birthing-woman and deadly archer, tended the hearth and minded the statue.

This Brig-ahn, a tall woman with crimson-stained hair and ear and lips plugs of jet readily invited the Merlin into the sanctuary, as was the wont of her cult; no one seeking succour or solace was ever turned away from the Shrine of Fiery Arrow. Merlin made his offering to the Lady of that place — a gleaming lucite arrowhead with long barbs, so thin and painstakingly crafted it could only be used by the spirit-world — and then sat in meditation, breathing in the herb-scented smoke that coiled round the chamber. He had chosen to come here because he wished to follow the footsteps of another Merlin, who had visited Brygyndo's shrine countless lifetimes ago, studying the God-stones that guarded the sanctuary. An ancient forebear Merlin who had brought his followers to the peaks of God-of-Bronze, where they quarried pillars of bluestone, a type of doleritic stone speckled with white flecks that made them resemble a starry night sky. These stones were dragged to the coast and sent on a perilous journey to the south, where they were used to build the inner circles of Khor Ghor, the Dance-of-Great-Spirits, on the barren expanse of the Great Plain.

The priestess Brig-ahn gazed at the youth, cross-legged amid the smoke, and her eyes were hooded, thoughtful. "Times of change come to our sister isles," she said. "The world is changing, as the world must. Rumours have come that many great cities in the hot seas of the south have fallen into fiery ruin, that corsairs harry their shores and survivors have taken to the hills. We are more fortunate here, in our isolation, but even so there has been an increase in Sea-Raiders in the last year — black-bearded men from far in the East, the likes of which we have not seen before. Some call them demons, but they are only men. Greedy men. They seek gold, they seek tin, but they wish to take all for themselves and not to engage in legitimate trade. Several villages on our coasts have been burned by these raiders when they were denied access to our mines."

Merlin nodded. "The rumours of these Sea-Pirates have come to my ears too, brought by the traders on the Golden Path that runs through God-of-Bronze, whose peaks gaze out towards Ibherna. But in the valleys my people have not encountered them; we have kept safe. The mountain regions have always repelled unwelcome visitors."

"They will come, nonetheless," said Brig-ahn, sighing deeply. "Their greed and fury will eventually make them leave their boats and fare far ashore. Even mountains will not hold them back, if they think there is plunder to be won, and foolish, timid people who will offer them no challenge."

Merlin rubbed his chin, with its haze of youthful stubble. "If you can, Great Lady, give me counsel in this matter, as your predecessor of ancient days gave wisdom to the Merlin of old, the Merlin who raised the temple of Khor Ghor with arts learned from Ibherna's own Stones."

The priestess sighed. "Our peoples are fractious and have ever been so. Prydn needs a chief who will be strong enough to gather the tribes together, to lead them against these incomers, using new ways of warfare that the invaders will not expect."

"You are not thinking of my chief, Vhortiern, are you?" Merlin laughed mockingly. "He dreams of his days as a warrior, but his belly grows fat and his arm trembles."

Brig-ahn shook her head. "In the south of Albu, men still gather every year at Khor Ghor. Back many lifetimes ago, five chiefs — Samothos, Sarron, Longho, Harbron and Gorbonian — came to that place, marked by five settings of stones that stretch to heaven, and they forged the laws that men of the Isle of Prydn lived by. Samothos held supreme sway above the rest, as king of the Great Trilithon, the place where the Sun dies at Midwinter, and under him the isle grew strong and prosperous. But then, plague laid the kings low and their line was extinguished. No high-king has ruled Albu the White for many generations. The time without a strong leader must come to an end, and a king return to Prydn. A king...and another Merlin like the Merlin of old."

The young shaman was silent, but his heart suddenly leaped, beating like a wild, trapped thing against his ribs. Khor Ghor, the temple of the Ancestors, receptacle of Sun-Face and Moon's eye! Khor Ghor, a mighty marvel begun by his own namesake, the Merlin of ancient times, one of a

11

long line of Merlins. Perhaps he would be next in that illustrious line, the next to reap undying fame amidst the frowning pillars of that great structure, unique among the monuments of the tribes of Prydn. A place some called, in dread, the Tomb of all Hope, with its five inner trilithons forming portals that led into the Otherworld.

Brig-ahn smiled at him, almost slyly, cobweb creases fanning out from her pale blue eyes and too-rich mouth. She had seemed quite youthful at first, with her flame hair and painted cheeks, but now she had suddenly grown old, an ancient crone, both wise and deadly, hiding behind the veneer of youth. She might be twenty summers old, or two thousand. "Your eyes are on fire at the mention of that dread place! It is in your heart, is it not? And so it might well be. For are you not known as the Merlin, like he who raised the first stones? Are you not Chosen, the child of no mortal man? Yes, even here, the rumours have come of a fatherless boy who found two Wyrms that fought beneath the earth and tamed them."

Merlin scowled, looking like a petulant lad rather than a powerful, albeit youthful, shaman. "My chief, Vhortiern, has bound me to him, by my blood. I may not leave Faraon while he lives. So I have sworn"

"Blood." The Priestess stoked up the sacred fire. Shadows leaped around the thatched temple, stretching long from the triadic carving of Fiery-Arrow on its plinth before the hearth. "Blood bond may be broken in many ways. Think on this. You know it to be true, and you will know, when the time comes, what you must do... But do not think too long; for if action is delayed, the sea-men will come and destroy all you hold dear."

Pondering the Priestess's words, the Merlin left the sanctuary of Fiery Arrow the next morn and began his arduous journey back to Prydn. Journeying to the seastrand, where men fished along the shore, he gained passage across the waters by offering a fisherman a weather-spell to protect his coracle from the tumultuous tides of Mah-nan the Sea-lord.. Reaching the coast of Prydn after a long but uneventful crossing, the shaman bade the old sailor farewell, then shouldered bow and staff and began a forced march toward the stark silhouette of God-of-Bronze. He reached the boundaries of Vhortiern's territory close to the Time of Balance, just as he had promised.

As he arrived in the village, coming on weary feet down the long track over the moor, he felt a creeping unease. All looked the same, the clustered huts with their belching smoke-holes, the pigsties and the heaped midden, the little stream where the women beat clothes on rocks. But he felt a change, subtle and indescribable, as if, in the time he was absent, all he knew best had been wiped away, making it a very different place to that which he had left.

His unease heightened when one of the village children, recognising him, rushed forward with a loud squeal. "Merlin, Merlin, you've come back to us! Look what I've got, Merlin!"

The child, a little lad named Starn, held up his arm. On his wrist was a beaded bracelet. Merlin had not seen its like before, tiny seed-like beads in rainbow colours sewn on to a strip of cloth. He knew, though, that it was cheap and ill-made, and there was a smoky, unknown fragrance that clung to it, an alien perfume that reeked of faraway places.

"Starn, where did you get this thing?" he asked sternly.

The child looked afraid; he hid his arm with the cloth bracelet behind his back as if fearing Merlin would snatch his prize from him. "Just some traders, Merlin. They have been in Faraon since the day after you left. They are funny men, Merlin. Their hair curls like sheep's wool, and they pour oil on it — how it stinks! They paint their eyes too, like women. But they are rich; they have many good things that we have never seen before. They tell such wonderful stories of faraway lands where the Sun is always shining."

"They have been here a long time for traders," Merlin muttered, half to himself.

"Yes. But that is because chief Vhortiern plans to wed one of the stranger's women."

Merlin's eyes widened in shock and anger, but he fought to hide his rage from the child. "You have done well to tell me, Starn. Now, run along, I must see Vhortiern at once."

Grasping the hilt of his dagger, he slowly entered the village and approached Vhortiern's large hut with its carved doorposts all bloodied from offerings to household spirits. The skin flap across the door was pinned aside, and he could hear raucous laughter and the clink of drinking beakers within.

He pushed his way into the hut and stood blinking, forcing his eyes to adjust to the gloom. Vhortiern sat cross-legged on a fur, decked out in his chieftain's finery, three golden buttons on his tunic, his dagger and axe on one knee and Good Striker upon the other. His wives, Kymidei and Tyndri squatted beside him, dripping with necklaces of blue and honey-coloured beads. They were entertaining several well-fed men with wiry black hair and prominent features, whose long curled beards gleamed under coatings of scented oil. They wore tunics in colours Merlin had only even seen in rainbows, and the swords at their belts were long and grooved.

13

"Merlin, my friend, you've returned!" shouted Vhortiern, his face flushed from the honey-drink he had imbibed. "Meet Kaash and Ven, traders from afar. They have come seeking tin. Our tin. They have offered us great things in exchange, barrels of the magic drink of their land, fine jewels that will make us the envy of Albu...Even a fair daughter of the tribe, the Rho-han." He pointed to a sullen dark girl crouched by one of the woolly-bearded strangers, her brown eyes mutinous, her lower lip in a sullen pout.

Merlin did not like the look or stance of these men, or the girl, and wouldn't have even had not Brig-ahn warned him of the Sea-Raiders. "I would not rape the wealth of our mountains for a mere tub of foreign drink," he said harshly. "Or the unwilling flesh of a woman scarce better than a slave."

One of the foreigners, Ven, spread his be-ringed hands and flashed a wide grin. His face was long and his teeth were large, like a horse's teeth. "Do not fear, my friend." He spoke the language of Prydn in a thickly accented voice. "I forgive you your distrust and harsh words. But your folk have so much tin and gold, what little we take will not harm your supply at all. As your chieftain," he stressed the word, "has realised, your tribe will most fortunate if you cooperate with us. Just think of the treasures that we could bring you from our homelands! No enmity need be between our peoples; once Rho-han and Vhortiern wed, we will be almost as kin."

Merlin's face darkened with fury. He was young but no fool. Unlike Vhortiern, he could see the cold insincerity in Ven's eyes, the disdain for northern savages who would gladly trade their tribe's freedom for a few baubles. "Our tin lies in the heart of the mountain known as God-of-Bronze," he said between clenched teeth. "It is a sacred mountain. It is said to be one of the entrances to the Deadlands of Ahn-un. If you strangers go there uninvited, I will call the wrath of the mountain down upon you!"

The dark-bearded men cast each other angry, darting looks. Vhortiern's face purpled. "Merlin! They are to give us swords and spears, arms such as we have never owned! We could rule the entire West — or more! None surely would have the strength to stand against us, with the sea-strangers at our backs."

"At our backs, ready to stab us with their sharp daggers!" cried Merlin, and he whirled around and grabbed the tunic of one of the foreign men, dragging him from the mat where he squatted and hauling him to his feet.

"Where are the rest of your men? What have you planned? That we show you our mines, then you slaughter us all?"

The man flailed clumsily, his teeth bared like a mad dog's against his raven beard. Merlin slung him towards Vhortiern and the girl Rho-han. He fell with a crash at Rho-han's feet, crushing pottery beneath him. The girl leapt up with an angry shriek and fled from the hut into the twilight while Ven shouted furiously after her.

Vhortiern bellowed and drew his dagger from its horn sheath; it glowed like a tongue of flame in the gloomy hut. Merlin's eyes sparked in his thin, dark face, already weather-beaten despite his youth. "Do you dare, chief? Do you raise hand to one who speaks with the spirits? Think deeply before you strike, what that deed could bring you!"

At that moment, the hanging in the door of the hut was torn aside and two village youths tumbled in, panting and wild-eyed. "What do you want?" roared Vhortiern, striding towards the pair with dagger in hand, ready to strike anything, anyone, in his anger.

"There are men in the wood, armed men!" cried one of the boys, waving his arms frantically. "We've seen them! They attacked Yde when she was washing clothes by the ford, but she got away...

"I warned you, chief!" cried Merlin, rounding on Vhortiern with flashing eyes. "This is the price of your greed!"

Immediately Vhortiern's attendant warriors sprang into action, grabbing Ven and Kaash and binding them. Vhortiern himself staggered out into the smoky twilight, axe in one hand, dagger in the other, shouting 'To me, warriors, to me!' One of his older sons blew on a great cow's horn and the rest of the warriors of Faraon poured out of their huts, raising knives and axes both of ancient stone and new-wrought bronze. Shouting in fear and excitement, eager for action, they streamed down the hillside toward the wooded valley below, cloaked with a cap of mist that concealed both friend and foe.

Merlin did not follow them. His heart felt heavy, his mind troubled. All his learning, his natural-born arts, yet he was oath-bound to a fool who would sell his own people for a girl and a few trinkets. A vision entered his mind of the other Merlin, the one who had used his Arts to build the circle of Khor Ghor. He longed to be such a one, whose power would be remembered forever, whose memories were whispered from the stones to the grass to the everlasting sky.

In that instant he knew what course he must take. Oath or not, he had to leave the oppressive atmosphere of Faraon. Maybe he would become a priest of Khor Ghor, as he desired... or maybe he would be slain as an interloper by unfriendly priests, shot full of arrows and dumped in the ditch... His fate, his future, was in the hands of the spirits. What he would not do is waste

15

more time in a backwater where he would grow old and die with his potential unrealised.

Snatching up his staff, he stalked from the village and hurried to join the Golden Road that wound past Din-Amnon and curled like a Wyrm's tail across the ridged brow of God-of-Bronze. Women and children called after him — he could hear Keine weeping — but he did not glance back at them least his resolve was lessened.

As he reached the soul-stones on their lonely moor, the first stars were coming out, dancing over their dark tips. He paused and bowed in respect to the Ancestors, remembering how close he had come to joining them, aware they still might be angry because they did not receive the gift of his blood. He noticed that a piglet's carcass had been placed at the foot of the mother-stone, its eyes plucked by the ravens.

A pig when it should have been a child…

Suddenly out of the wispy night fog a figure rose, lurching and lumbering, malevolent. Despite himself, Merlin jumped in alarm, his breathing ragged… and then he recognised Vhortiern.

Vhortiern bloodied to the shoulder, the Good-striker a gory mess in his hand.

"Why are you here?" asked Merlin. "Should you not be in the valley, seeking to undo the evil you have wrought?"

"The battle is over. I have killed the foreigners — all of them," panted Vhortiern. "Ven's head." He reached under his woollen cape and flung a gaping severed head to the ground. It bounced along by Merlin's feet, and he stepped away in disgust. "I brought it here to appease the Old Ones, who will be angry at me, for it was I who let these wolves in amongst our people."

His eyes suddenly narrowed. "But why are you skulking around by the stones? Where were you during the battle?"

Merlin's face turned hard as flint. He raised his arm, and his Merlin-hawk flew down with a cry and flutter of wings. "I leave Faraon again, Chief. This time for good. I will not stay in this place. You have sullied it with the blood of those sea-devils that wanted our tin…and our freedom as a people. I go to Khor Ghor, to see if they will have me, and maybe the wise there can raise a force against these ill-starred men who will seek our shores as long as there are men like you to let them get a foothold!"

Vhortiern made a strangled sound, half-enraged and half-surprised. "You are my magic-man. I forbid this! You have brought luck to Faraon, and if you go, all I value may fail…" He grasped Merlin's shoulders, shaking him, spittle flecking his lips in fury as he shouted, "You swore to stay with me…"

"Until the day you go to the Ancestors…"

Merlin's copper dagger leapt out of the dark like one of the stars above the mountains. It pierced Vhortiern's chest, drove deep. "You are old, Vhortiern; old kings must die before their dotage causes crops and the wombs of beasts and women to fail," he said coldly. "Go now to the Ancestors; your sons are young and hale and will be better rulers than you."

Vhortiern sank to his knees, face white with shock. He grasped at his chest; blood welled between his fingers and splattered the ground like red rain. He staggered against the long Man-stone, then thudded to his knees. Good-Striker rolled in the grass beside him.

Merlin picked up the chief's axe, beautiful, polished, its head jade-green beneath a slime of blood and brain. It was a fine thing, ancient and full of power. He raised it to his lips and whispered, "Make it swift, great Ancestors. Take the life of this one as final payment for sparing mine, and may my blood-debt to you be finished forever."

He swung the axe and it crashed into Vhortiern's temple. The big man crumpled silently, his skull a shattered ruin, and Merlin watched his death-throes in solemn contemplation, divining the future from his last twitching contortions. He noticed, with a sense of elation, that the already stiffening fingers on Vhortiern's out flung arm pointed to the south — toward the gentler lands of Albu and the pathways that led to the fabled temple of Khor Ghor.

CHAPTER TWO

Merlin wound his way up to the spires of God-of-Bronze, the Golden Road a pale ribbon beneath his feet. He passed the outcrops where the first Merlin had quarried the bluestones of Khor Ghor, and bathed his feet in the healing springs that sprang around the sacred dolerite. Then, to pay the stone-spirits for his safe passage, he sheared off a single lock of hair to leave as an offering on the capstone of the tiny ancestral tomb on the summit of the mountain. The shorn strands blew away like smoke, towards the South.

Towards Khor Ghor.

Descending from the mountains into tamer lands, he abandoned the Golden Road, fearful of encountering traders heading West, who might give information of his whereabouts, willingly or not, to Vhortiern's vengeful kinsmen. He set out across open country instead, climbing banks and fording streams, sending his hawk ahead and following its shadow on the grass.

He passed through the Valley of Wolves, where he walked with drawn bow and watched every rock, and crested the Bald Hills and the Black Hills, where no trees grew and the earth was dark and ashen as if it has been burned in ancient fire. Then he began a slow journey South into lower, flatter lands covered in deep vegetation, until, at last, he reached the banks of the mighty, green-brown river sacred to the spirit Ha-bren, who every year caused a great tidal bore to roar inland, sweeping all before it. Ha-bren could be dangerous and capricious, but not to all men — she allowed many to sail and fish her waters unharmed. Still, in order to ensure her favour, Merlin tossed her a quartz pebble from the magic-bag at his waist before continuing his journey along her banks.

Ha-bren must have been pleased by the gift. Not long after he deposited the pebble, Merlin saw smoke rising from a gaggle of huts near the riverbank. He had been guided to food and lodging. As he drew near, he noted the pungent smell of fish, and wrinkled his face in disgust — fish was taboo to his people, who ate only meat and grain — but he forced his revulsion down and approached the village's wattle fence. His hawk gave a disgusted cry and soared away, as if he, too, found the reek of the place foul.

Immediately scavenging dogs and fishy-smelling children poured from huts and surrounded Merlin, the children wide-eyed and bouncing with excitement, the dogs barking and snuffling at the hem of his robe. They were followed by a pack of curious women, all rather unappealing and smelly, and then several warriors, who left off drinking, snoring, and boasting round the evening fire to see what the commotion was about.

They gazed at Merlin suspiciously, fingering their axes, till he cast back his cloak to reveal the robe beneath – a knee-length sheath of tanned hide painted with mystic symbols, the edges sewn with ancient teeth of dog and wolf and boar. Buan-ann had aided him to paint it and sew the points on in the proscribed order, and it was obvious even to these strangers that the robe was the attire of a magic-man.

The people drew back then, gasping, slightly afraid, especially when Merlin's totem-hawk suddenly appeared, dropping onto his wrist and uttering a challenging scream to the throng.

The chief of the tribe, an old man with stringy grey hair bound in a knot high on his head, ambled forward, hands outstretched. His face was leathery, his mouth toothless. He walked with a limp, but despite this defect, his clothes were carefully crafted, with expensive conical buttons of jet fastening the front.

"Welcome, holy man!" he cried. "You may dine with us this evening, and stay the night if you so desire. My son had gone hunting and will be away till the new Moon — his hut is empty."

Merlin smiled. The tribes of Prydn had a custom that favoured a lone wanderer on the road. They were generous to a fault to those with special gifts: magic-craft, tale-telling, metallurgy, healing or dagger-play. A chief who was stingy, whose hearth was unwelcoming to guests, would soon be a laughing stock for miles around. No one would willingly besmirch their honour by being niggardly, and especially they would not do so before one who spoke with the spirits, lest he call a blight to wither the crops or spirit their babes off to Ahn-un.

Surrounded by the curious children, Merlin entered the communal feasting hut, his hawk still flapping on his arm. He was handed a beaker of honey-mead and a haunch of pig. It tasted good, and he realised how weak and hungry he had become on his long journey. Across the room he spied the tribe's shaman, an ugly man with a sly, canny face shaped like a crescent Moon, with a jabbing chin and bulbous brow that strove to meet. Moon-face must also have had a dedication to the Lady Moon, for he had a crescent tattooed between his brows, and his deerskin cloak was patterned with the lunar phases picked out in tiny beads.

The Shaman was kneeling by a hearth, cooking something that sputtered and sizzled on a spit. "Come, young stranger and man-of-magic," he wheedled. "Come, hawk-man, and see what we do here in Ha-bren's village."

Merlin had little interest in what Moon-face was doing. Nevertheless, he did not wish to offend his hosts, so he sent his hawk flying back out into the night, causing the gathered women to scream as its wings brushed their heads. He then squatted by the shaman, and saw that Moon-face was cooking a fish over the fire. Its juices foamed and spat; its mouth gaped and its big luminous eyes seemed to bulge at the young watcher. Again, Merlin fought his instinct to gag at the sight and smell.

Moon-face smirked, obviously aware of his discomfiture. "Is it 'gesh' for you, do you have a taboo on sea-flesh?" he cackled. "'Tis a pity, for this fish is the Salmon of Knowledge. Eat its flesh and you will have greater knowledge than any mortal man." With that, he grabbed the fish himself and bit into its shining scales. Juices spurted out and ran down his skin, but he had evidently miscalculated how hot it would be, for he let out an agonised howl and flung the fish from him.

The flopping, sizzling thing landed straight into Merlin's lap, as the villagers nudged each other and sniggered with mirth. He slapped it away, but his thumb sank into the roasted flesh, and he bit back a pained cry as the hot juices burnt him. Instinctively he placed his scalded thumb in his mouth, and the essence of the taboo creature passed into him.

He sprang up at once, glaring angrily at those gathered in the hut. "You think me some poor man of the mountains to jeer at," he snarled. "Beware, I say, lest you be cursed for your inhospitable ways!"

The people parted as he stormed from the tent, burnt thumb in his mouth like a petulant child. He heard snorts of laughter behind him, which both riled and concerned him. Safe passage in these unknown lands depended on his ability to convince the tribesmen that he was untouchable, worthy of honour and hospitality. He had not convinced these folk.

In the hut the chief had loaned him, Merlin lay down with his staff and dagger close by his side. The strange taste of the fish lingered in his mouth; he spat onto the ground once or twice but could not rid himself of it. At least it had not killed him or turned him in to some foul beast!

When he finally found sleep, after many hours, he began to dream... He was a fish, like the one he had tasted; the Father of all fish, the Salmon of Wisdom with the Fire in his Head. As he swam, he felt the presence of pursuers, dark men along the water line who prodded the water with barbed spears, seeking to hook him, kill him.

Using the Salmon Leap, the champion's leap, he flew up through the water in a spray, soaring high above the heads of his foes. And as he leaped, ringed in the light of the rising Sun, he began to change. From fish that leaped high, to a bird of the air.

A hawk. His hawk.

A Merlin that soared over the forests of Albu toward a conical green hill that filled him with strange excitement and longing…

"I must go!" He sat up in the fuggy dark, eyes shining like a wild beast's. It was silent in the riverside village, with only the occasional wail of a babe or the bark of a dog breaking the stillness. Yet something was stirring, coming his way. Merlin could feel it with a new, inborn sense.

He gazed at his blistered thumb. "The Salmon of Wisdom… Knowledge given me by my enemy's own mocking."

Quietly he crept between the dark huts, making his way towards the river. He halted, slinking into the shadows of one round hut, as two warriors swaggered past in a haze of alcoholic fumes. "He's not one of us," he heard one say. "He's ill-starred. Did you see the magic crystal he carried at his belt? It would go well in my hut, a gift for my new wife. Why should such as he have it? We should throw him to the fishes he despises so much."

The other man's teeth glinted in his coppery beard. "Let us do it. You can have the bright ball. Just let me search his pouch for other wealth…"

The two warriors picked up pace and Merlin swirled by them, silent as a breath of wind, a trick he had learned from Buan-ann. His fears had been proven; these men had no honour and were out to rob and kill. His lip curled in a snarl of outrage; in these lands even a magic-man was not safe…surely an affront to the spirits themselves!

Reaching the river, he spotted the tribesmen's canoes, tethered like animals to pegs in the thin, Moon-bathed mud. Cutting one free with his dagger, he paddled it into the centre of the flow, the sound of the oar no louder than that of fish leaping in the dark

A few moments later there were angry shouts from the village. Torches flared. He grinned and spat in the direction of the huts, murmuring a powerful curse on the faithless and the false. As if it already had taken effect, a stray spark from the watch fire landed on a thatched roof and it burst into sudden, unexpected flame. Screams of fear and anger filled the night. Merlin watched for a moment more, coldly satisfied, then paddled

21

on into the shadows, with the flip-flop of fish all around him and the soft laughter of the spirits soughing through the bushes to speed him on his way.

Merlin abandoned the canoe many miles upstream. His arms ached, and he knew, if he pursued, he could not keep up the pace against experienced boatmen. So he decided to proceed inland on foot.

Using his staff for support, he walked for what seemed an eternity, until the soles of his skin footgear hung in tatters. But still on he walked...

And walked...and walked...

Villages came and went; he made cautious stops to gather supplies and ask directions, but he never lingered. Like a man caught in a dream, he shouldered his pack and wandered on...

And on... And on...

His shoes soon disintegrated utterly; he caught a cony with help of his Merlin-hawk and made its pelt into a pair of new boots, which he padded with grass woven into a matt. He fed the cony giblets to his eager bird, then walked on, quite proud of his new footgear.

And still the path wound on, seemingly endless, deep into the strange southern lands far from the mountains of his birth.

Eventually, he felt the ground changing beneath his feet, becoming soft as a maiden's pliant flesh. It was Woman's land here, void of the harsh masculinity of his homeland of gods and giants. In his nostrils he could smell water and earth intermingled — women's elements, unlike fire and air, which were male.

Cresting a low rise, he suddenly spotted a conical hill on the horizon. It dominated the surrounding landscape, looking somehow unnatural, as if man, or maybe a god, had sculpted its form. It was the hill of his dream — deep green, with a spiral-path winding up to its crown and water pooling at its feet. The evening Sun was passing over its shoulder, and the lake below gleamed dark as jet, sucking in the lingering light.

Entranced, he hunkered down and watched as the Sun fell from heaven and the water at the base of the hill turned scarlet — a lake of blood, the birthing-pool of the holy hill. Slowly, the gory welter of sunset faded from the West. Jewel-like stars now glimmered on the surface of the lake, reminding Merlin of the white speckles in the stones on God-of-Bronze.

"What is this place?" he whispered. "Surely it must be one of the Hallows of Prydn."

Rising, he continued with renewed vigour toward the holy hill, skirting the edges of the now-sullen lake. He trod carefully, for the ground became even-wetter, saturated with rank marsh-water. Glancing down, he could see that he walked on a mesh of ancient withies, laid down in some bygone time to aid passage across the fen. A little god-doll carved from a slab of bog-oak squatted in the marsh near the head of the track, its quartz-pebble eyes glinting in the dusk. Fireflies ringed the figure's head, making a crown of dancing light. Merlin bowed to the effigy in respect, but could not sense if it welcomed or warned him.

Further along, he spied the pointed roof of a hut set on an islet in the heart of the marsh. It was so quiet he guessed at once it was the house of some idol or spirit rather than the dwelling place of mortal men. Respecting its sanctity, he avoided its lintelled doorway and continued to skirt the boggy lake.

Just as he was beginning to despair of ever walking on solid land again, he spied a trail that led from the water's edge. Mist was rising around him now, as the cool of the night strove against the warmth of the day, and some of the stars went out, blotted by the opaque cloud. Merlin scanned what he could still see of the sky and realised it was very late; the Moon had Westered. It was time for him to sleep like the sunken Moon, least weariness make his steps clumsy and he ended up sinking in the bog amid the slimy marsh-eels.

He peered around, eyes straining in the murk. Off to one side, he could see a tree on a rise, guarding an entranceway or passage formed by several natural boulders. He stepped towards the gap and nearly bumped into a wooden post covered in carvings that he could not decipher. He ignored it, although he realised it might be perilous to do so, and entered an enclosure surrounded by close-set, stunted trees. They were laden with small ripe apples, and the grass below their boughs was full of fallen fruit that gave out the sickly-sweet smell of decay.

He could hear water running and stumbled through the gloom towards the sound. His feet splashed into the stream before he saw it. Ice-cold water swirled around his calloused soles, soothing them. He sighed in utter pleasure.

He followed the small stream further into the enclosure. A sharp tang hung in the air, stronger even than the fug of the rancid apples. Recognising the sharp coppery scent, Merlin felt the hair on the back of his neck prickle.

23

Fumbling in his belt-pouch, he drew out his flint strike-a-light and a piece of tinder. Swiftly he kindled a small torch and held it aloft.

Shadows swirled about the garth, retreating from the flame. Merlin stood on the edge of a pond fed by the tiny stream. Offerings lay on its shores: wheat sheaves bound with twine, a broken pot with spiral designs, the upended top of a skull that rocked mournfully, ominously, in the wind. The sharp tang rose even more strongly here and Merlin knelt and cupped the water, bringing it to his lips. It was pale, pure and clear, seemingly untainted, and yet…the waters tasted of blood.

There was no mistaking taste and scent. It was as if he were drinking the blood of the Earth itself, of Great Ahn-ann whose breasts were hills, whose body spawned all living things. This spring, and the coiled hill beyond, was very holy places indeed. Holy, but fearsome and filled with dark mysteries, women's mysteries of which he knew little.

Awed, he knelt to pray to the patron of the blood-water spring…but he heard a harsh breath in the dark, a swish of long robes.

Before he had chance to react, the cold blade of a bronze dagger pressed against his throat. Warm breath tickled his ear, and a woman's voice said, "Who are you stranger, who have come unbidden to the Garden of Afallan? To enter here without the permission of the Lady of the Lake makes your life forfeit!"

He froze, scarcely daring to breathe. "I am friend, I mean no harm. I am a wanderer who comes in search of wisdom. The Ancestors have guided me here."

"Have they now?" the woman said mockingly. "The Ancestors are capricious, or did you not know? Perhaps they guided you here to be sacrificed to them."

The dagger poked his neck; he felt a drop of blood slide over his collarbone. He was filled with real fear. He had not envisioned his life-force going to feed this bitter, metallic-tasting pool. "The land may want my blood," he croaked, "and if that is what the high ones decree, that is my fate. But I would not gladly die before seeing Khor Ghor."

The woman's breath railed between her teeth. "Khor Ghor? What business do you have with that mighty place? If it is merely to gawk, there are screens to shield the holy of all holies from unworthy eyes. You would not be welcome there — you are, by your tongue, a rude mountain man."

Anger kindled within Merlin, overcoming his fear of the woman's dagger. "I seek the priesthood. Barbarian I may be to you, woman, but I tamed the Wyrms of Faraon, I have studied in the groves on Mhon, and I've

24

held counsel with the priestess of Brygyndo in Ibherna."

The knife suddenly dropped away. "Interesting." A hint of mirth deepened the woman's voice. "Maybe you are more than just a hapless wanderer after all. Maybe you were guided here for a reason. Turn around, slowly mind... If you disobey, my dagger will strike your heart quicker than lightning."

Slowly Merlin turned around. A girl stood on the green grass, a deadly copper rapier in her hand. Autumn-brown hair wound with strips of blue felt tumbled to her waist, and a white-gold lunula circled her neck. Spirals were painted on cheeks and chin. Fringed by dark lashes, her eyes were as green as the conical hill of his dreams. A thin robe blew floated around her, ephemeral as the mist, hiding little of the slim, wiry body beneath.

"Who are you?" he breathed. She seemed so beautiful, standing in the starlight; she put all the women of his tribe to shame. But there was a deadly, dangerous quality to her beauty. It reminded him of a snake, mysterious and exotic with its piercing eyes and dappled skin, but with fangs ready to bite the foolish hand that reached to touch. He would not dare touch this lady. He half wondered if she was human at all, or one of the Everliving ones, who could take on human form at will.

The girl was looking him up and down with her unsettling, grass-green eyes. "You are younger than I thought at first, and less ugsome. Though you could use a meal...and a bath. But not in the sacred lake...unless you wish never to come out again." She giggled quietly, her laughter unsettling. "My sisters and I alone can swim there and live. I am Nin-Aeifa, priestess of Afallan, the Apple-garden, and guardian of the Tor where Hwynn the White Fire, lord of the mortuary and son of Nud Cloudmaker, rides every Sovahn to collect the shades of the dead. With my sisters we form the ring of Nine Maidens who tend the Sacred Cauldron of Inspiration, boiled by fires that never wane."

"I am known as the Merlin," Merlin said simply, and at that moment his hawk descended from the clouds to flutter round his shoulders. Merlin was oddly pleased to see Nin-Aeifa jump at the sight of the bird before regaining her regal composure.

"You continue to surprise," said Nin-Aeifa. She sheathed her rapier. "Follow me."

The young priestess led Merlin to a round hut outside the enclosure, within sight of the great cult house that stood on the artificial island in the lake, but not too near it. She gestured Merlin onto a pallet of furs, then reached for a drum made of gut stretched taut over a wooden frame. She tapped out a sharp tattoo, bringing a flurry of younger girls, who carried in trenchers heaped with pork, and beakers brimming with a drink made from fermented apples, the likes of which Merlin had never tasted before.

"Eat, Western stranger," commanded Nin-Aeifa, "and slake your thirst to your heart's content," and Merlin did as he was bade, uncaring in his hunger that juices smeared his face and dripped onto his clothes. As the apple-ale hit his belly, his tongue loosened in a way that was unusual for him, and he began to tell Priestess Nin-Aeifa about his old life, of the serpents that caused the godstones to fall, of Old Woman Buan-ann and the warnings of the priestess of Fiery Arrow. He even told her how he had slain Vhortiern and given him to the stones.

Nin-Aeifa sat cross-legged, stroking her chin thoughtfully. Merlin was amazed; she was so young yet appeared so wise, as if the knowledge of centuries was locked within the body of a girl. "Rumours have come to Afallan," she said, "that Eckhy, one of the elder priests of Khor Ghor, is ill with a disease than thins his blood. It is thought he will not last more than one more Winter, two at most. When he passes to the West, magic-men from all over Prydn will gather to compete for his position in the Great Temple. Maybe his death will be new life to you, outlander — perhaps it is true, that the Ancestors sent you from your mountain realm to take his place. This may be a good thing. Many of the priests there are old both in body and mind, and seem not to see the perils of these troubled times. Maybe Khor Ghor needs new blood." She laughed again, the not-quite-pleasant laugh of the garden. "And if not, the Stones may well have your blood anyway. They do not like pretenders there."

"I am no pretender," growled Merlin, flushing with annoyance.

"Well, good." She smiled impishly, tossing her blue-streaked hair over her shoulder. "You will have nothing to fear then."

"I will press on to Khor Ghor at first light," said Merlin. "I will make myself known to the priests before this Eckhy passes."

"No, you will not." Nin-Aeifa sidled up to him; suddenly he noticed how sweet she smelt, but it was the cloying scent of the rotted apples in the enclosure, a scent dark and earthy and unsettling, an overwhelming brew both fair and foul. "You have eaten my food — the food of Otherness — and drank my ale, brewed with the waters of Life and the apples of Afallan. You are mine for a year and a day. But no, do not cast me those angry looks; yours will be a fine captivity. I will teach you many things that you must know before you reach Khor Ghor. Right now you are but a boy of some talent...you must go there a man of Many Talents."

26

He dared not defy her; knew he could not, that her bright blade would snake out to seek his veins if he resisted. And he was not entirely sure he wanted to resist. The offer of learning appealed; his inquisitive mind was fast as flame and, like flame, craved more fuel to burn. He felt strange other yearnings and longings too, in his chest, and in his loins. He had not had much truck with women of his own clan, who had seemed like dull, dumb oxen, worn down with care. But this creature, fire and water and cloying apple-scent, she was a match for him, one of the Touched Ones, an equal of his own kind.

"I will stay," he whispered hoarsely. "I want you to teach me... everything."

"Oh, I shall..." In her hand she held a small round cup laced with perforations; she lit its powdered contents with a bit of kindling from her hearth and the room was suddenly wreathed with curling, pungent smoke. Enchanted smoke that went to the head and gave men visions of the Otherworld.

The clouds wreathed her and he saw her face, haloed by the smoke, a face serene and young, yet cunning and dangerous. A goddess's face. Her crescent collar gleamed like the Moon as she took it off and raised it, kissing it before setting it aside. Then her flimsy robes slithered away, pooling on the floor, and she flung herself down upon the furs, her supple legs and floating autumn-leaf hair tangling with his limbs, and her lips, apple-laced, burning hotter than the fire against his yearning mouth.

The days marched on into months, and the trees in the nearby groves turned red as blood, then became thin as skeletons in a barrow. The Year Turned, the Sun falling into the sacred lake on the shortest day, and the dance of the seasons began again, with new buds sprouting on the trees followed by flowers and leaves, and gradually, the gold and reds of yet another Autumn.

Merlin and Nin-Aeifa lived as lovers in her hut below the Tor, and as she had promised, she taught him all she knew of magic and the spirits of the water and the dead, and he taught her of his mountain ways, and the gods of sky and stone. He gave to her his secret name, Lailoq, and she whispered that she had been born Hwyndolona, child of a priestess of Afallan, and she was consecrated to Hwynn, god of the Mortuary, by both name and upbringing.

27

"When I leave this place, will you come with me, be my wife?" Merlin asked one day, when they lay beneath her sheepskins, with a wind that bore the first bitter hint of winter whistling about the roundhouse.

She glanced at him, eyes fathomless. "Never. I am a Maiden of the Cauldron. If I were to go with you, my honour would go too. I would have to kill you."

"Maiden!" His hands slid over the rises and valleys of her lithe body. "I hardly think so."

She gave him a glare that immediately stopped his ministrations. "Maiden merely means that the servants of the Cauldron never wed. It does not mean we must remain virgin, though some choose that path. Every year at Midsummer we bathe in the lake on the first full Moon after solstice, and it is said the Lady of the Spiral Crown purifies us anew."

Merlin settled down into the warmth of the furs, pressing against the swell of her hip. "Forgive my rash words. I am but a man and do not know the women's mysteries. Women…the doom of the Merlin!"

"It may be so," she whispered, and turned away into the dark.

The next morning Merlin went to gather healing plants in the nearby woods. He was alone, for Nin-Aeifa had gone to the cult house in the lake, attending to matters of the Cauldron. Distantly he could hear his lover and her fellows singing and chanting, as they began the preparations for Savhan, the night when the dead came from their barrows and walked the dark beyond the firelight. It was when Hwynn himself rode forth, head burning with White Fire, and collected new spirits to take into the Deadlands.

Merlin had gathered half a basketful of fungus when he became aware of a faint rhythmic vibration in the earth beneath his feet. He lay down and pressed his ear against the ground. Yes, something was coming. Something large…far larger and heavier than a man or even several men. Winds arose, and the fallen leaves eddied as if dancing in anticipation. Shoving his woven basket beneath a bush, he hastened to the ancient trackway that wound through the marshy woodland where he collected his mushrooms, mosses and herbs.

At the end of the track a figure appeared, mounted on a great black horse. This sight frightened Merlin at once, for men seldom rode those great wild beasts; they were sacred to the spirits, and had hooves and teeth to fight off the advances of men. Some tribes captured them and kept them as totem animals, and it was said the kings of Ibherna ate their flesh after boiling them at their inauguration feasts, but his people just avoided them... they were the children of the Lady-of-Horses whose head was a woman's but who ran on four legs.

The galloping animal drew closer; he could now see its wild eyes and the froth on its muzzle, and a shaggy, raven mane plaited with what looked to be human finger-bones. Astride its back was a man, or something man-like, with silver-white, bleached hair that billowed like a cloud of fog. Its face was narrow, lean, painted in black and white, its contours those of a skull...or was it paint indeed, for there seemed to be no human eyes in the darkness of its sockets, just pinpoints of bright blue light?

Merlin shuddered and dropped to his knees, heart pounding with both terror and elation. Surely this was Hwynn the White himself, riding to the Holy Tor to bear the souls of the newly dead back to Ahn-un, where Hwynn and his sire Nod would judge them, before sending them on to the Plain of Honey, or casting them back into the world as vengeful ghosts. Fearfully he peered up, and saw with terrified excitement, that there were now three great dogs bounding alongside the unearthly rider, their coats white as untrodden snow and their flapping ears the hue of old blood. They bayed and howled and snapped at the air, frenzied by the mad flight of the skull-faced rider.

Fighting down his fear at being in the presence of such a holy one, Merlin struggled back to his feet. "Oh Great Lord!" he cried. "What tidings do you bring to Afallan this day?"

The skull face turned, white hair foaming around it. "I come from the lands where Abona makes the waters swell." A gravelly voice rang out, reminiscent of the clatter of winter icicles, of long bones in rifled cists upon the hills. "I come bearing the spirit of one who has passed, one who will now live forever with his mighty forefathers from the Times-before-Time. Eckhy the old, the wise, priest of Khor Ghor, has now lain upon the mortuary platform for the prescribed turning of the Moon, and will now come to rest for a while under the Hill." He parted his cloak of shredded black pig-skins, and revealed a drum-shaped chalk box upon his knee, decorated with surprised, watching, faceless eyes. "His heart, his spirit, lies within."

The vision of the sinister reliquary box was gone in a flash and the unearthly rider with it, pounding on his sweat-stained steed along the track toward the Tor, domain of Hwynn, son of Snatcher, Son of Snarer.

Merlin stepped onto the path and stared after the fearsome figure as it dwindled into the distance, the attendant hounds yammering around the horse's hooves. "So...Eckhy is dead," he whispered. "And as the Moon accounts it, it nigh on a year and a day since Nin-Aeifa bound me to her. I am free of her constraints, and I must go."

There was a shriek from above and his totem-hawk descended from the trees and dug its talons into his uplifted forearm. He was surprised, for the bird had not come to him for a while, though he had oftimes spotted it circling in the sky, wary of the settlement of the Ladies of the Lake yet still tied to its mortal brother.

"You have returned, my friend," he said, stroking the feathered head. "You will be my one companion on the road to the Temple of the Ancestors."

A stab of pain needled his heart as he spoke to the bird, but he forced it away. Nin-Aeifa had made her choice, and he had made his. Quickly, without a backward glance, he hurried away into the wintry woods, his hawk flying up above his head, spiralling and screaming as if goading him on.

And in the cult house in the lake, the Nine Maidens paused while stoking the fire round their sacred Cauldron, and they heard the hounds and hoof beats of Hwynn the White upon the beaten path, and suddenly Nin-Aeifa cried out with knowledge and loss, "He is gone!"

Her Sisters, thinking she spoke of the spirit of the old one that Hwynn carried, began to keen for the dead, and to tear their hair and faces. Nin-Aeifa joined in their mourning, her hands clawed and a shroud across her face.

But it was not for any ancient temple priest she wailed.

It was for the death of love, and the end of youth, and the twisting of destinies in the unassailable hands of fate.

CHAPTER THREE

Darkness shrouded the Great River than was known simply as Abona —
the River. It was the prime waterway of Albu and the most holy, hence the
simple, defining name; the recipient of ancient soulstones on a long journey
from the West, and a source of life and death and cleansing.

Merlin sat in a canoe while a lean, wiry, river-man poled the craft through
weirs, past tall stands of reeds and round islets where strange birds, disturbed
by splash of the paddle, rushed up shrieking into the shadows.

Overhead the stars wheeled in the vault of sky, their white points
scattered amid the tangle of trees on the riverbank. Fish flopped in the water,
their passage leaving rings on the swell, and Merlin, listening carefully,
fancied he could hear the song of the river-mother who lay, green and
weedy, on the beds below:
"Lay di lay, for a thousand lives' span
The river will run where the river ran
I was here ere great stones stood
I saw them borne on rafts of wood
But I shall flow while stones may fall
Old Mother shall outlive them all!"

"Where am I now?" he asked his guide, whose services he had hired at a
village upriver in exchange for a handful of bluestone chippings.

The man grunted, continuing to pole the craft. "Not far from the Temple.
On the left..." he paused, waving one arm into the blackness, "are the
Resting Places of great Kings, and the Giant's Dance beyond them, where
their shades may look upon it. Continue to follow the river and you will
come to the Old Circle, where the Spirit-Avenue begins, leading over the hill
and across Moy Mor, the Great Plain, up to the Stone of Summer itself. If
you turn your back to the Avenue and following the river South, you will
soon see the Place-of-Light upon a plateau, marked by posts and lit by
torchlight. This is where the folk who are not priests dwell."

Merlin craned his head around, smelling the air, eyes seeking in the deep
darkness. "Pull into the bank," he ordered, nodding towards a spot where the
reeds were thin.

The man bared his teeth. "I would rather take you to the settlement. There
will be ghosts walking in the fog. Not all are happy to be dead, not all have

joined their Ancestors on the Plains of Honey!"

Merlin grinned, his eyes twinkling. "I fear no Wight. Indeed, I would gladly talk to the dead tonight!"

"You are mad," said his companion morosely, but he pushed the coracle in again the bank as Merlin had asked. "I do not suppose I will ever hear of you again. My wife will thank you in her prayers for the lucky bluestones."

Merlin climbed out onto the bank, his skin shoes slopping in the mud. "You will hear of me again. Remember the name of the Merlin! Remember it, and pass it to your sons and to your son's son's sons! My name will live forever!"

"Mad!" the boatman repeated, as Merlin vanished into the scrub growing on the riverbank. Then, as shivers that were not brought by the chill of the wind rippled down his spine, he began to paddle madly toward the wholesome, welcoming fires of the Place-of-Light.

Merlin wandered a while, before finding a track. Cut into the chalk, it wound up from the verdant banks of Abona and snaked north, glowing faintly in the starshine. Hoisting up his heavy, tooth-fringed robe so that his legs were bare and free, he began to follow it. The night was cold, and rags of mist fluttered past him like the souls of the dead that the boatman had warned him about.

Suddenly, one of the dead men's barrows came into view, huge and round, blocking out the starlight, circled by a white chalk ditch that kept the spirit of the corpse — if he still lingered on the mortal plain — within its sacred boundaries. A decaying memorial pole loomed on the mound's summit, facing North-East, where the Sun rose at Midsummer.

Merlin felt power flow from the tumulus, cold lines that twisted like serpents beneath his ill-shod feet. Approaching, he crossed the ditch and knelt by the pole, examining carvings of axes and chevrons and spirals. Around him the air sighed, and he suspected old barrow-man was stirring; that he, loving life as a warrior of Khor Ghor, had not yet crossed the Great Plain to the Deadlands of the ultimate West where the chosen played eternally on the Plain of Honey.

Hastily, Merlin fumbled with the pouch at his belt and drew out some dried herbs wrapped in a large dark leaf. He crumbled them between his fingers, thrust them into his mouth and forced himself to swallow, despite the bitterness that caused him to grimace and gag.

For a while he sat cross-legged, the wind hissing in the grass and in his sleek black hair. Gradually, a dull cramping sickness gripped his belly and he forced back the urge to heave. Zigzag flashes obscured the edges of his vision, while the centre of his gaze became an undulating black tunnel. His heartbeat grew loud, echoing in his ears, while a fine sweat covered brow and torso, to be licked away by the rising breeze.

A splitting pain gripped one side of his head, almost as if some primeval monster was squeezing it with vicious claws, trying to rend his skull and steal his brain as a man might suck a wild bird's egg. He closed his eyes against the throbbing agony, and when he opened them again...He was there.

The warrior. The grave-wight. He was one of the old ones, one of the first men of tin. He carried a bow, and golden baskets glittered in his hair. His face was green and glowing, alternating between a skull and livid flesh, and in his hand he brandished a dagger of ancient style, phospherus flowing from its blade in a stream like a comet's tail.

Merlin felt a surge of both fear and elation. "I welcome you, mighty Ancestor!" he cried, kneeling with his head almost upon the bony feet.

"Why do you wake me from my sleep of a million nights, from my dreaming with my beakers and my arrows and beloved gold?" asked the Wight, his voice the eerie sough of wind in bare branches. It was the inhuman rasp of one who has no throat, no tongue of mortal flesh with which to speak.

Merlin gazed up, suddenly fierce. "Because I can!"

The dead face looked almost surprised. But then the jaw dropped and a grating screech came from the desiccated throat, a terrible sound that Merlin only just recognised as laughter. "You are not as other men if you, in truth, wish to gaze upon such a creature as I!"

"I am not as other men," replied Merlin. "Indeed, some say I am not a real mortal man at all, for my sire was of the spirit world. Hence I do not fear you. It is learning I seek."

"To what purpose?" The creature leaned over him, smelling of cold earth and long-dead flesh. "You have hawk's eyes. I do not trust you. Hawks rent my flesh when I was dead."

"Tell me the secrets of Khor Ghor. It is there that I go this night, to become a priest — the greatest priest ever — of that temple. I must have knowledge in order that they will accept me, a youth and a foreigner."

The Wight's teeth grinned through rags of flesh. "Secrets should stay secrets, but as you have compelled me here, know this — I lived when the lintel-ring was raised. The great stones came from the north, from near the temple of the Eye. Many hands pounded these stones into shape — the work of men, not gods, brought with blood and hard labour. Wooden platforms were built skyward to put the capstones in place, a work never seen among the stone buildings of men, truly a fitting tribute to the Ancestors and to Bhel Sunface and Mother Moon. And when it was done, we carved upon some of the stones, putting marks upon them from our respective beliefs — the image of She-Who-Guards, the Axe that bears the power of the Sun, the Blade of Power. And the priestesses, the dancing women, came and honoured the Great Stones, weaving in and out until their cries of ecstasy greeted the dawn..."

"You honour me with your knowledge." Merlin bowed, awed by this being who had witnessed the raising of the greatest temple in Prydn, who had walked in an era when stone fell before metal and Midsummer became secondary to the great feast of resurrection in Winter's heart.

The cold wind blew more fiercely; goose bumps sprouted on Merlin's bare legs beneath his robe. The mist went sailing in great ragged loops down the valley, while stray leaves tumbled and fell like dead men on the valley sides. He swayed and fell, and went tumbling with the leaves, rolling over and over, unable to gain footing, while behind him the ghostly, ghastly laughter of the barrow-man split the night until, suddenly, his gaunt, surreal figure flickered out as a flame is extinguished in the wind. Only the night and the wind trod upon the lowering bulk of his great barrow.

Merlin staggered dazedly to his feet and trudged on, heavy-headed and unsteady, his vision still distorted from the effects of the potion he had consumed. Up ahead, he noticed a lofty rise crowned by an unassuming earthwork and lit by the hard crescent of the Westering Moon. The place looked deserted, but its height would enable him to survey the lands below and plan his route.

Breath a cloud of white before his mouth, he clambered up the rise. As he climbed, he could smell a sickly tang, the same sweet but hideous scent he had recognised beside the Holy well in Afallan. The scent of decay, of dissolution.

The scent of death.

Cresting the bank of the earthwork, he immediately knew why. The hill was covered by excarnation platforms, some with hunched figures lying upon them, others bearing completely skeletal bodies, their rib cages stark beneath the cold, thin, bone-light of the Moon.

As he stumbled forward, his feet shifted millennia of teeth and small bones fallen from their owner's corpses into the grass. They tumbled like shimmering pearls in the muted starshine.

Merlin noticed one platform that loomed higher than the rest, and seemed to be of recent construction. The body lying on it was furled in the shredded remains of a blue robe that fluttered like a sail in the breeze. The face had been picked clean by birds and other scavengers, but the hands, still retaining some flesh and tendon, grasped a boar's tusk and a shard of magic quartz.

Suddenly he realised who this sky-burial must be. "Eckhy the priest," Merlin murmured.

There was a rushing sound, another skirl of wind, and suddenly the spirit of the old man appeared, thinner and less substantial than the Tin-man in his ancient mound, and less threatening. He was like a dim reflection of life, ready to break apart like an image seen in a raindrop or on a puddle. "You have come, I know you would," he said. "It was foretold a Merlin would return to the Temple."

"Do I have your blessing, old one?"

"Aye, but your desire will not come easy. Many covet a place in Khor Ghor. But you alone will have spoken to the dead of the Stones, as well as the living priests. You belong to our world as well as the world of men. Look, Merlin…look over and see the Dance-of-Spirits in its majesty."

Merlin peered out from the height, gaze sweeping over rises and ridges dotted with barrows, some overgrown with spiky thorns, others glowing white, their chalk faces still bare and their ditches newly dug. Beyond them, pallid in the starlight, on a plain long denuded of forest, stood the Temple; the Year's Turn, the Circle of Eternity. Its lintels rose into the night, beacon bright, while its barrier-ditch glowed with an eerie earth-light. The worked, smoothed stones of the outer ring grinned like a row of even teeth, with utter darkness gathered in the spaces between them.

"It is not a place for the faint hearted," said Eckhy. "Some have come with foolish posies and gifts of pebbles, but this is not a place of simple charms and cures. Khor Ghor is a place of power, a place of Kings that were and Kings that will be."

Merlin stared at the gigantic structure, hot and cold chills rippling down body. He felt as if his very spirit was being sucked from his chest into the unearthly blackness between those massive stones. He was afraid…yet he wanted to plunder that blackness too. He too was part of the darkness, the mystery that lay beyond safe firelight, and if any could tread those paths unscathed — it was the Son of No Man.

"Do you fear what you see, boy?" asked the shade of the old priest, pointing to the Stones, while the substance of his thin arm unravelled like mist. He was being drawn back into the darkness, back across the Plain to the Holy Hill where Hwynn had taken him to enter the Otherworld, to begin his long journey from Ahn-un to the Plain of Honey.

"I do," replied Merlin. "But not a fear that would put me to flight. It is a fear that has also set a fire alight within me — I want to know more."

"Then you, like your namesake, will surely become one of the great priests of that hallowed Place," said the spirit, and he abruptly vanished with a hiss like escaping marsh-gas, leaving only a bird-ravaged body high on a wooden dais.

Merlin stared at the bundle of bones that had been a man, and placed pebble offerings in the dead man's empty eyeholes as a token of thanks and respect. Finishing, he swiftly left the hill and hurried across the chalkland on a well-worn trail. It led between the upturned bowls of warriors' barrows and the disc-shaped tumuli of forgotten queens, before petering out a respectful distance from Khor Ghor's bank, which formed a stark boundary between the profane world and the world of the Ancestors.

Heart drumming against his ribs, he cautiously approached the earthwork, watchful for any guards. Mere feet away, the outer sarsens were like pale, malformed giants dancing in a ring, joined together for all time by their lintels. Beyond them the mighty five trilithons that were symbols of both death and power roared up into the night, the largest man-made structures Merlin had ever laid eyes on. He knew their names from age-old lore: Throne of Kings, decorated with dagger and axe; the Arch of the Eastern Sky; the House of the North Wind; the Western Guardian, and tallest and most imposing of all, the Great Trilithon, Door of the Setting Sun, with its massive lintel towering high above the rest. More ominously, this trilithon was also known as the Door into Winter and Portal-of-Ghosts.

Not yet daring to approach the heart of the sanctuary, Merlin wandered Sunwise along the edge of the bank. His eyes scanned the shadows; he saw ghosts, watching shyly, but no living men, or any guards. He had heard that though Warrior-Priests traversed the Plain all night, they did not tarry long in the Stones themselves — it was too fearsome a place to linger after Sunset.

Indeed, at that moment Merlin's own heart quailed and he wished momentarily to be very far away, where there was fire and the comforts of men. But, then, unexpectedly, there was a rush in the dark, a brush of wings against his cheek. He nearly screamed, but took control of himself at once, watching as a huge white owl, its eyes the colour of amber beads, beat

36

shadows back with its wings before vanishing amid the Stones.

The Owl was the totem of the Guardian, the Lady of the Watching Eyes, whose rectangular symbol was graven high on the Western trilithon.

Merlin had his omen, his welcoming.

Taking a deep breath, he crossed the divide and passed beneath the lintels of the outer sarsen ring.

A hedge of bluestones greeted him, crowding around him like old friends. Stones from his own lands, the jagged mountain that was God-of-Bronze, with its views across the waves to Ibherna. Damp with dew, the stones gleamed bluish-green, the Western ones tall and elegant, the others more roughly formed, though two, one pointed and the other broad, were exceptions. They were the Old Father, with his peaked head, and flat, broad-faced Grey Woman; progenitors of the tribes of Albu embodied in stone.

Leaving the bluestones, Merlin crossed the circle and came before the Altar, the Stone of Adoration, the godstone that held the very essence of the Circle's power. Green and faintly glittering, it was backed by the enormous Door into Winter, which opened the way for the spirits of the departed to fly across the Great Plain, following the path of the setting Sun.

This was the centre of all things, caught in a circle that had no beginning and no end. Awed, Merlin knelt on the chalk floor and bent his head to the ground in homage to the Stone of Adoration. He could feel energy rushing through the earth, the beat of life itself. It soothed him, comforted him

as if he was a child. Sighing, he stretched out beneath the dark skies, watched over by the guardian Stones.

Heaviness crept over his limbs; his body went limp as a babe's. He feared nothing here, not spirits, not angry guards. His eyelids dragged down, and the darkness of sleep overcame him.

###

"Should we kill him?"

The prod of an arrow's tip between his shoulder blades brought Merlin to wakefulness. Biting back a cry, he struggled to wake from his potion-addled sleep. The world tilted. He could see he was still in the centre of Khor Ghor, lying slumped against one of the sarsens, but the sky was blood red with approaching dawn.

Turning his head, he saw two men glaring at him. He guessed they were warrior-priests of the temple, both young, clad in woven tunics and with bronze bands holding back their hair. The one prodding him had some kind of northern ancestry for his long locks were corn-coloured, braided in front and hooped by gold rings. The other had wild, curling russet hair, and dark tattoos ringing his eyes, giving him the semblance of Owl's eyes. Both carried bows, and daggers with hilts of horn.

"So, the sleepy one wakes!" The tattooed man nudged him with a toe. "How dare you, ragged one, come in here and lie like a dog at the fire in the holy of holies."

"You are lucky you are not dead," said the blonde man, lip curling in a sneer. "What have you to say for yourself, stranger?"

"I say… who is leader here? Neither of you I would wager."

The men glanced at each other with mingled expressions of anger and perplexity. "You must be Moon-touched, boy!" choked the tattooed man. "To speak so to the guardians of Khor Ghor, when the very arrows that mete death are pointed at your heart!"

Merlin stared into the man's eyes. "If you had really sought to kill me, you would have done the deed by now. You don't know what to make of me, do you? You don't know how I got here, passing your careful guardianship…" He smirked mockingly. "You wonder if I am a spirit, or a sorcerer… after all, you could not tell your superiors a mere mountain boy slipped into Khor Ghor and slept the night among the holy Stones, while you huddled outside like frightened women!"

The tattooed man gritted his teeth. "Stop playing with us, boy. Who are you, who comes here with such audacity, mocking us?"

Merlin flashed a vulpine smile. Suddenly he looked older than his captors, as old as the Stones themselves, and somehow sinister, with his beak-nosed and strangely archaic face, its high planes streaked with sweat and dirt, the deep-set eyes bloodshot from his magic spirit-brew. "I'm son of no Man. They say my father was a spirit from the forest. I have studied the mysteries within earth and within the sky. I have made stones stand that have fallen. I have killed a chief and have tasted the apples of Afallan. The Salmon of Knowledge has blessed my tongue, and the Lady of the Lake my body. And so I come here to join the priests of Khor Ghor and replace Eckhy the old."

The warrior-priests glanced at each other, anger replaced by surprise and even a touch of fear. "If what you speak is truth," said the tattooed one, "you must come with us right away, to meet the leader of our Order."

Dragging him from the centre circle, they skirted the Summer Stone that marked the year's longest day, before hurrying down the parallel arms of the processional Avenue, which led over the fields before curving sharply toward the River Abona. However, the priests did not take Merlin this way. Instead, they left the safety of the Avenue and herded him along the top of a ridge studded with huge, swollen tumuli, some of the largest burial mounds Merlin had ever seen. Cow carcasses rotted in their ditches; offering to placate restive spirits.

"Seven kings sleep here," said the yellow-haired priest. "Lords who wrought Khor Ghor of old. This is not a Land of the Living, stranger-boy; it belongs to the Dead, and there may be horrors in the morning mist that freeze your heart."

"Not mine," retorted Merlin. "The Dead have been as much friend to me as the living, priest."

The party journeyed onward in an Easterly direction. The rising Sun was a burning red eye through the dwindling night-fog. In the distance Merlin could see a range of sloping hills, curved like a woman's body, the chalk scars on their slopes gleaming in the growing light. And not far away, facing the hills, was a settlement on an escarpment that overlooked a shallow dell and the river beyond.

The sight of this holding awed him, but he kept his expression impassive, not wishing to appear a gawping and unsophisticated country fool. He had never seen a settlement so large, never really knew that one existed. Standing on the highest point of the plateau was a great round temple, lintelled and open to the sky in similar fashion to Khor Ghor, but wrought from stout oak timbers instead of stones. A scatter of barrows hugged the temple's sides, as if the dead sought to press in upon this place where the living worshipped.

A short distance away, a circular earthwork shone white as bone in the half-light. Hundreds of rectangular houses clustered around its edges, and at the centre stood a mighty cult house, once again circular and open to the sky. A pair of soaring totem poles fronted this house of the spirits, and a wide pathway, smoothed by the passage of countless feet, curved from its doorway toward the river lying in the dip below the settlement.

The blonde warrior-priest gestured with his bow, pride and the rosy light of dawn bringing a flush to his face. "Look and wonder, newcomer. You gaze on Deroweth, place of oaks, place of the wise seers — the greatest dwelling in all of Albu, maybe all of Prydn."

"It is a mighty place," Merlin agreed, his gaze sweeping over Deroweth. "Though quiet, considering it has many dwellings."

"You have not seen it in Midwinter, when chiefs come from all over the Five Cantrevs, bringing their women, children and herding beasts. Laws are passed by the priests, disputes settled, marriages made… but best of all is the Great Feast on the day Bhel Sunface dies and is reborn! Even the dogs of Deroweth are glutted with meat on that night, and beacons burn on every hill to greet the rebirth of Bhel from Ahn-ann's womb."

The warrior-priests and their captive soon reached a house standing near the entrance to the great henge. It was of highest quality, long and rectangular, with stout oak walls — the dwelling of a man of status. Smaller huts straddled its sides, with middens at the back and strong scents of cooking wafting from them — but there was no midden near the big house or signs of domestic life. All was clean and perfect and holy.

The fair priest rapped on the door, before entering the house without further ado. "You had best be respectful," his companion hissed into Merlin's ear as he shoved him forward, jabbing him in the back with the tip of a barbed arrow. "You don't know how lucky you are that we've let you live to come before our High-Priest!"

The interior of the house was dark, wreathed with smoke from a large fire-pit at the centre. A sleepy-looking old woman, bunched-up hair straggling from a bone pin, was stoking the flames. She didn't even glance up at the newcomers. Merlin's eyes darted about, taking in everything: the painted symbols on the walls, pots sealed with clay plugs lined up on wooden shelves, rich furs and weavings that enshrouded the boxed-off sleeping cells. The opulence confirmed his first impression that whoever dwelt here was indeed held in high esteem.

"What have we here?" A hoarse voice sounded from the back of the hut, bodiless, its owner shrouded by the roiling smoke. "Why this intrusion so early in the morning? Bhel has hardly risen."

"We have a captive, great one." The blond guard shoved Merlin forward. "He was caught in the Stones. The disrespectful dog had spent the night there, curled up at their feet! We would have punished him in the usual way, but he claims he is a magic man come seeking admittance to our Order."

"I am eager to see this brave or foolhardy one!"

The smoke eddied, and a tall man stepped from behind a skin curtain. He was one of the oldest people Merlin had ever seen, well beyond his fiftieth summer. His hair was so white and fine, it was almost a shade of pale blue, the colour of snowfall at twilight. His long beard was equally pale, tumbling in tendrils over his floor-length robe. Serpent tattoos slithered round his frail arms and coiled in knotwork designs above his eyes, which were shrewd, sharp, grey flints beneath a ridge of frosty brows.

"I am Ambris, Speaker-to-Immortals," he said. "High priest of Khor Ghor. Is it true what my priests tell me? That you broke the sanctity of the Stones and lay amongst them while you slept?"

"It is true, Great Lord." Merlin bowed to the stately elder. "I was in the Stones. But not to desecrate or bring dishonour. They called to me, and all the mighty Ancestors of old called to me too. I come from the mountains far away, but that is my home no longer. My home, my heart tells me, is here, serving the temple of Khor Ghor. I know the number of your priests is less by one, and I would fill that empty place."

Ambris stepped forward and caught Merlin's face in his withered hands, staring into the youth's eyes and searching the depths of his heart, his soul, with a glance that cut like a dagger-blade. After a few minutes, he let his hands fall. "I can see no falsehood in you. Fervour, aye…and maybe, just maybe, some kind of power. Who are you?"

"I am called the Merlin. The hawk that also bears that name is my totem; one travels with me, he comes and goes with the wind, as I do."

Ambris's brows lifted slightly. "There have been other Merlins here, before our father's, father's, father's time. One came to Khor Ghor when the land was forest; he danced the Horn-dance with the Moon, and raised great poles as beacons to the spirits above. He gave his name to these isles — the Merlin's Precinct. Later, there was the Merlin who brought the skystones from the West; floating them down rivers while wolves howled on the bank and strange men flung spears. Three is a magic number, Merlin. Maybe, as the third Merlin, you will be the greatest and most famed Merlin of all."

The priests who had escorted Merlin to Deroweth were gawking. They had obviously expected anger from the High Priest, maybe even an ordered execution. "High One," owl-eyes muttered, "You speak like he's one of us already! Surely he will have to pass the test!"

Ambris glanced at the man with irritation. "Do not fear; he will have to pass the test like every other priest." He turned back towards Merlin. "There is a bed and food here, within my hut. You may make yourself at home. When the next full Moon comes, it will be time to choose a new priest to replace Eckhy, who is lost to us. A competition of wisdom will take place. No man shall have an advantage above the other; no priority is given for status or age. You have as much chance as any other competitor, young stranger. But if you fail, you must leave in the dawn and never return on pain

41

of death. The Stones will have chosen and if they reject you, you must never set foot in their presence again."

The night of the full Moon rolled round after what seemed an interminable time, during which Merlin had stalked around the settlement like a beast trammelled in a cage. He explored the entire settlement, guided by one of Ambris's many attendants, and committed to his mind and heart the places of power: Woodenheart, with its gateway facing Magic Hill at Midsummer, and the Hallows in the centre of the great chalk ring, which was focussed on Midwinter Sunrise in reverse to Khor Gor, where the dying Sun was framed by the arch of the Door into Winter.

He knew he must not fail in his testing, least he be cast into the wilds, a tribeless man — there was no going back to God-of-Bronze and those far off Western lands, not with Vhortiern's blood on his hands. Sighing, he reached to his belt-pouch, brought out Buan-ann's crystal ball and wiped it on his fringed cape. He held it up and stared at the sky through its heart, but today the magic stone was misty and vague, showing him nothing.

"Master Merlin, it is time to make ready." One of Ambris' acolytes appeared from a hut and gestured to Merlin to follow him. "You must be prepared and purified for tonight's testing."

"Are the other men who seek a position here also?" Merlin asked, following the acolyte as he was bidden.

"Aye, Lord Tyllion arrived yester eve from Peak-land, and Uinious from the East this morning, just before the Sun was up. That is why there is so much activity here today. Most of the year, except at the times of festivals, only the priests dwell in Deroweth. The common folk live in the Place of Light, on the Hill of Golden Graves where the tin-men set up their tent-camps long ago, but some have been employed by Lord Ambris to come down to tend to the newcomers."

Merlin glanced over near to Woodenheart, where a gaggle of children, women, robed priests and priestesses, dogs, pigs and even a roving ox milled about in disarray. A cacophony of noise filled the air: geese honking, dogs yapping, babies wailing, women laughing and shrieking, and suddenly he saw a man the size of a black bear sweeping around the circle of onlookers, touching the foreheads of children, laying hands on the bellies of women in blessing. "Is that one of the would-be priests?"

"Aye, Tyllion from Peak-land, which is a land of high hills many miles

42

north, bounded by the Great Dark Forest and guarded by the Mother Mountain and Shining Tor. His folk have blood-ties with Khor Ghor going back many generations to the days of Samothos. Jet is much traded through Tyllion and his people, who purchase it from the Brighi along the northern coastal cliffs."

"And the other man? Uinious?"

"He prays in Woodenheart. He is less boastful than Tyllion of the Peak, but no less determined! Come now, O Merlin, we must make you ready so that you can stand proudly with the other two."

Merlin followed the solemn youth to one of several smaller wooden buildings that stood between Woodenheart and the Hallows. These round huts were for the priests and priestesses, where they washed themselves, performed purification rites, and meditated before commencing with their daily lives. Like the larger wooden temples, these cult-houses were aligned on events in the sky: one on the Moon, which was for female initiates only, one on the rising of the Seven Sister Stars, and another with opposing entrances that faced Sunrise on the quarter-days when light and dark were balanced.

He was taken into the Circle of the Seven Sisters, where several priests awaited him. "Kneel," ordered a hard-faced man in a peaked red hood, and he roughly pushed Merlin to his knees beside a lit fire. Other priests came forth and stripped him of his robes, beating his body with willow-switches, to purify the flesh and drive out any evil humours that might linger in him. Lips taut, he bore the pain without complaint, while sweat mixed with blood upon his bare back.

Once the ritual beating was done, the priests raised him up and painted him from head to toe with symbols, the marks of his tribe and the mark of an initiate. Then they brought back his robes and draped them around him, and gave him his crystal to hold, and they bound his raven hair with a long pin made of bone.

"You are ready," said the red-hooded one. "You may go to Woodenheart to join the others."

Merlin walked across the frosty ground. Dusk had begun to fall, and tendrils of mist curled up like the reaching hands of the untold generations of dead that lay in the barrow cemeteries just beyond Deroweth. Across the field, the bulky Khu Stone, or Hound's stone, sank down into an eerie white cloud, with only its grizzled tip sticking out, sharp as a spear.

On the far side of the plateau the Moon was rising, fat and cold and pale as a skull, casting chill light over Holy Hill and the lands below. "Oh Eye-

Goddess of Moon and Dead Men," whispered Merlin, "look kindly on me this night! They say you were here even before Bhel Bright-face, and that you see into the hearts of all men. Then see I am the one who best who best shall serve Khor Ghor and the Isle of the Mighty!"

Prayer finished, he tore his eyes from the Moon and entered the lintelled gateway of Woodenheart. Inside, a forest of posts and standing stones confronted him. Priests glided between posts and menhirs, ghostly in their rustling robes and fantastical masks. They beckoned Merlin forward, toward three stones that leaned in toward each other like conspirators whispering secrets.

A cove. A sacred space that resembled the mouth of a tomb.

Ambris stood within the cove, his flowing hair a nimbus of red in the light of fires that burned in hearths on either side, the flames fanned by attendants who cast strange powders and oils upon them. On the floor, before a cairn of flints, squatted barrel-chested Tyllion, looking more like a strongman than a shaman, but wearing mystical symbols on his face, and with a holy man's rattle in his hand. Uinious, contender from the east, was kneeling beside him. He was more suave and smooth than Tyllion, with a sandy, bifurcated beard sewn with blue beads, and a strangely-cut tunic fastened by toggles and a fancy bronze pin that must have come from beyond the Northern Sea. He was younger than Tyllion, and his shrewd hazel-green eyes darted everywhere, measuring the mood in the temple.

So this was the competition... Merlin's lip curled contemptuously. He knew he was the right candidate, that these others cared mostly for their own prestige, but how was he to convince the assembly that he would be a greater asset to the Temple than they would? Beads of nervous sweat popped out on his forehead, and he clutched his seeing stone, damp fingers streaking the quartz as he begged the spirits for a sign.

Ambris clapped his hands, and the temple priestesses brought round the Beaker of Peace, brimming with the fermented honey-mead that only men were allowed to drink. Each one of the priestly candidates took a draught, savouring the rich golden taste and the rush of fire in the belly that followed soon after.

Uinious was first to speak. "I come from the East to the West, and will bring new ways and ideas to Khor Ghor and its peoples. The gods have always been with me; I killed a wild cat at nine and my first man a year later."

"I shall bring new ideas too!" roared Tyllion. "Northern ideas!" He took another swig from the Beaker and wiped his red, dripping lips. "The gods have always smiled on me, as much, if not more, than you, Easterner. I have wrestled a bear in a darkling forest, and overseen the bringing of the black jet from the sea cliffs. I have seen the Antlered Man ride from Dark Dale and up the shivering slopes of Mother Mountain, and welcomed the Moon home in the cove of Ar-bar. I know the lore of all living things; I know the names of kings and chiefs who ruled on Albu's shores since time immemorial!"

He stood up, cleared his throat and began to half-sing, half-chant reams of names of people long barrowed away, dust in the wind. The list was obviously pleasing to a few onlookers who doubtless fancied themselves the direct descendants of these ancient worthies, but Merlin grew bored and restive. Any decent storyteller could recite the annals of the Ancestors as well as fat Tyllion.

Uinious grinned savagely as the cumbrous man finished his litany with yet another slurp of honey-mead from the ceremonial Beaker. He tossed back his long, thin head, making the beads in his oiled beard clack like bones. "I have skills that can help us grow closer to the gods and gain their favour. I am skilled with herbs and plants; my knowledge of these is beyond compare. I know of plants that can make a man fly high enough to kiss the icy lips of Mother Moon — and others that, with a mere drop, could fell every living creature in this settlement. I will tell you their names: hemlock, henbane, deathcap..."

Merlin leaned forward, supporting his chin with his hand, eyes glazing over at the prospect of another lengthy bout of posturing. Uinious's plant-lore was hardly new; he had learned the same years ago, when Buan-ann first took him to the woods to train him in the shamanic art. He was so bored, listening to the old ones' flapping tongues, he half-wished the Sea-Raiders would attack that very moment, so that he could test his wits and powers against them.

As Uinious droned on, prattling about his amazing studies of Sun and stars in the wooden temples of the East, Merlin reached for the Beaker of Peace. In its depths he could see the Moon's reflected eye, watching him. Careful to remain unseen, he dropped several mistletoe berries into the brew before draining it to the dregs. The Moon had called to him, with her white horns; he would commune with the spirits, not with these two fools, eaten up by a quest for their own glory.

A few minutes later, his head began to throb, one-sided, in the usual manner. His central vision became a spinning tunnel that guided him toward the spirit realm. The walls of the world fell away; Woodenheart's posts grew huge, spiralling up into the starry sky. The heat of the fire vanished abruptly, the flames turning ice-blue, and the big sarsens that stood in the cove seemed to be rocking in their beds. Across from him, Tyllion had butted in over Uinious and was droning out some stale, ancient folk-tale, much to the annoyance of his rival, whose eyes had narrowed dangerously. Tyllion's rumbling baritone seemed to have become unnaturally slow and deep, wobbling in and out of Merlin's hearing.

"I have something to say…" Merlin's voice rose above the drone, distant and unearthly in his own ears. It was like the voice of someone else, someone older, stronger and more powerful. An ancient, long-gone Merlin, speaking from beyond the veil… "It is my turn, and I have words of greater importance than these pretty tales!"

"You are an insolent brat!" Tyllion roared petulantly, heaving his huge bulk up and clawing for the haft of his axe, but Ambris laid a firm hand on his shoulder and pushed him back to the ground.

"Remember where you are, Tyllion. Under our Law, the boy has the right to speak. He has said nothing so far, while you and Uinious have spoken enough for ten!"

Merlin glanced around him, in strange ghost-world born of his potion. At his feet, by the little cairn of stones on the Midsummer alignment of the temple, a ghostly child was playing with a pebble. She was a small thing, bird-frail, with eyes of mismatched colours. She was touched by the gods, like Merlin himself, but her fate was not his — though he nearly had shared hers, at Vhortiern's circle.

"Help us, Merlin of Albu," she said in her whispery ghost-voice. "Or my sacrifice will mean nothing, and my grave will lie forgotten beneath burnt timbers." She knelt on the cairn of flints before the cove, stroking the stones with thin white fingers.

Merlin reached out to touch her cheek, but his hand went through her and touched the flint that topped her grave instead. "A child lies here," he murmured, quietly but loud enough that the surrounding priests could hear, "her head was split so that her spirit could guard this place with her ardent innocence. She will weep for an eternity if either of these blusterers becomes a temple priest; they are old and the world they knew is passing. It is time for youth to triumph, for youth to build this land anew!"

The onlookers gasped at the young man's presumption. Ambris smiled behind the rim of the Beaker of Peace. Merlin rose, gesturing for the gathered assembly to follow him. Arms held aloft, he walked between the posts of Woodenheart and out into the night, where the rising gale went screaming around the settlement and over the plain, dispelling the last scraps of ground-fog on its boreal breath.

In the distance the hump of the Great Spirit-Path, a linear earthwork far older than Khor Ghor itself, stretched out across the fields like the white leg-bone of a fallen giant. A thousand stars crowned its bank, twinkling like watchful eyes. Some said stars were the most ancient of the dead, set in the firmament to watch over their descendants. If so, they were all out to witness the events of this momentous night.

"Why have your brought us here?" Merlin heard Uinious's dismissive snarl. "There's nothing to see... it is cold, and dark...A waste of our precious time!"

"Silence!" ordered Merlin. "And behold!"

In the North-Western sky, beyond the end of the Spirit-Path, a flash of light tore the blackness asunder. Merlin went cold, then hot, then cold again, as if spirits were touching him, passing through his body. He gave a shuddering cry of ecstasy and, ignoring those around him, began to run towards the light in the heavens. Behind him he could hear shouts and cries, but he paid them no heed.

Out in the field beyond Woodenheart he paused by the Khu Stone, the Stone of Hounds. He could now see the guardian spirit-dogs, snarling around the menhir, red-eared and red-eyed, their bodies white as the chalk of the plain. They ceased their growling and yipped in delight as he raced towards them and sprang upon the stone, teetering on its tip with his arms outstretched toward heaven.

"Sacrilege!" he heard someone bellow and he knew that many arrows were aimed at his back. He did not care. They would not slay him. The signs were in the sky, and he could read them.

He, alone.

"Look you!" he cried. "In the North-West there sails a comet, an omen from the gods! It is a portent."

Behind him he heard puffing and mumbling, and he was vaguely aware of a growing crowd, furled by the shadows.

"And what do you think this comet betokens, Merlin?" He heard Ambris's muffled voice. "Speak now, or speak never again in this company."

Merlin took a deep breath, the cold night air searing his lungs. His head reeled and his tongue felt swollen, hanging heavy in his dry mouth. Letting the trance-state of the mistletoe engulf him, he rocked drunkenly on the Khu-stone, and gestured to the sky.

To the comet with a great bright tail that sailed through the Western heavens, emerging from the Deadlands to betoken new Life.

"The Armed King-Dragon rises in his chariot of stars…" Words tumbled from his lips, flowing like water from somewhere deep inside him, without thought or rehearsal. "But ascending his realm, he shall fall, crown shattered, while Firetail, the Dragon of the Flaming Star beats the drum of War with his bright tail. Strife is coming to the shores of Prydn, but so too the Bear in the Wain, the Dragon's heir with his shield of the sky; and he will be known unto you as Bronze-Wielder, Hammer-Hand, Stone Lord. But the child who will become the man is not yet born upon earth, and those who will give him blood and sinew know not yet their part in destiny's play. I, the Merlin, shall be the one who moves them in this game, and when the Stone Lord is grown to man, he and I shall weave a tale betwixt us that will last ten thousand years!"

Face flushed with ecstasy, Merlin turned from the streaking comet and stared down at the gathered sea of faces, some approving, some shocked, a few openly hostile. But none disbelieved his words, his prophecy; he could see fear and elation, hope and worry within their watchful eyes.

The stars spun above, and suddenly he felt the world lurch, and then he was falling…falling…tumbling from the top of the standing stone, while the phantom hounds bounded in excitement. His brow caught an edge of the sarsen and blood sprang out, which the hounds lapped with their ghostly tongues.

"Blood," he murmured, as black spots spun before his eyes, "is this what you still want from me? Well, I swear if you will give me what I desire, you will have me in the end — not in one death but Three."

The stone seemed to shudder under his touch, and then Merlin fell down into merciful blackness.

Merlin woke around the middle of the next day, his head pounding like a solstice drum and his hair clogged with dried blood. He was lying on a bier of woven withies inside Ambris's house, with a warm and woolly sheepskin over him. The high priest was sitting cross-legged on a fur by the fire-pit, arms folded and eyes closed as he meditated on events beyond the world. Slowly he opened one keen eye, and fixed his young guest with a stare. "So you are awake."

Merlin sat up, clutching his cramping stomach. The headache and nausea

48

always came after close contact with the spirit-world. He could barely recall all that happened the night before, only that he had spoken words of prophecy to the gathered priests. Tidings of a king, yet to be born. A Great King that was to come. "It is dawn... that means the choosing is over. Where are Uinious and Tyllion? Did they..."

Ambris shook his head. "They are gone."

"Gone? Gone where?" Merlin had an unsettling vision of both men striding arrogantly up the Avenue to be initiated as priests of the Temple, congratulating each other that even though neither had been deemed supreme, they had both trumped the mad boy from the West.

"Gone home," said Ambris quietly. "Where else?"

Merlin sprang to his feet, despite his heaving guts and reeling head. "You... you mean..."

"Aye," Merlin," said the high priest. "It is you who passed the test. After that show you gave us last night, few supported those two tedious bores from afar!" He laughed quietly, his face breaking into a thousand merry lines.

Merlin staggered out of the hut into the hazy morning mist that hung over the settlement. A thin trickle of black smoke rose between the oak pillars of Woodenheart, while away in the culthouse a drum was beating, its rhythm matching the beat of his blood. Overhead the Sun's eye was a bleary orange ball, looking down upon him with favour.

Merlin fell face forward onto the packed chalk, kissing the blessed earth, taking the crumbs into his mouth. He belonged here, he had always known this was so, and now he had proved it. "Ancestors, Lord Bhel and Lady Moon, I thank you for this honour. I will not shame you. I will honour you in life and in death."

Ambris came up beside him, and raised him from the ground, brushing the chalk from his clothes. Merlin leaned over and grabbed the hem of Ambris's robe, raising it to his lips. "I will serve you and the temple well; I swear it, my Master. I am young but I beg you — do not doubt me."

"I do not doubt you," said Ambris. "The truth is clear for those who have eyes to see."

"I am here for the sake of Albu, high one. I am here to usher in a time when the people will have no fear of raiders from afar... Though it will not be through feats of arms on my part. I am many things, but no warrior."

"No, and neither am I, nor many who have followed the path of communion with the spirits," said Ambris. "Like you, I have been looking for many years among the tribes, seeking one who can take the role of High Chief of Albu. Five hundred years has it been since there was one ruler over the Five Cantrevs of the West; the Great Trilithon has stood empty, home only to the spirits and the dying Sun. I have searched and have seen many chiefs with strength and heart, but none have been the One who can lead all men, rallying their hearts, and strengthening their hands, no matter their differences of birth or custom.... Our people have one great fault, Merlin, and it is that they spend too much time fighting amongst themselves to see the danger all Prydn faces if the Sea-Raiders are not halted."

Merlin clenched his fists. "The omens in last night's sky foretell the ascendance of the King we seek. He will come, even if the Wise must meddle with the hearts and minds and flesh of ordinary men."

Ambris leaned heavily on his oak staff. "I am old now, Merlin. The quest, I fear, is no longer for me to pursue. But I shall tell you of one that might be of interest... my sister's son, who dwells in the land of Dwr. I read the stars at the hour of his birth, and saw portents there, although there was…weakness too, a shadow in him that I do not understand."

Merlin glanced up with interest. "Tell me more of this kinsman of yours, Lord Ambris"

Ambris's eyes glinted beneath his snowy brows. "He is fourteen summers, tall as a spear and good enough to look upon. His hand is steady on the bow and he fights with the courage of the bear. His name? It is U'thyr. U'thyr Pendraec of the Dragon Path of Dwr."

PART TWO — U'THYR: MOONSET

CHAPTER FOUR

U'thyr marched along the long white back of the Sacred Dragon mound, the winter wind clawing his dark braids back from his face. On side of him the fields of the Dwr, the People-of-the-Water, undulated and rolled away into an icy fog. Near the sides of the Dragon mound, a spirit-road that ran nearly a mile across Dwr territory and dwarfed the similar monument near Khor Ghor, burial mounds clustered like children round a great mother, their summits yellow with old dry grass that had withered after the summer.

Reaching to his belt, U'thyr lifted up a severed head, gaunt and stinking. He dangled it on high by its thick bush of tangled black hair. Its tongue protruded as if poking out disrespectfully at the ancient dead in their clustered mounds. "Ancestors!" shouted U'thyr. "I bring you the head of the leader of those scavengers who dared set foot on Dwr soil, bringing violence and grief to its rightful peoples. Let it be known that while there is breath in my body, none of this creature's kind shall ever settle on Dwr lands, or even have the right to walk here as free men!"

He tossed the head from him; it bounced on the mound's bank, and rolled into the half-silted ditch. Immediately a flock of rooks descended, eager to taste its flesh.

U'thyr, the Pendraec, the Terrible Head, stood upon the top of the bank, feeling the current run beneath his feet, in the soil. He spread out his arms, buffeted by the wind, and, he was sure, by the fleeting spirits of those who had passed before, generation upon generation, their bones mingling with the earth, making it rich and fertile for their descendants through the ages.

He felt good. There was nothing he liked better than a good battle, and to slay a few of the hateful invaders. Smiling, he took his dagger from its calfskin sheath and examined it. Bright bronze, the colour of the dying Sun, reddened and strengthened by the blood of enemies of Prydn. Carefully, he took the flint knife he always carried at his belt as a back-up weapon, and used it to make a notch in the polished antler hilt of his dagger. Eleven Sea-Pirates under his belt. And he was still only ten and seven years old.

He longed to tell Merlin, high priest of Khor Ghor, of his latest victory.

51

Merlin had mentored him since U'thyr was a boy, taking over from his Uncle Ambris, when Ambris sickened with fever one winter and went to the heavenly Ancestors. Merlin, in fact, took a bit too much interest in him, always questioning him about when he would take a wife, wanting to know what girls he bedded, or wanted to bed... and then chiding him if he thought they were 'unsuitable.' Embarrassing stuff, for, as young chief of the Dwr, he was enjoying having his choice of the willing village girls, and heard no complaints from amongst them.

Still, he would be glad to see Merlin again and share meat and tales of battle with him at the Great Midwinter Feast of Deroweth, when the Sun died and was reborn at Khor Ghor, and men could celebrate that winter and shadow would not endure. The feasting would go on for over a week; there would be dancing and drinking and song, and babies and marriages would be made and alliances between clans forged... and sometimes broken.

Slipping his dagger back into its sheath he headed for his village, tucked into a hollow in the side of The Pen or Head hill, which overlooked the great twisting dragon-path as it snaked across the downs. He could smell the hearth-fires burning, and hear the village women singing as they packed for the long trek to Deroweth.

Passing the first hut, he saw his mother, Indeg, directing her serving girls to load the best woollen blankets and sheepskins on to a large wooden cart. All around was hustle and bustle: other carts being loaded, women chasing over-excited children, sheep and cattle driven hither and thither by flushed-faced shepherds with their yapping dogs. Only the very old and the sickly would remain at The Pen, guarded by a few unlucky men chosen to miss the festival.

U'thyr slipped up behind Indeg, made a playful grab for her. "I am back, mother, just in time for the Winter Celebration. The beaches are safe, probably till spring. The stories and tales of the strength of the men of Albu should keep the intruders away."

Indeg hugged him, her face flushed. "I heard of your victory. The entire West knows that Indeg's son is master not only of the Dwr, but of all Albu! Did you bring anything for me from your travels, my dearest son?"

"You will have an amulet made from the skull of the black-bearded leader of the Sea-Raiders," promised U'thyr. "I will carve it myself and get my friend the Merlin to place charms upon it to benefit you. But first our friends the ravens and the rooks must feast upon the ugly creature's flesh to clean it away... And now..." U'thyr nodded toward the weighted-down carts, groaning beneath excited celebrants and their goods, "we should put our thoughts to happier things, to meetings of friends and kin at Deroweth."

"Maybe you will find a nice wife of noble status this year," said Indeg hopefully.

U'thyr snorted. "You're nigh as bad as Merlin, marrying me off to every girl who has half-decent lineage and a face slightly more comely than an aurochs' arse! When the time comes, it will come. Now let's get a move on! I've been travelling several days and look forward to feasting with my men and the other tribes of the West."

Nightfall three days hence found the people of the Dwr arriving at Deroweth. They were not the only arrivals; chieftains major and minor from all over the West and South of Albu had begun to descend on the site. A few had even journeyed from beyond Peak-land, tall men sweltering in furs too heavy for the temperate south-western climes. Tents and yurts were set up on the downs, while families of high status crowded into the empty wooden long-houses that thronged the bank of the Great Circle; their homes this time of the year alone. The whole site, usually reserved for the priests, was a buzzing hive of activity: traders setting up stalls, women and children thronging outside the temples, dogs running about half-mad with excitement, herdsmen driving wild-eyed cattle and shaggy brown sheep into pens where they would be either sold or slaughtered. In one corner, a huge wattle enclosure held dozens of half-grown pigs that squalled and dashed around crazily as children lobbed chunks of mud at them, eliciting the wrath of the pig-boy, who chased the giggling youngsters away with a big stick.

All the longhouses were decorated with holly and ivy, while the great cult houses gloried in renewed splendour, their timbers painted red and their internal hearths alight and puffing out great clouds of dark smoke into the faded winter sky. Skulls of beasts were affixed to their broad lintels, amid bunches of white-berried mistletoe, the plant none but the priests dared touch, sacred to both Sun and Moon, the symbol of peace and fertility. Drums were beating within the great circles, shaking the earth and summoning the tribesfolk to celebrate and chase the darkness of winter away.

Down by the banks of Abona torches glowed in the icy fog as womenfolk poured the ashes of their Ancestors, saved especially for this occasion, into the cleansing swell of the holy river. Their keening and lamenting rose to mingle with the primal thud-thud-thud of the great drums inside Woodenheart and the other cult houses.

U'thyr squatted on the chalk bank of the Great Circle, surveying the activity below him. People in all manner of array strode past. Beakers were raised and honey-mead and beer consumed until men went rolling down the banks into the ditch. There was much laughter and a lot of shouting, as a pair of young hotheads started pummelling each other over a whey-faced girl with yellow hair, who was simpering and feigning horror, when one look at her round, flushed face told how much she was enjoying the whole sad spectacle.

U'thyr snorted in bemusement. To think his mother and Merlin wanted him tied to some wench and acting just like those besotted fools! He'd trust no woman. A man's trust should lie only in his dagger and axe.

His attention was drawn from the fighting youths by the sound of a horn, blown repeatedly, that cut through the dwindling twilight. Peering through the smoke toward the Khu-stone, he spotted a party of newcomers, a good sized troupe with many sheep and cattle, fronted by warriors in stout leather jerkins and red woollen cloaks, one of whom was blowing on a huge ox-horn bound with copper. "All hail to Gorlas of Belerion!" the warrior shouted between discordant blasts of the horn. "Lord of the farthest West, master of tin, tamer of bronze, trader of axes…"

"King of braggarts, by the sound of it," murmured U'thyr, who had arrived at Deroweth with little ceremony. Still, his interest was piqued, for he had never met this Western chief, and he leaned forward straining his eyes into the growing gloom.

The red-caped warriors marched past, followed by Gorlas's shepherds with their flocks for trade and slaughter. Pushed by two youths, an enormous wooden keg trundled by, sloshing some kind of alcoholic drink, followed by a gaggle of sweaty, red-faced women rolling a gigantic Moon-like disc of cheese — both obviously gifts to the Temple to declare Chief Gorlas's wealth and power.

A whip cracked, and the horn blasted with even more furious intensity, and two chunky carts rolled into view, shuddering and juddering across the uneven ground. On the first lay a man, big as a bear, reclining on a bed of rich furs. His hair was blue-black, almost like that of a Sea-Pirate, falling in coils almost to his waist. A golden Moon-collar circled his throat, and his bare chest was tattooed with fantastical animals. His beard was cut short but it was thick and bushy and covered much of his broad, thick-jawed face. Rings and ornaments jangled in his tresses, proclaiming his wealth and rank.

"So that's the man who thinks so highly of himself!" laughed U'thyr, not very impressed. The man was so fat, he looked as though the only way he could kill an enemy would be to crush him with his bulk!

U'thyr let his gaze wander from the corpulent tin-lord to the cart behind. Sitting on a pile of soft sheepskins was a woman clad in expensive blue-dyed linen. She was young and very small, almost child-like in appearance, but there was toughness in the set of her shoulders and the arrogant tilt of her jaw. She had long, loose, wavy dark hair that held a hint of copper fire, and her brow was bound by a diadem of a pale, Moon-coloured metal that U'thyr had never seen before.

"She is a comely woman, is she not?" U'thyr glanced over to see Merlin walking toward him, dressed in his robes of priesthood, a long tunic of tanned hide fringed with the claws and teeth of foxes, badgers, boars, dogs and even the canine of a great wolf that the local villagers had brought down one Winter. A staff topped by a human jawbone was in his right hand, for when he wished to speak to the Dead. Around his neck hung the skull of his long-dead totem-hawk, bound in bronze, with chips of faience for eyes. "But do not stare too much…I've heard Gorlas protects her as a bear protects its young! And can you blame him?"

U'thyr looked over in surprise at his friend, his mentor. He usually thought of Merlin, with his grey-flecked hair and craggy visage, as an old man, unlikely to talk of the charms of women, but he remembered that in truth that the priest was only a handful of years older than U'thyr himself. "Is she his daughter?"

"No, his wife! Gorlas is lord of a tin mine in Belerion and very rich; in fact, he sometimes trades with our enemies to swell his riches, which is why you have not seen him here before; he is not popular amongst the other chiefs. And the girl... the girl is daughter of an ancient family of Belerion; they say her Ancestors' Ancestors came from the Drowned Lands where the Little Sea now flows. He saw her dancing within their holy Circle on Bhel's Eve, and was so overcome by lust that he ran into the stones and snatched her away, kicking and screaming, right in front of the shaman. Her father was so vexed he came here to Khor Ghor to ask the priests to intervene. We decided to let Gorlas keep the girl if he would wed her honourably and pay reparations in gold and cattle to her sire and to the dishonoured temple. He did as asked and within nine Moons the girl bore him a daughter. This secured her position with him, for all his other three wives proved barren — a sure sign the spirits were angry."

"Why has Gorlas come here now, when he is unpopular through his dealing with the sea-folk?"

The corner of Merlin's mouth quirked upwards. "Can you not guess? He has a daughter but that is not enough. Now that the spirits smile on him, he has come to ask them for a son."

U'thyr nodded toward Gorlas's wife, who had climbed down from the cart and gone to the fat man, stretching a hand to help him ponderously descend from his fur bed. "And what is the name of this Western woman, with her silver brow and fierce eyes?"

"Y'gerna," said Merlin. "That is her name. The Queen."

Gorlas and Y'gerna began walking slowly toward the great portal pillars of Woodenheart, surrounded by their followers and the curious crowds of Deroweth. U'thyr was possessed by a sudden desire to see more, and scrambled to his feet, almost tumbling down the bank in his haste.

Merlin frowned at him. "Where are you going, U'thyr? We have only just met and off you run like a deer in the wood! I need to know of your doings in the land of the Dwr, of the raiders and the outcome of your battles."

"Merlin, forgive me!" U'thyr bowled humbly, hoping he appeared suitably apologetic. "But I... I must also ask a favour of the spirits in Woodenheart. Very urgent. I mustn't delay. I will be back as soon as I may."

"A favour, eh?" Merlin tapped the jawbone on his staff with a fingernail, making an annoyed click-click-click. "Just make sure this 'favour' is asked of the gods... and not that girl! Or about that girl!"

"Girl!" U'thyr felt colour flood his face. "I am not... I swear it..."

Merlin waved his hand dismissively. "Go, U'thyr. But be careful. I need your arm against our foes; I don't want it hacked off by bull-headed Gorlas of Belerion!"

U'thyr slid down the bank and pushed his way through the milling crowds. He could feel a tension rising in the tribesfolk, charging the air like lightning. They were almost hysterical with mingled joy and fear: knowing that if the gods so willed the warmer days would soon return, yet terrified that their prayers and sacrifices would not suffice, and Bhel would die upon the Altar at Khor Ghor and never rise again.

Thrusting the wild-eyed revellers, the endless yapping dogs, the trundling sheep, he stepped over the threshold of Woodenheart. Its posts soared around him, as imposing as living trees and red from the heat of the great hearth at its centre, where the little child's grave-cairn lay crossing the Midsummer alignment.

A priest and priestess stood on either side of the cairn, listening to the supplications of a line of men and women. Unlike Khor Ghor, which was the gathering place of spirits on their way to eternity, this temple was a place of life as well as death, its pillars like fossilised trees, permanent and undecayed. People came to Woodenheart to pray for the easy passing of dying elders and sickly babes, and for the birth of strong infants and the continued fecundity of both the womb and the field.

Ahead, half-shrouded in the smoke that billowed from the hearth, U'thyr spotted Y'gerna's arrow-straight back, draped in her long dark hair. Gorlas was clutching her arm as if he feared she would run away, but U'thyr scarcely noticed him. Just a fat old man, puffed up with pride, not worth noticing.

The tiny woman approached the priest and priestess. They turned her around three times, chanting, before leading her deeper into the temple, to the three-sided cove of standing stones that were both tomb and womb. She knelt on the floor, hair spilling like midnight water around her. "Grant me a son, O ancient ones, spirits of earth, spirits of grave!" she cried. "My lord desires a son to rule after him, strong and healthy."

The temple priestess, whitened by chalk from head to toe, stepped forward carrying a set of old, bleached antlers, symbol of the feminine. The priest, painted such a shade of dark blue he looked almost black, moved alongside her, bearing a huge stone phallus decorated with mistletoe. The priestess laid the antlers before Y'gerna and began to chant, holding up her bone-white arms to the sky. The priest's deep voice sang out in answering incantation, and he began to whirl and dance around Y'gerna, waving the phallic sceptre and thrusting it at the heavens and at the supplicant and her husband, who stood staring at the spectacle, his face red and sweating like a piece of cooking meat.

When the priest was done, the priestess took Y'gerna's hand and raised her to her feet. Her eyes rolled and she leaned on the girl's shoulder. A tendril of drool trickled from the corner of her lips. "Yes... yes..." she croaked in a voice coarsened by the smoke of the pyre. "A child shall come to you.... A male child... a special child..." Her fingers caught in Y'gerna's blue robes, clutching at the girl's stomach. "Within the month he will be conceived; he will be a great hero beyond compare. His name will be sung for eternity!"

The priestess stumbled away, shaking, worn out by her prophecy. She dropped, panting, to all fours beside the fire. The priest lay down the sacred phallus. "It will be so," he said. "The spirits have spoken. Go now!"

Y'gerna turned on her heel, her long locks swinging. Gorlas followed her like an eager dog, his podgy face florid and smug. "Well, that is good news. Come, wife, let us go to our tent and make sure the prophecy comes true!"

Y'gerna scowled and lashed out at him with a small, clenched fist. "Don't bother me, you uncouth oaf! I am tired; we have been travelling for days. Let me have at least one night in peace where I may forget my 'duties!'"

Gorlas sprang away from her as though he'd been burnt. His face so suffused by blood it looked as though his bloated cheeks might burst. Y'gerna seemed not to care that he was angry. Without a single glance at her furious, shamed husband, she swept from Woodenheart and out into the frosty winter night.

Intrigued, U'thyr followed, skulking in the distance among the festive solstice crowds. He did not want Gorlas to spot him. Or Y'gerna, for that matter. He just wanted to watch her, light and lithe as a river spirit, brave and fierce as a she-bear. And so pleasing to look upon, with her narrow waist and arrogant but lovely face…

Stop it! He chided himself, feeling foolish. He was near as bad as the two lads fighting over the yellow-headed trull…There were plenty of good women available who were not bound to other men.

He paused, hiding behind a greybeard who was dragging a stubborn goat along and cursing as the animal butted him with stubby horns. Over the man's bony shoulder, he could see Y'gerna walking down the wide path that led to the banks of Abona — the Path of the Sun, which would light up on the morn of the shortest day. But it wasn't the Sun she went to greet, hours away in His bed in Darkness, but Mother Moon, sailing across the distant tree tops. She raised her arms and began to dance, tossing back her hair, moving her slim hips. She sang in a low voice, in a language U'thyr did not know but recognised; the tongue of the Firstborn, who came to Prydn after the Great Ice melted from the land, and hunted great elk and wolves and bear in forests that had now vanished. Later, others speaking new tongues came to Albu, bringing a settled way of living that supplanted the old hunting life. With the end of the hunter, the old language died too, and languages of trade became paramount. Still, a few words of the First Tongue were heard occasionally on the lips of certain sturdy, dark men who still lived a semi-nomadic existence, and some rivers and hills bore names that had no meaning in the common Western tongue.

He paused, watching, and felt a fire burn in his loins unlike any such longing he had ever experienced before. The other women he had lain with seemed dull and trivial, creatures of lowly clay. Y'gerna was a being of the Moon and the night, flitting to and fro like the fireflies that buzzed over the walls of Deroweth.

Like a man possessed, he stumbled forward onto the metalled Path of the Sun.

Y'gerna must have sensed his presence; she ceased her frenzied Moon-dance and turned. Her eyes were midnight hollows; the shadowy webs of her lashes dark on her cheeks. "Why do you stare, stranger? Do you always go about gawking at women you do not know?"

He suppressed a grin. "Not always. Never in fact, before this night."

"It is not seemly."

"Then you should find a place to dance alone, lady. Only a man made of stone would not be entranced by your grace and beauty."

She laughed sharply, and then snorted, "You have a honeyed tongue! What are you... a singer of songs?"

He approached her, shaking his head. He could see stars reflected in the dark pools of her eyes and caught in her damp-frizzed hair. His heart thumped madly. "No, lady. I am head chief of the mighty Dwr. My lands stretch from the sea to the Great Fort of the Plain, Maigh Dhun, to the spirit-path that is known as the Dragon's Back."

"You are young to hold such a vast realm." She looked impressed; he could feel her sharp gaze scanning his features, running approvingly over his torso and down his slim, leather-clad legs. He flushed furiously; he was used to appraising women, not the reverse.

"My father recently passed to Otherness," he said, attempting to hide his embarrassment in words. "He fell to the arrow of a Sea-Pirate. And so his lands are now mine to rule."

Y'gerna chewed her lips. "I am sorry for your loss. I do not like the Sea-people. My husband curries their favour, but I can read deceit and hatred in their eyes."

U'thyr stepped up to her, touching her blue-clad arm. "Why are you with that treacherous fool? He is old and foul, with one foot in the barrow! He does not deserve you."

Her lips pursed, a small hard bud. "He is wealthy and he is powerful, lord of tin and master of many cattle. He is the father of my daughter, Morigau. He claimed me by conqueror's rights and gave my family much-needed wealth. Is that not enough for any woman? Or can you offer me more?"

She tossed back her hair and stared intently into his eyes, her stance fierce, with her legs braced apart and her arms folded. He was all too aware of the Moonlight shining through the fabric of her gown, and the beckoning play of shadows between her breasts.

"If you leave him," U'thyr said gruffly, "I will make sure you and yours will never go short. I will bring you gold from Ibherna, amber and jet from the north and blue star-beads from the south. You will want for nothing, nor will your kin, and you shall not have to endure the lusts of an old, fat, failing man."

She leaned toward him, her hair brushing his cheek, her breath a whisper against his ear. "You will have to kill him, you know."

A fierce, hard look came into U'thyr's gaze. "If I must." He reached for her, breath heavy, wanting in that instant nothing more than to pull her down into the grass, Gorlas and Merlin be damned

She danced away from him, light as a linden leaf in the starshine. "You are a bold fellow, aren't you? I like that. But you need to prove yourself to me by brave deeds, not by brave words. I will leave you now to think on this, U'thyr Pendraec. And on this, least you forget me when the mead wears off." She sidled up to him and let her fingertips drift seductively down his skin-clad thigh, and then, laughing, she sprinted off into the crowd of late-night revellers, leaving U'thyr staring helplessly after her.

Merlin found him a short while later, sitting on the bank staring moodily into the night. "Where have you been?" chided the High Priest "You said you were coming back to discuss important matters with me. But no, I find you moping here with a face sour as an unripe apple! What's wrong, U'thyr? Has the drink curdled in your belly?"

U'thyr leaped up, a sudden spark of green fury in his eyes. Merlin almost stepped back, but did not; he would not show such weakness to his young protégé. "Merlin," snarled U'thyr, his voice harsh, "I must have her! No other will do!"

"Who? What?" the shaman frowned, and then, as realisation hit him: "By Bhel's blood, I knew this was going to happen from the moment Gorlas and his party arrived, and you were there with your eyes where they shouldn't be! This is folly, U'thyr, folly and madness! She is his wife, you fool! We need to be making alliances, not breaking them! Start fighting amongst ourselves, and we are doomed; the Sea-pirates will overwhelm us!"

"I do not care!" U'thyr's tone was hard, dangerous. "It is as if the gods planned the hour of our meeting, and gave me a quest to take her for my own. If I can steal her from Gorlas, maybe the words the priestess spoke in Woodenheart will be relevant to me, not that slobbering half-man!"

Merlin's face grew very solemn and still. "Words? What words were spoken? Tell me, boy!"

"The priestess said Y'gerna would bear a son...a child who would grow so great he would be remembered when we are all dust in our barrows!"

Merlin's eyes grew distant, black; he thumped his staff against the packed chalk. "So... it is her... it must be her. How the Ancestors toy with us! Well, if it must be, then it must be, broken alliances or not. U'thyr Pendraec, I will do what I can to get you this woman. But you must make me a promise..."

"What promise is that?"

"That the firstborn son, this special child, will be given to me at birth, that I might raise him in my own way."

"Yes, yes, whatever you wish." U'thyr waved his hand as if swatting at flies. He was not interested in some putative child, god-touched or no, other than the honour it would bring his line. All he wanted right then was to quell the flames of his passion between Y'gerna's promising thighs, and of that alone could he think.

"Give me two days...the Solstice is upon us," said Merlin, "It will do not good for any of us if the Sun does not return in spring!" He flitted off into the shadows, leaving the younger man burning with his unfulfilled desire on the banks of Deroweth henge.

U'thyr eventually sought the Merlin's hut, where he invited to sleep as a token of friendship. Under sheepskin rugs he slept fitfully, until, shortly before dawn, he was woken by the sound of mournful horns blowing. Groaning, he clambered to his feet, tugged on his boots and trews, and took from a small wooden box the symbols of his chieftaincy, passed on through many generations; gold tresses to clasp his hair, arm-bands that twisted round the biceps like copper-coloured snakes, a bronze diadem decorated with serpentine spirals — the crown of the Head Dragon. He donned them swiftly; fastening the gold buttons on the tunic with chilled fingers, then wrapped his warm fox-fur cloak around him, and went out into the dark-before-day.

Outside the sky was lightening, the night-fog turning violet. Frost glittered on the ground. A solemn drum was banging inside the cult-house in the centre of the earth circle, while Woodenheart and the other smaller timber temples were silent and dark. All around the people of the plain and visitors from the Five Cantrevs flitted like grey ghosts, some with faces painted into skulls, others ash-smeared, dark and sombre. Quietly, with none of the laughter of the night before, they hastened toward the Hallows to wait for the imminent dawn.

U'thyr followed the crowd, alert for any sightings of Y'gerna, but he saw neither her nor Gorlas. He castigated himself inwardly, unsettled by his own weakness where she was concerned; he must strive not to think of her till after the ceremonies were done, least the spirits be angered and play cruel tricks on them all...

Silently he entered the cult-house, stepping over a crescent of skulls which had been chosen from the many sacred bones carried to Deroweth from afar, and took his place among the great of the Five Cantrevs, who stood ranked between the oak posts that stood open to the sky. The common folk crowded outside the circle, silent, and expectant.

Down by the river, the sound of chanting started, and the drummer at the back of the cult-house began to tap out a faster rhythm. The sky above Magic Hill in the East flushed crimson, and suddenly a solitary flame flared beside the waters of Abona, slashing through the mist, chasing back the night and any malevolent wights that might reside in it. The chanting grew louder, and the tongue of flame became a glowing circle of fire, round as the Sun himself, casting out sparks and fiery tendrils into the gloom. Slowly, as the flames intensified, it began to bob up the slope from the great river toward the East-aligned temple.

At the embanked entrance of the Great Circle, U'thyr could now see the source of the flames. Surrounded by a score of priests, Merlin was bearing aloft a huge, spoked wooden disc that had been set alight. Symbolic of the Sun, it blazed into the darkness, imitative of the solar events that would soon occur.

"Today Bhel Brighteye dies and is reborn!" the Merlin cried, holding the solar-wheel aloft. "His Mother is angry, for she is now the Old Woman of Gloominess, The Watcher of the Dead. As a Great Sow who eats her own farrow, she has chased him and bitten him till he is weary and wounded, for he is growing old and weak. He will bleed upon the stones of Khor Ghor this Winter's eve... and then he will be reborn, the Young Son, growing fairer and stronger. If ever it was not so, then the world we know would perish!"

An awed moan rose from the waiting crowd. Women began to wail and tear their hair. Men stomped and cried out to the heavens, raising bronze axes to the still-twilit sky.

Merlin stepped into the cult-house and cast down the firebrand, which was extinguished by the other priests, who flung crumbled chalk upon it, burying the ashes under a mound that resembled a miniature barrow. Then he turned back toward the undulating bulk of Magic Hill and opened his arms wide, his voice rising in a wordless cry of both joy and despair.

At that very moment, the rim of the Sun peeped out from a small gap in those distant snow-crusted hills, a red burning eye, sullen and without warmth. It ascended swiftly, a ball of blood, livid colours staining the sky around it. Sullen beams struck the metalled path that led to the river, and a shaft of wavering, uncertain light streaked into the heart of Deroweth, cutting a path across the grass and entering the lintelled archway of the great cult-house, piercing the shadows beyond.

Another moan came from the crowd, and the drummer inside the temple beat on his drums in a frenzy. People fell on their faces, bowing toward the East, while warriors blew on horns and waved bullroarers that made a terrific, thunderous sound.

Merlin made a jerking gesture with his arms and the noise ceased abruptly. The drums started again slow, steady, but with an added beat, a touch of menace. One of the priestesses ventured forward, her face and naked body blackened with ash, carrying a black-feathered chicken below one arm. She was Night, her hair a snarled tangle of darkness, her teeth in her ebony face as sharp as the fangs of the creatures that prowled the midnight hours. Another woman joined her, body striped with yellow and crimson ochre, bearing a squawking red-feathered bird in her hands. She was the Day, the dying day when Night held mastery over the weary Sun.

Together they entered the cult-house and promptly sacrificed the two chickens, cutting their bellies with flint knives and mingling their blood as day mingled with night at that auspicious time of the year. The women then painted each other with the blood, the essence of life, and daubed it on the carved faces on the stout posts of the unnatural forest that surrounded them, while Merlin read omens and portents in the birds' entrails that lay coiled across the chalk floor.

Heading back outside, the priestesses began to dance a circular, halting dance, and the women of the tribes joined them. The men clapped and shouted. Suddenly one priestess stopped and pointed to the entrance of the Circle: 'Look, he comes, he comes — the cursed one!'

Through the gap came a black billy-goat followed by a man wearing a hideous bull-horned mask. He bore a club, which he used to swat the goat, forcing the frightened beast forward. The animal was dressed outlandishly; a garland of holly on its brow a mock crown that slipped over one rolling, terrified eye.

"Evil!" shouted a priestess, gesturing to the bewildered goat. "Cursed. Drive him from this place, so that he will take away your sins, your pains, your wickedness. Let him take away famine, plague and death… Let all the ills men suffer fall on his cursed head!"

The tribesfolk began to hurl lumps of chalk, handfuls of grass, a finally stones at the frightened animal. They screamed with rage, cursing the goat and cursing every ill that afflicted them — aching bones and abscessed teeth, children who died in infancy, wives lost in childbirth, husbands slain in strife. Their eyes became fierce and wild and they would have run forward and torn the animal to bits had not the priests held them at bay.

This unfortunate beast was not for their pleasure. He would go to Khor Ghor, to please the Old Woman and her Son and take the troubles of Albu's people into the West. At one time, in days long gone, it was a Man who made this sacrifice when the land was invaded, when crops withered and babes went hungry... but for now, a fine, healthy animal crowned with holly would do to appease the forces of heaven and earth.

Merlin looped a rope round the beast's neck and led it toward the river, where waiting rafts and coracles bobbed along the banks. The masked Teaser shuffled behind, swinging his club, forcing the goat onto a raft, where it was trussed up with hemp ropes. Next, the temple priests processed to Abona, singing and chanting. A group of elite suppliants followed them, warriors, chiefs and high status women who would be permitted to enter the stones of Khor Ghor on that night only. Many bore funerary urns packed with cremations; others carried bones scraped clean that would be interred around the ditch. They clambered into the boats, and they party set out into the purple morning, the goat's bleating becoming fainter and fainter as the current carried it farther downstream, to the Old Circle and the start of the Avenue.

The rest of the celebrants spilled out along the verdant banks of the great river, tossing in cremations, wailing and praying, splashing themselves with the cleansing waters of old River-Woman. U'thyr walked along proudly with members of his warband, long-shanked Kol, swift-handed Rivan, Govna the smith of the Dwri, who wrought doughty blades. He tried to keep his mind on spiritual matters but his thoughts kept slipping back to Y'gerna dancing under the Moon. He glanced around surreptitiously, hoping to spot her, but could not see her in the heaving throng milling about on the banks of the river.

After a long walk, the tribesfolk reached the start of the Sacred Avenue. They hurried along it, crying out to the heavens, beating the path with the thighbones of Ancestors. Mothers with babies strapped to their backs held up yellowed, age-worn skulls, clacking the jawbones and making a sinister,

64

rhythmic noise amid the ululations of the mourners and the reedy skirl of bone pipes.

Reaching the bend of the Avenue below the ridge of the Seven Kings, where mighty white barrows stood glittering with frost, the celebrants paused, gaping and awe-struck. The great sanctuary of Khor Ghor rose up on the Plain before them, shining like a beacon, its stones warm in the crisp winter light, the shadows of trilithons and free standing menhirs running like black fingers across the grass. Two fire-pits glowed before the entrance, and priests were driving long-horned cattle through in rites of purification. Drumbeats came from within the circle, slow and steady, bouncing from stone to stone, while deep, otherworldly horns blew in the heart of the sanctuary, almost sounding like chthonic voices as the great megaliths reverberated to the sound.

The celebrants halted outside the henge bank, for this was as far as was permitted for most. Excitement hung in the air, and men drank heartily from beakers before ritually breaking them, killing them as the Sun was killed on this day, and soon the people of the five Cantrevs became very noisy with the shouts of boasting, cheering, intoxicated men. The women did not drink the honey mead — a man's drink — but they had a thinner brew of their own that made them just as merry as their menfolk.

Like the others, U'thyr hastily imbibed as much of the mead as he could. The more a man could drink without vomiting or unconsciousness, the higher he was held in the esteem of the others. It was also thought that the effect of the mead could put one into close proximity with the spirit-world, while also giving a warrior courage and unnatural strength.

He had just downed his fourth beakerful when he saw Y'gerna caught within the ring of revellers, her hateful bloated husband flapping about her like some sinister, flesh-gorged raven. She was clad in a tight dress of tanned deerskin, and her hair was braided many times and set off by blue beads. A great chunk of honey-hued amber from the north rested on a thong between her breasts.

He could not keep his eyes off her, and he felt both the fire of the mead and the fire of his lust well up in him. Heat suffused his face, although the air around him was cold.

As if sensing his stare, Gorlas turned his head towards him, his piggy black eyes full of anger. It was almost as though he sensed that here was a rival who could bring his whole world crashing down. He scowled evilly, his face twisted like that of some hideous demon from the Otherworld.

The sight of Gorlas's contorted visage turned U'thyr's lust to white-hot rage. He wanted the man dead, and his hand stole to the antler hilt of his dagger. His companions milled about him, seeing the murderous look in his gaze, and tried to calm him. Violence among rivals was forbidden at the temple, with harsh penalties exacted, especially on this sacred day.

Knowing of this prohibition, Gorlas swaggered over, his beard split by a white gap-toothed grin. "You stare at me…at my wife," he said. "Maybe, one day, when you are grown, you will get yourself a woman as fair as Lady Y'gerna. That is, if some angry husband does not cleave your skull first. I would smite you myself, but it is Solstice. And Gorlas of Belerion is magnanimous."

U'thyr made a lunge at him, but Kol and Govna grabbed his arms and dragged him back.

"You will be sorry you spoke those words," U'thyr snarled. "When I split your skull and let your spirit out, and lie that very night between Y'gerna's thighs!"

Gorlas laughed. "Idle threats, from a boy who is a chief but has gained it only through lucky descent from his betters! Prove yourself a great warrior and then maybe I will battle you. I could use some sport! But now, I would not even raise my dagger to you, it would be an insult to the might of my arm. I do not fight children!"

U'thyr flushed; he knew he was the youngest of all the chieftains in the Five Cantrevs. "Prove myself I shall!" he spat. "Tonight, back in Deroweth, I will claim the Champion's Portion, in the way done of old, and be lord of the feast with nothing denied me! Then you will be sorry, old man!"

Gorlas's face went pale but he promptly regained his composure. He laughed harshly, dismissively. "I hardly think so. If you follow such a course of madness, my young friend, you will be dead before the night is over!"

CHAPTER FIVE

U'thyr made another lunge at Gorlas but his warband pulled him back, keeping him from committing an act that would have been seen as sacrilegious, especially outside the very portal stones of Khor Ghor. Kol yanked U'thyr's arms behind him, keeping his fingers well away from his dagger, while Govna poured a brimming beaker of mead over his head, making him roar with rage but having the desired effect of distracting him from his enemy.

"Hush, my chief," said Govna, as U'thyr bellowed and kicked at him, his sodden hair straggling in his drink-maddened eyes. "You must cease this fight with Gorlas — for now. It is almost time! The Sun is almost dead!"

There was a sudden blast of noise from the shielded heart of Khor Ghor: a cacophony of chanting, wailing and blowing horns, flat and sinister.

Merlin appeared in the central arch, seemingly in a trance, holding up a bloodied dagger of harsh black stone — an ancient artefact from a thousand years past. Standing between the Watchers, he wiped the gore in streaks upon his face and licked the blade. Behind him, the Sun was going down in a welter of blood, setting puffy-ridged clouds on fire. Slowly, slowly the orb tumbled through the firmament, until it was framed, the bloody eye of the dying winter-god, between the immense arches of the Great Trilithon, Door into Winter. It hovered briefly above the shimmering head of the Stone of Adoration, and then sank into the West, utterly vanquished.

"He is dead...but he will rise again!" Merlin held his sinewy arms up to the sky in ecstasy. "And so too will a great Chief, greater than the men of today, a man like unto our blessed forebears, those mighty ones who braved the seas to come to Albu the White! I have read this in the entrails, in the death throes of the Chosen Beast and I have read it in the patterns of the sky! It will be, and Albu shall be great once more! As Bhel Sunface will rise on the morrow, strong and renewed, so too shall the fortunes of Prydn rise!"

The crowd cheered. Some men began to leap and stamp their feet before the pit-fires and the gross bulk of the Stone of Summer. Women joined hands and danced a circular dance around the outside of the bank, singing to the Sun that was gone into the Land of the Dead, and to the Moon, the woman's planet, that was rising in ghostly majesty over Magic Hill in the East.

The priests and supplicants inside the stone circle began to process out of the ring, two acolytes dousing the fires at the entrance, as the Sun itself was extinguished. The crowd began heading back down the Sacred Avenue, mood lighter now that the Merlin had foreseen the rebirth of the Sun and a new dawn for Albu. The drummers came along behind, still playing, while masked flautists leaped amongst the crowds blowing on their bone pipes.

Back in Deroweth, the warbands of U'thyr and Gorlas sought desperately to keep the two chieftains apart. Now that U'thyr had, in Gorlas's opinion, doomed himself by boasting of the deeds he would do, the older man took the opportunity to make U'thyr's boasts known to all the peoples of the Five Cantrevs. Waving a beaker about, with mead slopping down his arms and torso, he pointed to his young adversary. "Look over there!" he slurred. "A young pup who thinks he's a hero! Who thinks he has right to my wife. MY wife! Ah, I cannot wait to see him humbled. He said he'd claim the Champion's portion! "

Red-faced and furious, U'thyr tore himself away from his men and stormed towards the leering Gorlas.... only to find his path blocked by a herd of squealing young pigs that were being driven by two acolytes of the temple. The animals were fat and rosy, fed with honey to make their meat taste sweet. They would be slaughtered today, chased by the young men of the tribes, who would shoot them with arrows, making sport rather than mere slaughter, with the man who slew the most being awarded 'the Champion's portion' — the right to eat the first of the cooked flesh, from the largest, juiciest pig in the herd.

Raising his arms to the sky, U'thyr cried out in a great voice: "Let no man speak me ill this day…for I will claim the Champion's portion! I will be Lord of the Feast, the Winter King! But... he paused as the sea of faces around him grew thicker, deeper, interest piqued by his show of bravado, "I will not be testing the strength of my bow arm tonight! I will become one with my quarry, I will become the Sun himself, chased by the Hag of Winter, his dam and his bane! I will run with the pigs!"

A gasp rose from the crowd. In their father's father's day, it was customary to have a man run through the heaving, squealing herd of pigs, while the youths let fly with their barbed arrows. If the man lived — and most often he did not — he was feted as King-for-a-day, and had his every wish granted and the Champion's portion on his platter. If he died, pierced by many arrows, his remains would be thrown under the pig bones in the great middens around the settlement.

"Do not do this, my son!" U'thyr's mother Indeg staggered up to him, face twisted in anguish. "What madness has possessed you? You are a chieftain, not some callow boy out to prove his manhood! You must not risk yourself this way!"

"Begone from me, woman!" snapped U'thyr. He was beyond reason now, the mead and the day and his passion bringing him almost to the point of what some called the warrior's madness, where a man might foam in rage like a beast gone mad.

The crowd stirred restlessly, their faces flushed and a strange primal eagerness in eyes that sudden grew bright and small and dangerous, desirous of excitement and blood. They jostled each other, elbowing and pushing to get a better view.

The acolytes rounded the pigs to one side of the white chalk walls, while helpers set up temporary fences, forming a long straight avenue similar in appearance to a spirit-path. The village youths fetched their bows and their most lethal arrows with translucent quartz tips and goose feather fletchings. They hollered and yelled, strutting like peacocks before the village women in bright headdresses and paint, setting arrows on fire and shooting them high above the waters of Abona in brilliant barbarous display.

U'thyr stepped forward, handing his beaker to Kol. Slowly he stripped off his tunic with its rich gold plate, and handed it over, too, followed by his armbands and diadem. Govna ran up with a pot of ground ochre and drew protective designs on his torso, zigzags and whorls, the surprised eyes of the Guardian. When this ritual was completed, U'thyr bound up his long leaf-brown hair with a pin of bone, and unsheathed his dagger.

"I am ready!" he shouted. "I will run with the pigs and be the Winter-King!"

The crowd roared its approval; beakers clashed and clattered. Vaguely U'thyr could hear Gorlas yelling, "Die, die, DIE!"

Face set, U'thyr swung over the fencing and dropped in amongst the pigs. They squealed frantically and dashed in all directions, bashing into walls and each other. U'thyr launched himself forward, his calves slamming into the slower pigs' bottoms, almost making him fall. Mud and faeces oozed under his feet, as he swayed, struggling to keep his footing as the frightened beasts swarmed around him.

Suddenly he heard a sinister hiss, like the sound of a dozen snakes. Out of the corner of his eye, he saw the young men draw and release their arrows.

The race was on.

The first arrow took out a pig just in front of him. The animal fell, stricken, a clean kill. The people watching on the sidelines and the henge bank loosed a roar of unanimous delight. U'thyr leaped over the twitching carcass as the rest of the arrows whistled around him, some hitting the ground, others finding their marks among the terrified pigs, who were now almost screaming in fear, their voice high-pitched and surreal, almost like the shrieks of tortured human beings.

U'thyr darted forward again, zigzagging from side to side of the run as more arrows whistled overhead. One nicked the tip of his shoulder, drawing blood, but he hardly noticed. He just ran faster, weaving in and out of the mass of frightened beasts. Faster came the arrows and more thick, their fletchings momentarily dimming the Moon, but U'thyr eluded their barbs and only the pigs lay dead and dying in the run.

The people began to chant his name, "Pendraec, Pendraec, PENDRAEC!" over and over, and to stamp their feet in rhythm with the chanting of his name. It spurred him on even more. He leaped high into the air now, while arrows whizzed below him, then went into a roll as flint tips thudded into the earth around him...

Leaping back up, he bounded toward the far end of the run. Up on the banks he could see the stout frame of the hated Gorlas silhouetted against the stars, with Y'gerna a smaller silhouette at his side. Merlin was hovering several feet in front of them, his face inscrutable in the flickering torchlight.

Another arrow hissed by, the wind created by its passage caressing his cheek like the cold finger of death. He dropped to all fours, crawling amidst the blood and entrails and shrieking animals, whilst another volley sailed overhead and thudded into pigs near the end of the run. They dropped, twitching in their death-throes.

U'thyr tossed the bodies aside. He was near to completion of his task now, unscathed except for the small wound to his shoulder. Blood streaked his chest but he paid it no heed; it was like protective war paint. He was so close to the finish he could see his men; his mother's anguished face; the impassive visage of the Merlin. Hands reached over the rails, trying to touch him, the day-king, the Champion of the Winter feast, and to lift him out of the blood and filth to safety and to glory.

But no, he had one more act of courage to perform as Champion of the Feast. He must choose the animal from which the sacred portion would be carved. Glancing around, he saw one particularly large black pig rushing back and forth, grunting and foaming in fear. Its eyes were red, almost mad in its terror. For a moment man and beast looked each other in the eye, and then they came together in brutal conflict, rolling amidst carcasses and steaming dung.

U'thyr reached to his belt and snatched out his dagger. "Brother, you have fought the good fight tonight!" he whispered into the pig's bristly ear, as he put his knee across the fleshy neck and yanked back the head. "Be pleased that your spirit will be honoured, and that your flesh will go to nourish the people of the Five Cantrevs!"

With that, he slit the pig's throat and released its life force into the night. Standing up, he grabbed the carcass and raised it over his head like a trophy. Blood showered over him, mingling with the red stream from his own wound.

The crowd cheered again and hurled down boughs of holly and mistletoe, for he was without question the Winter-King, king for a day.

U'thyr heaved the pig's carcass up, flinging it over the fence toward Gorlas and Y'gerna where they watched on the bank. It fell with a thud before them, split throat showering blood. U'thyr then vaulted over the rail and stalked over to his kill, dragging it up by the head. "I claim the Champion's portion!" he cried, his voice guttural, almost animalistic. "Does any here gainsay me?"

There was no answer. Gorlas's face was a twisted mask of rage — and fear. In silence, Merlin strode over and began to paint designs on U'thyr face and shoulders with the warm blood of the pig. Then he flung out his arms and shouted, "Hail the champion, lord of the feast, Midwinter's King! Let nothing he asks for this eve be denied him!"

A wolfish grin split U'thyr's bloodied visage. "I ask but one simple thing…" He stepped toward Gorlas and Y'gerna, noticing that the girl was staring at him with dark, admiring eyes. He stretched out his hand, filthy and red. "A kiss from the lips of this queen who has driven the cold of winter from my flesh with her presence."

The crowd muttered; Gorlas's face was thunderous, but he knew he could say nothing to the winner of the Champion's portion. Y'gerna reached out and placed her slim fingers on U'thyr's bare shoulder. "For the Champion," she said, and she tilted her face to his, her dark hair raining back like a waterfall, past her slim hips, almost to the backs of her knees.

U'thyr devoured her red mouth like a wolf, tasting his own blood, salt, the mead they had both drunk that night.

The moment was broken by an enraged scream from Gorlas. "This is outrageous! Champion of the feast or no, I won't be made a fool of by some young idiot! I shall leave at once, and I will never come here again! Khor Ghor is corrupt and the gods will soon speak their anger. And you…you harlot…" He snatched Y'gerna's arm and yanked her away from

U'thyr, "you've had too much to drink! Go find your attendants, and make ready for the journey back to Belerion!"

He pushed Y'gerna out into the darkness and followed after, cursing and shoving her to make her go faster.

U'thyr turned to Merlin, eyes wild. "I must kill him now! I cannot let her go…"

"Silence!" The Merlin laid a warning finger to his lips. "You will have what you want, I will see to it, but we will do this my way, so that there will be as little blood spilt as possible, and none here in this holy place of priests. As I said before, we do not want war with the men of Belerion, who have long been allies of Khor Ghor and also of Ar-morah across the Short Sea. Meet me at Moonset, by the Khu stone… and put your trust in me."

The rest of the night dragged for U'thyr, despite his position as Champion. He feasted, tearing off huge chunks of meat then throwing the half-eaten remains to the hungry dogs, which ran from reveller to reveller, tongues lolling and tails wagging frantically. He drank deep heady brews that made his head spin. He dandled women on his knee, some dark, some fair, some red as fire… but they could not drive out his lust for Y'gerna. It was as if she had bewitched him with some ancient woman's magic.

At last the fires started to die away and the people disappeared in twos and threes to seek their huts and tents. U'thyr called his warband to him, and, with their weapons concealed under their cloaks, they wandered through the smoke and mist to seek Merlin at the Khu-stone.

The shaman was waiting by the hump-backed menhir, wrapped in a skin cloak with a hood pulled up to hide his face. "Follow me…" he said, and he led the small party out across the night-cloaked expanse of the Great Plain.

"How far has Gorlas got, think you?" U'thyr strode next to the older man, dagger unsheathed and jaw tense.

"His rage carried him swiftly for a few miles," Merlin smirked, pushing back his hood. He had repainted his face; it looked frightening beneath the Moonglow — skull-like, a symbol of death to come. "But he's not so young, and his bones ache…and I slipped a sleeping drought into his drink at the feast, and he took three draughts of it!"

U'thyr laughed sharply. "His gluttony may have served me well!"

Merlin's eyes glimmered. "I then sent a tracker to follow his trail… Gorlas has camped for the night at the old fort of Sarlog, which lies

72

betwixt the plain and the lands of the Willow."

"Sarlog... never did I think the site of its broken ramparts would be so sweet to me," murmured U'thyr and he lengthened his strides, knowing that Y'gerna was waiting for him there. Waiting for him to free her from her husband, to take her to his bed, to claim her as his own woman

Soon the crown of Kar Sarlog appeared on the horizon, a whitish blot against an obsidian sky. Vast earth ramparts, partly ruinous, spiralled upward to form a vast black cone. The sides were chalky and strewn with bushes, attesting to the fort's desolation, but on top tents rustled in the breeze and fires flickered. U'thyr would have rushed for the main gate then and there, but Merlin held him back. "No. That would be folly. Gorlas will be half-expecting you to follow him, and his men will be on guard."

"We should have brought more warriors!" snarled U'thyr. "Stormed the place, and killed them all..."

Merlin's eyes flickered. "I told you — no more blood than is necessary! You will get what you desire... I promised I would help you, did I not?"

"Then work your magic, wizard!" snapped U'thyr.

Merlin knelt on the ground, hands splayed on the earth. He closed his eyes and began to chant. He rocked back and forth, teeth grinding, calling on unearthly forces to help him, to help U'thyr. Reaching into his belt-pouch he brought out a switch of rowan and beat himself with him until blood beaded on his flesh — his own sacrifice, himself to himself, on this night of power and destiny.

For a long while nothing happened. U'thyr began to stalk back and forth, his eyes wild as a caged beast's, the cold wind licking droplets of sweat from his agitated brow. His men looked helplessly one to the other; they did not ken the ways of sorcerers or even of their lust-maddened chief.

Suddenly Merlin leaned back on his heels, panting, drooling, his face-paint smeared. His eyes were black as coal, inhuman, the pupils distended and the whites full of red veins. "It is done!" he rasped. "Look into the valley!"

U'thyr and his men gazed into the vale that swept down from the Western side of the hill-fort. A white mist was curling, rising, rolling toward them. Higher and higher its tendrils reached, blotting out the stars, sucking in bushes and trees and rocks. The men huddled close together, warriors or no; for they half fancied they could see faces in that mist — cold dead faces, eyeless skulls, yawing mouths of beings that detested the living that walked beneath the Sun.

"The mist is the Faeth, the fog of Oakseers," said Merlin. "It will last but a few hours. Go now, U'thyr and call Gorlas to combat. When he is vanquished, take his battle-helm and place it upon your own head. You will seem as Gorlas to his people, and you can go to the Lady Y'gerna without detection."

U'thyr looked at his mentor, suddenly grateful. "Merlin, my friend, my helpmeet, I have been acid-tongued towards you this eve. What can I give you, to repay all that you have risked for me?"

Merlin inched up to the younger man, his dark gaze locked with U'thyr's. "I told you before. One thing only will suffice. A child. The child. The first male child that you get on Y'gerna. That is all I ask."

"Yes, yes, whatever you want, it is yours…"

"Then go… and may the Ancestors smile on you!"

U'thyr scrambled up the hill, tripping on rabbit holes and roots hidden by the sorcerous Faeth.. Ahead, he could see the gateway, undefended, open like a mouth inhaling the unholy mist of Merlin. Fires flickered beyond, hissing in the sudden damp.

"Gorlas of Dindagol!" he shouted, drawing his dagger. "I, U'thyr son of Kustenhin, call you out for single combat! You have insulted me, who became Winter's king through my prowess, and you have shown disrespect to the Temple of Khor Ghor. You are not a man in my eyes, but a beast — a foul, rutting boar that needs to be culled!"

There was a roar of rage from within the encampment, and moments later U'thyr saw the helmeted figure of Gorlas silhouetted against the guttering fires, a huge stone battle-axe in one hand and a bronze rapier in the other. His warriors milled around him, bleary eyed, not sure what or who was attacking

"Where are you, U'thyr Pendraec?" Gorlas shouted. "Show yourself!"

"No, you come to me — alone!" cried U'thyr. "Or are you so fearful that you must surround yourself with younger, doughtier men!"

Gorlas roared again and launched himself through the gateway. His warriors blundered after him, uttering war cries that fell dead in the mist. They crashed down the slopes of the fort, tripping on stunted shrubs, sliding on winter-rotten leaves as cold and slimy as dead flesh… and then at the bottom, the enchanted fog curled up to engulf them, all arms and legs and twisted faces full or sorrow and hate. There came a soft whirring noise, like the fluttering of a bird's wings wildly beating — or the wind through the fletchings of an arrow in the dark — followed by a series of muffled shrieks and then deathly silence.

U'thyr and Gorlas found themselves alone on the hillside, the mist forming a circle, an unearthly arena, around them. Purposefully, U'thyr stepped toward his adversary, his dagger held in ready, every muscle tensed. Gorlas dropped into a crouch, growling like a beast, and indeed he looked much like an animal in his rude fur cloak and grotesque helmet fashioned from a boar's head.

For a few minutes they circled, each getting the measure of the other, and then, uttering an unearthly yell, Gorlas barrelled forward, head lowered, the boar's tusks on his helm thrust forward like a pair of additional weapons. U'thyr sprang back in surprise; he had expected an axe swing or a slash from the rapier. He stumbled against a tree, and Gorlas rushed past him, the impetus of his attack carrying him beyond his intended quarry. Slipping on leaves, he managed to halt himself and turn around ponderously... in time to see U'thyr bearing down on him, dagger upraised.

Panting, he flung up his axe and U'thyr's blow smashed against the wooden haft, cutting a great gouge. There was a crack and the wood parted. and the black polished axe head thudded to the ground.

Gorlas yelped in fury, but his anger turned to mirth as he saw that his opponent's weapon had suffered a similar fate. The bronze blade of U'thyr's knife had bent with the power of his blow and was in danger of breaking in two.

"I have you now, young fool!" he grunted, raising his rapier. "You should have stayed in Deroweth with the womanish priests. You would have reigned as chief for another year...but now the Dwr shall have no ruler and I shall make a drinking cup of your skull. I shall make that faithless whore Y'gerna drink from it every night."

"I am not done, Gorlas," said U'thyr, falling into a crouch. "I still have one weapon — the strength of my arms!"

Gorlas laughed. "You! Thin as a reed! Know you that I once wrestled a wild boar unarmed and won — hence the head upon my helm!"

"Looking at that mangy token, the battle was many long years ago," U'thyr retorted. "Once your limbs were doubtless strong.... Now they are merely fat!"

Gorlas snarled and leaped at his adversary, his blade making slashing sounds through the chill air. U'thyr ducked and swung a balled fist into his stomach, making the older man double over and gasp for breath. Purple-faced, Gorlas stumbled in his direction, dagger stabbing aimlessly, free hand groping for a handful of cloak, tunic, hair...

U'thyr darted behind him, trying to kick through the banks of sodden leaves on the ramparts of the fort. He slipped and fell heavily amid the slimy mulch, and Gorlas made a wild lunge with his knife, thinking his luck was in... but U'thyr grabbed a handful of the mouldering leaves and rammed them into his face.

"You fight unfairly!" screamed Gorlas. "You fight like a maid afraid of being tupped!"

"You are the one who fights like a coward — a man with a weapon against one with none!" U'thyr shouted back.

"I have had enough of your tongue!" Gorlas yelled, and he lunged at U'thyr once more, adrenaline giving him a speed unnatural in one so fat and indolent. Like a maddened ox, he charged at U'thyr, arms flailing madly, pointlessly, his mouth open in a frothing, mad shout.

And U'thyr, with the litheness of youth, once again sprang up into the misty darkness, swinging on the bough of a shrivelled hawthorn tree above the reach of Gorlas's sword. The fat man, as before, blundered forward, carried along by his mad, headlong rush and the weight of his own corpulent frame.

He began to slip on leaves, as U'thyr had done, his legs bowing and his cloak billowing and tangling with bushes. The hillside beneath him was tilting, while around him rose the Faeth; its coiling tendrils full of sneering, jeering faces and hooded, accusing figures. "What evil magic is this?" he screamed, and he slashed wildly at the phantoms with his rapier.

Still he was propelled forward, unable to stop himself, toadstools crushing to pulp beneath his boots, branches whipping his cheeks, cobwebs breaking over his eyes and obscuring his vision. He was gathering speed, sliding, slipping, knee-deep in mud and mulch...

And then, suddenly, his feet were free and kicking....

In cold air, with no solid earth below him.

He hung in mid-air for a moment, as if dangled by some giant's child, and then suddenly he began to fall, to plummet like a stone toward whatever lay below, shrouded in the eerie fog. He shrieked once and the faces in the mist twisted with mirth and anticipation.

Through tearing eyes, he saw the mist opening below him, parting to accept his heavy frame. There was grass, and mud, the bottom of a ditch ... and the fallen trunk of a hoary oak, with bare branches radiating out from it like sharpened spears.

"No!" he shrieked, clawing at the mist, the sky... and then he hit the fallen tree and lay like a sacrifice upon an altar, head back, eyes wide, the spoke of a huge tree branch jutting up through his belly. Blood pattered on the floor of the ditch.

U'thyr slid down the embankment to the side of his fallen foe. Gorlas was clearly dead, his eyes already glazing. Carefully U'thyr removed his helm with its ugly mask and placed it on his own head. Unfastening the dead man's cape, he wiped it free of blood spray as best he could and wrapped himself in it.

"May Merlin's magic make me seem enough like Gorlas!" he muttered, and he began to climb back up to the entrance of Sarlog fort.

He passed through the gates unchallenged. He saw some men looking at him quizzically, and snarled in a gruff voice, the sound distorted by the swirling fog: "He is dead... the fool who mocked me is dead. Go back to your rest."

"But lord, what of the warriors who went out with you tonight?" asked one old man, his face creased with worry. "Where are they? Why are you alone?"

U'thyr kicked a water bucket over, spraying the man. "I've fought a battle for my life and you pester me with questions? They are chasing my enemy's men, hunting them down. They will not be back for hours yet for I have ordered that they slay every last man."

Gorlas's people murmured, nodding, glad at his words, and comforted to think that their enemies were put to flight. U'thyr turned from them and blundered through the sea of hastily thrown up tents, looking for one that seemed as if it might belong to a chieftain. Sweat poured down his face under the reeking helmet of Gorlas.

Up ahead he spied one tent that was larger than the others, its sides painted with chevrons and zigzags. Two small braziers glowed before the doorway and he could smell the scent of burning herbs, sweet on the night air.

She was in there, waiting for him — he knew it.

Breathing heavily, he approached the door and flicked back the entrance flap. Inside a stout woman was poking a fire with a stick, and he felt his stomach knot with anger and disappointment. But then, behind the woman, he spotted Y'gerna lying on a bed of sheepskins. She was slowly, languorously, combing her dark locks with her fingers. Coyly, she looked over at him, and a small smile touched her lips.

The woman by the fire had stopped stoking the flames and was peering nervously at her mistress. Y'gerna flicked a hand at her. "What are you gawking at, drab? Get out, you know my lord is always filled with ardour after his conquests."

The woman bowed and scurried away. Y'gerna rose, letting the sheepskin round her shoulders drop to the floor. She was lean and lithe; her wiry body scarcely showing any signs that she had born a child nigh on a year ago. "Let me undress you, my lord," she said hoarsely, reaching out to unfasten his cloak, and as it dropped to the floor: "My lord…U'thyr!"

U'thyr said nothing, he had no flattering words, no pretty lover's speeches, but that did not anger Y'gerna — she did not want them, this fierce Western princess of the old blood. He jerked her towards him, and she kissed him as fiercely as he had kissed her on the ramparts of Deroweth, drinking of his mouth as if she meant to draw out his very soul.

Maybe she had done exactly that. He had never felt like this before, possessed by a kind of madness.

Gasping, he fell forward, bearing her down into the mounded piles of furs and skins. Her hair streamed out, dark as night-time water, tangling around his arms, flowing over the hard peaks of her high, round breasts. She was like some primeval deity lying there, a goddess of earth and love and war, with her dark eyes glowing and her lips red and wet. She could be his life… or his death.

Outside he could hear Gorlas's folk beginning a dance round their fires, a victory dance that would soon turn to tears. Drums started slowly and rhythmic, and so too did he move with Y'gerna, twined in the oldest dance of man since time began.

###

Out in the valley beyond Merlin heard the drums and glanced up at the darkened hilltop. Making his way across the ramparts, he spied the body of Gorlas of Dindagol lying as it had fallen, his blood feeding the hungry earth below him.

"So U'thyr has succeeded!" The shaman glanced up toward the shadowed gateway of the ancient camp. "He must be lying with the woman even as I stand here."

He clapped his hands and slowly, slowly, the mists receded. A great joy overcame him, as in his mind's eye he beheld a vision of the future, of the great man that he would mould to his will from childhood. He began to dance and whirl, stamping in time with the drums from the hillfort, calling on the Ancestors to bless this night, to bless U'thyr and Y'gerna's loins, to bless the child that would be born to give his strength to Albu the White.

CHAPTER SIX

The Sun came up in a cold, watery haze above Sarlog. In the encampment, the folk of Belerion lay sleeping, worn out by their long trek and the dancing of the night before. Even the dogs slumbered, twitching by the remains of the fires.

Only one woman stirred, bleary eyed, her heart filled by an unknown sense of dread. The warriors had not returned.. On silent feet she crossed the centre of the fort to the unmanned gateway and stared down the hill. The fog of the previous night had burned away and the naked branches of trees stuck up like the denuded bones of skeletons.

She cocked her head, trying to focus. There seemed to be something lying in the bottom of one of the mighty defensive ditches, a crumpled bundle of rags slung over a tree. More bundles lay scattered through the woods beyond, empty sacks of clothes. A sick fear suddenly rose in her gut and she strained her eyes into the morning Sun.... and began to scream.

Her shrieks brought instant wakefulness to the rest of the tribesfolk. Leaping up, they ran to the gate and peered down. More women started to wail, and the men rushed down the slope, drawing daggers from their belts. In horror they found their best warriors dead, slain by arrows in the night, and their lord, Gorlas, lying impaled upon the great tree, the birds of carrion already gathering about him, squabbling over morsels of eyes and nose.

They dragged his corpse free and, howling and keening, hauled it back up toward the encampment, his dead weight resting upon their shoulders.

"This is madness!" wept the woman who had first spotted the corpses. "I saw Lord Gorlas enter my lady Y'gerna's tent last night...saw him with my own eyes! Or maybe it was not a living man I saw, maybe it was an evil wraith out to bring death to us all!"

"No, it was no spirit!"

The folk of Belerion halted in their tracks. The Merlin, high priest of Khor Ghor, was standing in the centre of the camp, leaning heavily upon his shaman's staff. He looked hard and hawkish, his face tired but triumphant. The hawk's head in bronze upon his breast glimmered in the strengthening light. "It was no spirit that wrought this doom upon you — it was the hand of man. But it happened because the Ancestors frowned upon you, for blindly following Gorlas, who consorted with our enemies, and slighted the priests of Khor Ghor just yester eve. Now, because of his folly, you will have a new lord over you, and you will work your tin mines and pay a tithe to Khor Ghor and the spirits to atone for Gorlas's errors."

The people murmured, looking at each other with not a little relief. When they found the warriors slain, they had been certain the killers had slated them for a similar end. Gorlas's death they could come to terms with; he had been feared and honoured, but never loved.

"Who is this great warrior who has killed our chief and will rule us from this day forth?" asked one old woman, her voice high and tremulous.

"I am that man."

U'thyr stepped from Y'gerna's tent and stood before the tribesmen. He still wore the helm of his fallen foe, with its curved tusks and harsh bristles, and in his hand he held both dagger and axe as a symbol of his authority. "I am U'thyr Pendraec, the Terrible Head, chief of the Dwri and the great Dragon Path. I have killed treacherous Sea-folk and I have killed your black-hearted chief and taken his woman for my own. You need not fear me — unless you try to raise hand against me, or do me disrespect."

At that moment Y'gerna herself stepped forward, hair in disarray, wearing only a skin she had hastily wrapped around her. "Listen to him!" she cried. "This man may seem fearsome, but I swear he will treat you all with fairness. He has no wish to harm you, that I know."

The serving woman whose husband lay dead at the foot of the hill spat at her. "A curse on you...you who are tearless though your husband lies dead! You let him in, didn't you? You contrived this between you, you bitch-in-heat!"

She stumbled forward, trying to lunge at Y'gerna, but Merlin stepped into the way. "No, it is not the girl's fault. I spun a glamour that gave U'thyr the semblance of Gorlas. And so he entered Y'gerna's bed. If she is tearless, it is because she knows what her duty must be. She has no choice but to cleave to U'thyr."

Y'gerna bowed her head, hiding her smile beneath the curtain of her hair. The old man made her flesh crawl, but she was grateful that he had spared her the tribesfolk's wrath.

"Now..." Merlin turned to U'thyr. "We should return to Deroweth. You can make preparations to send these poor wretches back to Belerion with one of your men, who can oversee them and get the wealth sent to you in Dwranon."

U'thyr stepped uncomfortably from foot to foot, his jaw tightening. "No, Merlin, I have thought long into the night, and have other plans. I will go to

Belerion and live with Y'gerna in the fort of Dindagol. Think of it...the Sea-folk come most often to those regions; I can make sure they get no more footholds in our land!"

"What of your own lands?" Merlin shot him a dark look. "Who will defend them? The chief of Duvnon's kingdom lies between Dwranon and Belerion; it will not be so easy to cross between the two without conflict. To say nothing of taking many days."

U'thyr shook his head. "My mind is made up, Merlin. I will go to Dindagol, and leave the management of Dwranon with men like Kol and my young cousins."

Merlin poked a bony finger into U'thyr's chest. "You...you disappoint me! I had such hopes once, but you were always hard-headed and rash. But, be that as it may, I hope you are not trying to escape because of the promise you made me!"

"Promise?" He looked genuinely puzzled.

"The promise about the boy. Your son. Born of your night with Y'gerna."

U'thyr tried to laugh; it came out a hoarse croak. "What makes you so certain there will be a child? If it were so quick and easy, any young fellow might get half a dozen each new Moon!"

Merlin stared into his face, his eyes black with anger. "There will be a child. And you will give him to me. Just remember that, U'thyr Pendraec. You will give him to me."

The months rolled by. Winter bloomed into the fairest spring men could remember, then a blazing summer with blue skies and red sunsets. By Autumn the folk of Belerion were bringing in a bumper harvest, and Y'gerna gave birth to a boy-child just after the feast of the Corn-Lord, where men and women bundled together in the furrows as the last sheaf was cut down. There was rejoicing among the folk of Belerion, who had grown loyal to U'thyr Pendraec and his lady, after their initial reservations after the bloody death of Gorlas.

But U'thyr was not happy, though all about him celebrated. Her turned his head away from the flower-topped cliffs and the blue sea and looked inland... Waiting... Dreading...

The thing he feared most happened one night when the Moon was full and men could feel the hint of old magic in the air, touching the standing stones, awakening the spirits, drawing back the barrier between the world of men and Otherness. U'thyr woke from a deep sleep in the chieftain's hut high on the hill at Dindagol with its rampart ring of lichened boulders. He felt strangely uneasy. Outside, at the foot of the cliffs, he could hear the waves crashing, smiting the land as the hammer smote the anvil — a sound that still unnerved him even after all these months. It was an alien realm here, surrounded by the magics of the sea-god Man-ahn, who rode the wave-caps on a seal's back, and blew fog and storms in on his bitter breath.

Rolling over, he saw that Y'gerna was still fast asleep, her head pillowed on her arm. Whatever it was wakened him had not bothered her in the least.

Quietly he rose and walked over to the cradle of woven birch boughs in the corner, where their infant son slept wrapped in a sheepskin. The baby was silent, also in deep sleep. He had no true name as yet, but his parents called him Art'igen, the bear-that-is-to-be, the Cub, in order to fool passing evil spirits into thinking he was not a human child and hence of no consequence. Call your babe 'brave' or 'fair-face' at birth, and the old dead ones in their barrow-tombs might become jealous and spirit them away, leaving gnarly, unseelie things in their cradles instead.

"Sleep on, my dark one," U'thyr said, ruffling the infant's hair with a finger, and then he left the hut and stepped out into the shadows.

It was a pleasant night, with the warm orange Moon burning over the sea, its light making an enchanted road across the waves. The wind was a warm caress against his face, and the air tasted of salt.

Silently, U'thyr left the confines of the dun and walked along the rugged coastal path atop the cliffs. Sea-grasses whipped his ankles, and his hair was a banner in the breeze. He stopped by the little waterfall that tumbled over the black bastions of the cliff and knelt down, surveying the land and the endless waters before him. For all its beauty, it made him shudder — the cliffs seemed stark, frightening, the sea too deep, too fierce, frothing up like a dog gone mad. Strongly, he felt that there was something out beyond, waiting for him, something that he did not want to face.

He almost hoped it would be another attack by Sea-People, in their long fast ships that darted like fish down the Western coast of the mainland, skimming past the lands of ancient kindred tribes — the Iverri, the Vasca and the Albianis who looked out toward the Isles of Prydn from across the Little Sea.

He could deal with Sea-Pirates. It was a promise made in the heat of lust he could not deal with.

His heart skipped a beat. Down on the beach he caught a glimpse of movement, a greyish shape contrasted against white shingle. The figure was standing in the mouth of a sea-cavern men called Mahn-ann's Maw. An ill-starred place that sucked in dead bodies lost at sea, and where exploring children often drowned in the fast-incoming tides. It was whispered Fhann, wife of Mahn-ann, would sing the children into enchanted sleep, then hungry Mah-nan would flood the cave and carry their drowned bodies into the deep.

But it was not the Sea-god he feared tonight.

It was a man. But a man unlike other men.

His fears were realised as the figure below left the cave-mouth and started in his direction, climbing a well-worn path up the cliff-face He could see a flutter of stained robes, flowing silver-streaked hair, and a staff topped with a jawbone.

Like a craven, U'thyr hid in a wind-stunted bush, praying to all the spirits that the old man would stumble and fall down the cliff side.

The gods didn't listen,

The Merlin reached the top of the cliff and gazed straight at the bush where U'thyr hid, with his hard, black, bird-like eyes. "Come out, U'thyr," he said mockingly. "It is not fitting that the lord of Belerion and Dwranon hides away like a fearful girl."

Shamefaced, U'thyr stepped from the shrub to face his old mentor. "So you have come."

"As I said I would. I speak no lies, U'thyr Pendraec. Are you able to say the same? Are you an honourable man who keeps his bargains?"

U'thyr flushed. "Do not doubt me. You will have what you want…but are you sure you must do this thing? The child…there will be others later, he is my heir…"

"And so he will remain," said Merlin dryly. "But I will foster him. Many tribes practise fosterage. Now give him to me. I am not here to pass the time, my duties lie elsewhere. Reports have come that both raiders from Ibherna and Sea-People have been harrying the coasts in Duvnon, and I have been trying to rally local chiefs to band together and fight them, although the battles may not be in their own lands. This was a job I had hoped for you, U'thyr, to be the high war-leader of the tribes. But you have lost the fire, between your dark queen's thighs!"

U'thyr hung his head, angered by Merlin's words but unable to find any words of his own to answer him. In silence he walked back to his hut, the Merlin walking briskly at his side. Entering the door, he saw Y'gerna sitting by the glowing embers of the fire, feeding the baby Art'igen, the bear-cub. "Merlin!" she said with surprise and some trepidation as the shaman swept into the hut. "What brings you to Belerion unannounced?"

Merlin paused, his brows raised. "Has he not told you? Has U'thyr, the brave and terrible Head, been too fearful to tell his own wife about the will of Merlin?"

Y'gerna whipped around to face U'thyr, her eyes darkening with alarm. "No, he had told me nothing! U'thyr, what is the meaning of all this?"

U'thyr's face reddened and his lips moved soundlessly.

"I shall tell you if U'thyr cannot," said Merlin. "When U'thyr first became enamoured of you, he asked for my help. He would have done anything for an hour in your arms. And so he promised me the fruits of your night together, Lady Y'gerna... he promised me your son."

"No!" Y'gerna put Art'igen down and sprang to her feet. For a moment it looked as if she would attack Merlin, but instead, she turned on her silent, shame-faced husband. "You bastard!" she screamed, launching herself at him, tearing at his tunic and hair, biting at his neck like a crazed animal. "How could you do this to me? How could you keep this terrible secret from me? I despise you..."

"Shut up, woman!" U'thyr grabbed her wrists, holding her away from him as she spat and struggled, kicking out at him. "What's done is done. The boy will come to no harm; you know the Merlin will treat him well. Many lads are fostered out to great men's families."

"But you didn't tell me..." she sobbed, the fight suddenly gone from her. She sagged at the knees, looking faint. "How could you? He is so small, not ready to be taken away..."

U'thyr grabbed her as she started to fall, gathering her close. Tears were streaming down her face, hot, helpless, angry tears. "I promise you I will make amends. Gold, amber, garments and circlets imported from over the sea. I'll put another six strong sons in your belly! But we must let the Merlin take the Cub — I cannot break the promise I made."

His strained gaze flicked over to Merlin and he nodded, mouthing the word, "Go, now!"

The older man picked up the baby from the rush-mat on the floor, wrapping it in a fur, then tying it in a sling across his chest. Without a further word to U'thyr or the sobbing Y'gerna, he left the round house and walked back through the courtyard of the fort toward the sea.

As he reached the last hut of Dindagol, nestled against the ramparts, he suddenly sensed eyes upon him. Turning, he beheld a small girl child, no more than three, watching him from the entrance of the hut. She was black-haired and dark-eyed, her face a tiny, petulant heart. She was observing him intently, her thumb in her mouth. Merlin noticed she had copper bangles on her wrists; so he guessed she must have some status among her people.

"Where you going?" she asked, letting her thumb drop.

"Far away, to lands near the great temple of Khor Ghor," he replied.

"You take baby?" She toddled over, and grabbed at the furs that wrapped the Cub.

"Yes. I am to foster him."

A strange expression crossed the elfin face; a look too old for such a young child. A look of resentment...even malice. "Good... no like him! My da not come back, and new man is with mam... and baby. I sent to nurse."

"Ah..." Merlin let out a long exhalation. He knew the truth now — this strange dark child was Morigau, Gorlas's daughter by Y'gerna, replaced in her mother's favours by the U'thyr and the new baby.

"Would you not take Morigau too?" the child asked, hopefully.

Merlin knelt down, staring into her eyes. "No, you must stay and look after your mother. She will need you now that Art'igen is gone."

Again that troubling expression of malice crossed Morigau's face, making her look almost like some small demon. "Me should go to temple... not brat!" Her eyes glowed, green-brown in the wan Moonlight, and Merlin felt his heartbeat quicken.

It was as if she had a bad spirit within her. Perhaps her father's ghost was angry about his death and had possessed her. Young as she was, she already exuded a kind of darkness, and he knew, instinctively, if she was left unchecked, she would attempt to bring all his plans crashing down in ruin...

He glanced at the seawall, the bright stars beyond. The sea was rumbling over pebbles on the beach. It would be easy to snatch her up, muffling any cries, and hurl her down into the waters. Mahn-ann would take her, and her malignant spirit would no longer be there to threaten her brother and Merlin's dreams.

But...he could not do it. He would kill when the spirits demanded their due, but she was no sacrifice, no Chosen One — the spilling of her blood would be cursed, not made sacred. Such an act would cause dissension, even war, in Albu, and he had no doubt U'thyr and the men of Belerion would hunt him down without mercy.

No, he had to leave her be... but he would remember the darkness in her, and try to make sure she was kept well away from the swelling rises of the Great Plain and her younger brother.

Turning from the child, he hurried out through the gate of the fort and down the hillside, slipping on the long sea-grasses with their crusts of glittering salt. In his arms the baby began to grizzle, his voice high and thin on the night breeze, the cry of a gull, the wail of a spirit out of the cold cairn.

"You'll wish you took meeee, old one!" Merlin heard Morigau's voice rise up like some malevolent death-spirit in the night. "Not him! Meeee!"

Unsettled by the vehemence of the fey dark child, the high priest of Khor Ghor hurried on toward the boat moored in the shadows of Mahn-ann's Maw, and the safety of the lands he knew.

PART THREE: ARDHU — SUNRISE

CHAPTER SEVEN

The horse galloped across the green field, flanks rippling, nostrils flaring in the chill wind. Art'igen watched, taut as a bowstring, transfixed by the grace and power of the animal before him. He wished he had the same kind of fluidity, the strength of rippling muscles and powerful flanks, but he was still just a boy in training, in his own eyes ungainly and clumsy.

Just wait, his foster-father had said, and you will surprise yourself.

Wait! It seemed Art's life was all about waiting, and he was growing impatient.

Art'igen was fifteen and had not yet been made a Man of the Tribe. He lived with his foster-brother, big, ugly but amusing Ka'hai, and his foster-father, Ech-tor, who was a smith. At one time, being a metal-worker, Ech-tor would have been regarded as a magic man, just like the great Merlin of Khor Ghor (who often came to visit Art'igen, teaching him the magic patterns of the skies and many other things). Smiths knew how to make the sword come from stone, and how to turn dull base metals into the axes and daggers of kings.

Now, in Art'igen's day, a smith was still a most honoured trade, if not thought to be of otherworldly mode. Ech-tor, however, was spirit-marked by another art unrelated to the forge — his love of horses, those fearsome animals who ran free in the wilds, some hunted for meat by tribes who wanted to ingest their strength, the rest being shunned by those who deemed them creatures that only the gods dared sit upon.

On Ech-tor's little steading, a few miles from the important settlement of Marthodunu, lying between Khor Ghor and the stones of Suilven, the Crossroads-of-the-World, the Smith kept six horses which he had captured and tamed. Hence his old name of Tor had been changed to Ech-tor, Tor the Horse-Man. And men came not only to watch him make the daggers of bronze and serpentine armbands, but to watch him and Ka'hai slip twine bridles onto their horses' heads and ride them up and down amid the frightened sheep and pigs in the yard.

Art'igen was considered too young and callow to partake of this sport, but

Ka'hai told him that soon this would change. Indeed, it was almost time for his initiation into the tribe, and the time of choosing of a new name, his adult name. This was a fraught time for Art'igen, not knowing what would be expected of him when the priests gathered the boys of the tribe together in the Sweat Lodge of Marthodunu. What name would they give him, to identify him forever more? It could be Tall Spear or Stag-fleet, which would be honourable names to bear, but likewise it could be Scowling-Face or even something as grotesque as Pig-eyes. Art'igen knew a Pig-Eyes, a fat, red- haired boy who puffed and grunted when he ran, hence the unflattering name.

"Art!" He heard a familiar voice, and looking around saw Ka'hai riding toward him on his horse, Hen-gron. He had rounded up the golden-maned mare that Art'igen had watched in her wild race across the Sunlit meadow, and slipped a twine bridle over her ears. "Art, come here, I have something for you."

Art'igen ran over to his brother, a big bluff lad with sandy, rough-cut hair and light, light eyes that spoke of some strange northern ancestry. Despite his size he was quite a shy, gentle youth, who preferred horses and dogs to strutting around with boastful lads of similar age. "Here." He grinned at Art'igen, "I have a present for you, since you are now fifteen summers old and about to become a man. My gift for your naming day is this mare, Lamrai is her name."

"Mine?" Art'igen gasped, astounded.

"All yours, little brother," replied Ka'hai, handing him Lamrai's reins. "Now, let us see if you can ride her! Father and I have already taught you crafts of wood and metal, and the use of dagger and bow. Now, we will teach you how to ride — a feat seldom seen in Prydn. It may be of great help to you one day — or so said the Merlin."

Carefully, Art'igen grasped Lamrai's Sun-honeyed mane, and with the litheness of youth, vaulted onto her back. He yelped and slid about for a bit, while she snorted and danced at his unfamiliar clumsiness, and Ka'hai covered his mouth with a hand and suppressed a laugh.

But Ka'hai's eyes were kind when his mirth was quelled. "Go on," he said. "Touch her sides with your heels. Ride her up to the Hill of the Old People on yonder rise..." He nodded towards a distant round barrow that stood on the crest of a nearby slope, marking the territory for the past few hundred years. "You must become one with her, as you would with a beautiful woman..."

Kauai's big, plain face broke into a grin as he saw Art'igen squirm in embarrassment. Youths of Art's age were not permitted to dally with village girls, even if the girl was already marked as a woman of the tribe. That could come only after Art had a name and status; then he could take a wife or wives if he could afford more than one... But Ka'hai had seen him looking at the girls of the nearby settlements, and knew it would soon be time for him to do more than just look.

Art'igen querulously tapped his heels onto Lamrai's flanks. With a toss of her head, the mare trotted forward. Another tap, slightly harder than the first. Llamrai broke into a canter.

"That's it, brother!" Ka'hai yelled. "Ride like the wind!"

Face flushed with excitement, Art'igen slammed his heels into the mare's sides. She leaped in fright at the sudden punishment, and Art'igen let out a strangled yelp as she suddenly bolted from the yard, heading toward the desired rise but at a breakneck gallop. He clung desperately to her mane, the coarse golden hair whipping his cheeks and stinging his eyes...while behind him Ka'hai stood, hands on hips, roaring with laughter.

After the initial panic, Art'igen became used to the hard beat of the gallop. He steadied his position, moving with the movements of his steed, raising himself up to see above her head. Trees flew by, a green blur, while up ahead the hump of the marker-barrow rose, a black blot against the cloud-strewn sky. It was a moment of magic — Art felt as if he were indeed one with the horse, a mythical six-legged man-beast that could fly over ground that would take an hour's walk on foot. He almost fancied that Lamrai's heart was beating in time with his own, symbolic of their joining on that day. Any chief who could learn this art, this communion with a beast of four legs and broad back, would surely become great beyond words, especially if he ordered his men to take mounts as well. They could ride hither and thither to protect their lands, fighting with bow and long spears from horseback.... Dreamily he thought of it — an army of men with himself at the fore, travelling the Four Corners of Albu.

His reverie was brought to an abrupt end as Lamrai mounted the slopes of the barrow. A rustling noise came from the bushes sprouting in its ditch, and the mare suddenly threw back her head and shied to the right, eyes rolling in fear. Art'igen was sent flying over her head, his arms and legs flailing at air, and landed in a hunched ball on the grass, bruised but unharmed. Lamrai, now seemingly calm, trotted off down the side of the barrow, cropping grass that grew rich and green from the nourishing bones below.

"Stupid beast!" Art'igen muttered petulantly, his pride wounded more than his flesh. In the distance he could hear Ka'hai bellowing with laughter. "What could have made her behave in such a way?"

He rolled over, groaning…and then he saw what had frightened the mare. A man was standing atop the barrow; lean and wiry, with grey-dark hair in long braids round a lean, sharp face. A hawk's skull plated with copper hung round his neck, and a staff topped by a worn human jaw rested in his right hand.

"Merlin!" Art'igen shouted joyously, leaping to his feet. He was always glad to see the old shaman, proud that such a one, chief of the holy men of Khor Ghor, would take an interest in him. Despite the distance from Marthudunu to his abode at Deroweth, Merlin came at least once a year to see Art'igen, to teach him various lessons and to instruct Ech-tor as to what he wanted for the lad. Art wasn't sure why Merlin was so interested in his education, but a boy his age did not ask questions of the great ones. He simply assumed that his closest kin had died when he was a babe and hence he was given to the temple, and that Merlin had placed him with Ech-tor to ensure he would grow up useful to the tribe.

Merlin nodded toward the youth. "I did not expect to see you rolling in the grass like a babe," he said dryly.

Art blushed. "I was riding, Merlin. Riding a horse! I fell off…but that won't happen again! Ka'hai is teaching me! Just think, would it not be a great war-tool, to ride horses…"

"Indeed," said Merlin, with a taut smile, "but not if you dream away so much you fall off and are trampled by them!"

Art's blush deepened and he stared at his feet. "I will learn… I will not fall again!"

Merlin grinned again. "You will fall. We all do along the long, hard paths of our lives… but you will rise again as all strong men of Albu must!" He stretched out a veiny brown hand to Art'igen. "Come, rise, young Art, I have news for you. Exciting news!"

"And what news is that?" asked Art'igen, excitedly. Few diversions came to Ech-tor's holding, with the exception of the occasional traders or warriors seeking new weaponry. Art had only been to the great henge of Marthodunu once or twice, despite it being only a few miles hence. As a boy, he was not entitled to join the rites and had only viewed it between festivals, when it was empty, its huge banks covered in mist from the nearby river.

"It is the time for your manhood rite," said Merlin. "I have put your name forward and the priests there have said to bring you."

Art'igen's eyes gleamed; he tried to control his excitement, and not look childish and over-eager. "This is great news, Merlin! I had not expected the call till the autumn, after harvest fest, at earliest. "

"The priests listen to me — I am the Merlin," said Merlin. "I want to see you made a man-of-the-tribe as soon as possible… because much is afoot in Albu, and it is men the tribes need, not sheltered boys. After some years of peace, the Sea-Raiders have been harrying the coasts of Belerion and Duvnon again. Some have even sailed down the rivers, making paths inland. The chieftains are uneasy, and in their fear they may grow some common sense at last, and stop fighting petty quarrels amongst themselves! They have agreed choose a high chief, the supreme Head, as we had of old; he who will be Stone Lord, Master of the Great Trilithon and Son of the Sun. This event is something I want you to witness."

Art was nearly jumping with excitement. He'd heard the tales of chiefs and warriors around the fires, of men who painted themselves blue and men who spoke different tongues, of some who pierced their noses with bone, and some who were tall as giants, their great arms a-clatter with bangles of polished shale. He had only seen the few travellers, cloaked and dusty, who sought smith Ech-tor's wares, and as a boy, he had not been allowed to speak to them. He had watched them from afar, men with Sun-bronzed faces and scars, all the while burning with impertinent youthful questions that went unanswered.

"Ah, Merlin, my friend, I thank you for this gift! It is a great honour," he cried. "When do we go?"

"As soon as possible." Merlin glanced at the Sun's position in the sky. "The chiefs of the Cantrevs and their wains are on the move even as we speak. Go collect Ka'hai — he will also want to witness this great day — and gather whatever possessions you need. And bring the horse; it will make you look good!"

"If I don't fall off," said Art'igen sheepishly, with a small grin.

"I will pin you on there with my magic if need be," said the Merlin fiercely. "Just that one time!"

The Merlin, the two youths and their mounts departed the Ech-tor's holding and headed across the downland of the Valley-between-Hills. It was arable land and they saw farms dotted about and lone shepherds driving their flocks of woolly brown sheep. As night fell, they came into a thin grove of silver birches, their branches whistling and whipping in the wind like the hair of a dancing maiden. Merlin stopped and sat down in a little rounded bowl formed by the roots of several ancient trees that had lashed themselves together, strangling each other as they fought for purchase in the rich, deep earth. He scraped together some dry twigs and lit them with his flint strike-a-light, murmuring a short prayer to the flame to keep it bright and warm.

Ka'hai tethered the horses to a tree, and then slumped against its trunk, wrapped in his piebald cowhide cloak. Almost immediately his head drooped and he started to snore; the day was warm and he wasn't used to walking so far from the smithy. Ignoring the big lad, Merlin handed Art'igen some strips of dried meat from the bag at his waist, then stretched out his thin legs until they were almost in the fire. He chewed a mouthful of jerky in thoughtful silence, his sharp eyes locked on the dark-haired youth across from him.

Art felt mildly uncomfortable. Merlin had never subjected him to that kind of silent scrutiny before. It was embarrassing… especially as he did not know why the priest stared with such intensity. Measuring him up. Judging.

Eventually Merlin spoke. Night was drawing in now; the thin fingernail of the Moon hung suspended above in a swaying web of ghostly branches. "Art'igen, what do you know of the making of Khor Ghor?"

"Only what the storytellers sing. That the first Merlin…blessed be his spirit…" He glanced anxiously at the older man, who was possibly — who knew? — reborn with the spirit of that much Esteemed Ancestor. "The first Merlin brought the stones from the West by magic, after winning them from Ibherna in a terrible battle! It is said that he floated them through the air all the way to the Great Plain!"

Merlin's eyes were hooded. "A pretty tale, but just a tale. Wiser lore-masters will tell that you how he dismantled the stones with cunning devices, and raised them again in the same way — with the wisdom of his thought, not any magical art. Art'igen, come follow me. We will not be long. Ka-hai will be quite safe."

Merlin got up and entered another section of the darkling grove. Art'igen followed, carefully picking his way between snarled roots and animal burrows. Up ahead he spotted a stone, furred with moss: the capstone of a mighty burial cist, a chamber to contain the bones of some great warrior, his knees drawn up in foetal position as he awaited rebirth, his long-fleshless face turned toward the rising Sun in the East. It was not a particularly pleasant place to visit in the dead of night, with the wind rushing and dancing about, keening through the moving branches of the trees. What if the old barrow-man was lonely, hungry, seeking to draw the unwary living into the Lands of the Dead?

"Art'igen," said Merlin, "do you think you can move that stone?" He

92

gestured to the capstone with its cupmarks that held the tremulous Moonlight.

Art stared at him as if he had gone mad. "Of course not! Many men would be needed to drag such a heavy slab!"

"So it may appear... but watch me, Art'igen." Merlin approached the stone and set his hand upon it. He shut his eyes; the wind lifted his hair, Moonbeams turning it to a mist of silver and shadow. His lips moved soundlessly, invoking who knew what beings. He gave the capstone a small but sharp shove... and the stone moved. It swivelled round, grinding on pebbles beneath its underside before settling again with a dull thud.

Art was silent, but his mouth was hanging open. He forced his jaw to shut, afraid that he looked like the village fool, gawping and incredulous. "Great is the magic of Merlin!" he gasped.

"Magic? Some would see it as such," said the priest. And then, leaning close to the youth, his eyes hollow as those of a skull: "Others would call it an art. Remember this, Art'igen, and if I ever ask you to move stones for me, do not hesitate and have faith. Remember this night, and cast all doubts away."

Merlin was so ardent, so impassioned, that Art felt a thrill of fear run from head to toe. But he bowed his head gravely, and said, "Whatever is the will of the Great Merlin, my mentor."

They returned to the encampment, where Ka-hai still snored beneath the tree, and the horses contentedly cropped grass beneath the Moon. Merlin eased himself onto the mossy ground with a groan — already he suffered the chronic bone-ache that afflicted almost all older folk in Prydn — and soon he was snoring as loudly as Ka'hai, his cloak thrown over his head.

But Art'igen could not sleep, not after seeing that huge stone moved by one man's hand. In silence he sat staring at the changing sky, thinking on what he had witnessed, while growing excitement knotted the pit of his belly. It was only after Moonset, when the wind sank to a sigh and the little grove was black with unbroken shadow, that he finally allowed himself to sleep.

And as he lay curled on the grass, Merlin got up and sat over him, singing and humming, casting his spells, treating with the spirits and elements that they would protect and assist this dark young bear, son of the Head Dragon.

###

The three travellers reached the henge of Marthodunu early the next day.

93

The sky was fair and the huge banks towered high and bright beneath the Sun. Unlike Deroweth, there were timber building actually built upon the earthworks, their roofs shining in the early light. On one side of the settlement, the coiled snake of Abona made a natural watery boundary before winding its way across the flatlands: following its course, a traveller would eventually reach Deroweth and the Place-of-Light. It was the umbilical cord that bound the holy places of the land together.

Merlin entered Marthodunu first, through the great Northeastern gap. Art'igen and Ka'hai followed, all eyes, trying not to gawk at the unfamiliar sights around them. To one side, a priestess sat moaning and incanting, her face blue-grey with clay, mimicking a corpse's pallid visage. She squatted above the unmarked tomb of the guardian of the gate, a young girl whose stunted bones had marked her as chosen many centuries ago. Merlin tossed a chip of bluestone at the priestess and she smiled a toothless grin and bowed, swaying on her bony painted legs before placing the chip on a gathered pile of offerings given my incoming travellers — shells, pebbles, bones, flints.

Further on, at the heart of the huge complex, was a mighty mound, raised by the hand of man, but nearly as big as a natural hill. A ditch surrounded it, and water glistened palely at its foot, a sheet of blue mirroring the morning sky. Beyond the mound stood more timber buildings and an earthen enclosure that resembled a small arena or amphitheatre. It was here that most of the people were heading.

It seemed that many of the chiefs of the Five Cantrevs and their wives and warriors had arrived during the night or around dawn. They clustered by the amphitheatre surrounded by crude wagons heaped with furs and grain to offer to the priests of the henge and to use for barter with each other.

Ka'hai and Art were now staring openly, unable to feign adolescent disinterest any longer. These people, men and women alike, were as magnificent as the tellers-of-tales had painted them. One highborn woman had fire-red hair, caught up in golden wires, and a crescent necklace of imported jet from the north. Another was almost impossibly old, her wrinkled face dominated by tribal scars and a lip-stud that distended her mouth, but she appeared to have much power and prestige — thick cones of pure, decorated gold fastened her dress, and amber droplets swung from the ends of her grey braids. One lord was tall as a spear, with tattoos of beasts on his body, and he shaved his face and the sides of his head, which left a huge tufted plain of grain-golden hair on top, waving like a flag in the breeze. Yet another was muscled and dark of aspect, with a plate of fine gold stretched out upon a linen tunic and jet plugs in ears and the bottom of his nose. They all jostled and shouted, trying to establish dominance, along with their equally bright contingents of warriors, all boasting, bragging, and strutting in their finery, while their less lordly companions, wrapped in undyed sheepskins, unloaded the carts and started bargaining with the crowds of onlookers who had come in from the nearby farmlands. Some had even brought girls to marry off — the maidens giggled and tittered, making eyes at the handsomest, most gold-rich warriors.

A lanky priest in a brown robe approached Merlin and spoke to him earnestly. A moment later he came over and beckoned to Art'igen. "Come," he said in a sharp voice. "You must prepare yourself."

Art was led away by the priest, but not before Ka'hai has whispered, 'Good luck to you, little brother!" in his ear. He was taken across the great enclosure, up to the earth-turfed house that squatted like a crouched beast on its lofty banks. The house had a low door, its gable painted with chevrons. The priest thrust aside a screen barring the doorway and pushed the lad inside.

The interior of the hut was boiling-hot; Art had never felt anything like it, even on the hottest summer's day. A huge fire roared in a pit sunken into the ground, and around it clustered half a dozen lads, stripped and shining with sweat, all looking decidedly uneasy. Behind them clustered some priests, greasy-haired in the heat, faces florid above their long beards. The chanted and sang; one drummed. Behind them, where the flames from the pit cast little illumination, were a row of bowed heads...bald heads, heads devoid not only of hair but flesh: Ancestors brought out of old tombs to witness their children's children ten times over become men of the tribe. Some were merely bones, on others drying had caused bone and skin to fuse; some of the latter were dressed in clothes, as if they were living men, with ochre rubbed on their bony cheeks to give the semblance of renewed life.

"You — take off your tunic," ordered the head priest, turning to Art'igen. Art quickly obeyed, and the priests clustered round inspecting him for any flaws. A boy with a shrivelled arm, a clubbed foot or a sway back would never be a proper man... though he could sometimes find a haven amongst the priests and shamans.

"He will pass," said another priest, nodding. "He is sound and hale."

"Kneel," the chief priest ordered, gesturing to the other lads to also get down on their knees.

Art knelt down, sweat starting to trickle along his spine. The priests were chanting loudly now, lifting up great switches made of bound willow withies. Crying out, they struck the bare backs of the kneeling youths over and over again, beating any evil spirits from their flesh, making them pure before the watching Ancestors and the ever-present spirits that resided in the earth, the air, the water and the holy fire.

When they were finished, the cast the bloodied branches into the fire and danced around it as they were consumed. Then they took the hot ashes and rubbed them over the boys' wheals and painted symbols on their brows with them. Through all of this, the young men remained silent, not a sound passing between them — one groan of pain, one tear in a smoke-filled eye, and that lad would be considered a failure, to be returned to his mother's hearth for another year.

Once this face-painting was completed, the boys were led from the hut by the head priest and herded across the grass to the circular arena, the ring within a greater ring, which Art had noted when he arrived. It was still thronged with the visiting chiefs, who sat on sheepskin rugs in the fore; behind them clustered the humble people of the surrounding lands, craning to see the display. For boys from the outlying farmsteads and small settlements, this parade was a good thing — often, if they showed themselves worthy, they would be invited to join a chief's warband. This was Art's great hope...as much as he honoured his foster-father, he wanted to go beyond the forge, to see the great temples spoken of in song, to fire the bow and wield the axe in defence of the green hills of his home.

Inside the earthen amphitheatre, small and cramped in the shadow of the Great Barrowhill, the boys began to march in a circle. Pipes wailed and drums thumped and the youths danced with wild abandon — the fire-warrior's first dance in honour of the Risen Sun. High they leapt, nimble as the deer, supple as the salmon, reaching toward the Bright Lord of the Everlasting-Sky. The men and women on the banks shouted and catcalled, choosing favourites, jeering at those who were not light of foot or pleasing to look at. Art was glad he didn't hear any insults thrown his way.

The drums and pipes died suddenly and a cudgel was thrust into his hand. One older lad, already an adult, was coming toward him from amid the gaggle of priests and their followers. His face was painted in red and black stripes and his oversized mouth was grinning nastily. In his hand he held a spiky blackthorn club which he swung menacingly.

On the banks the tribesfolk and foreign visitors began to chant and stamp their feet. The dull thudding made the ground reverberate beneath Art'igen's bare soles, almost as if the earth itself had gained an audible heartbeat. Art's own heart speeded up, as both fear and excitement blazed through him, and then he made a rush for the older youth.

The lad sneered and hopped easily out of the way and Art stumbled past him, almost falling with the impetus of his rush. The crowd booed. Face burning, he whirled on his heels and lashed out again at his smirking opponent. He was obviously quicker than the other lad expected, and this time Art's cudgel met with his wrist. He jerked back in surprise and then red rage filled his eyes. He was very tall and long-legged, and he sprang high into the air, a warrior's leap, and aimed a vicious blow at Art's head with his foot. Art'igen anticipated his move; he had seen a horse kick out under an unwelcome rider many times on Ech-tor's holding. Dropping his weapon, he grabbed the other youth's leg and tipped him over backwards. He fell with a crash on the sandy soil, breathless and gasping in shock and dismay. Art'igen hurled himself onto his chest, pinning him down, and tore the blackthorn club from his fingers, holding it menacingly above him as if to strike a death-blow.

Behind him he could hear the chiefs and warriors from the Five Cantrevs shouting and clamouring: "Finish him, boy! It's an honour to be blooded on your first day as a man! Kill the weakling!"

Art looked down at his adversary, his face paint smeared, his chalk-whitened hair filled with dirt. He was only perhaps a year older than Art himself. His eyes were still defiant but fear had crept into them. Art raised the club, to an accompanying roar from the audience. It would be an honour; he could gift the youth's spirit to the ever-eager Ancestors who always welcomed new faces in the realm of the Not-living.

But no. He could not do it. It seemed too great a waste... He looked down at his vanquished adversary and prodded him with his foot. ."What is your name?"

The young raised his head. "Betu'or. Of the people of Marthodunu."

"Betu'or — a name of two meanings, am I right? King of Battle and Knower-of-Graves. Well, Betu'or, you will live this day and the knowing of graves may not be for many years yet. Be glad this day, for I give you back your life, which was mine to take. Some would not show mercy but I say it is better to keep a valorous man of the tribe to fight our true foes. Rise now, and go. "

Betu'or scrambled up and sped from the enclosure. Some of the men in the crowd booed in disappointment, but the women were laughing and clapping, and eventually their menfolk put their bloodlust aside and followed suit.

The chief priest of Marthodunu swept towards Art'igen and took hold of his arm, raising it on high. "This one today shall be proclaimed a Man-of-the-Tribe, free to wed, to wield arms, to participate in rites to please the Old Ones and the spirits. He is born anew, his life as a man just begun, and a new name he must have. What shall it be?"

"He fought like a bear out there!" someone yelled from the crowd. "Like a bear!"

The priest inclined his snowy head. "He was Art'igen...the bear-that-is-to-be. A true Bear he is now. From this moment forward let him be known as Ardhu — the Dark Bear."

"Ardhu, Ardhu!" chanted the crowd, and the sound of Art's new adult name echoed round the steep walls of Marthodunu and reached up to touch the very vault of heaven and the realm of Sun and Moon.

CHAPTER EIGHT

Ardhu and Ka'hai spent the rest of the night getting very, very drunk on beer and fermented honey-mead. It was the first time Art had been permitted to drink alcohol, which was deemed fit only for adult males, and he was going to make the most of it. The Merlin kept an eye on them both from a perch high on the henge bank, and pretended to give them disapproving glances (although he was secretly amused.)

Finally, when Ardhu fell over, clutching his belly, and started to retch, the shaman wandered over and poked him with the tip of his staff. "Enough for now," he said. "You need some rest. When the chiefs meet tomorrow to choose a High Chief, I want you to witness the event with a clear head and undimmed eye! Do you understand?"

"Yes, Merlin," said Ardhu meekly. "But I really haven't drunk that much…"

He rose to prove his steadiness to the older man, and promptly fell over with a yelp. Ka'hai bellowed with laughter, his big bluff face red and shiny.

"Come on, Ka'hai, help me lift him," Merlin ordered curtly, and together they carried the protesting Ardhu to Merlin's tent, which was pitched by the river. The tents and yurts of the lords of the West were all around, brightly decorated, some billowing pungent smoke from their smoke-holes. Torches and rush lights flared, while warriors paraded by with huge hounds trundling at their heels and beautiful sloe-eyed women on their arms. It seemed a magic world of nobility and splendour to a youth who had spent nearly all his days at Ech-tor's smithy, away from even the normal daily life of the local villages. "Merlin…" he said suddenly. "Now that I am accounted a man…I want to be a warrior. Like them!" He flapped his arm wildly in the direction of the men with their dogs and daggers and haughty amber-draped women.

A chunky man with a nose flattened by many a fight and a face as coarse and lumpen as a slab of weathered sarsen, scowled in Art's direction. "You looking for a good thumping? What are you staring at, boy?

"Not your ugly face I'm sure, Bohrs!" Merlin retorted, peering over Art's shoulder at the squat warrior. "Actually, my ward was…admiring you! Now come and help an old man, and cease your bluster."

The scowling warrior, not daring to cross a priest, especially one from

Khor Ghor, scowled ever deeper but obeyed without question. Joining Ka'hai and Merlin, he grabbed one of Ardhu's arms and dragged his dead weight over to Merlin's tent. "My thanks, noble Bohrs!" gasped Ardhu, clutching feebly at Bohrs' cloak, while the older man curled his lip contemptuously and tried to rip the cloth free. "If I ever become a great warrior, I would have the likes of you in my band!"

"That's about as likely as a flying sow!" snorted Bohrs, and he stumped off with great aplomb, his dignity hurt by the familiarity of this silly, young drunk.

Merlin dragged his ward inside the tent and pushed him down on a pallet of dry grass; his eyes shut almost as his head hit the floor. Ka'hai, exhausted by lugging his little brother about the henge, fell forward in a drunken stupor, half over Ardhu's bed, like some giant, shaggy guardian dog. His jaw dropped and the usual ear-splitting snores came out.

"Sleep now," Merlin ordered, making a sign of protection over both young men. "Tomorrow you must be bright and alert. It will be a great day for Albu, the day the high one returns to the Temple and the Men of the Cantrevs!"

Ardhu awoke with an aching head that beat like a drum. Outside the tent he could hear real drums, and the low, mournful bleating of horns. Scrambling up, his stomach lurched and he thought for a moment he would be sick.

Instantly the Merlin was beside him, thrusting a beaker full of a foul-smelling liquid into his hands. "Drink swiftly — it will ease the griping of your belly," he ordered. "Then you must get ready, we must hurry so that we can get a good position at the meeting."

Art hastily downed the brew and almost immediately felt less ill. Colour returned to his cheeks. He stood up and let the Merlin fuss around him like an old woman, greasing his dark hair with bear-fat and binding it back from his brow with a copper diadem wreathed in snake-like designs. Then the priest took a tunic of soft leather from a container of sweet-smelling bark, and pulled it over Ardhu's head, fastening buttons of amber with golden crosses on them that were symbols of the Eternal Sun. It was a regal outfit and Ardhu's eyes were round with amazement. Surely he would stand out a mile, and look too ostentatious amongst his elders and betters. But he dared not question Merlin's motives. He kept his silence as the older man reached into his belt-pouch and drew out a tiny clay box, which held two very ancient hair-tresses made of beaten sheet gold. They were battered from wear; ancestral goods handed down from generation to generation, gathering power as they gathered years. Deftly he clipped them on to two small braids he had made in the front of Art's hair.

"I... I cannot accept this gift!" Art was stunned, since gold was only for great chiefs and their kin, and men of magic and art. Not for poor boys of unknown parentage. "This gold is an heirloom, belonging by rights only to the children of the last man who owned it."

Merlin looked at him solemnly. "And so it does, Ardhu. All I have given you — the tunic, the armbands and the hair tresses are your legacy. They have lain in wait for you many a year. There were your father's possessions."

"My father!"

"Did you not think you had one?" Merlin's bushy eyebrows rose quizzically. "Did you think a spirit begat you, as is rumoured about the Merlin?"

Ardhu flushed. "I never much thought on my blood- parents; Ech-tor and Ka'hai were father and brother to me... And you, Merlin, acted as the kindly grandfather."

"Not so kindly perhaps," said Merlin, lips narrowing. "I had my reasons."

"So who am I?" Art turned and stared into Merlin's eyes as if hoping to read the truth of his lineage there. "Who wore this tunic and ancient gold in his hair? And where is he now? Is he here? Is that why you brought me, so that he could witness my initiation as a Man-of-the-Tribe?"

Merlin shook his head. "He is dead and in his barrow these ten years. He was a fine youth, but his head was hot, and the lure of the flesh led him astray. I had hopes he would be a great chief once, possibly the highest of all chiefs. But he locked himself away in his own little world with his woman, and turned his face from the greater matters of Albu... and in the end it proved his undoing. He trusted where no trust should have been given... and a feast in which he hoped to make pacts of peace, the men of the Sea pulled their curved knives and stabbed him to death."

Ardhu's face was taut, full of mixed emotions. This news scarcely seemed real; it was like something from a tale told round the fires. "His name... you have not told me his name!"

"Ardhu, your sire was U'thyr. U'thyr Pendraec, the Terrible Head. You are Ardhu Pendraec, true scion of Uthyr's line and of the ancient house of

Belerion through your mother, Y'gerna. You will be a leader like your father. And who knows what else you will be, Dark Bear."

Half in shock, Art followed Merlin out into the enclosure of Marthodunu. He was the son of U'thyr! Who had not heard the tales of the young chief who had fought many battles and stolen the dark-eyed wife of Gorlas of Belerion? The chief who had been Prydn's great hope…until he vanished into the West, sequestering himself with his bride Y'gerna until his untimely death by treachery. They said that after his death, the tribe had feasted for ten weeks upon his burial mound, slaughtering cattle every night and tossing their remains into the ditch. Seven captive Sea-Raiders had been dispatched to the Otherworld with him, their cremations lying over his face in rough, squat urns, their spirits bound to serve him for eternity.

"Art, stop dreaming…we are coming to the meeting place," said Merlin, and glancing up, Ardhu saw that they were entering the amphitheatre where he had completed the manhood rites the night before.

The same crowd of chiefs and warriors were there, but the mood had changed. Darkened. Some men were openly arguing, and Ardhu was alarmed to see that many openly carried axes or daggers. No one laughed in this grey morn, the ribaldry and merriment of the night past was forgotten.

"Here is the Merlin, wise priest of Khor Ghor!" someone called, and Ardhu felt a hundred pairs of eyes swivel in his direction. He raised his chin, trying to look stern and unconcerned, despite feeling distinctly uncomfortable. "Ask his counsel in this matter!"

The chief with the horsetail of yellow hair who Art had noticed the previous day stepped forward. "I am Per-Adur. I believe I should be battle-lord of Albu… no, all of Prydn! I have never been bested in battle, and show my enemies no mercy. None will set foot on our shores without meeting my blade and my arrows."

"No, you are too young and green for such an honour. I have taken more heads that you!" Ardhu saw Bohrs strutting about, a whole row of gleaming daggers thrust into his belt. "Merlin! Tell this fool that he is unsuitable!"

Merlin frowned. "Same old arguments! Same old noise! I swear these fools would argue over each other's prowess even as our shores burned!"

The two rival chiefs were staring at Merlin, their faces grim and angry. "We have been talking and debating all night, magic man," said Per-Adur. "Do not accuse us of taking this matter too lightly! Where were you when men spoke of the fate of Albu the White and Prydn last night?"

"In my bed," said Merlin dryly. "But I am sure many lands were rescued and foes slain in the bottom of your beaker!"

"You mock me!"

"I do! I mock all those who think the loudness of their shouts will put a claim on the lordship of Albu! No, there will be another way; I am high-priest of Khor Ghor and I have talked for many Moons...no, Sun-Turnings, even...with my fellow priests from the Great Temple, and from Marthodunu and Suilven and Arb-ar in the Land of the Mother Mountain. We have communed with the spirits, and they have told us a test must be performed... Man must do what is seemingly impossible to do!"

"What is this test?" shouted Bohrs. "I will do it! I am not afraid."

Merlin crooked his hand. "Come, all those who would be master of the Isle of the Mighty. Follow me...if you dare."

Merlin, surrounded by a bevy of priests and seers from the various temples of the Five Cantrevs, left the entrance gap of Marthodunu, a crowd of warriors surging behind him. Ardhu and Ka'hai tagged along in the rear, intrigued, though Ardhu was less interested than he might have been yesterday. His mind was churning, filled with the wonder of his revealed parentage. He wondered if Ka'hai knew.

Before long, the party reached the grove of birches where Merlin, Ardhu and Ka'hai had spent the night on their journey to Marthodunu. Merlin and the priests went in first, chanting and hailing the spirits, then, when they were satisfied that no malign forces denied entry to the wood, they beckoned the rest of the party into the trees.

The chieftains poured into the grove, trampling the foliage, slipping on leaves and rotten mushrooms. Ardhu looked through the sea of foliage and moving bodies and saw the Merlin standing beside the huge burial cist with the cup-marked lid — the stone he had moved with his magic.

"Below this capstone rests the bones of a great warrior," Merlin said solemnly. "One who lived in the elder days, when men were as giants. Tall as a sapling he stood, so big that when he died the very flames of the pyre could not consume him totally, and his kindred had to pack his ashes into the straight bone of his back! But that was not all that was remarkable about him. He was a great man who knew the secret of bronze and the way of the warrior, and to mark his prowess he bore a knife from distant Ar-morah, land of our kin. Carnwennan it was named, and if his enemies saw it unsheathed, shining like the Sun itself, they trembled and quailed in fright. That blade lies in the tomb, waiting for a new great ruler to take it up. The man that moves this great stone and takes up Carnwennan shall be the rightful master of the Five Cantrevs. He will be war-chief of Albu, and lord of the Great Trilithon, Door into Winter."

The chieftains murmured darkly, looking one to the other as if Merlin had gone mad. He was, after all rumoured to have run wild once, during his quests for wisdom as a youth.

Then, slowly, they approached the capstone, long lines of men, grim faced and determined. Their usual bravado had vanished and been replaced by a steely determination. Their task was at hand — shouting and display would do no good. It would not move the impassive ancestral stone.

Bohrs was the first. He whipped off his shaggy cloak and flexed arm muscles bulging under a lattice of tattooing. "I am known for my strength. I'll wager that I am strongest amongst you. If any shall move this stone, it is likely to be me!"

So saying, he leaned down and set his shoulder against the mighty capstone. He pushed. Nothing. Grunted and strained. Nothing. Red-faced he grabbed the stone in both arms, clasping it as he would a lover, and pushed, grappled, struggled. Curses fell from his lips, sweat channelled down his face. Still nothing happened.

"Out of my way!" Another lordling pushed him aside. "You've failed. I will try my hand!"

And so on it went, with both the mighty and the lesser all trying to move the stone. It would not budge, not even an inch. Men sweated and swore and called on the gods and spirits and the priests to bless them, but nothing seemed to work

Ardhu, standing with Ka'hai at the back of all the activity, could only marvel at the vain display of strength. It seemed impossible that he had seen this very stone move under the hand of the ageing Merlin. He was beginning to wonder if he had dreamt the whole thing.

"That is enough for the day!" Merlin's sharp voice suddenly echoed through the grove. He stood forward, arm upraised to signal a halt. "The Ancestors have favoured no one who has tried to gain the dagger in the stone. You must retire for the night and begin again tomorrow when we are fresh and rested. I will stay here awhile to seek guidance"

Grumbling, the chiefs and warriors left the grove and set up a temporary encampment around its periphery. Ka'hai and Ardhu had no tent, unlike the highest-born chiefs, whose followers had brought supplies from Marthodunu, but that did not bother them. They merely wrapped themselves in their cloaks and nestled down on the grass near a fire, where they lay staring up at the night sky, unable to sleep, still fired up by the excitement of the day.

"What do you think will happen?" Ka'hai whispered to Ardhu sometime after midnight, when the fire at last fell to embers. Above the sky was a dark vault filled by pinpricks of light, a thousand watchful eyes, a thousand souls who had passed over the Great Plain to the Deadlands. "Do you suppose anyone will be able move that stone?"

Ardhu took a deep breath; a strange excitement was knotting his belly. "Ka'hai...Don't go to sleep just yet. Now that its dark and the fire's out, I want to show you something. Quick, while no one's looking..."

Silently the two youths rose. Around them the camp slumbered, save for a few tottering drunks and a couple of bored guards who leaned on their bows, staring morosely into the night and dreaming of warm skins and sleep.

Quickly and silently, they turned and entered the grove with its precious, hidden treasure. They glanced about furtively, in case they bumped into Merlin, who had still not returned to camp after the unsuccessful testing. "I don't like it here!" whispered Ka'hai, his face white. "The old one in his tomb might not be happy with all that's been going on. Merlin might not be happy either, to have us poking about..."

Ardhu put a finger to his lips. "Hush, Ka'hai. Be brave. Can you see Merlin? Wherever he is, it isn't here."

Side by side they approached the cist where Carnwennan lay amid the ashes of its long-dead master. Moonlight, slanting through the tree branches, danced on its capstone, the immovable stone that had been the cause of so much pain and frustration during the day. Fireflies wheeled in the air, filling the glade with an eerie, iridescent light.

"What are you planning to do?" asked Ka'hai uneasily. "We've looked at this thing all day!"

"Ka'hai, the night we bedded down here, Merlin brought me to this burial-stone. He showed me something I thought I would never see."

"What was that?"

"How a man, an ordinary mortal man, might move a stone many times his weight."

"But Merlin...is half of the spirit world, you know that! The rest of us are of common flesh. You have seen how the mightiest warriors failed to shift the block."

"But Ka'hai, he told me, from his own lips, that it could be done. Told me, and showed me! He told me I could do it myself, if I had faith!"

Ka'hai laughed. "You must be dreaming, little brother!"

"Then if I am dreaming… let me wake!"

Ardhu sprang forward, placing his hands upon the capstone. It was cold to touch, ice-cold, the lichens and moss slimy with night-dew. "Spirits, be with me this hour!" he whispered, and then he pushed with all his might, using the sideways movement he had seen Merlin use.

At first nothing happened. Ka'hai shook his head. "Come away before we're in trouble!"

Ardhu ignored him and pushed again, shoving the cist-lid in a Sunwise direction as if he sought to spin it in a circle. And suddenly there was a noise, as before, a deep, ominous groan as if the stone itself cried out, then the sound of pebbles being crushed and stone grinding fitfully on stone.

"By the Everlasting Sky, it's moving!" Ka'hai yelped, his eyes bulging in terror and amazement.

Ardhu kept pushing. The stone was turning swiftly now, shifting to one side, arching out and away from the granite cist below. Air full of the scent of cold earth and ancient decay blasted up into his face.

"I… I've done it!" He dropped to his knees beside the stone, gasping, breathless with exertion and excitement.

Ka'hai ran over, throwing himself down beside the younger boy. He peered into the cist. "Look, there, I can see it, I can see it!"

He pointed downwards with a tremulous hand. Ardhu, still gasping for air, peered into the cist. Deep below, he could see carvings on the stone, a pattern of human feet that symbolised the walk of the dead from life. A broken urn, lying on its side, spilled out ash and bone… and a short, broad dagger of archaic design. Its bronze blade was green from the long passage of years, but the hilt, wrought of antler and affixed with rare, white-gold rivets, still gleamed like the rising Moon, as fair and unmarred as the day it was made.

"I can't believe it!" Ka'hai sprawled over the edge of the burial-chest, reaching down. Carefully he brought up the dagger Carnwennan, frail but beautiful in the Moon's misted glow. "Art, you've done it…This must mean… you…"

At that moment a torch flared in the glade. Then another. And another. The Merlin strode out of the shadows, his eyes like obsidian flakes, and his mouth drawn into a severe line. Behind him were other holy men from

Marthodunu and elsewhere, and, hard on their heels, packs of craning chieftains and warriors.

"What is going on here?" demanded Merlin, striking the tip of his staff into the earth with a noise like muffled thunder. "Why have you come to this holy place, unbidden, when all others are abed? This is not a place for childish games!"

The two youths sat motionless, dazzled by the torchlight and by Merlin's anger, too ashamed and fearful to speak.

It was one of the warriors who spoke instead: "Lord Merlin, what is in the big lad's hand?"

Merlin rounded on the youth. "Show me, Ka'hai!"

Ka'hai lifted up Carnwennan, proffering it to the priest. "Merlin, please don't be angry. Ardhu was just showing me...."

An expression of genuine shock rushed over Merlin's face. His visage became skull-white, drawn. "The dagger! The sign of lordship! Ka'hai...was it you who moved the stone to get it?"

Ka'hai licked his lips. A look of longing filled his eyes. "Yes... Yes... it was me... I moved the stone and claimed Carnwennan! Does that make me lord?"

He turned and suddenly met Ardhu's shocked, reproachful gaze. Instantly, he hung his head in shame, tears burning his eyes. "No, I lie. Forgive me. I did not touch the stone. Ardhu was the one who moved it... Ardhu is the one who rightfully has won the sword."

So saying, he turned to Ardhu and bowed low, handing the fragile blade to its rightful owner.

"The sword has been taken from the stone!" cried Merlin, striding over to Ardhu and holding out his torch so that the flickering light fell over the youth's face, revealing him fully to the throng. "The spirits have spoken. Prydn has a new leader, come to raise our isle to the greatness of old and to repel our sworn enemies!"

There was an angry murmur from the gathered tribesmen; a hum like a hive of infuriated bees. "But he is only a boy!" someone shouted. "A beardless lad!"

"Yesterday you saw this boy made a man," said Merlin sternly. "Now you see the man become your King. Praise him! Ardhu, lord of the West, the chosen one." Turning, he knelt in the leaf-mulch by Ardhu's feet, his head bowed. "I, the Merlin of Khor Ghor, do swear to serve you until the breath is gone from my body or the sky falls, whichever comes first."

"This is madness," another chief roared from the shadows. "Even if this callow youth was acceptable, who, by the holy Sun, is he? We do not know his father's house or mother-line. He may not even be a true son of Prydn, for all we know!"

Merlin sprang to his feet; smiling now, fierce and wolfish. His voice was the crack of a whip. "Ardhu's blood could not be truer. For he is the son of U'thyr Pendraec, the Terrible Head, who once ranked high among you. His mother-line is Y'gerna of Belerion, the Land of Tin. It was I who worked the magic that brought that pair together, I who took their child from his cradle so that he might be raised to become a great leader! I, the Merlin, tell you this — is there any man who would gainsay me?"

There was a stunned silence. The warriors still looked surly, but there was doubt in their expressions too. And in many of the more youthful men, there was building excitement. They had been chained too long, hanging on the cloak-tails of elder chiefs who wanted to drink and recount the old days rather than defend their territories from the peril from the sea.

"He looked on me with favour!" The harsh, deep voice of Bohrs suddenly rang out. Bohrs, who had scowled at Ardhu on his first night as a Man-of-the-Tribe. "Yestereven, after the festivities, the new King of Albu looked on me with favour! He asked me to assist him to his tent! I am truly blessed! I will pledge my dagger-arm to him!"

"And I too!" A lighter voice rang out; tall Per-Adur with his horse-mane yellow hair. "I would have moved the stone myself but had not the strength. The boy-king did. The spirits have spoken!"

Merlin smiled, sly and secret in the shadows of the grove. A victory. It was only one battle, and the very first, but he and his young ward had won.

At the next full Moon Ardhu, the Dark Bear, son of the Terrible Head, mother-born of the Tin-lords, was brought to the temple of Khor Ghor to receive the blessing of the Ancestors, and to accept the Sacred Signs of Kingship from Merlin.

The young man was dressed in his father's tunic and hair-tresses, and Carnwennan was bound at his side in a deerskin sheath, its rusty blade replaced anew by the arts of Ech-tor. Silent and stern, his body painted with protective symbols, he was guided by priests along the Sacred Avenue, past the great Sun-Stone and the Guardians, and into the sanctity of the Khor Ghor itself.

Merlin stood in the shadow of the Great Trilithon, beside the Stone of

Adoration. He was dressed in his full priest's regalia: a painted skin cloak and long robe fringed with the teeth and claws of many beasts. A bull's horn headdress sat on his brow and his face was wreathed in chalk spirals that circled his dark eyes, making them look huge and surreal. By his feet rested a woven basket, its contents shrouded by a skin.

"Come forward," he beckoned, "and kneel before the spirits of this place, who rule the movements of the heaven and confer fertility upon the earth. Be humble in their presence and those of the Ancestors who made you, their long dead flesh into yours."

Ardhu sank to his knees. He glanced upwards, trying to take in the sights few mortal eyes were permitted to see. The stones — how high they were, how massive! The shimmering, micaceous sandstone block of the Altar-stone loomed above him and beyond it the tallest of the blue-tinged Ancestor-stones, which had come from the Western lands, the birthplace of the Merlin. On his right, one cumbrous trilithon faced due West, and on its face he could see the rectangular carving of She-Who-Watches-the-Dead. She had no eyes, no face, just a carved crook springing from her head, but he could feel her presence watching him, deciding the plan of his life and the hour of his death. He shivered slightly.

"Look at me, Ardhu son of U'thyr." Merlin spoke, his voice deep with emotion. Today is a day of great portent, of great change. A new era is dawning in Albu, in all of Prydn, and you and I will be as Sun and Moon, rising in splendour and power before the people. Do you swear to follow my guidance is this venture?"

"I do swear it."

"And will you honour the Stones and those who have gone before?"

"I will honour them."

"And will you give your life for the land, if it is asked of you?"

Ardhu hesitated; a cloud streaked over the face of the Sun, and shadows suddenly galloped around the stones, turning their stark faces sinister, frowning. "I... I... will...

"Then you shall be granted the symbols of high chiefdom, which no man has borne for hundreds of years, since before our father's father's time."

Merlin drew forth from his basket a round shield embossed with bronze. The rectangular image of the Guardian was graven on its gleaming surface, which was the colour of the dying Sun at Midwinter. "This is Wyngurthachar, Face of Evening. Let it shield you as you shield the folk of Prydn."

Reverently he fastened the shield on Ardhu's left shoulder; it was heavy, and Ardhu staggered a moment at the unexpected weight before recovering his balance. "My shield," he said. "Shield of Albu against her foes."

Merlin reached into the basket again, drawing out an item wrapped in dried moss. The covering crumbled away beneath his fingers to reveal a golden lozenge, incised by mystical, geometric designs. He held it aloft, catching the Sunlight; it flashed as though in answer to the burning orb in the heavens. "The breastplate of the Sky. Some say it was once used as a tool to assist the architects of Khor Ghor, others that it plots the motions of the Sun, and the dance of the rising stars."

He fastened the plate to Ardhu's tunic with thin leather thongs, before lifting up the last item from the woven container. It was a ceremonial mace, its polished head wrought from a fossil. Five lightning-like decorations of bone encircled the wooden handle, their number signifying the five trilithons of Khor Ghor. "This is Rhon-gom, the lightning-Mace of kingship," said Merlin. "With it, you may smite down your enemies as lightning smites the earth."

Ardhu took the mace, running his fingers over its smooth dome, feeling its energy flow into him. It was as if all his forefathers, from their long houses under the hill, were passing their strength and courage to him. "If I can be even half as worthy a ruler as my Ancestors, I will not have lifted this mace in vain," he whispered to the all-seeing sky, the all-knowing stones.

Merlin gestured the young chieftain toward a screen raised before the left-hand stone of the southern trilithon known as the Gate of Kings. This trilithon had the finest tooling and crafting of the hard sarsen, giving the structure a very sharp and precise appearance above all the others. Art frowned; what could be behind the screen of stretched deerskin, shielded from all eyes except those of holy men and ghosts?

"One of the Hallows of Prydn lies behind that covering," said Merlin. "Only a true leader, a true king, can touch it and live."

Reaching out, the shaman thrust the screen away. Ardhu gasped. There, fitted within the stone itself, was a dagger of gold, longer and thinner than those used in the West — a thing of great beauty, shining brightly as the afternoon Sunlight slanted into the great circle. Beside it were several large flame-coloured bronze axes, also beat into the hard sarsen, and around them dozens of smaller axe carvings.

"Symbols of kingship," said Merlin. "The sword of the Sun and the axe of the Sky. Come, forward, Ardhu of Prydn and set your hand upon this stone, your legacy, your destiny."

Ardhu reached out a trembling hand. What if the Merlin was wrong?

What if he was unacceptable in some way? Would fire gush from heaven and smite him?

But no... his palm came to rest upon the shiny, smooth gold, hot from the Sun, and no angry rebuttal came from heavens or earth.

"It is done!" Merlin shouted, and now his voice was great, bouncing around the circles, carrying to the priests and chiefs and warriors gathered outside the banks of the temple. "The rightful ruler has set his hand upon the Sword-in-the-Stone! The kings of old have return at last to the green fields of Albu the White, and a new Age of Men has begun!"

CHAPTER NINE

"A king must have a suitable dwelling place, a pre-eminent camp where he may gather his warriors and confer with them." Merlin shuffled around his hut in Deroweth, his silvered hair incandescent in the watery early morning light streaming through the door. An acolyte in a grubby robe was attending his fire-pit, baking bannocks for the priest and the young king who still lay abed under a pile of furs.

"But why, Merlin?" Art rolled over, stifling a yawn with his fist, looking both sleepy and impossibly young. "I like being here with you, my friend and advisor. And Deroweth is well known to all as a place of great learning and might — and so it has been for many generations."

Merlin shook his head. "Your position is still precarious, because of your youth and the circumstances of your birth. If you stay here for too long, wicked tongues will wag and men will say you are my pawn, a puppet-king under the control of the priests."

"And do you not control me?" Ardhu said carelessly, flopping onto his back as he yanked on his tunic, trousers and boots. "Since you are telling me to get out, and I must obey whether I wish it or not?"

Merlin shot him a sour look. "If I did not know you were jesting, well, you are not so old or so mighty that I might not tan your hide!"

"Hah!" Art smoothed down his sleek dark hair and twined a bronze circlet around it. "Like to see you try."

"Do not tempt me beyond endurance, whelp! Now come... I will show you the place I think may be suitable for building."

The priest and the young chief left the hut and strolled down the metalled road to the river, joining the well-worn track that led toward Place-of-Light. It was a fine day, with Sunlight rippling on the swell, and dragonflies whirring and darting above the reeds on the water's edge. Halfway along, not far from the barrow-ridge of the Seven Kings, Merlin turned aside and lead Ardhu into a boggy field. The twin banks of the Avenue cut across it, running down towards the curving silver snake of the river and the robbed stone-pits of the Old Circle. Above, shadowing the sacred pathway, rose a mighty hill with a tip like the prow of a ship jutting toward the eastern Sunrise.

Merlin gestured to it. "Your domain, Ardhu. Can you not see it? A huge fort of stout oak, gazing out toward not only Khor Ghor and Deroweth, but to Holy Hill in the East. A place of warriors …a place of legends!"

Arthur stared up at the hill, its banks green with oak and elm, and silver birch with graceful boughs that fluttered like pennants against the rain-washed sky. His mind whirled, and suddenly he could envision all that his mentor had said — earthen ramparts and wooden palisades, and a mighty hall the likes of which had never before been seen in Albu. "What is this place called?" he asked.

Merlin starred at the high hill, shadows stretching down from its prow-like tip. "Kham-El-Ard. The crooked High Place."

"I am surprised no one has built here before."

"It has been thought of as a haunt. A pool gathers at the foot of the hill that retreats and then grows, like the tides, like the Moon…a place of women's magic. This magic has kept men away. That, and spirits from the hunters' time. In the time before Dreams they came to the pool and gave thanks for their kills with gifts of flints and weapons."

"I fear no ghosts." Ardhu stepped forward. "I am glad you have showed me this place, Merlin. I think much can be accomplished here."

Merlin nodded. "I have already sent for great woodworkers in both East and West to come here. They are following the Tin-routes across land even as we speak. Many men want to catch a glimpse of you, even beyond the Five Cantrevs. Word of a King returned to Khor Ghor has spread like a summer fire!"

"Merlin, let us explore this hill, and not return to Deroweth till late. If this hill is to be the place of my high seat, I want to know every inch of it."

The shaman nodded and the young king and the older man walked into the shadow of the great hill of Kham-El-Ard. Skirting its broad base, they reached an area where water rose from the ground and weeds and fronds waved in the wind. Trees and brush grew thickest here, twining and twisting, branches forming an impenetrable backdrop to a round pool formed between the bank and a wide curve of Abona. Tendrils of fog hovered over the seed-speckled surface, showing that the spring feeding the pool was warm, heated by some great furnace within the heart of the earth.

Art knelt on the shore of the pool, breathing heavily, eyes scanning the waters and the dark foliage beyond. Merlin stood motionless, his feet crushing the flint tools of bygone men where they lay on the bank, suddenly reminded of Afallan, where he had loved a bright-eyed priestess called Nin-Aeifa. The dark lake, filled with mystery, the waters of Life and Death…

"Ardhu… someone is here!" he suddenly rasped, and he reached for Art's shoulder with one hand and pulled his dagger from his belt with the other.

Ardhu rose, his gaze intent on the waters. The mist was rising more strongly from the surface; coiling up into vast ghost shapes that streamed out upon the wind. Merlin could smell the magic in it, the glamour of Otherness. Time did not advance; it was as if the movement of the Sun himself had stilled, and all the woodland was silent, as if even the birds and beasts held their breath.

There was an eerie tinkling sound, and the mists began to part. Out onto the lake glided a raft, poled by a stately woman. At first glance she seemed almost a creature of the Un-world, maybe even the spirit of the wild places. Braids stiffened with lime tumbled to her hips; blue faience beads danced along their length. She wore a long, green skirt of twisted thongs interspersed with what seemed to be dried aquatic weeds, and all down the front of her deer-skin bodice were sewn hundreds of tiny shells and quartzes, swinging and clashing and making merry noise as she moved. Her head was bowed so that her face was hidden, but her exposed hands and throat was daubed with paint made from a paste of fish scale and chalk, which gave her a faintly surreal glitter as the thin Sunlight wandered over her.

"Ardhu the Dark Bear…" Her voice rang out over the pool, a voice of wind and rushing water. "You come to claim your kingdom, and I, the Lady of the lake, come to greet you."

Merlin jumped and his face flushed then paled. That voice…he knew it, dreamt of it when he grew weak and the wants of mortal flesh came upon him, making him bitter and morose. Nights when he turned and groaned in his furs, the arthritis nagging in his back, his brain afire with dreams of long, water-scented hair and white limbs that coiled around him, taking his will, his powers, even as he took his pleasure.

He peered across the water, trying to control the tremble in his hands…Yes, yes, he could see her face more clearly now, and it was she, Nin-Aeifa, one of the Nine Maids of Afallan. But in the intervening years she had changed. Changed greatly.

Gone was the sprightly, quick-tongued girl who had pressed her dagger to his throat in one instant, then led him to her bed in the next. She was still beautiful, but it was a ruined and surreal beauty: her left eye was blind, milky, an orb that gazed only upon the Otherworld. The other eye was as he remembered, but full of care and sorrow. She was thinner and somehow more regal, the planes of her face sharp as flint beneath the bleached and plaited mass of her hair.

"Nin-Aeifa," he breathed.

114

"Merlin." She smiled and it was like the Sun lancing through clouds. "I thought we might be bound in some way to each other, even if not in the way I once desired."

Ardhu glanced at his mentor. "You know this... this woman?"

"Indeed," murmured Merlin. "I know her well."

"More than any other living man," said Nin-Aeifa.

"Why have you come here, from the far-off dreaming isle?"

She shook her head and smiled again. "Wise Merlin has been so busy with his young king; he has not noticed what has taken place around the Great Plain. The High Priestess of Afallan heard of the coming of the King, and sent forth a band of priestesses to minister to him, to bring him great gifts of great power. We have built a dwelling in the vale beyond, where the lakes mirror the stars and the Sun. I am chief of those holy women; I am the Lady of the Lake, second only to High Priestess Vy'ahn of Afallan."

She then turned from Merlin and stretched out a hand toward Ardhu. "Dark Bear, come and let me gaze closely upon you. I wish to see the chosen one!"

Ardhu hesitantly waded out into the water. Leaves and weeds curled about his calves. The water was warmer than he expected and strangely soothing.

"Nin-Aeifa, you be careful with him!" barked Merlin. "Remember — he is mine."

Nin-Aeifa smiled again, and this time her expression was cruel. "Yours? You take another man's son, when you will not beget your own? But fear not, the Lady of the Lake shall not interfere with the wiles of the Merlin. Not yet. But the Nine Maidens may claim him at the end, as all go back to Mother Ahn-ann."

Ardhu had now reached the edge of Nin-Aiefa's raft. She knelt down, catching his face in her glittering, glimmering fingers, with nails long and pearled as talons. Her blind, smoky eye, weird and unblinking, was almost pressed up against his own eye. "Yes, you are the one," she said. "I can see into your heart, I see your past and your future. King you will be beyond compare, if you fall not into folly. Merlin has taught you well and no doubt armed you well against your enemies. But I have a weapon beyond peer that waits for the touch of your hand. One of the Lords of eld bore it, its blade forged by magic smiths who came from distant lands of Ice Mountains, and at his death it was consigned to the waters of this sacred pool, an offering to the spirits of this most ancient place."

"And what is this talisman of which you speak?" Ardhu asked through chattering teeth.

"It is called Caladvolc, the Hard Cleft," Nin-Aeifa replied. "Look below you, Ardhu the Dark. It is there. Waiting"

Art stared down into the waters swirling around him. The Lady moved her hand and it seemed to the young chief that the mists lingering over the sacred pool parted, darting away like errant spirits. Below, the water was clear... and something burned orange beneath its surface, down among the waving weeds.

Maybe that's why the water feels warm! Ardhu thought dully. That... that glowing thing, whatever it is, is heating the pool...

As if of its own volition, his hand reached down below the surface of the water. Ripples ran out across the holy spring. He could hear Merlin shouting from the bank, but he couldn't make out the words; they were remote, unclear, like echoes in a cavern. In the trees above a bird screamed and he saw the limed hair of the Lady fanning out above him, turned to white ash by the backlight of the Sun. She was smiling... but the smile was not necessarily one of friendship...

He slipped under the water, into the land-under-wave, a kind of otherworld or underworld. All was green-tinged, the Sun above a sickly blob distorted by the swell within the spring. Weeds caressed him, drawing him down... down... into the dark... past broken beakers and lost flint tools, old bones and a half-mouldered wheel with fishes streaming between its spokes.

And there, amidst the detritus, an accumulation of offerings from the time before time, lay a rapier — the longest bladed weapon he had ever laid eyes on, longer even than the famed daggers of the princes of Ar-morah. It was wrought of fine bronze, and on its blade were the chevrons and magic insignias of the long-ago chiefs of Khor Ghor. The light filtering through the spring water bounced off its blade, causing the fiery glow Art had seen from above.

Reaching out, Ardhu grasped the pommel, laced with hundreds of gold pins, and pulled it from its nest of slimy fronds. With a cry, he kicked upwards, leaving that watery underworld and cleaving the surface of the pool like an arrow, the sword held above his head in victory.

"Merlin, I have it!" he cried. "I have the sword Caladvolc!"

"And so you do." The Lady of the Lake spoke behind him. "Soon you must needs use it. The Lake Maidens have received messages that the Sea Folk are raiding anew, coming in ships across the Little Sea and even into Habren's swell; the lands of Duvnon burn even as we speak."

Ardhu grasped the sword, glowing like a fire-brand in the Sunlight. "Then I must go to meet them. And prove myself beyond a doubt to the chieftains of this isle."

"It is too soon!" Merlin snarled as he stomped along the trail back to Deroweth with Ardhu following, barely able to keep up with the older man's long, angry strides. "Your camp not even built, the men still doubtful, training only just begun, both theirs and yours. I had hoped inclement tides would have kept the raiders away a bit longer..."

Art increased his pace until he matched tat of the priest. His face had suddenly lost its youthful candour and become a granite mask, hard as one of the standing stones of Khor Ghor. "We must manage with what we have. Ka'hai and Ech-tor have brought ponies and horses from the Western moors and they are reasonably trained, if not perfect. Anyone who can sit a horse will ride... even if they must be tied in the saddle! I will ride at their head, as is my place."

Merlin glanced over at the young man. He looked less a boy now, the lines hardening on the sharp planes of his face, showing the man he would soon be — if he lived that long. Gone were all traces of youthful indecisiveness, of deference to the man who had mentored him — there was a shadow of his father U'thyr in him, but more besides. Something sterner and greater than U'thyr. "So be it, then, my lord," the shaman said with a wry smile. "You will go, and the gods go with you."

By the next full Moon the men of Ardhu's warband were ready to journey to the coast. Dressed in leather jerkins studded with copper and cloaks sewn with insignias of their respective families, they gathered at Khor Ghor to receive rallying words from their leader. Each one, armed with a bronze war-axe, a dagger, and a bow, stood proudly in an archway of the circle, every man an equal within the curve of that never-ending ring, no man higher or lower than the other.

Only Ardhu was pre-eminent, the Stone Lord, master of the Great Trilithon. He stood with Merlin upon the height of huge lintel, with the Face of Evening on his shoulder and Caladvolc in his hand. His green-dark eyes were ringed by spirals of blue war-paint, while his hair was plaited ornately and fastened in a knot with a long bone pin. The Sun flashed off the Breastplate of Heaven, making him look indeed like a son of the gods, of the Sun himself.

"Today we ride for Duvnon!" he shouted, his voice echoing in the sanctuary. "Today is the day you set out for immortality! Today is the beginning of a great adventure for all of us, when brave ideals and brave words are turned into brave deeds. Together we will crush our enemies, and all of Prydn will praise us, for as long as the Stones shall stand!"

The warriors began to cheer, raising their daggers to their young lord atop the height of the trilithon. He in turn raised the Lightning-Mace Rhon-gom, and they marvelled to see it, shining pale against the broad blue sky.

Art scrambled down from his high perch, using the secret hemp ladder that hung on the reverse side of the trilithon, and beckoned the men from the sacred enclosure. He led them across the fields to where Ka'hai, Ech-tor and a load of boys in their service were gathered with the horses and ponies. "We ride," declared Ardhu. "Our enemies will not be expecting men on horseback; I have heard they believe we fear horses. Remember, if the speak, do not listen to their words, and do not gaze into their snake-like eyes lest they entrance you. Strike them down as you would strike down a maddened boar! Strike hard and fast for Albu the White... for all Prydn!"

The men cheered again, but some were looking a bit warily at the horses, who stirred uneasily, sensing excitement in the air. Ka'hai and Ech-tor had set to teaching the warband to ride, but it was early days yet, and many a proud would-be warrior had bruised his arse and his pride during a riding lesson. Merlin looked at the men thoughtfully, his brow knitting in a frown. "They are still not sure, they could break faith with you at any time... Ardhu, do you want me to ride with you, hold them in check?"

"No!" Ardhu's reply was vehement, his face stern. "You said yourself they will not heed me if they think I am merely a tool of the priests of Khor Ghor. I must prove myself to them in this battle — or perish."

He whirled away from the older man and reached for the reins of his mare, Lamrai. Swinging up onto her back, he held up Rhon-gom and Carnwennan, the two signs of his kingship. "We ride!" he shouted. "To glory, to a free Prydn... or to death!"

The other men and boys mounted, clumsy but eager, and soon the Great Plain was filled with the dust of thundering hooves and the cries of excited warriors, rising above the wails of the women and children who had come to see them leave. Those left behind huddled in the swaying grass, keening and sobbing, not knowing if any of their loved ones would return from those far distant war-torn coasts.

Merlin stared after the warband, his own heart filled with unrest and foreboding, no different to the weeping women. This was the test above all other tests, and he, great magic-man though he was, did not know if he would see Ardhu Pendraec again in that world, or only in the next.

###

The journey to the coast seemed to take forever. The company stopped in various villages along the way, some friendly, some less so. Occasionally one or two men would slide from their horses and slip silently into the darkness, their nerves broken as the coast approached...but usually some bright-eyed village youth would leave his mother's hearth to ask if he could ride with the young King Ardhu. And so defectors were replaced; indeed the numbers in the band swelled considerably. And, most importantly, Art's main circle of men remained stalwart and loyal: Bohrs with his blustering voice and brawny arms; Betu'or, whose life Ardhu had spared; Ka'hai, who was as good as a brother to his lord; the twins Bal-in and Bal-ahn, kin of Betu'or; tall Per-Adur with his golden mane and aristocratic manner.

One evening, as they rode through the foggy dusk, Ka'hai sniffed the air. His big, lunkish brow wrinkled. "Art... I can smell burning, somewhere out ahead."

Ardhu took in a deep breath and nodded. "Burning thatch. And worse, I fear. I can also smell the salt... it must be the sea."

"Aye, indeed it is, Lord Ardhu." Bohrs rode up, nodding. "I know it well. We are at the junction of two rivers the Glain and Duv'las, where they meet to flow into the sea. I'll wager the pirates have taken over the arm of the Glein; there were a few rich villages there, where they used to bring in gold from Ibherna and beyond, and export shale and axes."

"Well, there is but one way to find out." Ardhu urged Lamrai forward through the fog.

The band soon reached a cliff top covered with many scrubby trees stunted by continuous blasts of wind from the sea. The mists began to part, and down below they could see a river shining dully in the failing light. On its banks stood the smoking ruins of roundhouses, and the fields that ran up to the base of the cliff were smouldering. Dark shapes lay sprawled in the furrows; it was too far to say for sure that they were men, but Ardhu's band knew they could be nothing else.

Along the riverbank were moored three large foreign ships, their red and

119

black sails furled. The sound of singing and raucous laughter lifted on the night air.

"Let us kill them!" cried Per-Adur, from behind Ardhu and Ka'hai. "Look what they've done, the murdering scum!"

"Silence!" Ardhu raised his hand. "We must not behave as fools. We must approach with stealth, not shouting and rushing in like mad men, with anger taking away our wits! Bal-ahn, you and your brother Ba-lin, go down to the right, and circle the village where its meets the water. You are both strong swimmers, just like a pair of otters; I want you to go out to the raiders' ships. And burn them."

The two brothers — twins born at one birthing and hence thought to share one soul — grinned at each other and nodded. Pulling up the hoods of their deerskin cloaks, they dismounted their horses and slipped away into the shadows.

Ardhu likewise dismounted and passed Lamrai's reigns to Ka'hai. "I will go down first," he said, looking from his foster-brother to the other young men of the warband. "I want to speak to the pirate leader, to let him know that Albu is not his to do what he wills. To let him know there is a high king at Khor Ghor once again."

Ka'hai tried to protest but Art silenced him with a stern look. "Keep your bows ready but do not come seeking me until..." He gazed into the West where the Moon was hovering, a thin white sliver between fleeting clouds. Expertly he deduced its course across the sky, using arts taught to him by Merlin, at night amid the Stones. "Do not come to me until the Moon appears fully over the water. When you do ride down from the cliff, I want the enemy to see you on your horses. They will not be expecting such a sight."

"Take care, Ardhu," Ka'hai's voice was a cracked whisper; he licked his lips nervously." Don't do anything too stupid!"

Art grinned and clasped his foster-brother's shoulder. "You know you can trust me on that score!" Hefting Wyngurthachar onto his shoulder, he vanished into the shadows.

On foot he wound his way down the hill to the river. The stink of fire and death hung in his nostrils; he felt a cold rage rising up to clench the pit of his belly. Ahead of him reared a sentinel stone, the Ancestor marking the territory of that riverside tribe... but its face was smeared with blackened blood and it leaned at an angle, where the invaders had tried to topple it from its pit, desecrating the site and driving off the spirit of the place. That made the young king even more angry; it was as if all the generations of people of Albu had been violated, the land itself raped by these foreign invaders who cared for nothing but tin and gold.

Passing the teetering stone, he caught sight of a man by the river. He had a woolly black beard to his waist and an aquiline profile. Robes of a lurid purple hue Ardhu had never seen before frothed round his ankles; the hem was fringed with gold wires. He held an ornate cup from which he sipped daintily, almost effeminately. Indeed, Ardhu thought he looked rather womanish in his flowing, brightly-coloured garb; the rims of his eyes were also painted with dark smoky lines. He was talking to another man, with his head shaved like a slave, who sat scribbling on a tablet, an activity alien and rather abhorrent to Ardhu. He had heard rumours that men in far off lands wrote down tales of gods and wars, but it was not the custom in Prydn. It was considered taboo, even if one had the art — surely it was better to learn the lore of one's people and pass it down around the fires, than to write it on clay or bark, where any enemy might make use of it, stealing the sacred names of living things and sapping their power?

Shaking his head, he took another step forward. Blood begin to pulse in his veins and a light sweat broke out on his face. His resolve wavered momentarily as, for the first time since he left Deroweth, he felt fear tighten his belly. Merlin was not there to guide him…and he was just a fifteen-year-old lad who had not even been blooded. He had the arms and regalia of a king, but how would that help him against these strangers from across the sea?

In that second, the black-bearded man turned as if sensing his presence. His robes swirled and Art could see daggers at his belt, long and deadly. "Who goes there?" the man barked, first in his own tongue, which sounded like the cawing of crows, and then in a rough version of the tongue of Albu. "Show yourself…I know you are out there."

Ardhu stepped forward at once, moving into the ring of fire. The bearded one's hot little eyes raked over him, as black and oily as his long tumbled beard. They lit up slightly as they touched on his golden breastplate and belt buckle, and the helmet he wore

"Welcome, my young friend," the man said, extending a hand jangling with rings. "I can see you are a man of worth and standing in your community. Please, let me get you a goblet of wine. Who is it who does us the honour of this visit?"

"Kind words indeed," said Ardhu, his own voice coming out harsh and flat. "From a man who has slain the people of this village without reason and left their bodies for the ravens in their own fields."

"Ahhh…" The bearded man gave a huge, theatrical sigh. "That. It was a pity. We tried to make ourselves known to them, to let them know we were peaceful traders. However, they did not or would not understand us. They attacked. We had no choice but to retaliate."

"Women and children attacked you too, did they?"

The man shrugged. "Casualties of battle, alas. It was nothing personal. We did not make them suffer. Why does it concern you, stranger? Those lowly river-folk were obviously not of your status." He gestured to Ardhu's shield and gold adornments.

Ardhu's eyes narrowed. "You asked my name and you shall have it. I am Ardhu Pendraec, son of the Terrible Head, war leader of Albu and high king of the West. Those 'lowly river people' you slew were my people, and if I am too late to defend them, at least I will avenge them!"

The man's fixed smile transformed into a vicious snarl. With a lightning-like motion, he yanked a dagger from his belt and hurled himself at Ardhu. Art stepped back, yanking out his flanged axe and flinging up Wyngurthachar at the same time. The knife-tip slammed into the shield, cutting a brief channel, and then snapped off with a loud crack. The pirate grunted in dismay, but immediately snatched another dagger from his belt, this one with a wicked serrated blade.

Ardhu stepped back and spun in a tight circle so that his enemy could find no obvious place to strike. Then, unexpectedly, he dropped to one knee on the muddy ground.

His opponent's eyes glistened evilly. He assumed that Ardhu had slipped in the mud. With a ululating battle-cry, he launched himself at his adversary with his knife high in the air, raised for a killing stroke

Ardhu waited until the man was directly above him, the cruel blade beginning to descend. Then, uttering a war cry of his own, he struck out with his axe, shattering the bigger man's left kneecap in one blow, and bringing him down screaming in pain.

Ardhu rolled out of the way of his flailing body and sprang to his feet. Out of the corner of his eye he saw the open-mouthed scribe drop his parchment and run. No time to stop him… he had to finish what he had begun.

Bending down, he grasped his enemy's thick hair and yanked his head back. "Ask your gods for their forgiveness and mercy — you will get none from Ardhu of Albu," he said harshly, and he drew Carnwennan across the raider's throat and released his life force out upon the ground.

Ardhu stood for a moment in shock, as blood spewed from the severed jugular, soaking his leggings and felt boots, and the feral light in the pirate's eyes faded into nothingness, leaving him a lifeless husk, food for crows. Art began to shiver…his first kill, but he took no joy in it, despite knowing what the raider had done.

He had no time, however, to dwell on the less glorious side of death and battle. He became aware of other sea-pirates arriving on the strand, exiting their tents and coming in from the ships, addled with drink and bleary-eyed, angry as disturbed bees for being awakened from their drunken slumber by the noises in the village.

There were too many for him to take on, he knew that at once. Staring up into the vault of the night sky, he saw the Moon, a bent sickle, over the troubled waters of the Gleyn. The Moon had risen where he had predicted it would, using Merlin's skills…

A shriek ripped through the darkness, a blood-curdling war cry. Out of the night-mist galloped Ka'hai, Per-Adur, Bohrs, Betu'or and the other warriors of the warband, waving axes of stone and bronze, their faces painted with patterns and their hair full of feathers. Their mounts champed and rolled their eyes, unnerved by their riders' unearthly cries. Nonetheless, they drove them on with heels and hands, crashing them through the foreigners' watch-fires and barging straight into the line of confused pirates — who only just seemed to have noticed that their leader lay dead upon the shore, his blood seeping into the earth of the land he had violated.

The raiders quickly recovered from their initial shock, and tried to form a ragged line of defence against Ardhu's men. Most, however, had left their best weapons on the boats, and soon many fell beneath pounding hooves or the downward strike of an axe or stone hammer. Realising they were outnumbered and at a gross disadvantage on foot, they began to retreat toward the moored ships.

"Stop them, they're getting away!" Bohrs roared in rage, slamming his heels into his pony's side and spitting with fury as the frightened animal refused to budge.

"Wait! Look!" Art pointed across the water. "Ba-lin and Bal-ahn! They have reached the boats!"

Out in the dark a solitary tongue of flame appeared on the deck of each ship. It grew bigger and brighter, then whooshed upwards, following the line of riggings and folded sails. Fire! Sparks shot up into the air; smoke billowed in pale clouds over the river.

The sea-pirates knew their game was up. Some threw themselves from their ships into the Gleyn and tried to swim ashore, but the men of Ardhu's warband rode them down in the shallows, trampling them with their mounts or felling them with their huge, ancient axes. Bodies bobbed along the shoreline; the currents of the Gleyn turned a sickly crimson.

And so was the first battle of Ardhu Pendraec, the Stone Lord, the Terrible Head, won in the West. His first battle as king and the first time he had spilled blood.

It would not be his last.

CHAPTER TEN

Ardhu sat within a hut in the riverside village, recovering from the events of the night. He drank from a beaker, slowly, reflectively, while Ka'hai fussed about him like an old woman, combing blood-clots from his hair, and rubbing ointments and unguents onto his bruises and scrapes. This killing of men... it was a nasty business. Ardhu wondered if he ever would grow used to it — the stink, the screams, the sensation of the dagger slicing through flesh, and then that strange, fearful emptiness as the adversary's spirit slipped into eternity. He glanced at Ka'hai, himself newly-blooded that day, and wondered if he felt as disturbed and shaken as he — his foster brother who was so gentle with animals, but who had just killed five men. Ka'hai's visage showed no emotion; he just worked on, finishing his ministrations of Art's grazes, before wrapping a fine cloak around his shoulders and fastening it with a huge disc-brooch surmounted by a golden cross, the symbol of the Sun himself.

Outside there were yells and cries as the rest of the war band danced around the fire, drunk with victory, drunk from the contents of their beakers. They had raided the stores of the sea-pirates and had found new drinks to imbibe, among other delicacies, and they were enjoying themselves tremendously.

"Are you going to join the men?" asked Ka'hai. "They expect to go amongst them, praising the might of their arms."

Ardhu smiled wanly and got to his feet. He was bone-weary, his eyes gritty as if they were full of sand, but he dared not let go of his fragile hold on his warriors. "If they want me there, then it is my duty to go," he said, and he walked stiffly from the hut.

He was greeted by applause and joyous shouts from the men, who were dancing around a giant pyre made from the pirates' possessions. Trophies of war surrounded them: kegs of drink and dried meats, strange foreign armour and weapons... and a dozen severed heads mounted on stakes of driftwood.

The dead eyes of the heads seemed to glare balefully, reproachfully, at Ardhu as he approached through the smoky darkness. He avoided their blank gaze; he could not forget that although they were his enemies and deserved to die, they were also men who once breathed even as he did.

"My men, I greet you!" he said to his warband. "And I praise you, the greatest warriors ever known. Such courage will be remembered forever."

Deep in his cups, Bohrs staggered up to his chief. "Will you reward one of us with the Champion's portion?" he bellowed "One who was better than the rest!"

Art took his arm and guided him back to his place by the fire. "No, Bohrs, there will be no one champion. You are all champions. As there is no beginning and end to the Great Circle of Stone, so there is no one higher or lower in my band of men. We are equals, fighting toward one goal — the freedom of Prydn."

Another cheer went up, and Bohrs plopped down drunkenly, splashing the heady liquor in his beaker across his ruddy face. He laughed and shook himself like a wet dog, to howls of mirth from his companions.

Suddenly two warriors came through the smoke and river-fog dragging something between them. "My lord," shouted one — it was Ba-lin, one of the twins who had fired the pirates' ships. "We've found another man, hiding. He was unarmed and begged for mercy, we did not think it right to kill him. At least until we had your permission." He grinned wolfishly.

"Let me see this man," Ardhu ordered.

Ba-lin's twin Bal-ahn kicked the prisoner forward; he fell on his knees before the young warlord. Art recognised him as once as the shaven-headed scribe he had first spotted in the village. He looked thoroughly miserable, covered in mud, his teeth chattering with fear. Close, he saw that the scribe's features did not quite match to that of the raiders, and deduced he came from some other tribe.

"What do you have to say for yourself, foreigner?" he asked.

The man spoke slowly, in a broken version of the tongue of Prydn, "I beg for your mercy, young lord. I am but a slave; I had nothing to do with the injustices done to your people. My own suffered likewise many years ago, and I was spared only because of my skill with words — I can both read and write."

"A slave. I thought so by your cropped head. Well, you are a slave no longer. Your masters are all dead."

The man looked confused. "Do you take me for your own slave now, lord?"

Ardhu shook his head. "In my kingdom I prefer my men to serve me of their own free will. I have no use for men with your skills, either — only those who can wield a bow or dagger."

"Then what are you going to do with me," the man said flatly.

"What do you think? I am not a monster, like the wretches you served. You are free."

The man looked up, amazed, his mouth hanging. "Young lord, you are too merciful. How ever can I thank you!"

"In one way. I will give you safe passage across the Narrow Sea, and when you arrive on the mainland, I want you to spread the word far and wide that Ardhu Pendraec holds Prydn, and that he will tolerate no incursions from men who seek not lawful trade but thievery and murder. Take this message to the ends of the known world! But tell them too that Prydn is open to trade with all with all those who come with honest hearts, and that the King of Albu is stern but also just and fair!"

"I will tell them," said the slave, and suddenly there was a new light in his eyes. "My name... the sea-folk called me Pal. But I am Palomides. I was the youngest son of a lord who lived on an island called Delos. Years ago there were friendships between your Isle and ours, and much trade; two holy women of your race even settled in our land and their tomb is decorated and revered by local maidens even today. This was many centuries past, when these Pretanic isles were ruled by Brytto, who gave his name to them; and by his son, Blessed Brahn, big as a house, with a raven as his totem."

Ardhu clapped his hands and roared with laughter. "I like this, friend. A man from far across the sea who knows more of our history than most native-born sons!"

Pal gave a little bow. "As a younger son I was not desired as either warrior or statesman. So I became learned about the ways of men in the world around me. It was a good thing, lord. My learning probably kept me alive."

"And long may it be so," said Ardhu, placing a hand on his shoulder. "Now go, my men will see that you have safe passage."

"Wait." Palomides' eyes darkened. "I must tell you. There are two more Sherdan ships further along the arm of this inlet. The pirates on them have treated the locals as harshly as here."

Ardhu frowned and his men muttered and felt the edges of their axes; but there was a note of despair in their voices too. They were weary from long travelling and hard fighting; they had more than their fill of blood and slaughter for one day.

"And," Palomides stared at his feet. "There is even worse afoot, I fear, my lord. One of the leaders, Husrubal, was in meeting with some of your own kind — men from the northern islands off the tip of the land called Kaladhon."

127

Fury ignited in Ardhu's eyes. "Who? What are their names?"

"Forgive me if my memory slips... I heard but whispers in the night... One was... Loth... Loth of Ynys Yrch, the other Orion... no, Urienz."

"The pig from the Isle of Pigs and his kinsman," grunted Bohrs, making a rude gesture. "Do you know what they wanted, foreigner? They were far from their homes."

Palomides swallowed. "They asked the Sherdan for help. Help to remove a boy-king of the West, who had become too powerful for his own good." He looked at Ardhu. "I wager they spoke of you, lord. And it was with no love."

"Traitorous wretches," growled Bohrs through gritted teeth. "I knew they would turn way back at Marthodunu, even though they grudgingly swore to support you!"

Ardhu wiped his arm across his face. He looked tired and drained, purple circles underscoring his eyes "This is ill news but not unexpected. Our thanks, Palomides of Delos. You may have been more valuable than you realise. Go now, and farewell — maybe we shall meet again. And if you do ever come to these shores again, I will make you a man of my warband — the different one, with different skills and much knowledge."

Palomides bowed again. "If the Gods will it, it will be so."

Then Art beckoned to two of his men and they led Palomides away, toward the coastal settlements where sea-trade had been the lifeblood of the locals for over six hundred years and boats travelling afar with tin and copper were plentiful. Once he had crossed the channel safely, he could make his way across the continent using ancient trade-routes that led through the forests of the Middle-Lands to the mighty Rivers Rhinns and Rhon. With luck, and no attacks from hostile tribes or evil weather-spirits, he could then follow the rivers Eastward and be home with his long-lost family within two Moons.

Art quietly thanked the spirits for the Delian man as he mulled the information the slave had imparted. He had to move quickly, before the other pirate raiders became aware of the destruction of their fellows... and before Urienz and Loth's men arrived from the northern isles.

Turning to his warband, he said in a voice that grated like stones on the shore: "No time for celebrating! No time for sleep! We must go on and cleanse Albu of these invaders and traitors. When that is done then may we rest-whether it is in our furs or in our barrows!"

He raised the Lightning Mace to the sky, its white bone mounts shining in the dark; and above the sky suddenly answered, lightning flaring sullenly under the belly of the livid clouds that had been gathering in the North. The horses whinnied and skittered, frightened of the storm, and the men felt the energy in the air, the electricity crackling in their hair.

"We ride on!" cried Ardhu, and he ran to Lamrai, vaulting easily onto her back. Just as the storm broke, and rain slashed down like tears of a tormented god, the warband galloped from the riverside, and toward the haunts of their enemies.

The next two battles of Ardhu the Bear were harder won than the first. The Sea-Raiders had seen smoke curling in the air, and sailed into coves and sheltered areas where they set up watchful camps. This time there were no words spoken between the two opposing forces; the air instead was full of the sound of war-cries and then with the screams of the injured and dying. Art's men were, for the most part, young and unskilled, but their youth and strength gave them an added edge — that and their sturdy mounts, which they drove over their foes as they fell. As Ardhu had hoped, the Sea-Raiders were not expecting horsemen, and had no time to devise a way to stave them off.

Eventually the fighting was done. Again, Ardhu sat in the dark, hair and skin bathed scarlet, his garb purple with dark, clotted gore and the stink of death all around him. On the river ahead he could see fires leaping as a ship aflame slowly sank beneath the waves to the jeers and shouts of his victorious band. He wiped his face, his burning eyes, wishing for nothing more than sleep and clean clothes.

Ka'hai came to join him; he too was smeared with red blood and dark, his hair- knot crimson and his blue eyes startling and somehow almost monstrous against the scarlet-streaked mask of his face. "Art...you are hale?" he asked, hunkering down beside his foster-brother. "We have done it...no pirate is left alive; the warriors have taken their heads and hands and feet and placed them under boulders so they will never walk as spirits either here in Prydn or in the Otherworld."

"And our men?" Art looked at him grimly, leaning on the hilt of Caladvolc the Hardcleft. "What of our losses? This time, I know we were not so lucky."

Ka'hai sighed. "Lucky enough, considering that we are all green in the arts of war, save for Bohrs and Per-Adur. The main body of warriors from Marthodunu and Place-of-Light is unharmed save for scrapes and gashes. But some of the youths and new recruits picked up along the route to the Gleyn will not be going home to their green fields and forests. But such is the way of war, and they knew that. They are now riding over the Great Plain, young forever."

Art rose, gesturing to his torn, stained clothes with sudden anger. "This disgusts me… I reek of death! We have leather-workers amongst us… hunt down a deer and kill it, and have them make me a new tunic to wear. I am not such a savage I would rejoice in wearing my enemies' blood!"

Ka'hai glanced at him solemnly. "Wear your soiled robe with pride, Ardhu. From this day forward, garments of such hue will be the colour of royalty, of battle and sacrifice for the Land."

Ardhu shook his head bitterly. "Noble speech, but hiding the ugliness that is truth. I tell you, brother, although it may not be so honourable, the tilling of soil is preferable to the killing of men."

"Oh, I agree, Art — I'd rather be with my horses that here, stinking of gore — but that is not our lot, I fear. Wear the royal purple blood-robe, my friend, and remember its colour comes not just from the wounds of your enemies but from your own blood."

The two youths walked down to the water's edge. The fallen of the warband lay in rows, curled into foetal position by their fellows, their sightless eyes turned, as was tradition, toward the rising Sun in the East.. There would be no barrow-burial for them, nor cremation with urn-burial, for women were the ones who moulded containers for the ashes of the dead, and they were far away. No, the fallen would be burned, and their ashes given to the waters, the air and the earth.

"Gather the wood," Ardhu commanded, and Ba-lin, Bal-ahn, Betu'or and others went out into the darkness and came back bearing as much dried kindling as they could find. They stacked it around their fallen comrades and packed the crevices with chunks of dried moss and lichen. When the pile was heaped high, Ardhu used his flint-strike-a-light to kindle a torch. He thrust the brand into the driest part of the pyre and the flames leapt up, twisting and turning, illuminating the faces of the living and giving the false glow of life to the faces of the dead.

"There is no time to linger and mourn," Ardhu said as the flames spiralled. "The kings of the North are coming… We have no time for grief!"

Leaving the pyre burning brightly in the night, the warband of Ardhu the Stone Lord rode on toward the gathering forces of Urienz and Loth.

The warriors made camp in a little valley of pleasant aspect, with a winding stream and rocky ground scattered with rowan trees. The valley lips were high and ridged, making it an ideal place to pitch camp in safety, for it would be easy to spot any unwelcome visitor silhouetted against the backdrop of the vast, open sky.

"We'll rest here for a few days," said Ardhu. "Get some decent food into us, if the hunt is good, and tend our wounds. Ba-lin, Bal-ahn, you scout ahead and see what you can find out about the movements of Loth and Urienz and their followers."

The band set about making camp, some throwing up temporary shelters while others took their bows and headed into the deeply-wooded valley-side to hunt for game. Ba-lin and Bal-ahn, like two eager pups, grabbed their bows, and went bounding up and over the lip of the vale and away, their war-whoops echoing through empty spaces broken only by the cries of hawks and other passing birds until that hour.

Ardhu pulled off his ragged, bloody tunic, freeing himself at last of the sight and smell of bloodshed. He yanked on a long, baggy, yellow-brown kirtle his men had looted from one of the sea-raider's troves; it hung on him almost like a woman's dress, and he snorted in derision, and pulled his belt tightly around his waist, cinching the garment up an inch or two. Hah…in his eyes it looked fair fit for a girl, but at least it was clean! Thrusting Carnwennan into the top of his felt-lined leggings, he walked away from the camp and followed the stream, seeking a place where he might bathe and sit away from the noise and clamour of the others for a while.

Gradually he noticed the stream widening, fanning out toward a line of gnarled trees that ran up to a wall of grey, slate cliffs. The cliff tops were stark, ridged with fangs of wind-battered stone round which the wind made eerie moans. Above this piteous keening he could hear the rush of swift-flowing currents, and a churning roar, like a giant's grinding teeth, as that water poured into an unseen basin.

"A waterfall," murmured Art, picking up speed as his curiosity deepened. He had never seen water falling from height before; Abona ran smooth and deep, save for a few eddies round the weir when the river was full after winter storms. But Merlin, whose ancestral lands had held such wonders, had told him of the white foaming hair of the water-spirits that fell over the bones of the land, and the deep green tears they shed into the fathomless pools below them.

Ideal places for mortal men to wash away the cares of the world…

Hastily he entered the trees, splashing in the stream's shallows, savouring the coolness on his bruised and blistered feet. Sunlight dappled a carpet of deep, drenched moss and flickered on the little crests of water that played round his ankles and slapped the slime-streaked boulders in the swell.

The trees suddenly parted and there before him reared the falls: a frothing spout of water that jetted over a tongue of dark green stone before falling, ringed by rainbows, into a pool where bubbles broke over pebbles worn into fantastic shapes by the ceaseless pounding of the torrent.

And spoiling Ardhu's view of this earthly paradise was a stranger.

Ardhu felt a fearful knot arise in his belly as he stared at the unwelcome one. Was this truly a mortal before him...or was it one of the Everliving Ones, the spirits who lived in the hills, the stones, and the wild places of earth? For surely no human could have the face and form of the man who stood before him, balanced high above the falls on the jut of stone where the waters began their rapid descent, practising warrior's-arts with a long and deadly spear that he thrust towards the belly of the sky.

He was a Man of Bronze.

Red bronze was the head of his spear, and pale bronze the skin on his bare shoulders and lean, tightly muscled torso. His hair, a rippling mane of waves that hung down his back, was also golden-bronze, and there were rings of copper threaded through its length. The planes of his face were high and fair, without flaw or defect: the nose sculpted, the jaw — which he wore clean-shaven — firm without viciousness, the lips curved but not womanish. Under a noble brow, his eyes gleamed rich, tawny amber. It was as if the Sun himself had stepped down onto that high perch and taken on the semblance of a human being in order to enjoin with human affairs.

But then the perfect stranger stumbled, his foot slipping on sodden water weeds and nearly spilling him into the flume, and his perfect mouth loosed a florid and very human oath, and Art, watching from below, knew at once it was no god preening and parading on that lofty perch. Just a man. A man who had the temerity to look like a god to Ardhu's eyes.

Fear and awe changed abruptly to annoyance... an embarrassing stab of jealousy. He was King of Prydn, who, at fifteen summers had won three battles in as many days — how dare this man wander around as if he owned this wood and water!

Harsh words burst out almost as if from a stranger's mouth: "You! Over there! I wish to use this place. Finish your practice and be on your way!"

The Man of Bronze halted and swung round to peer over the edge of the waterfall, his sun-bright face calm but mildly curious. He caught sight of Ardhu and his tawny eyes narrowed, although his lips rose in a mocking smile. "Who is this boy who speaks to me in such a haughty manner?" he asked in Ardhu's own tongue, though he spoke with a strange, outlandish accent. "I thought by the tone that surely it must be some great warrior, some mighty chief. Instead I see a child in a silly robe that he must have stolen from his sisters!"

"How dare you!" spat Ardhu, face reddening with rage. "You know not know who I am?"

"No, I don't... and you certainly do not know who I am!" retorted the shining stranger, leaping down the stony outcrops of the side of the falls with the fluidity of a sure-footed wildcat. "I am An'kelet, He-of-the-Striking-Spear, Prince of Ar-morah, son of the high priestess Eilahn of the Lake of Maidens and King Bhan. And I may well be the greatest warrior in the West of the world."

"The greatest braggart, more like!" shouted Ardhu, and in a sudden frenzy born of exhaustion and frustration, he hurled himself at the taller man.

The bronze stranger seemed unconcerned and even slightly amused. "You want to fight ...so be it, young fool. I will douse your hotness in the waters of the falls by the end of the day!" With a deft movement he cast his great spear into a nearby tree where it stuck, quivering, its embedded point releasing a stream of sap as red as blood. "Let it be hands on then, no weapons. I would not raise a weapon against a child; it would bring no honour."

His words, as intended, inflamed Ardhu even more. The young chief rushed at An'kelet and tried to seize him, to topple him over into the pool and stop his prideful boasts. He was no great wrestler, but he had competed in fun round the fires with his fellows, and what he lacked in bulk, he made up for in swiftness of movement and wiry strength in his bow-hardened upper arms. Surely, one good headlong rush and he could wipe the mocking smile off that too-handsome visage...

A moment later Art was on his arse on the hard rock, gasping. He stared up, unbelieving and bewildered, at the tall fair man looming above him, who had shot round him with lightning speed and tripped him up, kicking his legs out from under him with a swift blow from a lean, hard foot.

"What evil magic is this...?" he mumbled, wishing he had his own magic-man, the Merlin, with him to do battle against this unnatural warrior from Ar-morah. "Fight me properly... you... you water-creature!"

An'kelet sighed. "What more do you ask from me? I have already laid down my spear! Would you have me tie my hand behind my back too? I told you, boy — I am the best warrior in the Western world. Be it with weapons or hands, I will win!"

Ardhu's eyes blackened; burgeoning jealousy and self-doubt grew large in him again. Surely he gods loved him; they had given him the sword from beneath the stone...not this foreign stranger with his lazy smile and conceited boasts. Uttering an enraged cry, he struggled up into a half-crouch and slammed his head into his opponent's stomach.

The blow hit home... but did not have the effect Art desired. The bronze man staggered back for a brief second, but was immediately on him again, pinioning his arms behind his back. "A nasty, angry little boy, aren't you?" he mocked. "I told you, you need to cool off by having a ducking!" And without further ado, he hurled Ardhu into the emerald pool.

Art sank into the green depths, the water churning like a primordial cauldron around him. Immediately he kicked out and began to swim, striking out for the foam-laden surface. He burst through the spume and bubbles to see his adversary hunkered down on the bank, grinning and laughing.

Laughing at him! At Ardhu, king of Prydn!

A cloud of rage descended on the young warlord. Irrational thoughts of revenge filled his head. Although he vaguely knew it was ignoble in a fight where weapons had been downed, he reached under the water and drew Carnwennan from its hidden place in the band of his leggings.

"You will laugh at me no more!" he shouted and he sprang from the pool and slashed wildly at his opponent's startled, perfect face.

The next moment he was on his knees, gasping for breath. An'kelet's hands were around his throat, fingers pressing hard on his windpipe. No longer was the bronze man playing, teasing — now he was full of deadly intent. His eyes were narrowed, his face serious and deadly.

"Who are you? Who sent you, assassin? Was it Loth of Ynys Yrch? You are not just some local peasant lad, are you? Not with that fine dagger! Speak now, or you will never speak again!"

Ardhu struggled to answer; black spots streamed across his vision. "I...if Loth and Urienz are your enemies, then in truth you must be a friend of mine, for they are my enemies also."

An'kelet did not release his grip; he dragged Ardhu up, his eyes boring into the younger man's. "Is that so? Who are you, if that is true? And how did you come by that noble dagger...How could it be yours, unless you are a man of worth... or a cutpurse and thief, a looter of barrows!"

"I am Ardhu..." Art croaked. His head felt fuzzy, the world was spinning. He had never felt the Otherworld so near. "Pendraec. The Terrible head. The blade is mine by right. It was won from its barrow-guardian by moving the great stone. I am the King of the West!"

Through dimming vision he saw An'kelet suddenly blanche. "My lord, forgive me, I could not know!" he cried, and at once he released Ardhu's throat from his death-grip.

Ardhu sank to the ground, eyes streaming and puke dripping from his chin, as, before him, the mighty Man of Bronze went down on one knee and bowed his head to him.

###

Ardhu and An'kelet walked across the field toward Art's war-camp. The tall foreigner had donned tunic and cloak, and although he looked less godly in his woven garb, he was nobility was obvious by both his mien and his possessions. A fillet of thin gold held back his hair, and a small, ancestral axe-talisman fashioned from polished jadeite hung round his neck. His felt boots were of many colours, his belt-ring of shale, and at his belt hung two great, long Ar-morahan daggers with golden pontille hilts — Arondyt and Fragarak the Answerer. On his shoulder rested the great barbed spear Balugaisa, which, he told Ardhu, was wrought from the spiky hide of the sea-monster Kon-khenn.

"Here..." he was rummaging through a fox-skin bag. "I have mosses that will heal your throat... where my fingers bit into you. It will aid the bruising."

Art smiled wryly. "You heal too? Are you the world's best healer just as you are the world's best warrior?"

An'kelet grinned. "My mother, the high priestess Ailin, said the ability to heal is one of the greatest of all arts. She showed me much healer's magic, once even cutting a roundel from a man's skull so that evil spirits can fly from his mind!" He pulled a tuft of moss from the bag and handed it to Ardhu. "Here. Try it."

Ardhu did as An'kelet told him, still wondering at this odd shining man from over the sea, who was unlike anyone he'd ever met before. Despite the hostility of their initial encounter, he found himself beginning to warm to the stranger. Although An'kelet brimmed with confidence, and was better to look at than a human man had a right to be, there was something appealing about his open manner, and his eyes, when not burning with the light of battle, were kind.

"So, Prince An'kelet, what brought you to Albu from our cousin-land of Ar-morah?"

An'kelet gave him a sideways look. "My father Bhan died before my

135

birth, hence none of his lands became mine. My mother, as I told you, is a priestess; she lives with twelve maidens on an isle in the heart of a silver lake, in the middle of the mighty forest of Bro-khelian. These women were rumoured to be the most beautiful on earth; they tended a holy cairn surrounded by eighteen cup-marked stones that represented the Moon's Great Year. When the time arrived that the Moon came down from the sky to dance over the temple, the priestesses would seek lovers from amongst human men, for that one night only. My father came to the isle, drawn by the rumoured beauty of the women — and by his own lusts! He coupled with my mother on the lakeshore and sought to carry her off to be his wife…but he did not know all of what took place upon that island. The Maidens of the Moon, driven into frenzy by their dance, tore him apart with their bare hands and scattered his bones into the lake. Nine Moons later I was born on the same silvered shore where I was conceived, and from it took one of my many names An'kelet-of-the-Lake. I was happy there for many years, but when my manhood rites were completed I was forced to leave, for it is forbidden for a grown male to dwell on that isle, and so I went to stay with my mother's kinsman, King Ho-ehl. I grew restive there too, though, as a landless man…and decided to seek my fortune in Albu. We in Ar-morah had heard rumours of a mighty young war-lord and I was curious to see for myself if he was worthy of the strength of my arm."

Ardhu grimaced. "And there I was acting the fool…"

"It is forgotten, lord," said An'kelet, wide-eyed. "There is no shame in it. My presence merely startled you when you were weary and sore-hearted, and you were not yourself. I am to blame."

Ardhu waved his hand, urging him to continue. "So, you had heard of me over the Sundering Seas. But here you are, far in the mountains of the West, near Sylur lands. And you speak of my enemies, Loth and Urienz, as your enemies too. How has this come about?"

"I set sail in the winter when the waves were high; I am no sailor and forgot how the winds of Prydn are fierce and its weather-spirits capricious! No wonder the men of the East call your people 'Dwellers Beyond the North Wind'! My ship was blown beyond its desired port in Belerion, and took beached on the coast near Mhon. I went ashore and continued my travels on foot, and came at the Feast of Lambing to the village of a chief called Ludegran. He was well glad to see me, for he had been plagued by evil neighbours, and looked to the sharpness of my spear, Balugaisa, Spear-of-Mortal-Pain. He is old but kindly, and I pitied him; his only son is dead, and his men, like himself, grow old; many of the tribe's youths have perished in raids from the sea. He spoke of you with great hope, lord, and said he had seen you lift the great capstone to reveal the magic blade."

Ardhu nodded. "Yes, I recall Ludegran from the gathering at Marthodunu. Old but keen-eyed and quick of wit. He never spoke against me, as some of the others did."

"I was just about ready to leave Ludegran and search for you," continued An'kelet, "but then further evil befell. A messenger came from the North — from the chiefs Loth and Urienz. Ludegran was asked to join them in rebellion against you, and to support Loth in a bid for High Kingship of all Prydn. He refused, and Loth threatened dire revenge, and now scouts have brought word that fighting men are issuing from the North, by sea and by land, to burn the villages of those who refuse to support them, and join forces with those miscreants who do. And when their numbers are swelled, they will march to the Great Stone temple of great fame, and cast you down."

"So, they are well on their way," said Ardhu bitterly. "I had word of their treachery, and it is because of their threats that I have brought my warband to this place. However, it is evil new that they are so near at hand, for my men are weary...having three times fought the Sea-Pirates and won."

An'kelet clapped a firm hand on Art's shoulder. "Well, you need not fear so much now, lord. I am here, the master of the shining spear. Together, all the evils of the world will fall before us!"

When Ardhu and the Ar-morahan noble arrived at the camp, Ardhu's warband were just as intrigued by the newcomer as Art had been. They gathered close, curious, eyeing his weapons, especially the great, pronged spear, which was not a weapon used much by the men of Prydn, who preferred bows, daggers, and axes of stone and bronze.

Ka'hai looked a bit wary, however, and rubbed his big, broad chin with a grubby fist. "I don't know, Art," he murmured to his foster-brother. "I wish Merlin were here. Oh yes, he's likeable... amazing, even, but what if the men take to him and desert you? Do not be offended! But men are fickle and he is like a light to which lesser moths will cluster."

"Yes, I know the foreign prince is a special one," said Ardhu heavily. "Knew it so much that I acted in a shameful manner when first I met him. Look..." He pointed to the finger marks on his neck. "He put these on me and brought me back to my senses. He has marked me now and humbled me;

137

no matter if the men are loyal or not, I will know in my heart he is the better warrior and more worthy."

"Then why did you bring him here?" snapped Ka'hai, brow furrowed with anxiety. "Surely that is madness!"

"Because it was his aim to join our cause... and because we need men like him, men beyond compare. Men who will inspire. We need him on our side, gathering warriors to us, to our cause, rather than drawing them to whatever quest is dear to him. Do you understand?"

"I... I think so... I pray you're right, brother." Ka'hai chewed his lip.

At that moment An'kelet cast his spear in a demonstration of its power, and the warband cheered as it split a rotted tree stump nigh in two. "A fine cast!" yelled Bohrs. "Ardhu, is this one to join us this day? We could use a long throw like that, to split a few raiders' black hearts!"

Ardhu inclined his head gravely and approached An'kelet, hands out. His voice was steady. "That is solely up to prince An'kelet...let the decision be his."

An'kelet drew himself up to his full height and smiled. He then drew his long dagger Arondyt with its gold-pinned pommel and presented it hilt-first to Ardhu. "I will fight with you, against the enemies of Prydn that are also enemies of Ar-morah. And please, do not call me 'prince.' There is only one lord-chief here and can ever be... Ardhu Pendraec, King of the West."

He sank to one knee, still holding up his dagger. Ardhu took it and touched it to An'kelet's brow and to his shoulder as a token that he accepted this bronze stranger as one of his own men, and then he gave the blade back to its owner, who rose with a smile that blazed like the Sun at Midsummer.

"My lord," An'kelet said. "Now that I am your sworn man, can we set off to halt these bastards, Loth and Urienz? My spear is thirsty and my spirit crying for battle!"

"I'm just thirsty!" grunted Bohrs. "Ach, man, we've been battling for days!"

"There will be respite, before the big battle," said An'kelet. "Come, I will show you the way to the dun of chief Ludegran, where you will receive meat and drink to cheer you."

They upped camp before the Sun had reached the noon position, mounting their weary steeds and heading northwards, while around them the countryside grew more rugged, the mountains taller and the air more clear.

138

Above their heads, the sky was alive with wheeling seabirds, sunlight flashing off their outstretched wings, their cries shrill and lonely like the calling of lost spirits. "I can smell salt in the air," said Ardhu, lifting his head and scenting the wind like an animal, in a way Merlin has taught him.

Riding alongside him on a pony that had belonged to one of the warriors who fell on the sea-strand, An'kelet nodded. "Yes, we are not far from the sea — the sea that divides Albu from its sister isle Ibherna. The sea that brought men to Prydn years ago, and still does — but now they are men with filled with plans of hate and conquest. Ludegran's holding is just over yonder hill; he has moved his people from the valleys to a high place that overlooks the sea — a shrewd move, for the sea is where the danger lies, and he can now easily keep watch. This fort is an extraordinary structure, I have not seen its like... I am sure, in the future, its merits will catch on."

"Alas, this is how it shall be in many places, I fear; men will hide behind stout doors in high places and leave their farms behind," said Ardhu. "I myself have built a hilltop fort, Kham-El-Ard — you will see it when we head back south. But back to this Ludegran: will he welcome so many of us, eating his supplies, drinking his mead? Although he supported me at Marthodunu, it is hard for men in these perilous times to feed unexpected guests."

"He will regard your presence as a great honour," replied An'kelet. "And your bows and daggers a great relief. You see, he has a reason greater than most lords' to want his walls unbreached, his house defended. Behind the stout posts that surround his holdings he hides a great treasure!"

"A great treasure?" Art's dark eyebrows rose. "What kind of treasure is this?"

An'kelet grinned and tossed back his golden-bronze hair, setting his hair-rings jangling. "A most unique treasure, and the old man guards it with his life. In his walls he holds the White Phantom, fair beyond compare!"

"White phantom? You mean like a barrow-spirit? What a strange thing to trammel within the walls of a dwelling; such should stay behind the walls of henge and ditch!"

An'kelet laughed, his white teeth flashing. "No, my lord-friend. A goddess! A queen! His foster-daughter Fynavir of Ibherna, who was set to marry his son as Harvest-tide, had the lad not died. Ludegran worships her and fears for her safety, should he fall in battle. As well he might; I saw the northern emissaries' lustful eyes when they saw her!"

"A girl!" said Ardhu, with some disappointment. "Is that all?"

An'kelet laughed. "You are young yet, lord, I imagine women are not as interesting to you as hounds, horses and swords. Not yet."

"And I suppose you are the world's greatest lover, as well as the greatest warrior," said Ardhu teasingly.

"If I chose to be," said An'kelet, face suddenly serious and his eyes vaguely shadowed "Both woman and men have offered themselves to me. But, in truth, I take a more restrained approach to…pleasures… than most. I grew up on the Lake of Maidens where most of the priestesses knew men only once in their lives, and killed the men who took them, in atonement for their virginity."

An'kelet pulled his short cloak tight around his shoulders; the wind was rising, cooling. "Death was the fruit of the lust of men; I saw this. My own father succumbed to it. I believe yours did too, my lord, if the tales are true. I swore as a youth I would not be swayed by such lusts; that I would only worship and love what was pure and holy. I will not, I pray, be taken by passions that bring only doom and pain for all concerned."

"But surely you want to continue your line. That's what the Ancestors desire of us!"

"Maybe. But I do not think they frown on me." He grinned. "Do I look as though I am in disfavour?"

"You are a strange one, An'kelet," said Ardhu, laughing.

"I know, young lord. You will never meet my like again!" An'kelet tossed his head again, and his clear laughter mixed with the jangle of the rings in his hair rang out across the grey, empty land.

The path ahead narrowed and the trees melted away to become clusters of thorny bushes. Over the steep ridges ahead the sea was now visible, slate grey and shining dully. Far to the West, the green curves and swells of Ibherna rested under a pall of cloud.

"Look," said An'kelet. "Ahead is the fort of Ludegran, ready for war."

Art peered into the Sun. High on a plateau before him rose a fort with earthen ramparts newly dug. Stakes sharp as spears bristled at the bottom of the ditches, waiting to impale the unwelcome. A wooden palisade circled it, made of stout oak. He felt a small thrill as he looked upon it; for surely this was what Kham-El-Ard would look like one day. Only his citadel would be twice as big, twice as grand, blessed by the rising Sun on its eastern flank, and on the other side facing the Temple and the Great Plain.

An'kelet set his heels to the flanks of his pony and joyfully thundered toward the gates. A multitude of heads immediately popped up over the ramparts; Art could see a line of drawn bows. "Peace! It is only I, An'kelet-of-the-Lake!" called An'kelet, waving his spear above his head. "I've returned to help you, my friends, and I have brought with me Ardhu Pendraec, King of the West, my ally and my friend. Unbar the way and make us welcome!"

There was scuffling in the entrance to the fort. Barricades of wood and sharpened poles were hastily pushed aside.

An'kelet rode through the gap, his bright hair streaming like a banner, and Ardhu and his band followed after to cheers and the blowing of ox-horns.

CHAPTER ELEVEN

"Welcome, Lord Ardhu, Terrible head, chief of Khor Ghor and the West."

An old man, his beard white frizz and his rheumy eyes the colour of rain-wet slate, walked up to Art and bowed deeply. He wore a checked tunic with a sash tied over one shoulder; the dagger at his belt was of an ancient type with a handle of horn, and he wore an ancestral wristguard as a bracelet, its red stone pierced by three great studs of gold. "You may remember me from Marthodunu. I supported your cause."

Ardhu nodded. "I remember. I wish we could have met here in happier circumstances. Your stronghold intrigues me; it should hold out many foes."

"I pray you are right, young lord." A shadow passed over Ludegran's gaunt face. "Foe-men are on the march. I see Prince An'kelet has met with you already; I trust he has told you of Loth's treachery, and of the threats he has made against my people. And against you too, of course. He resents that he could not lift the stone and take kingly blade."

"Yes, I know about Loth, and his twisted brother," said Ardhu. "We will deal with them, and if the spirits will it, few if any of their men will return to their unfriendly, wind-blasted homeland! Do you have any news on their movements?"

"Nothing as yet. I have scouts in the villages along the coast, ready to send warnings when they arrive. But come, you look weary; news has come from the West that you have already been victorious in many battles. You will eat and drink with me and mine, and we will make a fitting reception for your brave heroes."

Chief Ludegran led Ardhu towards a massive roundhouse that stood in the shadow of the fort's retaining wall. Torches lit a path to its door, and the Westering Sun turned the thatching of its sloped roof to flame. Carved household deities with eyes of flint capered at the threshold, and a bull's skull loomed above the door-lintel, horns poking the sky.

Following Ludegran, Ardhu entered the smoky darkness of the house. For a rural chieftain away from main trade routes, Ludegran lived in moderate opulence. Furs of bear, wildcats and beavers hung on the walls, making the room warm and cosy. Woven pennants bearing blue and red designs — the symbols of kingly clans — hung between the furs. Skulls of boar and horse lined the roof beams, and several human skulls, either enemies or Ancestors, hung suspended over the deep fire-pit, which was tended by ash-smeared women who continuously poked and prodded, and fed the flames with logs of ash and oak. At the back of the house, several screened off areas marked the sleeping compartments of the highborn, their floors strewn with rushes and mounds of goatskins.

An'kelet, who had followed Ludegran and Ardhu into the roundhouse, was peering around. "My lord Ludegran, where is your fair treasure, who brings joy to us all?"

Ludegran smiled. "When strangers are at the gate, I hide her away — as any man would do with such a lady of value. She is here, watching even as we speak! War-chief Ardhu, let me present to you the White Phantom, noblest and most blessed woman in Prydn: Fynavir, daughter of red Mevva."

A screen shifted aside, skin hangings stirred and a slender figure emerged into the sultry glow of the fire-pit.

Knowing that Ludegran's 'treasure' was but a maiden beloved by a doting foster-father, Ardhu fixed a polite smile to his face, fully intending to murmur a few pretty words and then get on with men's discussions of war.

Abruptly his smile faded.

The girl was indeed magic, a goddess, as An'kelet had said. Like her name, White Phantom, she was truly white — almost unnaturally white, the palest girl he had ever seen. Moon-silk hair drifted in a sea of cobweb strands to her waist, and her skin was pearlescent, rose-tinted on her high cheekbones. A red robe with a fringe of bronze was wound about her, while a great Moon-collar wreathed in magic symbols clasped her neck.

Ludegran noticed Ardhu's appreciative stare. "My fosterling Fynavir is a Princess of Ibherna, Lord Ardhu — her mother the great Queen Mevva, the Intoxicator, who men say is a goddess-on-earth. She was to marry my lad, Brokfel, and make an alliance between out people and those of the sister-isle, but...he died. We have not yet heard what Mevva and her husband, the Ailello, wish for Fynavir now. No doubt they will seek another match before long."

An'kelet standing beside Ardhu stepped forward and kissed Fynavir's on each of her pale cheeks, a brotherly kiss of friendship but one that made Ardhu feel strangely uncomfortable nonetheless. Strangely jealous. "The Sun goes down and we live another day — and the great King Ardhu is amongst us!" he said. "Will you aid in our merrymaking tonight, my fair friend, as we wait for the approach of our enemies?"

Fynavir smiled and nodded, then left the roundhouse with other girls of the village crowded around her. They soon returned with beakers that brimmed with honey-mead, roundels of aged cheese, and wooden trenchers of beef and pork for the men. Musicians followed close behind them, blowing on bone flutes and horns of cattle and tapping out a steady beat on small skin drums painted with chevron designs.

"Come, Fynavir," An'kelet teased, catching at the hem of Fynavir's rust-red gown, "will you dance for us tonight — a victory dance to inspire the men of the tribe? Your feet are as light as falling leaves and pleasing to the spirits."

"It is not up to me, friend An'kelet," said the pale girl, pulling the fabric of her dress from An'kelet's fingers but smiling at him nonetheless. "It must be as my foster-father wishes — and our revered guest, the mighty warlord Ardhu Pendraec. He is a man of dagger and axe, who may not be given to watching the dances of maidens."

Regally she swept up to Ardhu, who sat cross-legged on a skin beside Ludegran. "My lord?" she questioned. Her teeth were like pearls, her eyes, beneath curving silver brows were chips of green ice. "Would you have me dance?"

"Ah...uh... yes!" he stammered, flushing to the roots of his hair.

"Foster-father?" She looked at Ludegran, who was beaming, full of pride as if he was her true father.

"Of course! If my esteemed guest wishes it, it shall be done."

Ludegran snapped her fingers and the pipes and flutes and drums came together to form a loud and frantic tune, wild and sensual and unearthly. The onlookers of the household stamped their feet and chanted in time to the beat as the foreign princess let her red robe fall to the floor, revealing a strange ritual dress beneath — a short woven top that left her belly bare, a belt with a round bronze plate, and a short skirt of individual woven strands that barely hid her modesty and revealed long, milky legs and smooth thighs. Gracefully she began to twirl on the rushes, arching backwards and leaping into the air, using arms and hands to gesture and pose, whipping and tossing back her silken hair which coiled and frothed round her almost-exposed hips. She seemed almost in a trance as she danced, her eyes closed, her lips slightly apart, beads of sweat breaking out on her flesh and slipping down her neck, between her full hard breasts...

Art stared, transfixed, the contents of his beaker slopping onto his deerskin leggings as his fingers suddenly turned to jelly. His men laughed; he ignored them. A strange heat went through him, rising up to his face, making his ears burn. He had little experience with females; once he'd become king Merlin had warned him against being too free with willing girls — "You are a great chief now, and many will try to be your friend or lover in order to share your power and fame. This will not do for one of your stature. Take low-rank women if you must ease your flesh, but a proper match with a female of similar standing to yourself must be made. I will find you a wife who will bring you riches and no shame!"

Ardhu wished Merlin was here with him now to advise him. Surely, surely, the shaman would agree that this girl, a princess from over the West Sea, would be a fitting match for the Stone Lord, the Terrible Head... Oh spirits, but what madness possessed him to even think of a match so soon... he'd only just met her, and had grunted at her like some savage, and ogled her like some lust-addled oaf. She probably thought he was coarse, clumsy and thick, but it was as if a mad fire was burning in his brain, and even worse, in his loins... "Chief Ludegran, I must... get some air!" He dropped his beaker, spilling mead all over the floor, and pushed his way out of the roundhouse. Pausing by the door, he took a quick look back. Seemingly unconcerned by his sudden departure, Fynavir was now dancing for An'kelet. Anger and jealousy leapt up in him like a wild fire, and, ashamed, he hurried away, almost knocking over a startled serving-woman carrying a platter of mutton.

Face grim, he stormed over to the palisade behind the hut and kicked the wall with all the force he could muster. It hurt, but the pain brought him back to his senses. Slightly. He knew better than to go into the roundhouse right now least he behave in a way that was less than kingly. Sighing, he climbed up onto the palisade and stared moodily into the descending night, uncaring of the curious stares of the men positioned as guards on the wall.

"Lord Ardhu..." A voice soft as the Moonlight drifted through the shadows. He froze. It couldn't be...

Turning around slowly, he gazed into the glacier-green eyes of Princess Fynavir. She had donned her red robe and a cloak of sewn beaver-pelts, and had tied her hair into a long braid, but still she looked heartbreakingly lovely, there in the muted starlight.

"My lord, I pray I did not offend you with my dancing." She placed a gentle hand on his arm. He nearly jumped with the unexpectedness of her touch.

"Offended?" he laughed coarsely, trying to sound unflustered. "Of course not. It was just... different... to the dances of my people. As were your garments. They were... short."

She nodded. "My father was the third Ailello of my mother, Queen

145

Mevva, and he was a man from over the Northern Sea, and it was to his homeland I was sent in fosterage as a young girl. I was to marry a northern chief who would bring amber from the Sea of Beltis to Ibherna in return for our gold. I grew up in the Women's House there and learned the dances of spring, to invoke the Sun and the spirits who make crops and women's bellies grow. It is their style of garments I wear, carried home in a cedar box when my intended husband died of tooth-rot. My mother ordered me to bring the dress; she said prospective husbands would like it."

"Well, I certainly liked it," Art mumbled, and then reddened, hating his bumbling, foolish tongue. She must surely think him a stupid, callow youth, not only an unworthy ruler but useless as a man.

Fynavir smiled. "My mother is seldom wrong about the wants of men. She has had more lovers than I can count and men clamour to bed her for both her beauty and her reputation."

"Does your father not complain?" Ardhu looked shocked.

A shadow passed over her face. "He is dead. Every seven years the old Ailello is given to Krom the Bloody Crescent, that some call Stonehead, at his temple of thirteen stones, and my mother takes a new young strong Ailello as husband. All are pawns to my mother, who men say is goddess-of-the-tuath or tribe. Even I, her only living daughter, am but a useful tool. However, I am unlucky with husbands, it would seem, much to Mevva's dismay!"

"And what now for you?" His heart started to pound dully in his ears. He wanted nothing more than to reach out, to touch that soft pale face, the long, swan-like neck, and feel those white, half-revealed thighs against his...

"I do not know, "she said softly. "It all depends on if we survive the attacks of these chieftains from the North. If we do, I am sure my mother will find some other who wants a goddess' daughter for a bride, or a golden bride price. Or both."

Ardhu reached up, suddenly catching hold of her arms. She gasped ever so slightly, eyes widening, unsure as to his intention. "You won't be bartered like that... if it's not your wish," he said forcefully. "Do you understand? You are in Albu now, and if I say you are free to do as you will, then so it will be."

She shook her head violently. "No! You would not dare risk ten thousand spears sailing to your shores!"

His eyes darkened; suddenly he was his father's son indeed, scion of impetuous hot header U'thyr. "I would risk it! I am Ardhu, king of Prydn! I am the land and this land is mine! Do you understand me, foreign girl? Your redheaded mother with her paramours and scheming ways holds no terror for me! Understand?"

"My lord... forgive me!" She drew back and dropped into a position of obeisance.

His face softened; her caught her arms and drew her up to him. The Moonlight was shivering on her brow and in her eyes, bleaching them of colour; she was like a mist-wraith ready to vanish on the wind. But she was of earth too — all too well he remembered her pale, round thighs, their promise barely hidden by the swinging strands of her skirt. "You are forgiven," he said, "but do not doubt what I say to you again. I would never lie... not to you, Fynavir White Phantom."

She glanced up, wondering, and before she could protest, he took her in his arms and covered her mouth with his, while the guards on the ramparts nudged each other and muttered behind their hands.

"Ardhu..." Fynavir pulled away first, but her hands were still resting on his shoulders. "Lord, you honour me, but I fear I will bring no luck to you. As I told you, both my betrothed husbands now lie in their barrows."

"Three is a blessed number and I will break that fatal charm," said Ardhu dismissively. And when Fynavir opened her mouth to protest: "I warned you not to doubt me!"

He was about to say more, but suddenly a wolf howled in the valley beyond the fort. It was a lonely cry, long and drawn out, borne aloft on the bitter night-wind. A score of other howls soon joined it, rising and falling, peaking in intensity as the Moon shone out from behind a patch of flying stratus.

"Wolves," breathed Fynavir. "I'd heard they sometimes came into these hills but not in recent years; they fear the halls of men."

Ardhu leaned over the wooden parapet, eyes straining into the dark cup of the valley below. "The wolves are indeed running tonight, with sharp teeth and fierce bite," he said grimly. "But they are not the kind who runs on four legs! Those voices do not belong to beasts. They belong to men. Loth and Urienz and their lot of mad Northerners have arrived."

"To the gate!"

The cry went out into the night. Ardhu's warband and Ludegran's men assembled in the yard of the fort, while the women, including Fynavir, were hustled off into the roundhouses and placed under guard. Art stood with

147

An'kelet on one side and Ka'hai on the other, Caladvolc in hand, waiting. All around him his men and their allies began igniting torches, filling the dun with a flickering light that spilled over into the shrouded fields beyond. Archers climbed onto the top of the walls, positioning themselves, their painted faces almost inhuman in the sputtering torchlight. War-chants went up, and horns were blown, their mournful tone matching the eerie cries of the false man-wolves skulking in the shadows beyond.

Ludegran climbed up on the barricades in the gateway of the fort and gazed out. Shadows were swirling and leaping in the fields and forests. "Where are you, Loth?" he spat. "I know you're out there. Show yourself, if you are not craven!"

The shadows parted and two men strode forward. Ardhu, peering over the barricade, recognised Loth of Ynys Yrch and his kinsman Urienz. Loth had been a handsome man once and still had a roguish appeal, despite a scar than ran from the edge of his eye to his chin and a tendency to run to fat. He was tall and broad-shouldered, with a short, neat beard and glossy dark brown hair cut bluntly at the shoulder. Blue eyes cold as the seas around his island stronghold gazed out from under heavy brows. Golden sun-whorls were stitched to his studded tunic, while a necklace made of the serrated teeth of some sea-beast clacked around his neck. Over his shoulder was draped a wolf-pelt, the head used as a hood –a trophy he must have acquired far from his homeland — for no wolf-haunted forests grew on the barren, wind-blasted isles of the Northern seas. Ynys Yrch was known as the Isle of Pigs, for those hardy beasts, sacred for their oracular powers, were the only beasts that thrived in Loth's domain.

Beside Loth stood his brother Urienz, who held territories on the shores across from Ynys Yrch. He had been less favoured in his appearance, a big, barrel-chested man whose hair had receded from his brow and ran down his back in a thin, mud-brown plait. One eye had been lost in some long-ago skirmish; many of his teeth were missing too. He wore a bearskin cape, complete with claws and head, adding to his fearsome appearance.

"I am here, Ludegran!" shouted Loth. "You're still resisting me, I see, though now from behind walls and wood! What a fool! If you had joined with me and marched on that snot-nosed priest's puppet who has usurped the kingdom of the Great Stones, you could have shared in the glory, and your people would have lived as free men honoured for their part in our victory! Now you force my hand-I must slay you all down to the last woman and child. Except for the white maid you treat as daughter..." He grinned lasciviously. "If she is as fair as my messengers report, I have other plans for her!"

"Shut your foul mouth, traitor!" Ludegran called back, enraged. Red spots burned on his wrinkled cheeks. "Speaking with an evil tongue is all you are good at, you lord of a petty realm where neither trees nor beasts thrive, where the Summer Sun hides His face, and the cold makes a man's heart wintry and cruel! You speak ill of the Lord Ardhu, but he brings us peace and freedom from foes from beyond…while you and your like bring death to our own people!"

"Your loyalty to the boy-king is touching," Loth sneered, his eyes narrowing. "But what good will it do you? Is Pendraec here? Can he help you? No doubt he is tucked up in his warm house being coddled by that conniving old fool, the priest called the Merlin."

"No, he is here with you now, listening to the words that bring you shame!" Ardhu suddenly leapt high onto the barricade, with the firelight glowing red on his golden breastplate and patterning the face of Wyngurthachar. "I am here, false chief, man of serpent's tongue, creature of no honour. I will always be ready to defend those who are in need, and who are loyal and true, not just to my rule, but to Prydn. You are not one, and you will pay the price."

Loth looked startled for a moment but almost instantly regained his composure. "It is you who will pay," he snapped. "Come down and speak your brave words to my face… boy!"

There was a rush of wind in the dark next to Ardhu. A war cry split the air and a brazen figure flung himself over the barricade and hurtled headlong toward the two rebel chiefs. It was An'kelet, his spear raised on high, his face contorted with the warrior madness known as the 'warp-spasm.' Some men got this rage from drinking specially concocted potions wrought in the Moon's dark, but to others it came naturally, making them as strong as beasts, nigh as powerful as gods, terrible and implacable in their madness.

Whooping, he descended on Loth, thrusting at him with his great barbed spear. Loth shouted an oath and stumbled back, smashing at the spear haft with his big dolerite battle-axe. It was no good; An'kelet was twirling like a mad thing, muscle and fire and the flame of fury. Loth could touch neither him, nor his spear. As the bronze man of Ar-morah drew close, drawing his long bronze blade Fragarak from the sheath at his belt, Loth turned tail and ran into the midst of his milling warriors, vanishing in the sea of skin-draped figures.

On the walls, the men of Ludegran hooted and laughed derisively. Warriors began to pour over the top of the barricade and rush toward the war-party of the traitor chiefs.

149

Seeing that An'kelet was fixated on finding Loth, Ardhu went after the cousin, Urienz, who was still standing his ground near the entrance to the fort. They locked together in hand to hand battle, slashing at each other with their grooved blades. The edge of Caladvolc sliced Urienz's knuckles and blood flowed, black in the sickly Moonlight. The older man roared in rage and charged like a maddened bull at his young opponent, throwing both of them onto a patch of trampled, muddy earth. Caladvolc and Wyngurthachar tore free of Art's hands with the impact, the sword flying across the ground to land several feet away, just out of reach.

Urienz began to laugh, his huge belly wobbling. Mud was daubed on his florid cheeks like war paint. "I will crush you, worm! I am a wrestling champion... and you are nothing. I will smash your spine, then take your head and make your skull into a drinking-cup!"

Violently, he grabbed Ardhu's shoulders and slammed him against the earth. Art's head struck the ground and stars showered across his vision. Urienz's great knee slammed into his gut, knocking the air from his lungs, and then the warrior's arm pressed down across his windpipe as he sought to pinion him for a final killing blow.

But Urienz was slow and unwieldy, long past first youth and fat from supping on too many tender young pigs for too many years. He had also not looked to see if his young opponent had any other weapons.

He had missed Carnwennan — the White Hilt. The Sword from within the Stone.

In a lightning motion, Ardhu drew the small but deadly blade from its hidden spot against his leg, and thrust it into his enemy's back, just above the kidneys. Urienz screamed, and the blood poured in an awful waterfall from his yawing mouth to spill all over the face and chest of the youth pinned beneath him.

Ardhu heaved Urienz's bulk to one side and leapt up, gasping, as Urienz flopped and flailed like a fish on a hook. "You saw me take this blade from under the Stone!" he said, holding up the dripping blade. "You knew what it meant, and you swore to honour it. You and your vile brother have angered the Ancestors by your actions, and so you have paid the price. The sword you falsely swore to serve has now taken your life."

Urienz stared up at him. "Not... a boy..." he mumbled, bloody foam making a strange and horrid red beard on his trembling chin. "Was wrong. You are... a monster!"

"I am my father's son," said Ardhu darkly, and suddenly he didn't seem a boy at all but some dark god of death, powerful and ruthless. "The Terrible

150

Head. I am also the Dark Bear...and you wear my emblem, the skin of the bear, and that offends me. It also rightly makes you my prey."

With that, he retrieved the fallen Caladvolc, and in a brutal motion drew it across Urienz's throat and sent his enemy's spirit to the otherworld. Then with another downward slash, he took Urienz's head. Lifting it in a shower of gore, he carried it to the cliff edge and hurled it toward the night-clad sea from whence the traitor had come, dooming his spirit to wander aimlessly forever.

Returning to the sprawled body, he took Urienz's bearskin cloak as a trophy and wrapped it about his own shoulders, a final insult against the spirit of his vanquished enemy. The great bear's head, preserved by careful drying, loomed over his own head, while the massive paws hung down with huge nails still intact. He was the bear, not Urienz — the Great Bear of Albu, where even the constellations spoke of his might.

He suddenly felt as one with his namesake animal, almost as if its spirit had entered him. Casting back his head, he roared like a bear into the night, "I am the King! I am the Terrible Head and no foe of Prydn will withstand me!"

Shaking with surges of adrenaline, he hurried back through the trees and up the slope to see how his warriors fared against Loth's men. Reaching the lower rampart of Ludegran's dun, he found the battle nearing its end. It had been a short, sharp skirmish, and Loth's forces had not fared well. Most of the men of the North lay dead, shot with arrows or ridden down by the horsemen of Ardhu's warband. The air reeked of blood; the rooks and crows and ravens would soon feast.

An'kelet was standing in the centre of the carnage, like the golden effigy of some solar deity, a smile on his face and his right foot firmly planted on the neck of Loth of Ynys Yrch, who lay sprawled on the ground, weaponless and utterly helpless.

Seeing Ardhu, An'kelet beckoned him over. "Lord," he called, "I have saved him for you... It is you he betrayed so foully, so you must be the one to have the honour of taking his head."

Ardhu strode up to Loth, staring down into the blood-smirched face of his enemy. "Your brother Urienz is dead," he stated harshly. "I wear his garb as my own. I have hurled his head into the sea, so his spirit will now wander the misty strands incomplete and lost. What will you say to me that will make me spare you the same fate?"

"You are not what I thought you were!" panted Loth. "Neither the wizard's pawn nor a jumped-up boy of no skill! I was wrong about you, and

I was wrong to doubt the choosing of the old one beneath the stone, whose dagger White-hilt you wear. I have been prideful and foolish...and it has brought me to a sorry pass. Ardhu Pendraec, if you are as merciful as you are powerful... show me clemency this day and let me return to my islands. I will not bother you again; the mainland holds no more attraction for me."

"Don't trust him, Art!" cried Ka'hai, staring with hatred at the Northern chief. "He is as slimy as an eel. Kill him and put an end to it."

Ardhu beckoned to An'kelet. "Get him on his feet. Whatever he has done and whatever I chose to do with him, he will not grovel in the dirt like an earthworm."

The bronze warrior grabbed Loth by his tunic and dragged him up, forcing him to stand before the young king. Ardhu stepped forward, his face only inches from his opponents, the tip of Caladvolc touching his throat. He stared into Loth's cold eyes for a moment, then lifted his hand and struck him across the face with all the force he could muster.

"Get out of here," he said as Loth tumbled onto the ground with a thud. "Go, before I change my mind. And if you ever set foot in these lands again, I will not only have your head, but I will march North and set your bleak islands ablaze from end to end, and wipe every one of your clan from the earth and cast down your Ancestor-stones and break your barrows and grind the bones to dust, so that no one ever shall know that your treacherous breed ever existed in the world of men! Spirits, so hear me, and know that I will hold true to this if Loth of the Yrch islands should defy me again!"

Wordlessly, Loth scrambled to his feet and ran blindly for the trees on the hillside, his arms flailing and his teeth bared like a frightened animal. The warriors of Ardhu and Ludegran hooted derisively and called insults after him.

"You should have killed him, I reckon, "said Ka'hai heavily, shaking his head. "He'll never change. He may never set foot on the mainland again — but I'll wager he'll still find a way to cause mischief!"

"We'll just have to watch his movements." Ardhu stared into the blackness where his adversary had vanished. "I would not kill him and risk more dissension among the tribes. We spend too much time fighting each other as it is. I do not wish to give some Northern lordling cause to create rebellion in his name. We need some kind of alliance between the Chiefs, even if an uneasy one, if we are ever to defend this island from invaders."

At the moment Ludegran came up to Ardhu and clasped his shoulder, his fingers trembling. "Mighty is the sword-arm of the Terrible Head! You have surely saved us from what would have been certain doom, even with our stalwart walls and brave bowmen! Chief Ardhu, ask anything of me and I will grant it if I can, in token of my gratitude and endless friendship!"

Art paused, blood rising suddenly to his face. Only one thing interested him in Ludegran's dun. A girl white as snow, with a goddess for a dam. The Merlin might be angry... but it would be a good alliance, surely the old man could see the wisdom in it. The seas between Albu and Ibherna would be made safe, and a link forged to the goldmines of the fabled green isle.

"I ask for one thing only." Ardhu folded his arms. "I ask that I might take as wife the Princess Fynavir, daughter of Mevva the Intoxicator."

Ludegran looked surprised but pleased. "Her mother must be consulted, of course, but I am sure she will agree to this match. Who could be a better husband for her daughter?" Turning around, he motioned to one of the women who had ventured out to view the aftermath of the battle.

"Go, Edel, fetch Fynavir from her chambers!"

The woman ran back into the dun and appeared a few moments later with Fynavir, wrapped in thick furs against the night chill. She glanced around anxiously, not sure why she had been summoned. Seeing her distress, An'kelet smiled at her, and the worried lines on her brow immediately softened at his concern.

"Fynavir." Ludegran placed his hands upon her shoulders. "In the time you have dwelt with my people, you have become as a daughter to me. I had hoped you would enter my family, but alas, due to the death of Brokvel, it was not to be. I have worried what your fate would be, knowing that you did not wish to return to your mother's hearth, but now I can assure you that this will never happen, barring any objections from Mevva. The great Chief Ardhu, Bear-chief and Terrible Head of Prydn has brought great honour upon us both — he wishes to take you as his wife."

Fynavir's lips parted; no sound came out. Her eyes travelled to An'kelet, who had stopped smiling. "Foster-father, I know not what to say..." she finally managed. Her voice trembled.

"He pleases you, does he not? Girl, I am lord here, and know what went on upon the walls last night! Is there some reason why you should not marry King Ardhu?"

"No, he is a great warrior and a comely chief. But I... I..." Her voice faltered and again her gaze slid towards An'kelet, as if hoping he would speak, finding a reason why this match should not occur. Instead, he stared at the ground, leaning heavily on his spear.

"Then it is settled!" Ludegran clapped his hands. "You will marry King Ardhu. I will send messengers to Queen Mevva and the Aylello on the morrow. Fear not, Ardhu, Fynavir will not bring just her beauty to your marriage bed. She will also bring forty head of cattle and golden treasure from her mother's hoard."

Ardhu grinned like a mad thing. "So much the better. Ludegran, if Mevva agrees to the match, have Fynavir sent to me for the Feast of the Rage of Trogran at the Crossroads-of-the-World. That is an auspicious time for fruitful marriages."

"It will be done," said Ludegran, clasping hands with the younger man to signify a deal had been made.

The warband then set about celebrating both their victory and the forthcoming marriage of the king. No one even noticed that Fynavir had retired, alone, to her sleeping cubicle, or that the usually ebullient An'kelet had grown suddenly solemn and pensive, drinking from his beaker as if the only solace in the world was to be found within its depths.

CHAPTER TWELVE

The Merlin was angry. Ardhu guessed it as soon as he rode into Deroweth, and could see no sign of his mentor, only pale-robed priests flitting to and fro between the houses with countenances sour as unripe apples. "Where is he then?" he said curtly to one priest, as he slid down from Lamrai's back and flung the reins to Ka'hai.

The man frowned from under the peak of his white linen hood. "He awaits your arrival in his hut, lord Ardhu. He is aware that you are home."

"Is he? Well, not much of a greeting for his king!" Angrily, Art stormed towards the Merlin's hut, with its grandly decorated doorway facing away from the sharp winds that raked the ridge overlooking Holy Hill.

Flinging aside the deerskin hide that hung in the entrance of the house, he thrust his way inside, blinking in the gloom. "Merlin…why do you shun me? Have I not driven off the invaders? Conquered Loth and killed the treacherous Urienz? What is wrong with you, man? I come home expecting glory and celebration, yet see nothing but grim faces and bowed heads."

Merlin's face loomed out of the darkness. He looked wild and fierce, eyes scored by dark rings, lips twisted in a sneer. "Yes, you have done all the deeds I trained you to do. But that's not all you did, is it, Ardhu Pendraec? You did much more. Yes, much, much more. News came of your victories…but also of you taking a foreign prince into your warrior's fold. Even worse, it seems that you have arranged a match with the daughter of Mevva of Ibherna! Fool!"

Ardhu's eyes ignited, his anger matching the Merlin's. "I am not your pawn, Merlin. You said yourself it would be good for the tribes to see that I my own man and not some minion of the Temple. And so I am. An'kelet is the greatest warrior in the world — and he is my friend, with whom I would entrust my life. And, as for the girl," he faltered here, his cheeks growing red. "You…you have not seen her, Merlin…"

Merlin spat on the ground in derision. "You are no better than your foolish father, swayed by the lure of a woman's tits and thighs! I was working on a match for you, and now those plans lie in ruins."

"Good!" Art shouted. "Why should I lie with some trollop with a face like a pig's arse just because you have chosen her for me?"

"Because I know what is right for you! For Prydn!" Merlin practically

155

shrieked. Spittle flew from his lips, striking Ardhu's cheek and making him wince in disgust. "I have cast the bones, cast them many times. Each time it comes out the same... Look!"

He grabbed Ardhu's arm and yanked him down beside the fire-pit. On the packed earth lay a jumble of knucklebones, some new, glowing white in the gloom of the hut, some dark yellow, worn smooth from centuries of use. Merlin passed his long, brown hand over them. His eyes were hot, hooded.

"There it is, written in the bones of our Ancestors. Signs. Dire signs. See the centre? That is the serpent, with you, Ardhu Pendraec, at its head. The Terrible Head. Above your right shoulder is the Sun, brightly shining but burning with fierce power too — that is your stranger from Ar-morah. Above your left shoulder rises a crescent Moon, pale and deathly — the white phantom woman you have chosen in defiance of me. These two shall come together as the Sun and Moon come together at rare and terrible times when the earth plunges into darkness for a time. The shadows cast by their brief union may undo all we have worked to achieve."

Art felt a chill of fear run up his spine but forced himself to face his mentor. "Pah! Quivering with fear because some chance configuration of the bones! Why, the old women cast such bones for the price of a bead or two on feast-days; it is little more than an entertaining game to them!"

Merlin's hand shot out, grabbing Ardhu's tunic and dragging him towards him with a strength belied by his lean frame. "The destiny of this land is no game," he snarled "Or if it is, it is a game we must win. Do you understand?"

"I understand," said Ardhu frostily. "But I want you to understand too. I will have my own friends and companions. I will have the wife of my choice. If I have done wrong and misjudged their worth, I will pay the price and seek to make amends. Do you understand, Merlin?"

Merlin leaned back, his breath hissing through clenched teeth, rocking on his callused heels. He seemed suddenly old and tired. "Yes, I understand," he said, voice heavy with sudden weariness. "For all my hard work, you are still your father's son. I should not have expected otherwise. Go, and leave me in peace; in your absence I have been overseeing the workers who build the great fort of Kham-El-Ard, and I am weary from doing for you, you ungrateful whelp."

Ardhu left the shaman's house and returned to his men, who sat waiting on their mounts, a little dismayed that there had not been feasting and celebrations to herald their arrival.

"Trouble, Art?" Ka'hai raised one eyebrow quizzically.

"Yes," replied his foster-brother. "Merlin trouble! But he'll get over it. He'll have to. In the mean time let us move up river and look at the walls of Kham-El-Ard, then fare to the Place-of-Light. I suspect the reception there might be more welcoming."

Ardhu and the warband rode down river, stopping to marvel at Kham-El-Ard, where oak posts sprouted like trees on the heights, soaring up almost to touch the Sun Himself. It made Ludegran's promontory fort look humble and mean in comparison. Workers streamed in and out of what would eventually be a great gate with turrets for archers, while others dug banks with antler picks and shovels made of cows' shoulder bones.

Riding beside Ardhu, An'kelet looked impressed. "One day this place will go down in legend. I am glad that I shall play a part. Our peoples were always close through deepest time; may it always remain so, Ardhu."

The warriors passed on, following the banks of Abona, which narrowed and began to curve and coil like a serpent. Fording her waters at a weir where water boiled like a cauldron, they then rode East toward the settlement known as Place-of-Light. Standing on a slight plateau, this village was an ancient place of great renown, for here the first great smiths from Faraway changed Prydn forever with their knowledge of the riddle of metal. And more besides — for in their retinues they not only brought the knowledge of copper and gold, but the brewing of mead and ale, the manufacture of drinking-beakers worthy of great warriors, and a burial rite of individual graves, where a man's spirit could go into the West with his dogs and treasures, even his servants and children if that was his desire. The Galloen had not fought with the people of Albu and Khaledon, but they changed their lives irrevocably; the communal stone tombs of the Ancestors had been sealed, and circles such as Khor Ghor had been reused and remodelled, its vast structures of stone rearranged and made even more magnificent.

The warband spotted the settlement almost at once, rising on top of an escarpment that gave an unobstructed view across open lands from Holy Hill to Deroweth. A line of vast totem poles glowered on the lip of the scarp; behind them loomed the remains of ancient grave mounds and other holy places, some marked by posts, others by pits and deep shafts. Further behind, stood roundhouses and huts, where children and dogs played in the Sun. Cattle lowed in pens, fat with sweet grass, while woolly brown sheep trundled lazily between the wattle walls of the huts. Women sat weaving and making pottery, while men tanned deer and cowhides and dragged in sheaves of wheat to be ground for bread.

As soon as the band became visible a joyous cry went up. A drum started to beat, and every hut seemed to disgorge a stream of children and women, all clamouring to see the returning warriors.

"I told you the reception would be better here," grinned Art, nudging his foster brother Ka-hai in the ribs. "Look, there is father!"

Ech-tor the smith was striding across the settlement, shoving aside infants and yipping, excited dogs. His face was split by a huge grin. He had abandoned his smithy near Marthodunu and come to live permanently in Place-of-Light, in order to be near Ka'hai and Ardhu. As the village's own smith had been barrowed the winter before, his skill was sorely needed — and much appreciated. In fact he was considered special, having raised the young Chief himself, and he had even taken a new wife, Kerek, from amongst the villagers.

"My boys!" he cried, arms outstretched, as Ardhu and Ka'hai dismounted. They fell about in bear-hug embrace, while the other warriors laughed. "You have returned to us as blooded warriors of the People! You are true men now — ha, I swear, you even look taller! And Art, what is this we hear…that you have contracted a bride?"

"It is so," murmured Ardhu, aware that he was blushing. "It is said her mother is a goddess-on-earth. She is white as the Moon, and her name means 'White Phantom.' She will bring gold and cattle as her dowry."

Ech-tor glanced sideways at Ka'hai. "You next boy!" he teased. "You mustn't let your brother outdo you! Now come, we must all celebrate your safe return from battle and hear tales of mighty feats of arms!"

The feasting that accompanied the warriors' homecoming lasted for three days. Venison and boar was consumed and roast goose sizzled and spat over the fire-pits. Hazelnuts were cracked and consumed, and mushrooms boiled in broth flavoured by dried seaweed imported from the coast. Rare sweet treats were offered afterwards — wheat grains drenched in milk and left till they burst, then flavoured with honey, and possets of tansy leaves mixed with berries from the local woods. There was much merriment, and many a man back from his first battle looked with new respect at domestic life unmarred by war's violence, and set his gaze upon one of the unwed womenfolk. The girls themselves wove flowers in their hair and stained their

lips with berry-juice, and acted shy and coy until they got their chosen
warrior alone, when they then showed the female-starved men who really
held the real power in matters of the heart. That was, of course, the practical
older girls, eager to escape their mothers' hearths — the younger ones sat
sighing over Ardhu or An'kelet, who treated them all like sisters and
tolerated their constant Mooning and moping better than most of the other
young men.

At the end of the third day, as the burnt orange eye of the Moon soared
West toward the Stones and the Deadlands, Ardhu gazed down from the
height and saw a familiar figure, staff in one hand, climbing slowly to the
top of the plateau.

The young king ran forward eagerly. "Merlin! You've come! Have you
forgiven me yet?"

Merlin pushed back his hood and spat onto the feet-impacted chalk,
shining blue in the Moonglow. "No. But there is naught to be gained in
dwelling on your rash actions. I must try and make the best of this situation.
Maybe I can shield you from what I have seen in the pattern of the bones."

Ardhu lead Merlin into the headman's hut, and the feasting continued,
though slightly more subdued now that Merlin's stern eyes were upon the
crowd. The shaman was particularly interested by An'kelet and spent hours
grilling him about his life and lineage back in Ar-morah. After he was done,
he looked more relaxed; the faint hint of a smile even touched his thin lips.

"He is an honourable man," he said to Ardhu. "A great warrior...but
child-like in a strange way. He is ruled by his beliefs, and when he has set
his course upon something, he will follow his heart till the end, right or
wrong. This is his failing...a failing you must deal with if he is to stay
amongst your men."

Art sipped from his beaker, savouring the rich, fermented honey taste.
"And what would you advise?"

"He must go to Khor Ghor and swear absolute obedience to you. This
oath will bind him. If he strays from your path, the guilt will break his mind.
That is the kind of man this stranger of bronze is — strong as a stone on the
outside, but with a fatal flaw inside which might cause him to crumble as an
ill-made pot crumbles. Pray you do not lean on him too much least he falls
and takes you down with him."

Ardhu looked at Merlin through drink-misted eyes. He hated it when the
old man went on so. "He already swore to me, when we first met. He even
renounced his princely title. Surely, that is good enough for you!"

Merlin thumped the head of his staff against the ground. "No, it is not. I want him to swear before the Ancestors, before the spirits that are all around us. A man may make noises of obedience in moments of triumph or gladness — then have a change of heart when next the wind blows. I want to take no chances; as the son of a priestess An'kelet will be well aware of what his fate might be if he shatters the vows he makes."

"So be it," said Art, eager to keep the old man happy. "He will be sworn in at the Stones on the next auspicious day, under your guidance, Merlin." He counted on his fingers. "And then…it will be nigh on the time of the Harvest Feast, the Rage of Trogran, and we must set off for the Crossroads-of-the-World to meet my bride!"

"Aye…lurching from one folly to the next," Merlin mumbled into his beard, but Ardhu, eye him sharply, fancied that his lips bore the trace of a weary smile.

An'kelet's oath-taking at Khor Ghor took place after the death of the Old Moon, when there was no Moon to be seen in the sky at all. This was a time when the elder powers and shades were said to be strongest, crossing from their barrows into the world of men, rewarding their most faithful descendants and bringing mischief and even death to those who did not venerate them in the proper manner.

The Merlin and other priests of the Temple led the prince of Ar-morah from the Place-of-Light to the banks of Abona. The day was fair, the sky blue as woad, and a warm, surreal light clung to the leaves of the wind-tossed trees and set the waters of the great river sparkling like a breastplate of gold. Swans sailed on the surface, birds of Otherness which, legend said, often turned into beautiful women who entranced men but stayed with them for but a year and a day.

On the bank, An'kelet was divested of his garb, and had the rings taken from his long hair. He was guided into the clear green waters, amidst streaming weeds of green that felt like surreal hands against his skin. The priests and acolytes surrounded him in the river, invoking Abona, the great Cleanser, to take away evil or malice from his heart, to make him born anew that day in the service of his chief.

Then Merlin came up and grasped his head by the hair, forcing his head below the swell. Three times he did this, with three great cries, as An'kelet gasped and thrashed blindly around in the water.

"Now you are purified in the blessed way, and you may continue with

160

your great journey," Merlin said solemnly, after the third dunking. "Rise now, and take the Sacred Avenue to the Dance of Spirits where your fate awaits you!"

An'kelet clambered out of the water on the far side of the river, and the acolytes brought him plain robes of undyed wool, a token of humility before his lord and the spirits. Then the party of priests gestured him forward, and he was taken into a small, banked monument, black with the ash of burning. Empty stone holes still showed as pits in the earth. An'kelet sensed this was a very old place, perhaps even older than the famous temple he had yet to behold, and it was a dark place too, scented with the funeral pyre. He shivered, wet and cold, as the wind blew.

Merlin bent over and picked up a lump of charcoal. Approaching An'kelet, he drew symbols with it on his face, his exposed arms. "We can never escape what we are — that is, food for the pyre, for the worms in the barrow mound," he intoned. "Each day might be our last. So remember this, and wear with pride and knowledge the marks of those who have gone before, written in the ash that was their flesh."

Once he was done, the holy men and women surrounded An'kelet once more, guiding him towards a pair of parallel banks that streaked away across the fields like white, exposed bones of the earth — the Sacred Avenue of Khor Ghor that protected pious men from the malign ghosts that lurked in this haunted landscape of gods and Ancestors.

Halfway up the Avenue, the party halted and a priest came forward holding a blindfold which he tied around An'kelet's eyes. Once it was on, the holy men turned him in a circle until he was dizzy. He knew it was a deliberate attempt to disorientate, to add to the strangeness and mysticism of his committal to the Young Lord — and it worked. He did not know if he walked into the Sun or with it at his shoulder, did not know who walked behind him or at his side, or even if they were still with him, or had allowed him to wander through some gap in the Avenue bank into sacrosanct lands where men feared to tread without powerful talismans.

At last, after stumbling up and down the rolls of the Great Plain, the Merlin called for An'kelet to stop. Time had passed; he felt the air cooling against his cheek, the first vapours of the evening. Hands reached up to his head, carefully removing his blindfold.

The Merlin was standing beside him, dark and saturnine in headdress and long robe with its clatter of animal teeth and claws. "You look toward the East, where the Sun rises," he said, and true enough, An'kelet found himself gazing out past the swelling mounds of the Seven Kings to the misted blue hump of Holy Hill. "That is where all life begins, with the rising of the Sun. But now you must turn from that toward the West, towards eternity and death. To your fate as a warrior of the king, sworn to die in his service. Do you still wish to proceed, Prince of Ar-morah?"

"I do, Merlin of Prydn, the choice was made long ere now."

"Then turn and face the Tomb of Every Hope, the gates of the Sky, the circle of Sun and Moon. Face the spirits who guide us all, and face your sovereign King."

An'kelet turned, and a gasp was wrest from his lips. He came from a land where many stone monuments stood, of antiquity beyond all others: great marching rows of menhirs like jagged teeth, huge humped tombs with carven chambers, a single standing stone so large it toppled the very day it was raised, its ninety-foot length smashing into fragments — but he had never before seen a structure like Khor Ghor, the Dance-of-Spirits. For its was solitary, unique, and would remain so unto the end of days.

Viewed from his low position in the bottom of the valley, the temple soared up toward the sky in towering layers. Each stone in the vast outer ring was joined to its fellow by mortise and tenon joints, a technique used in the construction of wooden buildings. An'kelet had never seen such an art put to stone before, and he also marvelled at the smooth grey faces of the stones, beaten into shape by long labouring with stone mauls. Inside this outer ring were even larger structures — five massive trilithons built of sarsens weighing many tons. They soared several feet above the outer circle, with the trilithon at the far end being the tallest and most imposing. The Sun was setting and the red light angling down on the great megaliths turned them a magical shade of crimson-gold.

Filled with awe, An'kelet walked up the rest of the Avenue. A gigantic wind-beaten stone confronted him — the Stone of Summer with its wrinkled, natural inward face frowning in the direction of coming Winter. Striding past it, he stopped to reflect on the stone gate of the Three Watchers, also known as the Shadow-stones; sure enough, as the Sun tumbled in the sky, their shadows stretched long over him, black and cold as death.

Then he was beyond them and entering the sacred space of the circle. A ring and oval of small dark stones, some vaguely human in appearance, faced him like a stony army, while the trilithons and outer sarsens rose up and up, seemingly the very pedestals on which the heavens rested.

At the far end, beside a green monolith that glittered dimly, stood Ardhu Pendraec, Stone Lord and king of the West, bearing the insignias of his

Kingship — the sword, the mace, the shield, the dagger. The bearskin he had taken from Urienz was on his shoulders, too, snarling mouth open in silent roar.

Around him, framed in each archway of the great circle, were the men of his warband. An'kelet knew them all, but they seemed different now, no longer the battle-worn, weary lads he had met on campaign, but mystic warriors in cloaks of fur and feathers, with axes tied to their belts by bright peace bonds, and totemic talismans jangling around their necks.

His eyes slid from the men back to Ardhu, his lord, his friend, and a sudden chill went through him. He had honoured Ardhu before, as a man, and a valorous leader, but here in Khor Ghor he was more than that. Here he was a god, a sacred king, bound to the land, his destiny entwined with the very fate of Prydn. His destiny was in his face, suddenly both old and young; it was in his eyes, the green of the wildwood and the darkness of the tomb.

Awed, An'kelet sank to his knees on the bone-white chalk, his head bowed and his hands pressed to his face in supplication.

Ardhu approached him, his deerskin shoes making no sound on the packed chalk floor of the inner sanctum. "An'kelet of Ar-morah, you come here this day before the Ancestors and powers that move the world of men. Do you swear to renounce all others and follow my path, and join the Comrades of Albu from this day forth and ever after?"

"Lord, I do," An'kelet said hoarsely.

"And do you swear to be loyal to me, to protect me with the strength of your arm, to honour my wife and any heirs as if they were your own kin, forsaking your own rank or any desire for status of your own?"

"I...I swear it, lord."

An'kelet hesitated a moment as Ardhu mentioned his 'wife.' Fynavir. Briefly her image filled his mind, snow hair and glacier-green eyes, the hint of sadness that always lingered in the girl who had been bartered so many times by her ambitious mother. The maiden said to be a goddess's child, herself a manifestation of the sacred Land. The White Phantom of birth and death. The Full Moon.

But he must not think of her as anything but Queen. She was Ardhu's, and he had sworn his oaths to his mother long ago. Shutting his eyes, he sighed then murmured, "You will be as my god, Lord Ardhu, and your lady I will love above all other women — my goddess to worship and protect."

Ardhu lifted Caladvolc, its long incised blade incarnadine in the failing light. "Then I confer upon you the title of champion of the Circle of Khor Ghor, hero of Prydn. Arise, Lord An'kelet."

The sword descended, touching briefly the kneeling warrior's broad shoulders, and then it was taken away and swiftly sheathed.

An'kelet rose, and Art embraced him, suddenly a youth again and not the stern-faced being, lord of life and death, that stood beside the Stone of Adoration, and the men came in and clapped him on the back, and were merry and encouraging indeed.

But Merlin, standing between the tallest two bluestones, looked bleak and wan. He had pushed for this oath-taking, hoping it would deflect the disaster he had read in the bones, but he had heard something in An'kelet's voice that made him quail anew. 'Your lady I will love above all women...'

"I will not let it happen," he muttered, hands clawing the dark rough side of the stones. "Ancestors, give me strength to stick a dagger through both their hearts should they betray us as I have foreseen!"

CHAPTER THIRTEEN

Ardhu and his men reached the outskirts of the great and ancient place known as the Crossroads of the World a few days after the three-week-long feast of Bron Trogran had begun. They had travelled overland from Khor Ghor to Marthodunu, where they rested for several days before journeying onwards, their numbers swelled by locals eager to celebrate the harvesting of the crops. Leaving the huge protective walls beside the gurgling Abona, they continued North, following a line of green ridges where ancient long barrows and abandoned camps kept watch over the changing landscape and the ancient paths that led to Suilven, Crossroads-of-the-World.

Riding along a worn trade-track that had brought men to this area for a thousand years or more, the company first spotted a circle circular wooden building perched high on the edge of a steep escarpment. It had a vast thatched roof and was circled by a ring of weathered grey stones. Next to it, a line of barrows stretched out along the horizon, ominous against the bright sky. The afternoon was warm and golden, the air thick as honey and shimmering eerily around stones and posts. A fire was burning by one of the stones, casting up a greasy smoke, and people in masks were spiralling in and out, in and out.

One of the lead dancers was a young man who, to Ardhu's surprise, wore women's garb: a crescentric jet necklace and big hooped earrings of gold, each with a dangling blue star-bead. Tumbling to his bare feet was a long gown painted with odd symbols — rutting stags, phallic signs, the terrible Mouth of Mother-Watcher as Devourer who all men desire yet fear. His lips were ochred and so too his cheeks, while ashes made his deep eyes smoky and emphasised his brows. People were bowing to him, and touching his robes as if for luck.

Ardhu glanced at Merlin, who rode beside him, rather uneasily, on a small fat pony chosen for its placid nature. "What is this place we can see?" he questioned. "And what are those people doing with that strange half-man? We do not celebrate in this way at Khor Ghor."

"The temple is the Sanctuary," replied Merlin. "It is said it was a bone-house in the old times, where the Ancestors would be laid out while the flesh fell from their bodies. It has changed its function many times. Now the priests and priestesses of Suilven use it as a gateway to that hallowed

165

place the Golden-Men called the Crossroads of the World. As for he beautiful boy, he is the Fhir-Vhan, the man-woman. He is both outcast, set apart from the tribe, and holy — he brings both good and bad luck. He embodies the dual nature of all things: day and night, Sun and Moon, male and female."

The warband approached the Sanctuary and dismounted their horses, bowing before the mighty stones and laying down offerings of meat and drink for the spirits and the priests and priestesses of the temple.

The Fhir-Vhan danced up to the party, waving a rattle made of an infant's skullcap. He held out his free hand, its fingernails of unseemly length, and gestured to himself. "A cowry shell or amber bead for blessing of the Fhir-Vhan on the Rage of Trogran," he wheedled.

Ill at ease with this unsettling figure, Ardhu pulled on Lamrai's reigns, drawing her away. "I don't want your blessing!" he snapped.

The man/woman's beautiful face turned ugly, malign. "Then you shall not have it. Nor shall you have children of your loins that will live to come after you, just as I, the Fhir-Vhan, have no living progeny!"

Merlin flung up his hand, making a symbol to avert evil and curses. An'kelet, Bohrs and Per-Adur drew their daggers. The Fhir-Vhan stared scornfully down his long, straight nose at them. "I fear no knife. No Fhir-Vhan lives to see more than one lunar year — death means nothing to me. I already belong to the gods."

Merlin was the first to make peace. "I crave your forgiveness, Fhir-Vhan. The King..." he stressed the word, "is not worldly in some matters, for he is very young."

The Fhir-Vhan gave a haughty sniff and turned his back on the party before resuming his mad dance around a cairn of flints that marked, deep below, the ashes of a hundred Fir-Vhans spread over the skeleton of the very first — a young male with the pelvis of a girl placed over his hips.

"No damage was done," Merlin said to Art, who gestured for his men to sheathe their weapons. "My avert sign shielded you. But by the Sun, Ardhu, keep your mouth in check when you are far from home or you won't live long enough to bed that fair woman who has bewitched you! Discretion is a lesson you still must learn!"

The warband left the Sanctuary and continued toward the heart of the Crossroads-of-the-World, following a sacred avenue that snaked, serpent-like, across the countryside. It was vastly different from the earthen avenue at Khor Ghor, being lined with rough-hewn sarsen stones, some long and phallic, others broad and shaped like diamonds. Celebrants flitted up and down the line of stones, bowing and praising them, pouring libations at their bases.

At last the Avenue ended. A bank and ditch became visible, immense and glowing white. Cresting its height, Ardhu gazed into a chalk ditch that fell away to such a depth it was as if he gazed down into the very underworld. Beyond was a raised earth platform, and on it three immense circles of unhewn stones similar to those in the adjacent Avenue. In the heart of the far ring stood a setting of three enormous menhirs that represented the mouth of a chambered barrow, its function much like the trilithon arches of Khor Ghor — a place where the spirits could enter or leave the world of the living under proper intercession from the priests and shamans. In the centre of the nearest circle loomed a single mighty obelisk with a tapered point, taller than the Great Trilithon by a man's height, and garlanded by flowers and fronds. Girls were dancing around it, arms raised to the Sun, and wheat sheaves bound in their hair. Some were naked or partly clad; many seemed to have worked themselves up into a trance as they whirled and writhed to the steady beat of a drum.

The comrades rode back down the bank at Ardhu's command and began pitching tents amid the other temporary dwellings that sprawled for a mile across the field beyond the sacred space. Once the encampment was made, and the horses and ponies safely tethered in a makeshift corral, Ardhu, accompanied by Merlin, returned to the activities in the great circle. The rest of the men, freed from warriors' obligations at this happy festival, mingled with the crowds both within and without, some seeking the solace of drink and some of women.

Merlin drew Ardhu toward the entrance of the south circle, fronted by two cyclopean stones, one with a large cleft in it, forming a natural seat. On it sat the most grotesque woman Art had ever set eyes upon. She was short, nearly a dwarf, and old, almost impossibly so, maybe sixty summers. Her face bore ritual scars that deformed mouth and nose, and her wide mouth, distended by a clay plug, was void of teeth. She wore only a loincloth and a swathe of perforated shells that dangled between pendulous breasts heavy as great stones themselves. She was bloated, edemous, her skin painted a livid shade of grey-blue. In one hand she held a sheaf of wheat and in the other a serpent that circled her wrist like a living bracelet.

"Who...or what... is this?" Ardhu hissed to Merlin. He had heard that the Crossroads-of-the-World, especially under its older name of Suilven, Stones of the Eye, was highly attuned to women's magic, dark and primal. Most men feared this magic, for it was one they would never understand — how

167

women bled but did not die, and how the Moon drank this sacred blood, and how the women let spirits come into them with a man's seed to be reborn as new babies for the tribes.

"She is Odharna the high priestess," replied Merlin. "The Old Woman of Suilven, the greatest Old Woman of them all. In her flesh is the spirit of the one we call Ahn'ann, whose paps are the hills, whose Womb is also the Barrow-hill. Mother of Life, bestower of Death."

The priestess Odharna had spotted Merlin and gave a crowing cry of greeting. "Merlin, Merlin of Khor Ghor, long has it been! Come closer; let me see how many new grey hairs I can count upon your head."

"Too many I fear, Lady Odharna." Merlin walked towards her and bowed. "I have had my hands full these many years guiding my young friend here toward his life's destiny. Among other duties of course."

"Aye, aye, the boy-king!" Odharna rocked back and forth with mirth. "News has come here of his deeds, the Eye of Suilven is ever watchful across Prydn! Here, bring him closer, let me see him!"

Merlin shoved Ardhu forward; the young man hesitated, disconcerted by this strange figure, who seemed half of the very stone she sat upon. "Ah, don't be afraid." She grinned toothlessly, gums flapping. They were stained green-black from some leafy substance she had been chewing. "I shan't eat you… it's not the season to eat pretty young men, I am not the blade-toothed Hag till winter!"

Ardhu forced himself to bow to her, using the depth of his bow to avoid looking at her lumpen, clay-coloured body, which reminded him of a bloated corpse. "I like the look of you," the priestess was saying, while stroking the head of her snake as it coiled about her arm. "Like U'thyr, your father, but without his petulance. Still green though; still a boy in many ways, that much I can see by your demeanour — the fact you cannot bear to gaze into my face. But you will learn in time, you are bright enough." Her small, fat-enfolded eyes raked over him. "You come here to marry at the feast, do you not?"

"Yes!" he burst out, surprised. "How did you know?"

"There is little I do not know," she grinned. "I have heard of the party from Ibherna that comes with cattle and gold — but, more precious than that, a woman white as snow. 'White Phantom' is her name, and her mother rumoured to be a goddess, and men now say that the daughter is a goddess too, embodiment of the very soul of the land. You'll have to keep a good eye on her when you get her, lad…for many men would kill to lay with the Sovereignty of Prydn, and gain mastery of the this isle."

Ardhu's face darkened with sudden apprehension. What a fool he'd been! He should have sent the warband to greet Fynavir and her attendants...

Odharna laughed. "Don't look so stricken. I have sent out my bowmen to guide the marriage-party safely to the Crossroads-of-the-World. They are still a few days away, but fear not, my men shall see your white lady arrives unmolested."

Art bowed again, truly grateful. "I am in your debt, High One."

"I dare say by the end of all things we at Suilven shall be in yours," the priestess retorted. "So let us say we are even, Terrible Head. Go now, and join the festivities — the games of Trogran have begun this day and there are races and archery, wrestling and the hurling of stones. The fields will come to life, and the corn-woman will walk in her golden dress beneath the dancing Stars ...and all will be blessed for another year."

"But..." She leaned forward, lank hair coiling like black serpents around her enormous mottled bosom, "a warning — most come here for blessing but some for less noble purposes. Darkness walks among us. I can feel its presence. One comes whose heart is black with hate. Milk will sour and the corn fail and women grow barren where this cursed one walks. And it is you she seeks, and hates, above all."

With that, her great flat head fell forward onto her chest and she drooped against the stone, her mind winging into some great Otherness.

Ardhu and the Merlin walked away toward the city of tents that had sprung up beyond the banks of Suilven. "Merlin, do you think I am in danger?" asked Art.

"You are always in danger," replied Merlin dryly. "It is a requirement of your position. But yes, there may be added peril here at Suilven. I know the danger that Odharna saw, and hence it is time to tell you... that your family is here at the Crossroads-of-the-World. I saw the colours of Belerion on their tents."

"Family?" Ardhu's eyes widened. He had never asked Merlin about any living relatives. He had assumed that, like U'thyr, they were dead.

"Yes, boy, you surely didn't think you had no kindred at all? I will take you to meet them, and I can assess the situation."

"I don't understand. You want me to meet them, yet imply they might be dangerous. Why would they seek to harm me?"

Merlin sighed. "Not all of them wish you ill. Just one. One who is jealous of you and all you have attained. I gazed into her eyes long ago and saw something I feared. She is touched by the spirits, boy; a powerful woman of magic — to be feared more than any man. She is your half-sister, Morigau."

"My half-sister! I wish you had told me earlier, Merlin. I could have tried to make amends!"

Merlin shook his head. "You cannot make amends. You cannot bring her father back from the dead or restore her position in her mother's heart."

Merlin stopped before a tent painted with flanged axes, and gestured to a servant wandering about with a water-jug in her hands. "Fetch your masters and mistresses," he ordered. "Ardhu Pendraec would meet with his family."

The woman scuttled away, and Art could hear voices behind the skin flaps of the tent. A few minutes later the hangings were swept aside, and several figures emerged into the summer afternoon. Foremost was a girl who Ardhu immediately guessed must be close kin to him. Her eyes were the same brown-green shade as his, and the planes of her heart-shaped face had a familiar cast. A golden band topped her long near-black hair and she wore woollen robes dyed a rich green — colour of death, of the Ancestors in their mounds. Several men and youths of varying heights and sizes emerged from the tent behind her, along with a second young woman holding a crying baby in her arms. She alone of the group had blue eyes, and her hair held the warm hue of an autumn leaf.

"Hail, Ardhu Terrible Head, lord of Stones and hammer of our foes," said the first woman formally, bowing to Ardhu with utmost grace. "I am Mhor-gan, daughter of U'thyr Pendraec and Y'gerna of Belerion — and your sister. Behind me are your uncles and cousins on our mother's side, Emys, Baradir, Yltid, and your other sister, Gwyar, who is married to Gorangon of Brig-ahn."

Ardhu clasped her hands and looked into Mhor-gan's greenish eyes, filled with sudden joy at this acknowledgement of their kinship. "The Sun's Face shines on this day of our meeting, sister!" he cried. "Has our mother come with you to the feast?"

Mhor-gan laughed and shook her head. "No, she seldom travels. She has a third husband in Belerion, and prefers to keep away from the intrigues and feuds of her children! Ardhu, lord, come into the tent and all the questions you have shall be answered in time!"

Art let Mhor-gan lead him into her tent. It was cosy and warm, with sheepskins on the floor and bed-spaces laden with furs. An incense-cup burned in a corner, releasing a heady perfume. Mhor-gan offered her brother a beaker of ale and he drank it gratefully in token of their new friendship.

"So, tell me, sister," he said, when he had placed the mug back on the floor. "How have you fared these long years of our separation? Are you wed? Betrothed? And why do you wear the colour of the grave-mound? "

Mhor-gan smiled, long lashes veiling her eyes. "Can you not guess, Ardhu? I am like your friend Merlin, I see beyond the veil into the spirit world. I can speak with the Ancestors, and I know the movements of Moon and Stars and Sun. I can make potions to heal or to kill. I have danced on the hill with the Korrig, the shining ones; hence the folk call me Mhor-gan of the Korrig-han, the faerie, and it is their colour I wear. It is my desire to join the Ladies of Afallan, sisters in my art, and learn more of my craft. Hence I will marry no man. We may well end up as neighbours, brother, for I believe I shall be put under the tutelage of the revered Nin-Aeifa, who dwells in the lake-lands near Khor-Ghor."

"That would be a happy day; great is the wisdom of my sister Mhor-gan! But tell me more…" He gazed into her eyes, probing. "You introduced me to uncles and cousins, and to my younger sister, Gwyar. But there is one more, isn't there? One who is not as the rest. What of our older half-sister, Morigau?"

Mhor-gan toyed uncomfortably with a clay amulet around her neck. "Our half-sister… I suppose you had best know, for knowledge can give protection. Morigau hates us both, Ardhu. You for 'stealing;' her father and her mother; me, for being gifted with the shaman's art. She has powers too, perhaps even greater than mine, but Morigau is blighted, Ardhu, cursed. All she touches goes awry, bringing grief to her and those around her."

"I feel pity for her," said Art. "I would not see her sundered from us if a friendship can be forged."

Mhor-gan shook her head vigorously. "Hatred is what she lives on, Ardhu; it is her life's blood. She will never be your friend. She is about to be married, even as you are... to your enemy, Loth of Ynys Yrch."

Art spluttered in range. "Loth! How did this come about?"

"The moment Morigau heard that he disputed your claim to kingship, she travelled the length and breadth of the land, risking her life in hostile territories to reach his lonely isle. Obviously Loth was impressed by her tenacity…and other things." She laughed bitterly. "Like our mother, Morigau has many charms that certain men find irresistible!"

Ardhu shook his head. "Bitterness between kin is an evil thing. If she is so twisted that no hand of friendship can be offered, then I am glad she will be in the cold north with that bastard, Loth. I have sworn to kill him if he should ever cross into Albu, and I make no idle threats."

"But dare you ban Morigau from the south, too? How the tribes would laugh — the great king Ardhu fearful of a woman, and his sister, no less!

Morigau is clever; she is well aware of how things stand, and will use it to her advantage."

Ardhu frowned and stroked his chin. "You speak troubling words, sister."

"Forgive me," Mhor-gan said. "But you need to know the truth. But come, smile again, is it not true your bride is on the way to Suilven? Soon you shall be together. Surely that thought will help dispel the gloom brought by Morigau's hate!"

Ardhu reached forward and kissed her on both cheeks. "You are a wise woman indeed. I will turn my thought to what will be, rather than what may be. For all we know, once Morigau weds Loth, she may never again set foot beyond the frigid north!"

"We can hope," said Mhor-gan, lady of the Khorrig-han. "Hope is the best we have."

Later that night, Ardhu emerged from the tent and went alone into the great circles that made up the Crossroads-of-the-World. Fires roared between jagged sarsens, and the figures of frenzied dancers cast strange shadows over the trampled grass. In the far circle, wailing women were carrying skulls and jawbones in and out of the three-stoned cove. A priestess hunkered down, naked, head lolling and eyes rolling as she invoked spirits she alone could see. Around her other revellers danced, reaching their hands up to the great Cross-of-Stars that was rising over distant Hakh-pen hill.

Ardhu glanced around, hoping to spot some of his men, or the Merlin, but he had not seen any of them since he had gone to speak with Mhor-gan. No matter — they had served him well these past months, and it was their right to join the great feast of the Harvest as much as any other.

Ardhu noticed a flurry of people leaving the main circles and processing down a secondary avenue of stones that branched out toward the night-shrouded West. The revellers chanted and waved torches, and a hot, smoky lust burned in the eyes of both men and women, repelling and yet intriguing the young chieftain. He let himself be carried along with the flow of people, the river of humanity streaming out along the row of sarsens.

At the end of the avenue the surging crowd slowed, pooled. Art threaded his way through the heaving mass to see what was happening. Dimly lit by the torches, he spotted another mighty stone cove, and beyond it the dark hump of a large, ponderous long barrow.

In the heart of the cove a rite of the harvest was taking place. A figure wrapped round with wheat-sheaves danced wildly in the flickering torchlight, weaving and winding between the sarsens, casting handfuls of grain over the onlookers. A man, naked except for a bull's head mask, pursued the figure. He was painted with stripes, and in his hand he brandished a flint sickle, honed and deadly, an ancient relic handed down from generations past. He chased the Dancer-of-the-Wheat-Sheaves in a rough, clumsy dance of his own, hewing at the air with his sickle and stamping and bellowing like a real bull.

Art sat down cross-legged in the grass alongside other onlookers. A huge drinking vessel was being passed around. Ardhu drank deeply, mimicking those around him. The mead in the brimming pot rushed to his head almost instantly, and in a flash he realised it was drugged.

His stomach contracted. He was a king, not a priest...he did not seek to get closer to the gods by the taking of potions. He went to rise, to make his way back to the encampment, but hands reach out to pull him down.

Two young men about his own age were tugging on his cloak. "You...you're Ardhu of Khor Ghor, are you not?" one asked. "The Young King? Surely you won't leave before the dance is over? Your blessing would surely make the crops grow stronger next year."

Art flopped clumsily back into the grass. "Who are you?"

"Friends. Admirers. We have heard much about you. I am Ack-olon." A youth of middling height with a broad, confident face stepped forward and gave a short bow. "And this is my friend, La'morak." He gestured to the other youth, smaller and less stocky, his tawny curls braided with feathers. "Would you care to share our drink and food? It would be an honour."

Ardhu did not know how he should respond. His head was light from the draught of tainted mead, and the thought of not being quite himself made him uneasy, but if he refused the lads' hospitality, it might be bandied about that he was high-handed and thought himself too good for people outside of his band. He wished now that he had consulted Merlin before blundering off and joining in the celebrations. Or maybe taken An'kelet with him.

A brimming beaker was being pushed into his hands by La'morak. "Drink, my King! First taste to you, the wielder of the sword from the stone, who has so bravely fought our enemies."

Ardhu drank, the thick, cloying mead running down his chin.

"And more!" Ack-olon shoved another beaker his way, this one full of frothy ale.

Again, he downed it, all too aware of the hot eyes of the youths on him. Surely, this was some sort of a test by these two young warriors — seeing if he, younger than they, could compete with them in the man's world of the feast.

A sudden shout from the cove drew his attention away from his companions. The Dancer-of-the-Wheat-Sheaves was twirling within reach of the vicious flint sickle, and the bull-headed man was hewing frenziedly at the golden coat. Suddenly he nicked a strand of twine binding the sheaf and the whole casing tumbled away, showering onto the onlookers, who grasped at the tendrils and took them for luck.

Where the Wheat-Dancer had been was a young girl, naked save for her streaming red hair. Her eyes were huge, the pupils swollen with mushroom-potion, looking inwards to otherness and emptiness. Her lips moved faintly in invocations as she reached towards the bull-masked man.

A priest in a conical bronze headdress emerged from the crowd and tied plaited strands of wheat around the two, binding them together. The masked man cast away his sickle and grabbed the girl to him, all lust and fury, with no gentleness. She met him in like passion, clawing his bare back with her nails, crying out wordlessly toward the hag-face of old Mother Moon as She soared overhead, a bent crescent heading West to the land of the Dead.

Together they fell onto the trampled ground, coupling like beasts before the assembled celebrants. The priest with the tall bronze hat and seven acolytes danced wild rings around them, offering up the jawbones of those whose spirits they hoped would be reborn and casting down carved chalk balls that symbolised the fertility of man and beast. The onlookers cried out, moaning and shrieking along with the pair on the ground; men and women started to pair off and run out into the darkness, tearing at their clothes, their eyes full of Moon-madness and unbridled desire.

Hot blood rushed to Ardhu's face. He had never seen rites like this before. He knew of course how it was between the sexes; he was not ignorant. But he had grown up in a small homestead of a widower, and if Ech-tor had women, he had met with them on his trading journeys when Ka'hai and Ardhu were left at home to mind the forge and tend the animals. Then, since his coming of age he had been in the Merlin's care, and until he met Fynavir had hardly so much as spoken to a girl...

The youth called Ack-olon nudged him in the ribs. "Surely that should be you there with the Corn-Maiden, since you are King," he said, his voice an insidious whisper. "That's how it was in the old days. The King mates with the Lady who is the Land."

"I have a woman... I am to be married during the feast," said Ardhu. He cursed himself inwardly even as he spoke. He had been foolish, naive. His companions' behaviour had gone beyond harmless testing; their eyes were glittered with amused malice, and their whole demeanour reeked of arrogance and impudence. They had some grudge with him. He knew the sensible thing to do would be to retreat into the milling crowds before any more trouble found him.

But La'morak had hold of his arm, his fingers like a vice. "Surely you should have her here, this night. It is only right that you, as King, should make the great marriage with your Queen."

Ardhu groped at his left boot, seeking Carnwennan in its hidden sheath, and then remembered, with a sinking feeling, that he had left it at the encampment along with Caladvolc, obeying the rule that forbade weapons in the circles of Suilven. He began to struggle, but the drugs in his first bowl of mead and the alcohol in the second and third made his head whirl and his knees and arms jelly-like and weak. He struck out at La'morak and missed, plummeting forward onto his belly on the ground.

He could hear the two young men laughing, and he tensed, half expecting to feel fists rain down on him, or even weapons...but then a figure came drifting out of the darkness, as if from some shadowy dream, a figure that swayed towards him, hands beckoning, dancing on delicate feet, bringing welcome memories and a shiver of both fear and desire.

The dancer was wearing a heavy wooden mask carved into the semblance of a raven with a long bone beak and eyes of glittering jet. A vast cloak made of hundreds of shining black feathers floated around the figure, rustling in the rising breeze.

Leaning over Ardhu, the dancer tapped him sharply on the shoulder with the beak of the bird-mask. The feather cloak briefly parted and he caught a tantalising glimpse of white flesh beneath.

Art started to grin, a silly, lecherous, drunken grin. Surely, surely no girl would know to dance for him in such a way...except Fynavir. Fynavir the White Phantom, who had danced in her foster-father's halls for him and awoken the fires in his loins. She must have arrived sooner than expected and devised this strange meeting, though he had no idea why she would play such games with him. He knew so little of women! Maybe this teasing game of courtship was part of her people's tradition; in foreign parts tribes did things differently — in Fynavir's homeland of Ibherna, he'd heard it was even usual for a king to mate with a white mare, which was then sacrificed and boiled into a broth. He was glad such an act would not be required of him; he fancied girls not horses!

La'morak smirked and pulled Ardhu roughly to his feet, pushing him in the direction of the masked woman. "Your Queen awaits, King Ardhu," he said, his voice husky, harsh, tense with excitement. "The one bound to you in life, in death. Go to her, the Great Queen, and know your destiny."

Ardhu stumbled toward the raven-woman. He tried to lift off her heavy mask, but she caught his hand, and instead drew it under her cloak, pressing it against hot, bare flesh, a conical breast that, oddly, made him think of the shape of a grave-mound.

He almost cried out with surprise at the jolt of fire that ran from head to crotch, but she laid a calming finger against his lips. "Come, come with me," she whispered, and she drew him away from the firelight illuminating the cove, and out into the shadows of the darkened fields, away from La'morak and Ack-olon, away from the celebrating people of Suilven.

Beyond the firelight, there was total darkness save for the stars. To the left Ardhu could see the vague silhouette of a mighty stepped hill, an earthen pyramid shaped like a barrow but much larger than the tomb of any man. It was the Hill of Suil, the Wise Eye, one of the wonders of Prydn, and a Tomb of Tombs that held no mortal bones. Some said it was the sepulchre of the Sun in Winter, others that it was mighty Ahn' ann's own body, from which she birthed the holy springs that rose nearby to join the Head River Khen. Some gave the Winter Sun a name; they called him Zhel, and said he was Ahn'ann's son, and that when he died on the shortest day he was buried in a golden coffin in his Mother's earth-womb to await rebirth as young, virile Bhel, the Sun of Summer.

But to Ardhu, wandering through that dead land with the raven-cloaked woman, he could think only that it resembled one thing — the great white breast of a goddess, caressed by the four winds and the wavering starlight. A giant replica of the warm, living flesh his questing hand had touched. Cold chills ran down his spine, but fire leapt up in him too, a primal heat that matched that of the man who played the corn-king at the Cove.

"Where are we going?" he asked his companion, trying once again to get a look under her concealing mask.

"You'll see, my king," came the muffled voice. "Not far now and then…" She swirled her feather cloak, revealing for one second the pointed hills and dark valleys of the tempting flesh beneath. "Your desire and your destiny will become one!"

They walked further and the night deepened. The noise from the great henge was a mere buzzing on the wind. Rounding the flanks of the Hill of the Eye, the raven-woman set off across country, crossing the sacred stream of Suil and hastening for the hilltop above. Ardhu followed silently, wanting to rip away that cloak, to fall with her into the furrows of the fields, and to give up the last vestiges of his childhood in her arms. To become one with her as the Sun became one with the Earth, quickening the crops and all nature to life.

Nearing the top of the rise, he spotted a finger of stone, a dark hummock with the fading Moon hanging over its end.

A long barrow.

It was the mightiest structure of its kind that Art had ever seen. On the Great Plain most of these early burial mounds, some already two thousand years old, were mere earthen piles, their wooden mortuary houses, once draped with the hides of oxen, long collapsed and decayed. But here, the barrow had chambers and forecourt of stone, and at the front of all was a great, wide, sealing stone, its threatening bulk seeming to shout 'I forbid!' into the darkness.

The lust in him almost died away in the presence of that stern, frowning Ancestor-stone. This was a place of haunts and shadows, not a bed for lovers to lie in.

The woman at his side noted his hesitation and slid her arms around his waist, rubbing herself against him. "Don't be afraid!" she whispered in his ear, nipping the lobe with sharp little teeth. "Here the spirits can bless our union. Here a great Ancestor might come into me even as you will, and breathe soul into a child in making."

Ardhu flushed. He had not even thought of that possibility. But how good would that seem to the people, not only leader and conqueror, but founder of a new dynasty of kings..!

He let himself be led around the stony fangs of the forecourt to the blocking stone. There was a gap between it and the arched roof of the cairn, and Raven-woman wriggled into it effortlessly, again giving him a tantalising glimpse of white legs and smooth buttocks.

He followed all too eagerly.

The night wind shrieked over the hill as if laughing at the folly of a lust-blinded young man.

Ardhu awoke early the next morning in a tangle of bones...and living arms and legs. Daylight was filtering dully through gaps around the blocking stone. He stared. On either side in niches were stacks of bones, skulls in one place, long bones in another. Empty eyeholes regarded him. Their owners were long dead, but the air smelt damp, foul, still retaining the hint of death and decay.

Tearing his gaze away, he stared at the woman sprawled next to him. She lay curled on her side, naked on the feather cloak, but still wearing the bird-mask. She had refused to take it off during their love-making, and he supposed, as before, that this was some strange custom of her people, so he dared not press her too far.

But now, the union was done…morning had come and she need not hide any longer. He crawled closer to her, taking in the curve of her hips, the small but perfect breasts which had been painted with ritual signs, now smudged by hands and lips. She was thinner than he had imagined she would be, and darker-skinned, though it was hard to tell through the paint and dirt from the floor of the cairn.

Lovingly he reached out to remove the clumsy mask, to free the Moon-white hair and kiss the pale full lips of Fynavir…

A lock of midnight-black hair tumbled over his hand.

His heart began to thud against his ribs. What madness was this?

Less gently, he pulled the mask away.

And looked into a dark, fine-featured face that was a feminine copy of his own visage. Greenish eyes, wide-set and knowing, regarded him with amusement. A small but sensual mouth, red and languid, smiled.

"Who… who are you?" he cried, hurling the mask away. It shattered against a stone and feathers flurried.

The girl rose onto her haunches, tossing back her ebony mane. "Haven't you guessed? I am sure the Merlin and Mhor-gan warned you of me! I am Morigau… your half-sister."

Bile rose up in Ardhu' throat, burning like fire. Shame reddened his face. This… this creature had tricked him…tricked him into breaking a terrible taboo. One of the greatest of all taboos. If any of the tribes were to find out, he would lose his kingship, and probably his life; it might even start a civil war in Prydn, as other men strove for supremacy.

Morigau seemed to read his thoughts. "Don't worry," she said haughtily. "I am not going to go about telling the world. My fate would be worse that yours, which would be a clean death at least. Me — they'd pin me in a bog."

"Why have you done this?" Ardhu cried. "Hate I could fathom, but not this terrible act! You…you are surely a shape-shifter, a witch… I could have sworn you were Fynavir!'"

Morigau's lips tightened to thin lines; her eyes were glowing, cat-like. "You saw what you wanted to see! Like most men you were led by your man-thing… and not this…" She tapped her forehead. "Do you want to know why I deceived you? Well, hear my words, brother: I had a father, whom I loved — he was taken from me by your father. I had a mother too; she forgot me when you were born, and even when Merlin claimed you, she never loved me again. I am going to show you what it is to lose, Ardhu. To lose everything, as I have: my father, my mother's heart, Belerion, which would have been my birthright, had Y'gerna not wed U'thyr. All that is left for me is to marry a pig like Loth of Ynys Yrch, so that I may live with a queen's status. I blame you for that too, Ardhu Terrible-Head, bastard of U'thyr, whose barrow I spit on!"

"If I had my sword I would kill you!" Ardhu shouted, smashing his clenched fist against one of the great megaliths of the chamber. "You are sick, twisted."

"I'm not afraid of you," she said scornfully. "Rage, little boy! I have powers, just like your friend the Merlin. You would not dare touch me…especially as the Eye-Goddess, lady of the tomb, has breathed a spirit into my belly to mingle with your seed. Nine Moons from today a child will be born…"

He stared at her, horrified. "You cannot know such a thing for sure!"

She smirked evilly. "I am a witch — you said it yourself! I saw it in the bones, cast three times three. Once I was certain the signs were right, I arranged the time of our coupling to follow the phases of the Moon that guides all women. I will not be wrong. My Woman magic is strong."

She wrapped her arms round her knees and her eyes were filled with burning fire. "Traders visiting Belerion have spoken of great kings in sun-burned lands far away, who marry their sisters to keep the bloodline pure. That's what our son will be, Ardhu — a pure son of Albu. Through him I will claim back all the lands I lost, and he will love me as no other ever has. Never will there have been a child of such beauty and power. Be warned, Ardhu — brother — he will be the Dark Moon that eclipses your Sun!"

She leaped to her feet, her face warped with hatred but also ecstatic at the thought of the future she foresaw. "Today I will continue my journey north to the realm of my husband-to-be. I am sure he will be pleased to find out he has got an heir on me so soon. He will never know another's seed grows in his field. Farewell, Ardhu. Thank you for your gift." She leaned over as if to kiss him, but viciously bit his lip instead, drawing blood.

He cried out and sprang back, repulsed.

Morigau laughed, standing with her lips reddened with his blood like some malign war-goddess. One droplet rolled down her skin, pooling in the hollow of her throat. She flicked it away with a finger and, casting Ardhu a mocking and contemptuous glance, snatched up her feather cloak and climbed hurriedly from the tomb.

Ardhu staggered after her, his stomach heaving with the enormity of what he had done. He didn't know what steps to take… killing Morigau was all he could think of, but he was weaponless, and she was blood-kin, and a woman.

And a magic-worker, set to marry his enemy, Loth.

Standing on the barren hillside, with the cold morning wind blasting into his face, he watched as Morigau traipsed blithely down from the burial cairn and was greeted by La'morak and Ack-olon at the bottom of the rise. They hugged and embraced in a congratulatory way, and he realised that not only had the youths been sent to entrap him with drink, that the familiarity between Morigau and her henchmen was more akin to that between lovers than mistress and servants.

With a cry of grief and despair, he sank down onto the dew-drenched soil and pounded the earth with his fists.

CHAPTER FOURTEEN

Later that morning, Ardhu sought out the palisaded enclosure beside the waters of the Khen, a sorry, grim-faced figure with a cut and bloodied lip and shadows in his eyes. He had sat for hours in the cold wind beside the Old Ones' barrow, cursing himself, Morigau, the very gods who could allow such deceit. Eaten by shame, he would have stayed even longer, but suddenly he heard the blare of horns, and standing on the ancient mound saw a stream of unfamiliar banners heading toward the palisade, followed by the flags and pennants of his kin and his own warband.

Unnerved by this flurry of activity, he cursed and ran from the hilltop toward the palisade enclosures.

An'kelet met him at the great gateway of stout oak. "Praise the spirits that you are here! The Merlin has been searching for you. The men were growing uneasy."

Art glanced at his friend, his insides clenching with revulsion at the memory of the taboo that he had broken. He could tell no one the truth...not An'kelet, not Ka'hai, certainly not Merlin. "I was drunk..." he said gruffly. "I fell. I've been in the fields sleeping it off."

An'kelet gazed at his troubled face, and frowned, but kept his peace — who was he to pry if Ardhu wished to keep his secrets? "There is news, Lord, news that should gladden your heart. The Lady Fynavir has arrived, bringing cattle and other riches in her train."

The last vestiges of colour drained from Ardhu's already pale face. How could he face Fynavir, so soon after...? If it had just been a tumble with some willing local girl, even a temple priestess, no harm done, none would think of it ever again or hold it against him. But to break such a powerful taboo as that which bars the mating of close kin, with such a powerful magic-woman, in such a holy and dreadful place....

He ran his hands through his lank and clotted hair, over his pounding forehead. "I must make myself presentable for her, An'kelet. Come; help me dress in my ceremonial clothes so that neither she nor I will be shamed."

Ardhu went to his tent and An'kelet followed. As his lord's right-hand man, he washed Ardhu's face and painted it. He braided his long dark hair and placed his copper helm upon his brow. Carefully he buttoned him into the leather tunic with the golden breastplate of King Samothos fastened to the front, and girt Caladvolc about his waist. Lastly he handed him the Lightning-Mace with its gleaming mounts and fossil head.

Hiding his inner turmoil as best he could, Ardhu stepped out of the tent into the milling crowds inside the palisade enclosure.

The first thing he saw was Merlin descending on him like an angry hawk. The Shaman grasped his arm, fingernails biting flesh. "Where have you been? Why do you play the fool? You spoke to Mhor-gan; she warned you, as I did, of possible danger here at Suilven, and yet you ignored us, and vanished without telling a soul. You are lucky you are not lying in some ditch with your throat slit from ear to ear!"

"Merlin, enough!" Ardhu flashed back. "You will not chide me like some wayward child in front of my people! Take me to Fynavir and hold your tongue at least till we are alone!"

The older man fell silent, sparks of fury leaping from his eyes, but he obviously thought better of making a scene. Face dark as a storm cloud, he ushered Ardhu toward a large group of people hovering around a newly-raised cattle pen at the back of the enclosure. Cows lowed and stomped as men leaned on the rails, remarking on their size and heartiness.

"Before you, Chief Ardhu, is Princess Fynavir's bride-price, sent from Mevva of Ibherna," said Merlin. "There are also three hounds, a goblet carved from amber, and a gold clothing fastener for your cloak. Ka'hai is looking after everything."

"It is good to have received such wealth, but only Fynavir and her well-being matters to me. Where is she?"

"She comes… dressed in her bridal gown and ready to greet her husband-who-will-be." Merlin nodded toward a tent guarded by several foreign warriors in outlandish clothes, and ringed by girls and women straining to catch a glimpse of the mysterious white woman who had come to wed the young king of the West.

The tent flap was suddenly pushed aside and Fynavir emerged, attended by two young women from her homeland. The sight of her took Ardhu's breath away, deepening his guilt over his tryst with Morigau the night before. She was truly a vision, an earthly goddess like her mother, but where Mevva was red, the colour of blood and sensuality, Fynavir was snow-white and pure, unstained, a creature born of cloud or mist. He almost expected white trefoils to blossom and dance at her feet.

She was wearing the badges of nobility, of a queenly bride — a bronze circlet that glowed against the snow of her hair and a shining pectoral cape wrought from a single sheet of beaten gold, fashioned by great art to resemble pleated cloth. Linen marriage-robes fell from eyelets along the cape's edges, sweeping the ground with a fringe made of thin gold wires. As stunning as the cape looked, Fynavir was clearly uncomfortable wearing it, for the shoulders were so narrow and inflexible she could scarcely bend her arms. She moved at a shuffle, looking nervous and disconcerted, while women and men alike touched her for luck.

"Fynavir." Ardhu held out his cold and dirty hands, green with barrow-mould, and made to clasp her soft white hands.

Then he stopped. He was filthy. Contaminated. Unfit to touch her.

He dropped his hands abruptly, and stared at his feet, leaving Fynavir stunned and hurt with the murmuring crowds all around her.

A priestess of the Sanctuary came up, tall and thin in her hooded robe. "Shall I send for the Old Woman of Blessed Fame, and prepare the circle for your marriage-binding, lord?"

"N... no!" Ardhu objected more harshly that he had intended. "I have decided that the best place to wed is my own territory, at the Temple of Khor Ghor. I would leave for there as soon as possible."

A gasp went through the crowd, and the people suddenly shied away from Fynavir as if she was now accursed. The priestess's weather-beaten face was thunderous. "If that is your wish, you must go — you are the Young King," she said. "But some may see this decision as an affront both to Suilven and the spirits."

Ardhu made no reply but signalled for his men prepare for departure. Merlin's visage was livid, but he kept his peace and stalked along behind Ardhu, clutching his staff until his knuckles were bleached as bone.

Art nodded at An'kelet, who stood in white-faced silence, as shocked by Ardhu's rejection of the blessings of Suilven as the rest of the company but loyalty staying his tongue "Ank, escort the Lady Fynavir back to the Place of Light, will you? Make sure her men need for nothing, and that the animals are well tended and don't escape along the journey. I will ride ahead with the Merlin. We have much to discuss. Things I cannot even speak of to you, my friend."

The warband moved across country, passing the harvest-hill that was a miniature twin to Zhel's Barrow before following the wild borders of Savarna's wood toward the South. Merlin and Ardhu were far ahead of the rest, out of earshot and almost out of sight.

183

Fynavir rode on a fat pony that had been acquisitioned from one of the warriors; she had never sat astride a horse before, and so An'kelet led her steed on a sturdy twine rein. She glanced over at him, noticing how the hazy summer light shimmered on cheekbone and smooth forehead, and made a halo of his waving amber hair. She had missed him, her friend from Lodegran's dun, who, as a foreigner himself, had understood her sense of never truly belonging. He had made her laugh, had taught her to fire a bow and tame a hawk, and she had danced for him once, as she had for Ardhu, but he, bound by the oaths set on him by his priestess mother, had merely kissed her hand afterwards and walked away.

"I am not sure about riding," she said dubiously, trying to strike up conversation. "It seems unnatural...

"You will grow accustomed," An'kelet replied with a smile. His teeth were white and even, not worn down by grit like so many others'. "It is a swift way to travel — and for warriors, riding gives advantage in most kinds of battle. Ardhu wants us all to learn to ride."

Fynavir tensed, and she stared at the ground. "I displease him."

"Don't be foolish!" An'kelet shook his head.

"Then why... did he not take my hand? Why has he postponed our marriage, and enraged the priestesses of Suilven?"

An'kelet sighed and flicked his horse's rein, guiding it closer to Fynavir's pony. "Art is young, Fynavir. Sometimes he acts with no thought. He is... moody."

She laughed a little. "I thought only women were prey to their moods! But I will take into account what you say. I hope I can trust your word, and that you are not just trying to pacify me."

He gazed at her with seriousness. "I would never lie to you...my queen. Ardhu is as my brother, and I will serve and love the both of you until there is no breath left in my body. If I should break this vow, many the sky fall upon me, my bones remain unbarrowed and my spirit be bound to earth forever."

He spoke with such passion that she blushed and glanced away, embarrassed. Heat crept up into her face. She was all too aware, suddenly, of An'kelet's near presence ... his muscled arms, bare in the heat, his golden male beauty making him shine like a spirit born of the Sun Himself....

'You should not think of him thus!' she told herself sternly...

At that moment a hare bounded out of a mossy bank and dashed, legs pumping, in front of her pony. The stocky little animal reared on its hinds, while Fynavir grappled hopelessly with the reins then, in desperation, flung her arms around its neck. The pony rolled its eyes and bolted, thundering over the rocky terrain toward a winding brook lined with ash-trees.

"Fynavir!" She heard An'kelet's voice call frantically after her. Sunlight shattered on the rocks about her, rippling like golden fire on the free-flowing stream. Wind raked her hair and the world tilted, earth becoming sky, sky becoming earth …and then a hefty branch hung with lichens smashed into her shoulder and sent her crashing to the ground amid the pointed rocks.

An'kelet was at her side with such speed it was as if he had flown to her on the wings of a magical swan. Face pallid with concern, he flung himself on the ground next to her and lifted her carefully in his arms. She could feel the beat of his heart against her cheek, the beat of her own heart madly, wildly, against her bruised ribs…and suddenly the world seem to lurch again, but not in an unpleasant way. It was as if time itself had stopped, and all the world had become unreal, a place where only she and An'kelet existed, locked in a golden circle of light, far from the fights and troubles of kings and warriors.

And An'kelet…he gazed down at her in silence, her hair spilling over his lap like a cloud, and Fynavir knew he felt what she felt, and that he feared it, and yet desired it more than anything on earth.

"My Lady…Fynavir…" he whispered hoarsely, and he gently turned her around in his arms so that she faced him. The golden light was all around them, the brook beside them roaring, its spirit rising to protect them, embrace them. She closed her eyes, felt his breath mingle with her breath, the faintest touch of his mouth on hers, rich with the taste of honey and meadowsweet…

Suddenly a shadow fell over them, and the magic circle was diminished, its light smothered. They both glanced up as a raven soared overhead, its voice harsh and mocking, doom-laden.

"An omen!" Fynavir whispered, covering her face in fear.

An'kelet's hands dropped from her shoulders; his visage was white and drained. "An evil spirit possessed me…. I should not have acted so. Forgive me."

Tears sprang in Fynavir's eyes; coldness clutched her heart. She had nearly betrayed her husband-to-be, her king, and put both her own life and An'kelet's in jeopardy with her wantonness.

At that moment Ka'hai and Bohrs rode up. "Lady, are you hurt?" Ka'hai swung down from his horse.

"Only my pride." She wiped her eyes with the back of her hand. "But don't fear for me, lords of the West — I will not break from such a tiny

185

bump, I am made of sterner stuff than that! I have a wedding-alliance to make between your peoples and mine. I will not fail in my duty."

She got up, ignoring their proffered hands, and managed to clamber with minimal fuss back onto her pony, which was now cropping grass calmly beside the stream. She gestured to Ka'hai to ride beside her, and set heels to her mount, driving it back up to the main entourage waiting on the trackway.

An'kelet was left behind, seemingly forgotten by his fellows, kneeling on the cold stones under the branches of the gnarly ash, watching Fynavir's white tresses stream away into the distance like a trail of wind-blown smoke.

She did not look back.

###

The sky was dark with promised rain, the clouds bunched into fantastical shapes of giants and gods. Shafts of sunlight spiked through tiered cumulus, lighting up the rolling barrow-downs around the temple of Khor Ghor, illuminating first one mound and then another, making chalk ditches and half-grassed summits gleam with otherworldly luminescence.

Inside the great Stone Circle, the warriors of Ardhu Pendraec stood in their ceremonial robes, one in each archway, facing in towards the Altar-stone. Ardhu stood upon the height of the Great Trilithon with Merlin at his side, invoking the spirits of Everlasting Sky — Nhod the healer, Cloudmaker, lord of the milky way; Moon-Mother with her bone-white eye; and Bhel Sunface with his radiant head that gave life to all the world.

Below them, beside the Stone of Adoration, Fynavir stood in her bridal gown with its unparalleled cape of gold. She looked small and alone amidst the towering megaliths. She felt uneasy, for though these Stones were strange to her, in her own land she knew of Stonehead, the Black Crooked One, surrounded by thirteen pillars, who demanded a tithe of milk, corn and children every seven years. And so it was everywhere — the spirits always demanded a sacrifice; there was always a price to be paid…

What did the Ancestors who ruled Khor Ghor want as payment? And who would pay it?

She shivered, and it wasn't from the biting wind that seemed to blow, day and night across the plain, bringing inclement weather from the West and battering the stones on that side of the circle.

Glancing to one side, she spied An'kelet among the warriors. His head was bowed, the wind casting his copper-gold hair in wild disarray. A sudden shaft of light touched him, and he was instantly all gold, a scion of the Sun himself.

She looked away hurriedly, fearful that he would notice her furtive glance, afraid her eyes would reveal the fearful secret of her heart.

Merlin and Ardhu were descending from the Door into Winter using a rope ladder that priest-acolytes then removed and rolled up. The shaman was stern-visaged, and unwelcoming; Fynavir had sensed that he did not approve of her. She knew he could be a danger if his opinion did not change, and determined she would put no foot wrong and win him to her cause.

The Merlin stalked up to her and grasped her hand, thrusting it into Ardhu's with little gentleness. Art grinned at her shyly, looking like the boy he truly was beneath the warrior's veneer, and squeezed her chilled fingers. Merlin then drew a cord made of gold wires from his belt-pouch. He wrapped it about their twined hands, knotting it again and again, until it dug into their flesh, binding them together.

"By these bonds, you are joined, King and Queen of Khor Ghor and the West, high lord and lady of the lands of the Dwri, the Duvnoni, and other client kingdoms. The spirits have entrusted you with these positions and you are their representatives on earth — son of sky, the Great heavenly Bear who rules the Northern heavens, and daughter of Earth, the White Lady who lies within the chalk below us, the very bones of Albu, our fair land. Together it is your duty to rule the tribes well and to give them a strong line of kings from the joining of your flesh..."

Merlin gave Ardhu a sudden piercing look from under his brows, and both Fynavir and Art blushed profusely, neither gazing at the other.

"So it is done," said the Merlin, and he waved his staff over them, lightly touching them on brow, on breast, on Fynavir's belly and Ardhu's thigh. "Hail to the Lord of the West and his Lady!"

The warband cheered and drums were beaten. A sweet smell went up as priests lit incense cups and walked around the stones, bowing and supplicating them, pouring offerings of animal blood and alcoholic drink at their bases so that the Ancestors might also join in with the wedding feast.

Once finished, they halted and turned toward the North-East. Their drum fell silent — but another in the distance was beating, slow and sensual. Up from the river came a party of women to attend to the bride and prepare her for the wedding night ahead. Three times three they were: a holy number, three maidens, three women of childbearing age, and three withered crones. Naked save for short skirts and paint, they capered and shrieked and wailed, occasionally lifting their skirts and exposing themselves — an age-old gesture that was said to ward off evil spirits and protect against lightning.

The men within the stone circle stared at the ground, or else covered their eyes — it was ill-luck for males to gaze upon these women as they danced for the fertility of human and beast, and even a furtive, stolen glance could make a man blind, or, worse, impotent.

The women surrounded Fynavir, touching her with their stained hands, leaving red and chalky and ashen handprints all over her splendid robe. They guided her to a great flat bluestone at the front of the circle, standing beside a peaked 'male' stone, its mate through long eternity. They crowded around it, rubbing themselves against its rough surface, pressing Fynavir forward until she too was embracing it, this old Mother stone that had seen generations come and go. She could feel its rough surface through the thin linen of her bridal robe, and it seemed to grow warm as she touched it, making her body tingle, and her thighs grow warm.

For the first time since she had entered Khor Ghor she felt less afraid. Whatever spirit dwelt in this Ancestor-stone, it felt benign, even loving... unlike crook-backed Stonehead with his Moon-sickle that harvested human lives.

The women took her by the arms and drew her away from the female stone. Slowly they retreated from the great circle, holding hands and making a circle of their own, dancing Sunwise around Fynavir as they chanted and sang.

Down the Avenue they danced, and the Sunlight and shadows of that day enfolded them until they became mere dots on the horizon by the swelling mounds of the Seven Kings.

"Go now," said Merlin to the men of the warband. "Let there be feasting and merriment among the peoples until the break of dawn. King Ardhu of Prydn now has his Queen."

###

The men fared forth to high Kham-El-Ard, where Merlin's builders had finally completed the Great Hall, a structure unlike any other ever raised in the isles. Crafted to the specifications of the shaman, its design was influenced by past meetings with travellers from beyond the mighty river Rhyn and the Pillars of the Western World, who brought tales of the splendid palaces and strongholds of faraway lands.

The hall stood shining in the pallid Sunlight, a true place of heroes with its mighty gables and lintelled door that faced East to catch the rising Sun. Rectangular in shape, it resembled the small houses that clustered about Deroweth but many times their size and covered with carvings of gods and spirits that seemed almost ready to leap into life. Unusually, it had small high portholes cut in the sides to let out smoke and odours, and screens of stretched calfskin that could be bound over these slits to keep out inclement weather.

The men set about drinking, and many ribald jokes were told, and boasts made that would never be carried out. Warriors wrestled, and a young aurochs, standing nearly six foot at the shoulder, was dragged up the hill and pole-axed before the doors of Ardhu's Great Hall, its blood being used to paint the threshold and bring good luck to the consummation of the marriage. The beast's head was then buried in a pit by the gate, a silent watcher that gazed toward the terminus of the Avenue.

Gradually day faded to early evening, and the light became warm. Red rays of Sun shot through the bunched clouds in the West, making the entire fort of Kham-El-Ard glow like fire. Down below, in the twisted trees near the Sacred Pool, a horn suddenly blared, its voice rising eerily up to the heights. Birds scattered from their perches at the sound, soaring into the sky like the souls of the dead taking flight.

"It is time," said the Merlin, "for the purified bride to come to her husband to fulfil the sacred marriage and bring great blessings on the people of the West. It is time for all to depart save Lord Ardhu."

The warriors began to gather their possessions — strewn cloaks and beakers, lolling-tongued dogs. They streamed toward the gates of the half-finished citadel, hurrying before the light failed to get onto the riverside path that led to their tents up near the Seven Kings. They did not dare glance back towards the woodland at the foot of the hill, the haunted area where it was whispered the shades of the old Hunting-men still wandered, firing ghostly arrows across the mist-exhaling lake. Here their new Queen was being ritually cleansed before coming to the bed of the King — the beautiful white Queen who was on that night a goddess, not a woman made of mere flesh. A thousand years before, any man who gazed upon the chief's bride in her purification rites would have been strangled and deposited in the holy waters of the lake, and although that tradition had lapsed, no man risked the displeasure of the gods by spying on her unveiled beauty.

"An'kelet, I would have you stay with me." Ardhu beckoned his friend to his side. "The fort seems too empty. I know it must be so till the warband's dwellings are built...but still. I would not be alone up here."

189

"Alone? You won't be alone." An'kelet smiled wryly. The smile did not reach his eyes.

"I meant unguarded. I could have chosen to celebrate the wedding night at Deroweth, but that is a place of priests and the half-world. I am a man, and this hill and the structures upon it are of the now-world — and they are mine, as Ardhu Pendraec, King of Prydn. Hence I want to bring my bride here, to the hall where she will be the first Queen of many over long generations to come."

An'kelet shifted uneasily, making circles in the dust with his felt boot. His confidence seemed to wane like the dying Moon. "Ardhu... my friend, I beg you, choose another..."

Ardhu frowned, perplexed. "I thought you would be honoured to be the king's Man on this night — the guardian of the Marriage Chamber."

"Yes, An'kelet of Ar-morah, surely you would not deny your sworn lord."

Merlin suddenly flapped in, saturnine and hawk-eyed, his cloak and hair and beard straggling on gusts of the ascending breeze. His piercing gaze darted from An'kelet's pale, guilty face to Ardhu's perturbed one. "What an honour, to protect the bridal bed of your beloved King and his comely Queen!"

"I...I cannot..." A glistening bead of sweat trickled down An'kelet's forehead, despite the coolness of the impending night.

Again, down in the trees below Kham-El-Ard, the horn sounded its mournful note — closer, this time. The chanting of the women could be heard as they began to ascend the hill.

"Maybe you should tell Ardhu why, Lord An'kelet." Merlin's voice was a growl. "Tell him the truth."

An'kelet turned to his friend, his chief, his eyes pleading. "I cannot stay here tonight... What you ask is geish — taboo for me."

"Taboo?" Ardhu shook his head. "Why? What do you mean?"

"He's making it up." Merlin pointed an accusing finger at An'kelet. "I warned you, Ardhu. The bones do not lie."

"Be silent!" Ardhu blazed back at him. "An'kelet, I order you to speak!"

An'kelet drew a shuddering breath. "I told you of my mother, the Priestess Eilahn, and how I am sworn to purity, as she dictated, in order to keep the power of my arm. I must not, therefore, be party to the joining of the flesh, which could lead me to weakness."

"Nonsense!" Merlin stamped his foot. "He hides the truth, Ardhu!"

"Believe me or not, I must not stay!" cried An'kelet. "Punish me on the morrow, if it is your will!"

Face white with shame, he stumbled from the hall. Neither Ardhu nor Merlin called after him. As he ran, he spotted the women coming up the hill. Fynavir walked amongst them, proud and cold, a white, frosted flower. Her garments had been stripped from her, and she had been painted head to foot with symbols of luck and fertility, and blue flowers were twined in her unbound hair.

He paused for a moment, unable to tear his gaze away from her naked beauty. His breath came low and heavy; he felt stirrings he had kept long suppressed. And fear, a terrible fear... If Fynavir was goddess on earth, she could be death as well as life...His death, the death of all that An'kelet, greatest warrior in the West, had ever striven for...

He cast himself on the ground, covering his eyes. The marriage party passed, and the doors of Ardhu's Great Hall closed as the women brought Fynavir to the bridal bed with many women's charms upon her.

And An'kelet, scrambling back onto his feet, howled like a beast in pain, and ran like a madman out into the Deadlands of the Plain, where the barrows clustered and mortals did not walk. He had told his first ever lie, to his best friend and his lord; heart and mind and body had all betrayed him that night.

And in the sky the new-risen Moon watched his torment: a white and haunting ghost whose face was that of Fynavir.

CHAPTER FIFTEEN

A year passed at Kham-El-Ard. Carpenters and craftsmen finished work upon the halls and walls, and as Merlin had foreseen, the fort stood in unparalleled splendour — a mighty citadel with woven banners flapping above the gate and guards strutting along the ramparts. The prime warriors and their wives had relocated there from Place-of-Light, living in small houses around the periphery of the fort. Despite the loss, Place-of-Light continued to thrive as it had done for centuries, ever since the gold-men came from overseas; indeed, its population swelled as youths arrived from all over Prydn to join Ardhu's warband. Not every youth was suitable, of course. Many were hot-headed and ill-trained, so Ka'hai, Bohrs and Bet'uor took to teaching them the arts of war — the strike with the slingshot, the death thrust of the dagger, the blow of the war-hammer.

The coasts were free of the snake-like ships of the Sea-Raiders and Ardhu and Fynavir rode out in splendour as far West as Belerion, and wherever they went, they were hailed as gods-come-to-earth. The weather was unusually settled from the Winter Solstice on through spring and summer, and everywhere crops sprouted in abundance, promising a fulsome harvest. Few old ones passed into the Otherworld, and less bone-ache, tooth-loss and rickets plagued the tribes. Children were born, and lived in record numbers, along with their mothers.

It was as if the earth itself had become fertile with the union of the young King and his white Queen…but there was no sign that Fynavir herself would present the people of Prydn with Ardhu's heir. Each month the village crones looked to her and gossiped, but every turning of the Moon she stole away to the Women's House in the lake valley to spend five days away from her husband until the priestesses of the temple purified her and returned her to her husband's bed.

But Ardhu was none too worried by the absence of a child. They were both young, and not every coupling produced a babe — he knew that. When the Ancestors decided that a long-dead Great One should be reborn in flesh, then they would make it so, breathing spirit into the woman's womb. This could happen now or months hence; the Ancestors were capricious.

In some ways he was glad no child had come as yet — he was just enjoying being married to Fynavir. After initial shyness, even slight reluctance, she had warmed to his embraces, and her long, strong dancer's legs wrapped round him in the lovers' dance helped him forget the dark, wild lustfulness of Morigau, his eternal shame, and his hidden secret.

But shortly after the first anniversary of their marriage union, Merlin came to Ardhu as he sat beside Fynavir in the Great Hall. Torches lit the high, carved roof-beams and incense burners let off sweet fragrance, while Art sat with his queen upon a nest of furs and pillows stuffed with dried grasses. A warm fire burned in a pit before them, and they passed back and forth a fine imported cup carved from a single lump of amber

"Your sister wants to see you, Pendraec," said the high priest curtly.

Ardhu turned bone-white; he thrust the amber mug at Fynavir. "My sister! Where is she?"

Merlin glanced at him suspiciously, noting his discomfiture. "What ails you? You look as if I told you the Great Sow herself was rooting for your blood! I am talking of your younger sister Mor-ghan…Ana, who lives in the Lake Valley with Lady Nin-Aeifa. She has asked for you at the secret cave below the fort."

Ardhu relaxed, colour flooding back into his face. "Ana! Yes, of course! She has joined the Lake Maidens. What does she want?"

Merlin shrugged. "Her tidings are not for me, Ardhu. You must meet with her yourself."

Ardhu rose from the floor, scattering furs.

Fynavir made to rise too. "Shall I come, Art?" She quite wanted to meet this mysterious sister; she had seen the Ladies of Lake worshipping at the Sacred Pool below Kham-El-Ard, but they wore concealing veils and painted their faces white like the dead, and she had never dared speak to them.

"No, it is a private matter between my kinswoman and myself," Ardhu said distractedly, dragging his bearskin cloak round his shoulders. "I shan't be long. An'kelet will entertain you while I'm away…" He nodded at his friend, who sat to the right of the fire, beaker in hand, half-hidden in shadow. "Sing her a song for me, will you, Ank? A ballad from your homeland. Something sad that will make her miss me, and then welcome me home again in the best way a woman can!"

An'kelet bowed his head, expression hidden by the amber locks of his hair. "I will do what I can to please her, lord."

"Good — that is as it should be! Keep my place warm for me!"

Ardhu slid down the path that led from the summit of the hill, and walked around the base of the mound with its dry defences rimmed by sharpened poles. Passing onto the eastern side, trees rose up in leafy abundance, and the smell of water and old things, growing things, reached into his nostrils. Wind rushed in the treetops, making an eerie hissing, and lonely birds cried out, their shrieks reminiscent of the cries of lost spirits.

Ardhu glanced gratefully toward Carnwennan in its secret sheath against his calf. He was reasonably certain he would meet no hostile humans so close to Kham-El-Ard, but denizens of the spirit-world were another matter. He did not know how well his earthly weapons would fare against spirit-beings, though he had heard they were fearful of metal, since many came from the Time Before, when weapons and tools were of bone or stone.

Ahead of him he saw a gap in the ash, elm and holly, yawning like some prickly foliate mouth. Though it, the waters of the lake where he had gained Caladvolc gleamed silver-blue, a mirror reflecting the graceful, swaying branches and the scudding clouds in the sky above.

He walked to the edge of the water, feet sinking in the mud, feeling suddenly cold and alone. Perhaps he should have allowed Fynavir to accompany him...but maybe Ana had things to say that Fyn could never hear...

Ardhu took another step forward, into the long reeds that grew in the shallows. They clacked together, noisy as the teeth in a dried old skull. Where was Mhor-gan? He did not like these games; all his sisters played too much with such flummery and drama, while he liked things straightforward and plain.

He scowled, wishing he were back in the hall. Suddenly a whistling noise filled his ears, a high whine like that made by some particularly malevolent insect. He paused for a second, frowning, before recognising the sound for what it was...and with a cry he dived into the reeds, throwing his arm over his head for protection.

An arrow! It had just skimmed past the tip of his ear...he could feel the flesh stinging in its aftermath. Glancing over his shoulder, he saw the shaft sticking in a tree behind him, still vibrating from impact.

Drawing Carnwennan with a sullen flash, he began to creep slowly through the reeds. Mist suddenly rose up, curling from the water, obscuring trees, shrubs and landmarks. The waters rippled, and out of this mist came Mhor-gan in a narrow boat made of skins, poled by a tall man who seemed a creature of the wild, with a cloak made of hawk feathers fluttering around him, and a hawk-mask covering his face. Mhor-gan carried a bow, an arrow to the string.

"Mhor-gan!" Ardhu shouted in vexation, leaping from the rushes. "What kind of folly is this, shooting at me? You could have killed me!"

"I could have killed you, brother." She looked at him and her eyes were strange, feral, and he knew at that moment she was more than his sister — she was one of Nin-Aiefa's priestesses, possessed of the spirits. "But I would never have done so. Take it as this — a warning. My dart may not seek your heart, but the knife will forever be ready to strike you."

"So I am in danger, then? Is that why you have come?"

"Follow me to the cave and we will talk." The boat ground into the shallows and Mhor-gan stepped elegantly from it, her deerskin-clad feet scarcely seeming to touch water or mud. Her hair hung loose, dark as the shadows, but tinted red in the flame of the torch her companion kindled.

She led Art through the woods at the foot of a hill to a cave that stretched away into the hillside. It was not entirely a natural construction; great sarsens slabs lined the sides and had been hoisted up as capstones. The rocks were stained with lichens and painted with faded signs.

She went in and knelt by a small hearth, throwing dried mosses and other fodder on it. Deftly using a strike-a-light, she kindled a flame and fire rushed up with a great whoosh, turning the cavern roof black almost instantly.

Ardhu stared around in amazement. The walls were painted with many pictures — scenes of setting Suns and rising Moons, and men at the hunt, and women at the dance, and men and women in the oldest dance at all... And at the very back of the cave, almost worn away, were vague outlines of tusked and toothed beasts Ardhu could not name, from the Time-Before-Time of the Hunting-Men.

Mhor-gan sat down cross-legged and Ardhu followed suit. The Hawk-headed Man stayed standing, perhaps guarding.

"Ardhu..." Morgan's voice was a whisper. "News comes from the north. Our sister Morigau..." She paused, eyes shadowed by her eyelashes, swaying slightly as if she might fall.

"Yes?" Ardhu's voice came out a hoarse croak. What did he wish — that Morigau were dead? It happened often, even among the young — a sudden flux, an unexpected wound, and the barrow gaped...

Morgan's head shook. "She has given birth to a son on the Isle of Pigs. She has called him Mordraed."

Ardhu went cold, then hot, then cold again. His heart thumped so loudly he was sure Mhor-gan and her man must hear it. "And Loth of Ynys Yrch, he is pleased to have a healthy son?"

Mhor-gan raised her head, a bitter little smile playing on her lips. "He is pleased, or so it is reported. Even though some malicious gossips count their fingers and say that the brat was born too soon to be his. But you will know more about that than I, Ardhu Pendraec."

Ardhu was silent, and then said slowly, "Perhaps you know more than you should. Who told you? Merlin?"

"How I know doesn't matter," said Mhor-gan. "All I know is that Morigau will use this child against us as a warrior uses his sword. It is said he was born with a caul over his head and is marked. It is rumoured she has fed him blood with her milk to whet his appetite for war. I have looked into the waters of the cauldron and seen running blood, and Mordraed's face and the walls of Kham-El-Ard burning."

Ardhu shuddered. "I will kill Morigau...I will kill her and the child."

"No, you cannot." Her fingers gripped his arm. "A kinslaying would bring all of Loth's forces down upon us, and many others would join his cause. Even if you proved victorious in battle, a taint would lie upon you, and Morigau's plot to topple your rule would be accomplished."

"What would you have me do, then, Ana? You are a holy woman — guide me!"

"Always take care. Trust not even those you love the most." Her eyes became shadowy again, her jaw tense. "Harden your heart and steel yourself. Think of war, and do not spend too much time in the pleasures of the hall. This is not the time of a gentle earth — it is an Age of Stone! And so your heart must be. Never let your guard down, Ardhu."

She glanced over at the Hawk-man, standing still as a monolith, gaze directed toward the cave's mouth. "Come, cousin," she said softly. "It is time to introduce you."

The feathered figure turned towards Ardhu and lifted the beaked mask from his head. Art saw a face not much older than his own, framed by dark hair, with the look of Mhor-gan and his other kin from Belerion. "Who is this?" he asked. "And why have you brought him to me?"

"This is our cousin, Hwalchmai, Hawk of the Plain, son of our mother's sister. Since the day you ascended the throne, he begged me to send him to you. But I would not till the famed Skatha the Shadowy, who dwells on the northern isle that bears her name, trained him in the warrior arts. Nor would I send him hence until taught by the priestesses in the ways of the spirit. For we have seen that there is a great quest ahead of Hwalchmai, one that will be sung for a thousand years and more. Right now, he is but a young sapling, with roots still seeking purchase, but he will fight and take the crown of old holly... or perish in doing so. But that is long away. For now, he will be one of your chief men in the warband, the most courteous of your warriors; and

196

if An'kelet of Ar-morah stands on your right, Hwalchmai shall guard the left with an arm as strong as the oak-tree."

Ardhu frowned. "Ka'hai, Ech-tor and Bohrs train new men, and we choose the best amongst them. They would not be pleased to see a newcomer march into the hall and take a place without trial."

"Then a trial there will be, "said Mhor-gan. "Now, before your eyes, will Hwalchmai show his skills. The greater testing will come later, as was prophesied."

The slender woman nodded to Hwalchmai, and he bowed to her and to Ardhu. He then began the warrior's dance, the chant of the hunt. Taking his bow, he fired several shots in succession over the lake, and to Ardhu's surprise, he brought down game with every shot — a roe-deer springing through the foliage, a bird that soared between the trees, a fox slinking through the waving ferns. Running over to the fallen beasts, he slashed them across the throat with his honed dagger and caught their warm blood in a handled beaker, drinking in their power and essence with their life-juices. Finishing, he gutted and skinned them, preparing the meat for the hall of his king and taking the skins for his own use.

"As fleet as the deer, am I," he said, wrapping the skin around him, "and as wily as the fox." He tied the fox's red tail into his hair. "But I am also as loyal as the dog that lies by the fire and guards the homestead."

Ardhu smiled, and placed his hand on his shoulder. "I do not doubt it. And now, my hound, you will bark for me, and guard my fort and all who dwell in it."

Mhor-gan's lips curved faintly upward as the cousins began to talk in a less formal manner, discussing warcraft and horses and feasting. It was good to see the pleasure in Ardhu's face. She feared he would not look so if he knew that, at that very moment, Morigau, his one-time lover and his bane, was meeting with the Merlin somewhere out on the Great Plain.

Merlin huffed along the track in the twilight, the butt of his staff thudding against the firm earth. His bones ached; he noticed it now whenever he had to move with swiftness, a burning pain that gnarled his joints, especially in knees and back. He gazed down at his thin hand, clutching the staff; his knuckles were knotted and deformed, already an old man's hands, though, mercifully, not enfeebled as yet.

He cursed, his breath a white fog before his lips. He had no wish to come

197

out here on the summons of the she-hag, Morigau. But better he came, level-headed, than Ardhu, who was still callow enough to lose control in the demon-woman's presence, whether by killing her or falling for her dubious charms as he had at Suilven. He would like to ring her neck himself, no matter how pretty it seemed, but he dared not, for the same reasons he couldn't allow Art to kill her — she was Loth's woman, and he'd use her demise as the perfect excuse to come rampaging down from the north, bringing the wild tribes of the isles and forests with him. Even if Ardhu's warband rode out to meet him, taking in additional warriors from the Land of the Mother Mountain and the Brig-ahn who dwelt on the high moors, this would then leave the entire West and south open to attack or infiltration from the mainland coasts. Rumours had come that the pirates were sheltering in coves along the rocky shores of Ar-morah, just biding their time until they thought they could sails unchecked into Albu once again...

Up ahead, the slope of a bank rose up into the twilight, half-grassed, half-chalk — the Great Spirit path, built by the earliest Ancestors to separate the lands of the living from the places of the spirits. In the distance, he could see the sanctuary of the Stones, the massive sarsens violet-tinted in the dusk, slumberous giants that brooded over the Great Plain.

Watch over me, O Ancestors, he thought moodily, as he traversed the bank of the Spirit Path to the place he had arranged to meet Morigau, in this liminal area far from stones or settlement, the only fitting place to deal with this viper who had sprung from the same nest as Ardhu but sought to impale him with her poison fangs.

The rustle of a cloak made him glance around, and he spotted her, hovering like some malign imp atop the bank. Her hair was free like a young girl's, blowing in a black, tangled cloud about her. She had painted her lips and cheeks with berry- juice and her dark eyes, dominating her face, were smudged with ash that made them appear huge and dark, almost black. She looked at him and an expression of disappointment and then anger passed over her visage; she had obviously expected Ardhu to be there.

"No, he's not coming," said Merlin tartly. "He has no wish to see your face again after your foul deceit. It is me you will deal with, Morigau of Ynys Yrch."

She smiled sweetly. "So be it, Merlin. Maybe that is for the best. After all, we are cut from the same mould, you and me. We are ...equals."

Merlin's brows lifted until they vanished under his unkempt grey-streaked fringe. "Indeed? Interesting that you should think so!"

"Ah..." She ascended from the crest of the bank, coming to stand beside him. She was short, like her mother, and similar in feature, with the same haughty arrogance and barely veiled sensuality that had attracted U'thyr to Y'gerna. "Don't you know? I too commune with the old ones. I too know the secrets of plants that harm and heal. I too study the movements of Sun and Moon. I have become priestess on the distant isles where I am also Queen. So we are indeed equals, cut from the same cloth. I do grant to you, though, as my elder, that there is much you could teach me."

Merlin said nothing. Morigau moved round in front of him, staring up into his face. "Merlin, Merlin, don't look at me that way! We don't have to be enemies..."

"No? After the evil you have wrought?"

Morigau pouted. "I blame you and your wiles for much of that, Merlin. But, be that as it may... I have changed since I lay with Ardhu at Suilven. My life is different now."

"Different? In what way?"

Her lips twisted into a mocking smile. "Can't you guess, Merlin? I am the mother of a fine, healthy son — heir of Ardhu Pendraec and recipient of all that I can teach him. Unclaimed he may be by his father, but one day he will wrest away all Ardhu has won."

"And you dare to speak to me of a peace between us!" snarled Merlin in anger.

"No, listen, listen!" She raised her hand. "I do not mean to anger you. I only speak truth, from one who has the Sight, even as you do. Ardhu is weak, plagued by the follies of his fathers; my son is strong, made of stern stuff in the north. Ardhu has married a woman they say is a goddess, but no news comes of a child of his loins; the goddess-of-earth does not favour them. I have looked into the fire and seen betrayal and death; even among his so-called friends...Can you tell me that you have not seen this too?"

"And what would your course be, Morigau?" Merlin's eyes were hard as sarsen.

"This...." In a practised movement, she tore open the toggles at the top of her robe, and let it fall in a heap to her ankles. Naked, she stood in the dying daylight, brazenly unashamed. She cupped her swollen breasts, holding them up like offerings. "For us to join, as man and woman. For us, two of a kind, to meld our power and knowledge and take on the leadership of Prydn until my son, under our tutelage, could become ruler. If you said yes to me, I swear you would not regret it."

She moved closer while the older man stood frozen like a statue. She wound herself around him, sinuous as a serpent and as deadly, writhing her slim hips against his, nipping at his neck with her sharp white teeth. "I have heard you live an austere life, Merlin," she panted in his ear. "Surely you do not want to live your entire life alone, without the pleasures of flesh. Surely you would prefer this…" she let her hand slide between his thighs, "to congress with naught but ghosts and spirits. Or perhaps you prefer to tup the dead," she finished cruelly.

Her last jibe goaded him to anger. For a moment, he had nearly succumbed to her, to the warmth of her willing body, to the sensations he had denied himself since he had left Nin-Aeifa at Afallan. But staring down into her carnal, cruel eyes, he realised that no pleasure would ever really be found in her embrace — only devouring death. Strength and resolve returned to him, and that ember of traitorous desire that threatened to ruin him died like a flame under cold water.

With a cry, he grabbed her shoulders and flung her backward into the ditch. Drawing his knife, he fell upon her before she had the chance to rise, and pressed its blade to her throat. "I could take you and then kill you," he grunted, his free hand wandering roughly over her body, a motion meant to humiliate rather than excite, "and none would know your fate, for the animals and hungry spirits would chew your corpse to rags in the night. But, you faithless whore, you have nothing that I want or need, nor ever shall. I can see now what evil magic you wrought on Ardhu, but it has no power over me!"

He rolled away from her and Morigau, spitting fury, sprang up and dragged on her gown. "You will pay for this outrage!" she spat. "Doubly. I offered you a chance…it will not be offered again. Enjoy your feasting and merry-making with my brother in your great hall of Kham-El-Ard; it will soon be at an end. The land will be in turmoil again, and by my hand."

"Loth would not dare to step on these shores again," said Merlin.

"I do not speak of the armies of my clumsy husband. That useless fool is too busy cursing Ardhu's name to gather men to him so that he can break the constraints my brother has laid on him. It is I who have reaped the whirlwind that is about to descend — I, alone. Though who will put blame on me, a priestess and a queen in the remotest part of Prydn?"

Merlin snarled between clenched teeth. "I knew I should have thrown you into the sea when you were but a puling brat! An evil spirit dwells within you, gnawing your innards!"

"You helped put it there!" she retorted. "But I have grown used to it now. And I have put the fire in my head to much use during my lonely hours on Ynys Yrch. When not rutting with Loth — he is like one of the pigs that roam those blasted isles, slobbering and gross, interesting in only his beaker and bed — I have been raising a fine little boar bred from the most vicious sow I could find — a sow black as She-Who-Guards. I have whipped him and tormented him, and watched with joy as he became more vicious every day. I gave him potions to craze him, and fed him on the flesh of men — strangers who came unbidden to the isles, shipwrecked men from the north, unwanted brats..."

"You sicken me..." Merlin's voice was a groan.

Morigau went on animatedly, almost merrily. "He is eager to run loose now, my dear little boar. T'orc is his name, and along with his handler, Rhyttah, a man most loyal to my cause..." She smirked and Merlin guessed exactly what she meant by 'loyal.' "He will lay waste to the lands of Prydn. Ardhu will have never faced such a creature before, and Rhyttah himself is not like the effete men of the south with their perfumed hair and oiled flesh; his very cloak is woven of the beards of slain enemies. Soon Ardhu will join their numbers...not that the soft-faced whelp has much beard to add to Rhyttah's cloak!"

Merlin flung his dagger at Morigau, tormented beyond endurance by her mocking words. The throw was not accurate, but the point tore her dress and nicked her arm, drawing beads of bright blood. "You dare strike me!" she gasped, clutching the wound. "Just wait, Merlin, one day that blow will come back on you! I await that day with much longing! Now farewell!"

She sprang away into the darkness, running fleet-footed as a deer into a nearby stand of trees. Above the Moon was rising, crooked, the wane Moon, the death Moon.

Merlin stared after his adversary, Ardhu's bane, and felt sickness knot his belly.

CHAPTER SIXTEEN

"She was here on the plain!" Ardhu swept an agitated hand through his hair as he paced the Great Hall. "Why did you not tell me, Merlin? You devised this with Ana, didn't you? Sending me off with her to keep me out of the way while you treated with Morigau."

"Yes," said Merlin," and it was the right thing to do. Look at you, filled with fury. You would have fallen right into Morigau's trap, and done something you would later regret."

Ardhu slumped to his knees by the fire-pit. "I have already done things I regret. Merlin, Ana has told me that Morigau has...that there is..."

Merlin nodded gravely. "Yes. There is a child. She has passed him off as the get of Loth."

"If I could..." Ardhu's eyes blackened, and for a second Merlin recoiled, for the young man looked so like his half-sister it was disconcerting. "If I could, I would send my warriors throughout the land to kill any man-child born in the month of the Bhel-fires!"

"But that would make you as much as monster as Morigau."

"I know." Ardhu bowed his head. "And you know I would never in truth do such a thing."

Merlin raised his young lord up with a hand. "Now that you have shouted out your anger, we had best gather the warband and hold council. Morigau threatened not only you, but all the people of Prydn. We must be prepared for sudden attacks. It may be all angry bluster and wishful malice — but I fear not."

More than four months had passed before Ardhu had news of his kinswoman and her malign devices. The warband was gathered in the hall of Kham-El-Ard, drinking and carousing, most well into their cups. Some played foolish games with coloured pebbles, while others dandled their wives on their knees or pinched and pawed the serving women who brought them their beakers of mead and beer. The day was cold, the Winter Solstice gone by nearly a month, and the whole world outside seemed a bleak vista of grey and white — a haze of mist, a touch of frost, a sprinkle of trodden snow. Icicles clattered on the roofline of the hall, while in the valley below tree-boughs clashed together like skeleton bones, tossed on a bitter wind.

As daylight failed, the clouds gaped and it began to rain, an icy flow from the heavens that pattered on that thatching of the great chieftain's house and beat against the calfskin stretched over the window-slits.

Ardhu sat at the head of the hall, on a raised pile of furs, his legs stretched out before him close to the blazing fire-pit. An'kelet reclined on his right hand side, honing the barbs on the spear Balugaisa, while Merlin squatted on his left, impassive and ever vigilant, one eye fixed on the door, which shuddered in the rising wind, threatening to burst open and flood the hall with wintry chill. Fynavir knelt between Ardhu and An'kelet; eyes locked on the fire's flames. She wore her frost-pale hair loose like an unwed maiden, instead of in the customary hairnet favoured by married women — it was what Ardhu liked and expected.

And An'kelet too. She could feel his gaze travelling the graceful curves of her body, willing her to turn and face him. To let him know the truth of what she felt towards him...

Eventually she could bear no more, and she turned her head and met his ready smile. A small gasp left her lips and she hastily turned away again, clutching her handled mug with its watered-down beer.

"Fynavir, what ails you?" Ardhu leaned over, hand caressing her shoulder, running over the swell of her breast, past her hip to touch her stomach. "Are you...all right? Should I call a healing woman?"

She knew what he implied; his intimate touch said it all. Tears pricked her eyes. There was still no sign of any child. The only signs visible tonight were of her traitorous desires.

"I am fine, lord husband," she said. "A moment's giddiness... the heat... the drink... Perhaps I should go to our chamber."

Ardhu stared moodily at her. These turns were more and more frequent. She seemed, sometimes, to be drawing away from him, her embraces cold and less frequent, and her expression distant.

"Fynavir, do not shame me here," he hissed in her ear, suddenly cruel with too much beer and winter boredom. "Men will talk if you leave the hall. You are meant to be at my side. You are my Queen, and the spirit of the land is within you. If it is not right between us, the people will think that it is also not right with the Land itself!"

"And is it?" Tears stung her eyes.

"It would be if you would give the land an heir!" Ardhu snapped, and then, realising he had spoken too freely, wrapped his bearskin around him and glowered furiously into the smoke in the longhouse.

He had done it — spoken the unspeakable out loud before all. Merlin, tapping out a thin beat on a shamanic drum held between his bony knees, smiled a bitter, knowing smile. He didn't hate the white foreign girl, but she was the worst choice his young king could have made. Maybe, with luck, Art would now see the unhappy truth and put her aside.

Feeling a stab of guilt for his outburst, Ardhu reached for Fynavir's arm. She was startlingly beautiful, her hair like the frost on the trees, her eyes green and stormy as the distant seas. Jet beads shone darkly around her neck and in her ears, startling against her unnatural whiteness. "Why don't you dance as you did before," he slurred. "Back in the hall of Ludegran. Dance for me, Fynavir, and show everyone that it is still good between us!"

"I... I can't... she began, hand rising to her throat, but the spasm of anger that crossed her husband's face silenced her protests.

Reluctantly, she climbed to her feet, swaying as her head reeled. The men of the warband cheered; most secretly found her good to look upon, different in her whiteness to most of the native Prydn women who tended to brown hair or red. Musicians began to play on pipes, while Merlin's drum sent out a frenzied thumping.

Fynavir closed her eyes, imagining, as she always did when she performed her magic dances that she was other than she was. In her mind's eye she was a swan, faltering on the wing, trying to fly away over a long, dark lake to join a long-lost mate in the shadows on the other side. She soared and swooped inside her head, and her body took over and mimicked the scene in her mind. On graceful toes she leaped around the fire, her head flung back revealing a long neck as graceful as that of the swan she envisioned.

Ardhu watched, enthralled, the blood running hot in his loins. He had been unkind, but by the gods, he would make it up to her. Blue faience beads, a golden- buttoned gown from over the sea…anything she asked.

Suddenly she ceased dancing. The image in her head lurched. The swan flew into the dark, and suddenly an arrow pierced its breast, and with a dying cry it plummeted down, falling, falling, and falling, toward the icy lake…

"No!" she cried, and toppled forward towards the burning fire.

A serving woman screamed.

Swift as the wind, An'kelet was at her side, catching her before she collapsed into the flames. He lifted her as if she were a child, carrying her away from the heat and the sparks that threatened to ignite her hair.

"An'kelet!" Ardhu leapt to his feet. His voice was harsh. He did not know why he felt angry toward An'kelet, who had done only what a loyal warrior would do. "Leave her be — I shall take care of her!"

An'kelet hesitated. Ardhu's eyes widened then blackened with fury. What was the fool up to, making him look like some boor who could not be trusted with the wellbeing of his own woman?

At that moment, there came a crash from outside. A huge gust of wind smashed opens the doors of the hall, and extinguished the torches at the entrance and the lamps full of burning fat. Even the fire dimmed down to a pile of sullen embers.

In the sudden blackness, someone shrieked in fear.

There was the sound of daggers being drawn. An'kelet placed Fynavir on a fur and drew Arondyt and Fragarak, while Ardhu unsheathed Caladvolc and snatched up the Face of Evening.

"Who goes?" he demanded.

Raiders he could deal with, but his spies had brought no news for weeks, and the great Ridgeways were empty. So close to Solstice, it was more likely that any unwelcome arrival at the feasting hall would come from the malevolent spirit-world.

The sound of hoofbeats answered his shout. The men and women in the hall shrank back, even Bohrs and Ka'hai, as a dark figure on horseback entered the hall and rode boldly across the rush-strewn floor toward the king's dais.

The stranger looked indeed as if he harkened from the Otherworld; surely, no mortal man had a countenance such as his. He was green from head to foot, in both skin colour and the colour of his tunic. Wild thorns and sprigs of holly jutted from curled hair and beard, and blood-red berries dangled from antlers sprouting from between his snarled locks. Against the green of his face, his eyes seemed large and reddish, monstrous. His teeth were filed sharp and white as the Moon, glowing as he laughed. Above his head he brandished a great double-bladed bronze axe.

Ardhu leapt up, Caladvolc shining like a tongue of flame in the dimness. "Be you man or spirit, I will smite you if you do not leave my hall!"

The green rider ignored him and swung down from the saddle, swaggering arrogantly toward the young king and his men. "Fine words," he cried. "Fine brave words…but where is your hospitality, O jewel of kings! Ach, the warrior-circle of the famed Ardhu Pendraec is made of naught but mean men, holding their beakers and their dark plots close to their hearts!"

"You speak treasonously!" Hwalchmai, who had been sitting with Ba-lin and Bal-ahn, sprang from his seat and rushed towards the verdant apparition.

"The Lord Ardhu is most generous of kings! He offers no hospitality to you, because your countenance is vile... as is your uncouth tongue! You deserve to die for your slurs!"

The Green Man peered down his aquiline nose at the young man before him, at the angry face and fierce grey-green eyes. He then laughed, the sound rising up to shake the rafters. "If you think I have committed such a grave crime, take my head, boy. Look...I will make the deed easy for you!"

He held out his huge, double-bladed axe, its long haft wrapped in oiled leather. Hwalchmai snatched it from him, stumbling as he realised it was heavier than he thought. His dismay at the brief loss of his footing elicited another peel of laughter from the Green Man.

"Surely my weapon is not too much for such a noble youth!" he bellowed. "But behold, I still bow to your great prowess! I will go down on my knees and bare my neck to the kiss of the blade!"

Grinning, he sank down before Hwalchmai and parted his mass of hair with big green hands. His neck shone in the dying embers of the fire — pale green like a corpse's skin.

Hwalchmai hefted the great axe. Sweat broke out on his brow. The axe's handle was slippery, sweaty; he fought to position it, to prepare for the lethal blow. With a cry he raised it over his head, and then brought it down with all his might, aiming for the tree-like neck, bulging with knots of veins....

And missed.

As if enchanted, the heavy-headed, foreign weapon dragged forward in his hand, tearing through clawed fingers as if trying to get back to its master's belt. The axe tumbled in the air, a flash of red, before thudding into the packed earth a few inches from the Green Man's ferocious head.

"A... ha!" he bellowed, springing to his feet and snatching up his fallen axe. "Brave words, but wavering hand! Can you honour ever be restored, young hothead? Not by ordinary means. Only if you come to my abode in Lud's hole, and play the axe-game with your head!"

Hwalchmai stared at him, furious yet fearful, eyeing the stranger's axe as if it were some living creature that might suddenly spring forward and strike him. He could hear the other men in the hall murmuring, some even sniggering — he was not liked in all quarters, for some believed he had risen in Ardhu's esteem too quickly, and only because he was blood-kin. Well, he would prove them wrong. He would pass the greatest test of them all, or die in the attempt.

"I will seek you out at this Lud's hole," he snarled between gritted teeth. "And I will play your axe-game."

"Good!" shouted the Green Man, with a rapacious grin, "I look to the hour of our meeting!" and he sprang astride his steed and galloped from the hall, out into the driving rain and wild weather beyond. In an eye's blink, he was gone, lost in the darkness of a storm-wracked winter night.

"Hwalchmai, what have you done?" Ardhu shook his cousin's shoulder." You have sworn your life away."

"I had no choice," said Hwalchmai, hotly. "To nay-say him would bring dishonour. Already I am looked on as an interloper who rides upon the fame of my kin. I will prove that is not the case and find eternal fame among the singers-of-song. Or else my head will decorate the Green Man's dwelling in Lud's Hole."

Hwalchmai did not go after the green stranger for another week; a terrible winter storm blew in from the frozen reaches of Kalydon, where the painted people dwelt amidst high mountains and uncharted forests, and turned all the land into a vista of white. Ice came with it, not just snow, borne on a screaming gale that gnashed men's flesh like wolves' teeth and left the trees and rooftops of Kham-El-Ard rimed with glittering icicles that fell and shattered with an eerie tinkling. Several head of cattle, terrified by the wild weather, broke free of their pens and perished while stampeding over a thinly frozen Abona and several shepherds on the eastern downlands did not return to their homes in the Place-of-Light.

"There is evil afoot in this storm." Merlin frowned as he leaned on his staff and stared out from the doors of Ardhu's Great Hall. "It comes from the North, where the devil-woman Morigau dwells. How she must laugh at us, soft in the South, trammelled here like beasts while she wreaks her mischief!"

Head bowed, he murmured invocations to the Sun, to the spirits in the snow-bound stone circle out on the Great Plain. The winds answered him, but they were cold, droning about him with icy malevolence.

As the storm finally died away, and the first hint of blue returned to the sky, Hwalchmai began to prepare for his journey to Lud's hole, packing a bag and wrapping himself in his thickest furs, stuffing straw inside his boots of felt and skin. Ardhu begged him to let the warband accompany him but he refused. "I must do this deed myself or no respect with be mine," he stated.

Bow and quiver of arrows strapped to his back, two sturdy daggers at his belt, he began to make his way down from the heights of Kham-El-Ard. It was not long after the Sunrise and the snowdrifts were red-tinted, as if stained from some gory battle. The eastern sky burned with crimson fire as the Sun's bleeding eye slowly ascended the dark hump of Magic Hill.

Ten steps he took, feet crunching on frozen snow, and then he cried out, "Ardhu! Someone comes to Kham-El-Ard this cold morn! Look!"

The gate-guards sprang into action, running halfway down the hill with bows nocked. Sleepy-eyed, Ardhu appeared on the ramparts, his bearskin wrapped loosely around his shoulders, his black hair storm-tossed. Sure enough a figure could be seen staggering across the fields towards the hillfort, a shambling shape amidst the ghostly fog-tendrils rising from the waters of Abona.

Fleet of foot, Hwalchmai was first to reach the stranger. He skidded to a halt as he realised the man was not alone — in his arms he carried the body of a young boy. A boy, blue-faced and stiff, who had been dead some days. Ash and blood smeared his livid face. He was no more than ten.

Hwalchmai stared in horror. The man stared back, face grimy and besmirched and twisted with grief. His mouth moved but it seemed he had lost the ability for speech.

"What has happened? Where are you from?" Hwalchmai found his own voice. "Who has done this evil deed?"

The man spluttered, and wiped his eyes, before at last finding his tongue. His voice was ragged with sorrow: "I hail from Tarn Wethelen on the borders of the Dwri lands… and I come begging help from the Young King who men say protects the weak and helpless against tyrants and wicked men from afar. A week ago our village and temple were burned to the ground by invaders. They spared no one, not even unarmed children…" He looked at the stiffened corpse in his arms and began a pitiful keening that cut eerily through the morning.

By now Ardhu had reached the foot of the hill, with Merlin and An'kelet following closely behind him. Ardhu approached the man and placed his hand on his shoulder, while Merlin prised the rigid child's body from the man's grasp and laid it respectfully on the grass, head facing toward the rising Sun.

"If it is vengeance you seek, you have come to the right place," said Ardhu firmly. "The Warband will ride this very day, and your boy's death will be made good with foemen's blood. Who was it that attacked your settlement? The sea-folk? Or other Western chiefs?"

The man spat on the ground. "Neither. They spoke our tongue but with a strange twist. Northerners, I think. With them they had a totem-animal, a

208

monster from the pits of shadow in An-un, the Underworld. A great boar it was, eyes like flame, tusks like knives. It was mad and ran amok, even as they did, goring and biting, and after the battle they fed it on dead men's livers...T'orc Is-gurth they called the beast, the Chief Boar, and its master who goaded it on was named Rhyttah Bad-adun, the Chief Giant. He was as fearsome as his creature, a hand taller than most men and one-eyed, and he wore a cloak woven from the beards of men he has slain."

Merlin clutched his staff, face twisting with anguish at the newcomer's words. "So she did not tell idle tales," he muttered. "Morigau did not lie, but worked her evil well. But she will not prevail... no, I shall see to it."

Turning to Ardhu, he caught his arm. "You must go and fight this new danger and crush it utterly. It is the doing of Morigau, your sister."

Ardhu spat an oath. "So soon! She must truly be a creature of Otherness; she flies around Prydn as no mortal could. What is your counsel, Merlin, to defeat this Boar and its Master? Will axes and arrows be enough? The smell of magic is on this, wrought by the hands of Morigau."

Merlin's lips narrowed, tightened. "Ever since she was here, I have thought on this, conferring with my fellow priests and lore-masters at Deroweth. You are warriors, not magic men, and I would that you kept it so, and hunted down this fell beast with the tools of warriors made from sound stone and good, wholesome metal. But if all fails, and Chief Giant and Chief Boar elude you, there are others ways — but they are dark and perilous. If it comes to it, seek the Black Witch daughter of White Witch in her cave in the Uplands of Despair, and take from her the magic razor, tempered in blood, that lies upon her altar. It is will shear both the magic boar's bristles and the neck of cruel Rhyttah."

Ardhu turned back toward Kham-El-Ard, and ordered the men to go out into the fields and blow on aurochs horns, awakening all in the lands between the Place-of-Light and the circles of Deroweth. The fort on its height sprang to life, youths running here and there to get their masters' mounts ready and women packing bedrolls and provisions for the long journey. Warriors dashed amongst them, polishing weapons and making high boasts while attaching talismans to tunics or belts. Those to be left behind looked grim, but the warrior's faces were full of joy — the Solstice was over and they were half-mad with boredom and glad of this new challenge.

Fynavir emerged from her sleeping quarters, feet bare, a sheepskin wrapped around her. "Ardhu, what is happening... I heard the horns blowing!"

"It is time for battle again," said Ardhu briskly. "Not foreign raiders, this time, but our own kind. In fact…it is the doing of my own sister Morigau."

"The wife of the northern King? I heard from the jet traders that she recently bore a child… What harm could a woman fresh from child-bed wreak?"

Ardhu stared at his wife, scanning her face to see if she had any knowledge of the truth of Morigau's child, if any hint of scandal had reached her ears. Her green eyes were guileless. He breathed a sigh of relief. "She is not as a normal woman, Fynavir. A bad spirit resides within her. "

Fynavir pondered this for a minute, and her face clouded. She grasped his wrist. "Ardhu, why must you go? It is far away and you have already done more than any other chief in three hundred years. Wait till spring, when the weather is sweeter and if the trouble is still about, deal with it then."

Ardhu snatched his wrist away and reached for his mace, tucking it into his belt. "People — my people, are dying. I cannot leave them to their fate, or I would not be worthy of the title of High King."

"And An'kelet…he will ride with you too?" She hung her head.

"Of course. He is my battle-brother, and the best warrior in my company, though Hwalchmai soon shall be his equal."

Tears began to leak from Fynavir's eyes, as they did all too frequently. "I beg you… don't go! I have seen omens in dreams, and heard dead voices on the wind… I do not wish to be left here alone. Ardhu, let me come with you!"

Art burst into loud, frustrated laughter. "Now that would scare the enemy! Fynavir, the battlefield is no place for you. It is your duty as Queen to stay and attend to the running of Kham-El-Ard in my absence. There is a homeless man at the gate, and a dead child to be barrowed… these shall be among your tasks when I am away."

"Oh Ardhu, Ardhu…" she wept, pressing her hands to her face, and in embarrassment he pushed past her to gather his shield and the rest of his things. He would never understand the woman; one moment seemingly indifferent, the next weeping if he stepped beyond the hill-fort's gates.

Leaving Fynavir, he proceeded to the entranceway of the fort, thronged by milling warriors and war-steeds, which champed and stamped and threatened to trample the dogs of the settlement as they rushed around in circles in the snow, half-mad with excitement. A few of the larger hounds were on leads, ready to be taken on the long road to hunt Chief Boar T'orc. Ba-lin and Bal-ahn were there, alongside Bohrs with his war-club and An'kelet leaning on his spear. Ka'hai was checking that all supplies for the long road were in place, aided by Betu'or and the brothers Brathac and Nerthac and lanky Cacamuri. Drust Thunderfist, who had a huge war-hammer made of black stone, was shouting a boast, while Glu Mightygrasp, wrestler of great renown, swore that he would tear T'orc into pieces. Hluk Windyhand, famed archer, was inspecting the fletchings on his arrows while sharing a swift joke with Anwas the Winged, fleet-footed scout and messenger. Wadu, Naw and Sberin, youths on their first foray with the warband, jostled each other with ill-concealed excitement, along with Is'govan and Isgowuin from the settlement of An-Dwra in the East. Ohsla Big-knife, Gillah Stagshank, and Ellidur the guide completed the band.

Ardhu gestured to Hwalchmai, whose own departure had been delayed in the drama of the morning. "Cousin, I know you have other journeys on your mind, but I would have you ride with us. I think you will play a part in this exploit before its ending."

"I have already sworn to go to Lud's Hole and meet the Green-faced Man."

"And so you shall. But you will come with us upon the road, at least to a point. Is that not acceptable to you? We may well need the might of your arm."

Hwalchmai grinned at his cousin. "It is acceptable, lord. I will be glad of the company, and who knows, maybe we can each help the other in our quests."

The company was ready to depart by the next dawn. The riverbanks were thronged with well-wishers who had come down from Place-of-Light. Mothers held up small children to watch the warriors pass, and old men cheered and shouted, reliving their youths in these bright new champions.

Fynavir stood in silence in the great gateway of Kham-El-Ard, under the carved lintel with its grinning faces of gods and spirits. She looked a being of the underworld herself, wearing her gold pectoral cape with the long linen skirts billowing below like a shroud. Her hair was limed into a fantastic, white coiled shape, and she had chalked her face as a token of her sorrow, turning her soft, lovely face into a surreal, emotionless, mask. Some superstitious folk even made signs against evil at the sight of her, behind their backs; she was their Queen, but she was foreign and different, and although they honoured her as Ardhu's wife and representative of the land, they did not love her.

211

Ardhu took her cold hands and kissed her on both cheeks, tasting the chalkiness of her face-paint. It was like kissing the earth of the plain itself, full of the bones of Ancestors... He shivered. He longed to kiss her lips, but she had frozen him out again, had spent the night curled under her furs, weeping. How tired he had grown of the sound, just as he had of the soughing, sighing winds that harassed the walls of Kham-El-Ard, making him long for his upcoming journey, no matter how dangerous.

"I leave my kingdom and all that is in it your hands, Fynavir," he said solemnly. "Merlin will be at Deroweth should you need him, and Ech-tor will remain at Kham-El-Ard to assist with the running of the fort. Lads from Place-of-Light have also been recruited as guards."

"I will do my best to look after your realm, lord husband," she said softly, inclining her head. And then unexpectedly, she embraced him, anguish in her eyes. "You...and An'kelet, you must take care, do you hear? Don't take any unnecessary risks; you have both already proved your valour!"

Embarrassed in front of the men, Ardhu gently pushed her away. "Have trust in our skills, wife," he said, and then he turned to Ka'hai who was leading Lamrai toward him. She whinnied and danced on the half-frozen ground, eager to be away, to stretch legs cramped by the confinement of winter. Ardhu knew exactly how she felt.

Nimbly, he swung up on her back, and his men mounted alongside him, a gaudy crowd in feathers and furs, bronze and gold, with their mounts nearly as brightly decked out as the warriors themselves. Mounted on a mist-grey stallion, An'kelet rode on Ardhu's right, while Hwalchmai, seated on a beast as black as charcoal, protected his shield arm. As the warband drew ranks behind them, they unfurled the great woven banner of the Head Serpent, with its insignia of a golden lozenge between two spirals. A horn blew and then another and the company moved off toward the fords of Abona.

Fynavir watched them go, uncaring that those around her saw tears track down her dead-white cheeks. She felt their scorn, their eyes harsh as flails on her back. Some of the women were tittering, shaking their heads. "May the spirits bring you safely home," she murmured into the wind...but she did not know if was her husband she asked the Old Ones to protect or the Prince from Ar-morah who rode at his side.

CHAPTER SEVENTEEN

The warband moved rapidly across country. Day blended into night and the Moon faded and went dark, leaving only its attendant crown of stars. Dawn came again, slow and sullen, the Sun barely alive as yet, seeming not to have strengthened since Solstice eve.

At length they came to the settlement of Tarn Wethelen.

Or what remained of it.

All was charcoal and ash. A village turned from a place of light to a place of death and shadow. Not one hut remained, and scarce were the traces that they had ever existed, so thoroughly had they been burned. Corpses of slain villagers lay amid the charred remains; they too had been caught in the conflagration and their cremated bones were scattered in the scant ruins of their homes. At least the wolves would not feast on their flesh.

Turning away from the grisly scene, still emanating the roast-pig scent of the funeral pyre, the company journeyed on toward Tarn Wethelan's temple, a mile away on a bald broad hilltop visible for leagues around. As they had been warned, it too lay in smouldering ruins, a trail of sullen black smoke spiralling up from its shattered remains to mingle with the sleet-heavy clouds. Dazed, the warriors rode up the hill and stopped before what had been the temple entrance. Some started to moan and keen; a few had visited here in happier times and remembered the magnificence that was now obliterated, never to rise again.

Once, an enormous wooden palisade had run inside a mighty encircling ditch, protecting the sacred area; two entrances had faced East and West, the eastern one with an imposing lintelled gateway that framed the rising Sun. Four circular arrangements of free-standing posts had made an unnatural forest in the centre, guarding a cove of three tall stones where the priests would treat with the spirits and perform rites to ensure the risings and settings of Sun and Moon.

Now that splendour had perished, leaving charred lumps overlaid by a crust of ash-smeared snow. The fire had been so voracious, many posts had burnt right down into the chalk pits in which they had been placed. The standing stones of the cove had been toppled into the ditch, and fires deliberately set under them so that they cracked into many pieces.

An'kelet gazed bleakly at the devastation. "How did they dare wreak

213

such evil in a holy place? Surely they feared that the spirits would strike them down for their sacrilege!"

Ardhu's visage was grey as the surroundings…the smeared snow, the solemn sky, the lifeless winter-bitten hills in the distance. "My evil sister and those under her spell seem to fear nothing, my friend, be it in the sky, or in a barrow, or walking the green earth. I pray you never meet her face to face; she has the Aspect of the Old Gloomy Woman of Winter on her…."

An'kelet shuddered and made a sign against evil behind his back; the Gloomy Woman was a euphemism for the the Death Crone, the Guardian, who sucked life from her own Son, the Sun, in Winter

"Where next from here, Art?" Ka-hai rode up, struggling with his horse, which was reacting in fear to the stench and smoke all around it.

Ardhu nodded towards Bohrs and a small knot of men who held the great hounds of the tribe on their tethers. The animals were restive, snapping at each other and tugging on the lead, sniffling and snuffling at the scored and blasted ground, their tails swinging like whips. "The scent of the raiders must be here, somewhere. Loose the hounds."

Bohrs let go of his dog, with a shout of encouragement. The tan hound bounded away, barking, and the rest of the pack raced after him, crashing through the ash piles, leaping up onto the broken embankments, their noses thrust into the wreckage. Bohrs and other dog-handlers went after them, scanning the ground for traces of footprints or animal spoor from the Chief Boar T'orc

At first Bohrs found nothing, and his wide face became as dark as a thunderhead in frustration. But suddenly his dog, Drudlwyn, gave a sharp bark and sprang on a brownish lump in the grass, clasping it in her jaws and worrying it. "Give that to me!" Bohrs leaned over and wrestled the scrap from his dog's jaws with much growling and snarling from the hound. "Hmm, Ardhu, what do you make of this?"

Art took the matted clump from Bohrs. It seemed to be a wad of coarse springy hair braided and sewn onto a scrap of cloth that looked as if it may have torn from the hem of a cloak. "I cannot say for sure…but maybe this hair is from the cloak of Rhyttah, which is said to be made from the beards of vanquished chiefs!"

"Just what we needed then," said Bohrs, and he snatched the clump back from Ardhu and thrust it under Drudlwyn's wildly working nose. "Find him, my girl!" he ordered the dog. "Bring us to this Rhyttah and his fat Boar…so we can all have boar meat for supper, then shave Rhyttah's chin as he has done to many others!"

The hound's ears lifted in excitement and the heavy tail thumped. Then, baying, she loped away, the rest of the dog-pack eagerly following. The men of Ardhu's warband pursued, riding single file through the steaming, dismal ruins of what had once been the temple of Tarn Wethelen.

The warriors journeyed West then North, then West again, wildly zigzagging across desolate, wintry lands, through hills furled with mist and over rivers frozen solid in their beds. Right up to the peaks of God-of-Bronze they galloped, below the very crags of Kharn Mennyn where the Spirits of Sky dwelt amidst sharp fingers of bluestone, then back across the harsh terrain toward gentler, lower lands that lay further North. They did not come across Chief Boar and Chief Giant, but they found their leavings — ransacked villages, desecrated holy sites, ravaged corpses left for scavengers to feast on. They tried to make decent the bones of those killed, then continued on, ever more determined to wreak justice on Rhyttah and T'orc. But slowly they began to feel an edge of despair, as they crossed endless gloomy expanses by day, and shivered round fires at night with the howls of wind and wolves in their ears. They might call Rhyttah a coward in boastful talk, but they were growing unnerved by both his refusal to meet them, and his continued path of destruction with T'orc. On several occasions, An'kelet brought up the name Merlin had mentioned — Ah-nis the Black Witch, daughter of White Witch, who lived at the Valley of Grief in the Uplands of Despair.But Ardhu refused to seek her out, still putting his trust in keen blades and the smiting of axes against enemies' skulls rather than sorcery and dark dealings.

Riding with the company, Hwalchmai had almost forgotten his oath to find the Green Man and offer his neck to the axe. His quest seemed almost foolish, with the ruins of once-thriving settlements scattered across the land and widows and orphaned children wailing on the sides of the great Ridgeways that crossed Prydn. Fighting the enemies of his chief and land was surely a better cause than dying at a Moon-mad man's bidding. After all, what was the Green One, who had entered the king's hall unbidden that stormy eve? Maybe an evil spirit born from the cold and the darkness, maybe just an enemy seeking to cause mayhem and confusion… Honour in facing him? Maybe. But would the men of Ardhu's band think Hwalchmai an honourable hero, or just an honourable fool? Breaking his word was not a thing to be proud of, but neither was throwing life away on a whim.

Hwalchmai pulled his horse's reins and began the decent into a low-slung valley filled with tumbled stones and gnarled thorn trees. Ardhu and An'kelet were riding several paces behind him, discussing heatedly what the best course of action was with Rhyttah seemingly moving like the wind across Prydn. The rest of the warriors massed in the rear, three abreast on the narrow, stony trail that wound towards the valley floor. Hwalchmai could see the hounds in the basin of the vale, sniffing between boulders and skidding over the surface of a frozen brook. They seemed uneasy, almost afraid, their ears press flat against their narrow skulls and their tails down.

Suddenly he caught a glimpse of movement on the far side of the valley. Squinting into the gloom, he spied the figure of an old woman clad in black rags shuffling amid the boulders. As he stared at her, her hooded head swung round and she stared back at him with such malevolence he instinctively made a sign against evil with his hand. He couldn't see her visage clearly, due to the distance, but a brief glimpse had shown him a countenance mottled and twisted, abnormal. He now noticed too that the valley itself was abnormal, with no vegetation, save for thorny black scrub, and rocks that were white as bone, jagged as blades. An air of desolation rose from the barren and blasted earth, and by a stunted shrub a flock of crows were pecking at the denuded carcass of some hapless beast.

The place felt foul, worse than anywhere he had ever venture — could this be the fabled Valley of Despair? It certainly fitted the name!

Without waiting for the others, he drove his mare on into the valley. He heard Ardhu shout to him, his voice raised in annoyance, but a strange rash madness overcame him, and he paid his kinsman no heed. Going into the vale first and facing the hag in her den would surely prove his valour to the Men of the West for once and for all...

And then the mist came down. It came fast and it came suddenly, creeping out of cracks between rocks, from damp earth, from the ice of the frozen river. Cold tendrils swirled round him, rising into sinister shapes and yawing faces that melted in an instant. Chills rippled down his spine, and he drew his dagger and slashed wildly at the fog. He heard sounds deep in its heart... was it laughter?

"Ardhu? My lord?" he shouted to his cousin, but his voice sounded abnormal in that grey amorphous mass, a muffled lifeless groan, a voice out of a barrow.

Pounding his heels against his steed's flanks, he stumbled on through the thickening greyness. He could see shapes, or so he thought, heard the faint trace of voices shouting his name. Then suddenly he was completely alone in a still grey world. Beneath him his mount was trembling.

Before long the mist lifted slightly. He could see frozen water, a river course leading up to a small waterfall that had turned to ice. It shone blue, beautiful yet cold and perilous in the half-light, its motionless juts of water thrust out like spears in mid-flight. Below the icy prongs, sitting on a rock, was a woman — not the hag he had spied shuffling across the valley, but another. One much more pleasing to the eye…

She was older than Hwalchmai, but good to look upon, not toothless or sagging from bearing children year after year. Straight nut-brown hair hung to her waist and her wide eyes were earth-hued. Translucent skin made her eyes appear even darker, and freckles dotted her small nose like flecks of gold. She was dressed all in green, with a red sash tied about her waist.

Green. He shuddered suddenly, and his heart started to pound.

The woman rose and approached him. She held out a sprig of mistletoe, a symbol of peace. "You, young warrior, are the one my husband has been waiting for," she said. "The youth who serves Ardhu, High-King."

Hwalchmai nodded. "If your husband is the green warrior who comes and goes like a being from Otherness, then yes, I am the one who swore to come to him."

She smiled. "So formal. Please, be at peace. I have no quarrel with you. See! I have brought the sacred mistletoe, used in treaties between warring chiefs. Let us give each other the kiss of peace, and then, in trust, we will go back to my husband's domain at Lud's Hole."

Hwalchmai dismounted, and the lady approached him. "What is your name?" he asked. She was tall for a woman, close to his height, and she smelt of the greenwood, fresh and woody, underlaid by slightly acrid tang. He noticed why as he saw that her necklace, which he had first thought was made of coloured beads, was really a string of poisonous, inedible holly-berries. They oozed, white and yellow.

"You may call me Rhagnell," the woman said, and she kissed him soundly on both cheeks. He was all too aware of the proximity of her, the warmth that flowed from her supple frame.

She smiled and held out her hand to him. He marvelled at it, soft and white as if she had never worked in the field or skinned a beast for the pot. "Come, Hwalchmai of the court of Ardhu Pendraec. Come and face your fate, whatever it might be."

###

"Where, by the Sun, is Hwalchmai?" An'kelet whirled in circles in the mist, sure of nothing except that Ardhu was near him, a darker spot in the sombre sheet of greyness. "He was here one moment…."

"And gone the next." Ardhu's face loomed out of the fog, pallid but with eyes on fire. "There is magic here, An'kelet; I'd stake my life on it. Merlin can conjure such mists — he did once so that my father could carry off my mother — and I am sure he is not the only magic-user who has the skill."

"What shall we do, Art?" Ka'hai broke through the fog-bank, brow furrowed with worry and nose red and dripping. "We can't see a thing! We could run right into a hedge of daggers for all we'd know."

"We must move forward," said An'kelet. "If there is someone beyond this mist who has no love of us, they will surely try and hem us in at the valley's exposed heart, attacking from all sides."

"But which way to get back out?" Ka'hai scraped his work-roughened hands through his damp hair, his face red with frustration. "Should we retreat? Going back up will be difficult, the shale is loose."

"Forward — and on foot." Ardhu swung off Lamrai's back. "If we ride about in the fog, the horses might slip and fall. We cannot afford to lose steeds or men in such a manner."

The warband slowly dismounted and Ardhu began to lead the party across the valley floor, over the weather-washed rocks and twisting roots. All conversation died away, sucked into the swirling fog; the atmosphere seemed oppressive, unnatural, and surreal. The hounds, sensing something was amiss, whimpered and hugged the heels of their masters' horses.

Suddenly they saw the cave, gaping like a monstrous mouth in the slate strewn valley side. A rust-hued stalactite hung down from the centre of its roof, the fang of some earth-giant ready to gnash the unwary, while evil humours drifted from its depths, reaching into their nostrils and making them gag.

"Pah!" spat Bohrs. "It reeks of death here. This must be a burial place!"

"Or a place of sacrifice," said An'kelet solemnly.

As they drew closer to the cavern they could see that the place was indeed some kind of hideous shrine, though what spirit demanded such dark worship they did not know. Seven stumpy stones marched across the cave-mouth, forming a barrier against the profane world, and on them rested a line of tiny skulls — the crania of children. More children's skulls could be seen in the gloomy cave interior, some stuck in natural fissures in the stone, others teetering on rotting poles. Lit tallow-cups illuminated the sad, bony faces.

"Truly this is a place of great darkness and despair," Ardhu muttered hoarsely. "Surely this must be the cursed valley mentioned by Merlin, and this cave the abode of the Black Witch daughter of White Witch."

An'kelet stared at the forbidding cave-mouth, face twisted with revulsion. "I think no other place is so accursed in all Prydn, my friend."

At that moment a screech sounded within the cavern, a horrible, throaty sound that echoed on the dank, moss-furred stones. A torch flared, and a wretched, hideous figure shambled into view. It was a woman, old beyond any the warriors had ever seen, her back humped and her left leg dragging from some paralysing malady. Her face resembled a skull, gaunt and taut-skinned, the mouth open and yawing, foul with ulcerations that had eaten away one side of her lip and exposed the gnarled stumps of her teeth. Her eyes were red and rheumy, their unnatural colour made more striking by the blue face-paint she wore. A third eye was drawn in ochre on the centre of her forehead. Stinking rags fluttered around her like malodorous wings; they were dun-coloured and reeking...and looked suspiciously like strips of desiccated skin.

"I am Ah-nis, the Black Witch!" she cried, "servant of Kayagh, Old Woman of Gloominess, the Hag of Winter. Why have you come to my valley, you men of bow and blade? Have you brought an offering for my shrine?" She grabbed one of the skulls from its plinth and cradled it as she would a living child. "Long has it been since the little ones were fed to the Moon, under the wings of Owl-face, the Great Watcher with her wide open eyes! And so the land has diminished, the Old One grows angry, her winters grow wilder. Her Sun raises his head less freely; soon, he may remain in the dark underworld, defeated, and all the wailing of priests in Khor Ghor will not bring His Light to the world!"

"Blasphemer!" cried out Ka'hai from his position behind Ardhu and An'kelet. "You think the works of great priests like the Merlin of Prydn are less than the bloody sacrifices committed by a mad old hag!"

The Black Witch pointed a bony, crooked finger in his direction. "You mock me and recoil in horror, big ugly man, but do your deny your own Ancestors gave the best of their babes to the Moon, and that in those days the folk of our land were in the height of our strength and power?"

The warriors stirred uneasily. Many lives were given to the spirits in the Old Times, to encourage the Sun and make the crops grow, and please old Mother Moon with her bleak skull-eyes. The priests said that if the brightest and best were given to the Ancestors, the ancients would be pleased and ensure fine weather and fine harvests. These practices had dwindled over the years, with offerings of sheep and cattle being given in place of human flesh. Only in rare occasions, when there was famine or plague or war, would it be deemed necessary for the Great Sacrifice.

The hag hobbled forward, leering horribly. "You will fail, all of you. The land cries for your blood. It may not be given on an altar, but that sacrifice will you make."

One of the lower ranks of warriors, Nerthac, gave a shout and swung his horn-filted dagger at the crone's midriff. A terrible shriek left her tumour-swollen lips and she leapt upon him like some grotesque, hopping spider, tearing at his face and throat with her twisted nails, snapping at his exposed flesh with rank green teeth.

Nerthac fell back, screaming, with the hag on top of him. Nerthac's friend, Cacamuri, rushed forward and tried to seize Ah-nis by her matted hair, but she turned on him with startling agility and grabbed his own long braids, bouncing his skull off the valley floor until the blood rushed from lips and nose.

"Do not underestimate me!" cried Ah-nis. "I am She who is in every Shadow, who guides the fatal arrow to its target, who judges the fatal blow. See me and fear me, men of the West! I will have what has long been due to me, blood and honour."

The men were beginning to waver. Other men they would have attacked and hewed at until either they or their opponents were slain. But this creature, frenzied and hideous…they did not know how to react. She was a woman, but not just any woman; a priestess certainly, and maybe more. It might bring the wrath of the Ancestors if she was killed — a punishment of blighted crops and empty cradles. The risk was too great.

Ardhu saw the paling faces, hands reaching to clasp talismans, lips moving in silent prayer. Adrenaline pumped through his body. He had to act quickly, or the lines would break and the warband would break asunder, to become lost in the sorcerous mist in the valley.

Drawing Carnwennan in a flash of light, he suddenly urged Lamrai forward and hurled the dagger at the Black Witch daughter of White Witch. The blade took the crone in the throat, burying itself deeply. She stumbled back, releasing Cacamuri, who crawled away, moaning and clutching his shattered nose. Hands fluttering, Ah-nis collapsed against the stone stumps at the mouth of the cave, knocking over skulls and tallow cups. The flames from the cups caught her skirts of dry skin and they began to smoulder, releasing an awful reek that turned the contents of one's stomach to bile.

Ardhu threw Lamrai's reins to An'kelet, and leaping from the saddle raced towards the thrashing figure of Ah-nis. He grabbed her hair and dragged her up, plucking his dagger from her flesh with his free hand. "Whatever you are, it is time for you to meet yours gods," he said. "You have been too long living in your past. You will seal this place of dread with one final sacrifice — yours."

The witch grinned at him, light already dimming in her eyes. Blood bubbled on her lips as she grated, "So be it, it is as the Owl-faced one decrees. One cannot live till Eventide whom the Old One has touched at dawn! Remember this well, man. I can see Her behind your shoulder, looking with her wide-spiralled eyes. The land cries out for mighty sacrifice, and my old flesh will not suffice."

A shiver went up Ardhu's spine at all this talk of death and the ancient spirit-mother, whose plaque he knew so well on one of the five trilithons inside Khor Ghor. All men met her, eventually, for that is the fate of men, but it seemed that the hag was cursing him, bringing evil in where there was none before.

"Be still, you monster. If ever you served this land's good, it was long ago, and now you are nothing but a blight." He brought Carnwennan down again, glittering in the fog, and clove the witch's skull near in twain with the might of his blow.

The fear that had taken many of his men evaporated. They circled back round and crowded into the cave, casting down the pitiful skeletal remains in every nook and cranny, turning over the witch's big bronze cauldron and sending its rank, gelatinous contents spilling across the cave floor. The liquid mingled with Ah-nis's blood and a hissing went up like a thousand serpents.

At the back of the cave, Ardhu came across the Black Witch's sacrificial altar, a block of sandstone with a natural dip in the top. Livid stains marred its surface, and shrivelled offerings he did not want to begin to think about lay scattered at the base. On top, in the hollow, lay an ancient bronze razor, green with age, the surface decorated by ancient patterns. Old as it was, the blade was honed to sharpness; its edge winked wickedly in the dim light.

Carefully Ardhu picked it up and held it out to show his men. "The Razor of the Black Witch. Surely this will be the tool to shear the bristles of T'orc...though an evil thing it seems."

An'kelet gazed toward the entrance of the unwholesome cave. "It is — so let us fare forth and use it, then break it to make it dead. We must waste no more time; the mist is lifting."

Sure enough rags of fog were sailing by, shredded on a rising breeze. Feeble sunlight played off the pointed white stones that littered the bleak valley.

Ardhu grinned and ran out into the burgeoning sunlight, swinging lithely onto Lamrai's back. "Come, warriors of the West, raise your bows and keep your hands close to dagger-hilts!" he cried. "We go forward now to finish the task that has been laid upon us — to slay the boar from the North that plagues our land!"

CHAPTER EIGHTEEN

A hard ride of several days brought Hwalchmai to Lud's hole, the abode of the Green Rider and of Rhagnell, his wife. It stood in an area of ancient woodland, with a row of great natural rocks rising up behind it like a row of black fingers clutching at the skies. Clouds scudded over their tips, dappling their flanks with light and shadow, making the landscape truly look like the abode of gods and giants.

Lud's hole itself lay in a slight dip surrounded by dark trees. Serrated rocks stuck up, the bones of a fallen god, forming a natural barrier. At one end, the boulders gapped away revealing a dark cleft that plummeted straight down into the earth. Above the lightless entrance hung great wreaths of mistletoe and holly.

Rhagnell dismounted and beckoned for Hwalchmai to do the same. She led the horses to a ramshackle pen beside the cavern and hastily fed and watered them. Then she approached Hwalchmai, her brown eyes solemn, her long straight hair swinging in the breeze. "Do you still dare to set your head on my husband's block?" she asked.

"I am a man of my word," he said resolutely.

Rhagnell went to the cave mouth, beckoning for Hwalchmai to follow. The entrance was dark and gloomy, lit only by small flickering pots of tallow in crevasses on the walls. Incense-cups were billowing, filling the air with the exotic scents…but they did not hide the underlying reek, sweet and sickly, of decay. Of rotten flesh.

"What is that smell?" Hwalchmai grimaced, raising a hand to his mouth.

Rhagnell's lips turned up at the corner. "Can you not guess? It comes from the others who have played — and lost — the beheading game." She took one of the tallow cups from its niche on the wall and held it aloft. On a little ledge near the roofline sat a dozen human heads, preserved by drying or by rubbing them with unguents and oils. Their eyes were gone but had been replaced by coloured stones; their skin was like tanned leather, brown and ropy.

Hwalchmai winced and glanced away, his hand instinctively going to his dagger.

A flight of stairs descended from this gallery of death, leading to another antechamber. Rhagnell went down them, solemn, stately, and Hwalchmai followed, cautious, unsure of what he would find.

When the young warrior reached the room below, he was amazed at how welcoming it seemed. A fire roared in a hearth, the smoke funnelling through a channel in the rock to reach the outside. The floor was strewn with sweet rushes, and herbs hung from above in woven nets, their fragrance, mingling with the scent of the incense cups, blotting out the reek of the preserved heads. A bench ran along one wall, and at the end of it sat the Green Man himself.

He was not in full ceremonial dress, although his shaggy robe was dyed green. He wore no verdant stain on his face and Hwalchmai could now see that he was old, over forty summers by the deep lines round his eyes and the grey streaks in his beard. So, he was not a man even in his prime...and yet he showed no sign of weakness, his legs sturdy as tree-trunks, his belly broad, and his shoulders wide and straining against the material of his tunic. He did not glance up as Rhagnell and Hwalchmai entered the chamber, but toyed with something that lay across his knees, hidden by the fall of his clothing and the shadows in the cave.

He looked up as Hwalchmai drew close, and he grinned. "So you have come, boy! Good, I need some sport to pass the winter. See...I have prepared for your coming!" He lifted the object on his lap, and Hwalchmai saw that it was his magic double-bladed axe. The Green Man had been honing it, sharpening the blade with a whetstone until its edge shone like cold fire.

Hwalchmai shuddered.

The Green Man hauled himself to his feet. He was a big man, taller than most in Albu, perhaps due to some ancestry from the Men of the Ice Seas, who were often tall as trees, or so it was said. "Don't look so stricken, lad," he rumbled, still grinning in his unsettling way. His teeth, for a man his age, were very white and even, with long canines that gave him a wolfish demeanour. "I'm not going to eat you. Indeed, I am going to give you a fair chance. I will not ask you to lay your head on the block tonight — it is not the auspicious time, the act must be done when the Moon is dark. That time will be in three days, and until then you will be fed and given a soft bed and well taken care of by Rhagnell. You can even leave if you wish...that's if you could bear the shame of such cowardice. What is your name, boy?"

Hwalchmai held his head high. "I am Hwalchmai, Hawk of the Plain, cousin to Ardhu, chieftain of Prydn, and of the High-clan of Belerion."

"A noble heritage. I would be glad to have your head decorate my hall. I am called Bresalak...the Contentious."

"A fitting name for you, for so you are," murmured Hwalchmai.

Bresalak ignored his comment. "Tell me, Hwalchmai of the high-clan of Belerion… what gift did my wife Rhagnell give you today?"

Hwalchmai stirred uneasily, ill at ease with this unexpected line of questioning. "Nothing that would bring you dishonour."

"Did I imply that I thought it would?" Bresalak roared with laughter and smote his knees with a hand. "By the gods, you are a strange fellow, Hwalchmai. But come, I ask a question. Show me what Rhagnell gave you."

"Do as he bids…" Rhagnell, standing near his shoulder, pushed him forward. "He will know if you lie; he can read men's truth."

Grimly, Hwalchmai leaned toward the green warrior and gave him the kiss of peace on his cheek. "This token of peace was the gift of the lady," he said. "I trust you will honour it…until the time when the beheading game must take place."

Bresalak laughed again, but there was a strange, strained note in his laughter. "Of course. Now I must go hunting in the woods and leave you here in my domain. Rhagnell will feed you and show you to your sleeping quarters. We will speak again tomorrow. Have a restful night, lord Hwalchmai."

With that, he gathered up his green robe, tossed a cloak about his shoulders, and strode from the cave.

"Sit." Rhagnell pointed Hwalchmai in the direction of the bench. He sat down and she brought him a handled beaker of heather-beer and a wooden platter of meat and cheese. When he had eaten his fill, she took his arm and guided him into an antechamber, where a bed of furs and sheepskins lay on the floor. Tallow lights hung suspended from the ceiling, casting flickering shadows around the walls.

"You shall stay here until the beheading game takes place," she said. "Sleep well, Hawk of the Plain."

She retreated, her long skirts and long hair rustling. Hwalchmai lay down, pulling a sheepskin over himself, watching water bead on the cavern roof. He swore to himself that not only he would not sleep well in this eldritch place, he would not sleep at all.

But despite his vows to keep wakeful, Hwalchmai dozed off sometime in the early hours of the morn. He was woken, suddenly, by the mournful hoot of an owl in the woods outside the cave. He sat up, heart hammering. An owl's cry was no good omen; the owl with its huge flower-like eyes was sacred to the Guardian.

Crawling out of the sheepskins, he pushed back the hanging that fronted the chamber and slipped out. The tallow cups had burnt down, and the only light came from the sullen glow of the hearth. Rhagnell was there, sitting cross-legged by the dying embers, crooning words he did not understand to something that lay in her lap. Her face was painted with strange signs and suddenly looked old, like that of a crone. She turned as he came into the room, and he hesitated, grimacing, as he noticed that on her lap she held a human head. She was oiling it, rubbing preservatives into the tanned leather skin.

"Are you repulsed?" she asked calmly, putting down the grisly artefact. "Do I frighten you?" She rose and walked towards him. He could smell the scent of the unguents she'd rubbed on the skull oozing from her skin, saw where sweat had tracked through her ceremonial face-paint.

He was too polite, in this strange house, to say ill words of her and maybe offend. Admitting fear was also not for a man and warrior of Ardhu's warband. "I am not afraid," he said. "Although I find this a strange house. But I would expect nothing more when its master is the green-faced rider."

Rhagnell laughed. "Do you find me fair, lord Hwalchmai?" She whirled on her bare feet, and suddenly he was all too aware of the thinness of her robe and how it clung to her flesh with sweat and scented oil.

He stared at his feet. "I found you fairer without the paint," he said, trying to make light.

"Ah, but this," she pointed to her face, "is what I must wear, to speak with the spirits of the men my husband has killed. A face half of shadow, because I must speak with shades. It is something I have always done, for I have that gift. If you were my man, instead of Bresalak, would you forbid me to wear my dark face and walk only in the world of light?"

"Lady," he said, "if I were your man, I would give you free will to do as you would. It would not be my place to stop you from speaking to those beyond the Western Door."

She smiled, her teeth glowing white against her artificially blackened lips. "A good answer, my brave young Hwalchmai. "Now kiss me to prove your words are true, to prove that you are my friend."

He hesitated. "What of Bresalak?"

"He is far away on a midnight hunt, tracking down the wild one with his branching horns. Besides, there is no harm in it. Another kiss for peace and one for friendship." She reached up and plucked another sprig of mistletoe from a bunch that hung from a hook on the roof, and handed it to Hwalchmai. He took the green shoot, but to his embarrassment could think of naught but that the plant was also linked with fertility, its white juices resembling the seed of a man.

Rhagnell laughed. Hwalchmai almost fancied that she knew where his thoughts were leading, and he blushed red to the roots of his hair. The dark-eyed wife of the Green man reached out and touched his chin, drawing his face towards her with her finger. "Mistletoe is the key that opens all doors," she said softly, watching as he blushed even deeper at the double meaning in her words.

Struggling, he found his tongue. "I do not think its use is always well advised."

"Ardhu Pendraec teaches his warriors much in the way of courtesy and self-sacrifice," said Rhagnell, still caressing Hwalchmai's face. "He must be an extraordinary being... as he is barely more than a boy himself."

"He is extraordinary. And I am his kin."

"Go now, then, Hwalchmai." She leaned in and kissed him, first his cheek and then, grasping his shoulders, his mouth. "But remember, in two days the Moon will be in the correct phase. Bresalak will wish to commence the beheading game."

Hwalchmai returned to his chamber and fell into the sheepskins and furs. He tossed restlessly, sweat beading on his skin. He felt feverish; he hoped he was not becoming ill. The idea of offering his neck to the green-faced warrior seemed utter madness now...surely he must have been ensorcelled to follow such a doomed path. And then there was Rhagnell, loathly as she caressed the severed head of one of Bresalek's victims, but also filling him with a desire he dared not slake. He thought with both pleasure and despair of her dark, questioning eyes, and her wandering, oil-smeared fingers on his face. Fingers that had caressed a withered death's head...

Night passed into morning, and he heard the roar and bellow of Bresalek returning to Lud's hole. He wandered from his sleeping space, bleary-eyed, in time to see the massive man stride into the chamber, a deer slung over his shoulders. He hurled it to the ground and began to skin it, uncaring of the blood and innards that slopped across the floor.

Excited, Rhagnell knelt beside him, helping clean out the carcass. Her arms were red with gore to the shoulder; daubs of red marred her face. She was truly the loathly lady again, the tender of the dead, aiding her monstrous, surreal husband with the fruits of the hunt.

"There will be fine venison for your meal tonight, Hawk of the Plain!" boomed Bresalek, wiping his besmirched hands on his baggy trews. "Your last meal, maybe... if that is what the spirits will."

He got up from the floor, and approached the silent youth in the corner. "And what did you do when I was gone? Did my woman Rhagnell entertain you?"

"She entertained me as every woman should entertain a visitor in her household."

"Indeed. And did she give you anything? Anything at all... Come, show me, boy... I will know if you lie."

Hwalchmai stared into the inscrutable face, Sun-bronzed and leathery, with deep, green-flecked eyes under grizzled brows. "Two kisses, that was all, one for peace and one for friendship, and I give them in return to you." And he duly set the kisses of peace and of friendship on the Green Man's cheeks, though he felt inclined to neither.

The Green Man roared with laughter and stretched out his immense, muscle- bound arm, beckoning Rhagnell to bring him a beaker of mead. "Peace there will be until the Moon's phase is right," he said. "And aye, we can even be friends until that time. So for another day enjoy my home, and the company of my woman, and let us not think about the future."

Finishing with the deer, Bresalak went outside and did not return. Rhagnell continued tending to the meat her husband had left, and then turned her attention to the deer's skin, scraping it clean with an old stone scraper and stretching it out on a drying frame made from branches.

"Where has Bresalak gone?" asked Hwalchmai.

"He hunted deer, now he seeks boar," she replied. "Just like your lord, Ardhu."

Hwalchmai signed. "Who I should be with now! I am a man or honour and would not break my word, but tell me, Rhagnell wife of Bresalak, why should I die just for some whim of your husband? We have no real cause for enmity."

She sighed. "Bresalak was touched by the spirits when he was young. He ran wild in the forest. He saw He-who-is-Oldest beneath his thunder-oak, antlers springing from his brow and leaves spilling from his mouth. It changed him. He devoted himself to his Lord of the wildwood, but there was one thing he could not accept — that he, like the foliage, would wither and die and a new young king supplant him. So, every year, he has chosen the best and brightest to play the beheading game...when he takes the head he feels the mightiness of the slain pass to him, renewing him for another year."

"He is mad," muttered Hwalchmai. "No mortal man may live forever."

"No, no man may," said Rhagnell, and she would say no more.

The day passed as if in a dream. Hwalchmai wandered outside, walking the woods of that wild place in a haze of anxious anticipation. Wind buffeted him, the trees roared and swept down with long branches. Everything around him seemed unusually bright, unusually vibrant — the rich greens of the mosses and leaves, the violet blue of the winter skies. And the smells! Water and damp earth, cold frost, and distant snow being gradually swept over the higher moorlands. All fresh and alive, taunting him with their beauty... for unless fate intervened, this would be the last such beauty his eyes would behold, for tomorrow he must face the Green Man's axe.

He wandered back to Lud's hole later that afternoon, after watching the Sun impale Himself upon the craggy fangs of rock that topped the long moor beyond the deep earth cave. Inside the fastness, Rhagnell had cooked some of the venison brought home by Bresalek; Hwalchmai ate in silence, and Rhagnell said nothing either, but merely stared into the fire with a strange lost look on her face.

As the tallow cups sputtered, and shadows danced around the main chamber, Hwalchmai departed for his room. He lay down but had been there only a short while before a shadow filled the stone doorway. He reached for his dagger instinctively... but let it drop with a clatter when he saw that his visitor was none other than Rhagnell.

Her hair fell unbound around her, autumn leaf hued, gold and brown and red combined. It was smooth and shone like metalwork, like Sun on a shield. A flowing robe, white as the Moon, and tied at the waist by a sash of green-dyed cloth, tumbled loosely to her ankles. She walked with purpose and her eyes swallowed the feeble, wavering light.

Hwalchmai propped himself up on his elbow. "Lady, what do you do here? I beg you let me rest and dream, for it may be the last night I can do so."

She knelt beside him on the sheepskins. "I have been here near enough three times three years, Hwalchmai, ever since Bresalak brought me here as a young and frightened girl. My father was a prince of the north; he traded me like a piece in a game in order to avoid Bresalek's axe. I have been loyal to my husband, and tended to all his needs. I have been a good wife to him. But I can sense a change in him, a weakening, and my own heart is changing too, and for the first time I feel sullied, not like his wife, but his captive, his slave. He is no longer the great oak, stalwart against the wind — he is the vine withering on the ground, its sap spent. We have no children, Hwalchmai."

She spread her arms, the loose white linen floating around her so that she almost looked like a spirit. "Hwalchmai, untie my sash from my waist and keep it safe with you when you go to face Bresalek tomorrow. My token to you… maybe a help, and maybe not. It is in the hands of the gods and they can be cruel."

Hands slightly shaking, Hwalchmai reached up to untie the moss-green sash. It tumbled in verdant folds to the floor. His hands then drifted to the front of her robe, where the linen gaped with the unfastening of the sash, revealing a provocative slice of pale skin. Gently, he pulled back the robe from her shoulders and let it drop alongside the sash. She had a lean, athletic body, with narrow hips and round, firm breasts that had been tattooed with spirals. He let his fingers trace the line of the tattoos, seeking, exploring. She wrapped her arms around his neck and drew his face up to hers and kissed him on the lips, three times, but no longer was it the kiss of friendship or of peace, but the kiss of a lover.

He pushed her down into the skins, admiring the play of the softly flickering tallow-lamps across her nakedness. He ran his hands through her glossy hair, spreading it out across the sheepskin, noticing for the first time that she still bore mistletoe, but it was artfully threaded through her locks, the berries cool and soft against his fingertips — much like Rhagnell's naked flesh.

She realised he had found the berries and smiled, coiling around him like a cat, drawing him down against her pliant warmth. "I am the key, Hwalchmai," she said.

Rhagnell left Hwalchmai's bed just before dawn. He heard her go, bare feet slapping on the stone floor of the cavern. He lay still for a few more minutes then rose himself, dressing quickly and binding on his belt with its daggers and axe. Last, he picked up Rhagnell's discarded sash and tied it tightly around his waist.

He went from the cave and out to the green grass before Lud's Hole. A sprinkle of snow had fallen in the night, and the rising Sun glittered on frozen fronds and boughs. A clean wind was blowing from the West, bringing the promise of kinder, warmer days.

He wanted to live to see those days…

Suddenly a shadow fell across him, wide as a broad-backed bull. Bresalek stood before him, grinning, his huge hands planted on his hips. He had been successful in his hunt again, but this time he had downed a wild boar. It lay over his muscled shoulders, its blood trickling down his tunic. With a grunt

230

he heaved it away and beckoned to Hwalchmai with a red-stained hand.

"Come closer, boy. Don't stand gawping like some sheep! This is the morning of the Beheading Game. The game I always win."

Hwalchmai approached the giant as bidden. A strange calm filled him. The Sun was brightening, sending long shafts of light between the spindly trees that surrounded Lud's hole. Surely, surely, he could not die this morning....

"So what did you do on your last evening, boy?" asked Bresalak. "Did you drink? Did you hope? Did my dear woman Rhagnell try to assuage your fears?"

"Indeed she did."

"And what did she give you this time? No more kisses of peace, I'll wager, for this morn no peace can be between us, only rivalry and death."

"No, no kisses of peace..." said Hwalchmai, unable to restrain an ironic grin. To think he had cuckolded this green monster, in his own den!

Bresalek's countenance whitened as he guessed the meaning of his victim's words. His gaze fell to Rhagnell's sash, bound tightly about the young warrior's waist. His eyes turned black as obsidian.

"To the place of Beheading –now!" he roared.

He stormed into the wood and Hwalchmai followed him. Soon they reached a raised mound with trees standing sentinel all around it. A single squat stone stood on the summit, a block of worn sandstone streaked with ores that turned its surface red as blood. It was aligned on a gap in the crags beyond, where the Moon would rise and dance every nineteen turns of the Sun.

Bresalek gestured angrily to the worn block. "Kneel down and part your hair," he ordered, "as I did for you in the hall of Ardhu Pendraec. Otherwise, be known as craven, and un-man...and I swear I will kill you anyway, with honour or not — the choice is yours!"

"I keep my word," said Hwalchmai and he dutifully knelt before the stump and laid his head upon its surface. He wondered how many others had knelt in such a fashion, and how much blood had bathed that single worn-down monolith.

"Are you ready, boy?" Bresalak was swinging his great double-headed axe, the muscles rippling in his enormous arms. "Have you made your peace with your gods?"

Hwalchmai's eyes darted, as his mind frantically worked out ways to distract the giant. "Wait! Let me change the place where I kneel. I am ashamed that I die without great conflict of arms. Therefore, if is fitting I die gazing into the shadows and not at Bhel's bright and victorious face."

Bresalek snorted. "I care not which way you kneel, head to the East or to the West. All that interests me is taking that head and adding it to my collection. Be assured I will make that slut Rhagnell dress it and lie with it at her side…since she favoured you so much!"

Hwalchmai wriggled round the pillar until he felt the rays of the strengthening Sun warm his back. Bresalek stomped up in front of him, brandishing his axe. His movements were jerky, erratic, dictated by fury rather than by the rules of the Beheading Game. His hair and beard bristled and his cheeks were purple with simmering rage — uttering a strangled cry, he swung the axe upwards, preparing for the death-stroke. The axe-head caught the early Sun-light and turned to a ball of lambent flame…

The light was full on Bresalek's face, pure golden light from the East. He faltered, suddenly blinded, as the Sun rose even higher in the sky, its radiant beams smiting deep into his eyes like the spear of the Young Son who had been reborn at Solstice and now slowly grew towards the flame of his power at Midsummer. With an angry, thwarted yell, he lashed out wildly with his axe at the crouched figure of Hwalchmai.

And missed.

The deadly blade of the axe thudded against the earth, cutting into the icy ground and sticking there.

Before Bresalek had the chance to pluck it free, Hwalchmai leaped to his feet and charged at the giant man. "One blow you had….and yet I still stand and breathe upon the earth!" he cried triumphantly. "Now it is your turn to meet the fate you gave so readily to others!"

Bresalek cried out, a note of fear in his voice. He suddenly looked old, weak — as Rhagnell had said, a withering vine, ready to return to the earth, where he would moulder alongside a million fallen leaves, his flesh and bones feeding and nurturing all manner of living things.

He tried to flee, to make a mad dash into the trees, but Hwalchmai flung himself on Bresalek's back, kicking his legs from under him and bringing him to the ground. Tearing off Rhagnell's sash, Hwalchmai looped it around Bresalek's throat and twisting with all his strength. Breath cut off, the Green Man thrashed and flailed, his hands scrabbling uselessly at the ever-tightening garrotte. Hwalchmai continued to twist the sash with one free hand, while drawing his flanged axe with the other.

"Go now to the Ancestors, Green Man," he said. "On this winter's morn. I, Hawk of the Plain, have won the Beheading game."

With that he struck Bresalek between the eyes with his axe, releasing the life-spirit from his skull. The huge body slumped into the grass, and Hwalchmai knelt by it and cut off the huge scowling head. He carried it to the pillar on the mound and set it on top, gazing sightlessly into the strengthening Sun that had brought ruin to its owner.

Then, arms and face and garments streaked with blood, Hwalchmai walked back to Lud's hole. Rhagnell stood outside the cavern, anxious and pale. When she saw his gore-drenched visage, she sobbed briefly, then wiped the tears away with her hand. "So it is done. Bresalek is dead."

Hwalchmai nodded. "Yes, and I must now hasten to join my kinsman, Ardhu, in his hunt for the boar T'orc."

"And what of me? What will become of me now that Bresalek is no more?"

"I leave that up to you," he said. "I would not compel you to come with me, for once already a man compelled you to do his bidding. But if you would ride with me, and share my bed, and dwell with me at the hall of Kham-El-Ard as my wife, it would bring me great pleasure."

"So be it," she said, and she ran round to fetch the horses and provisions for their journey.

Before bright Bhel Sun-face had reached his midday height, they were away toward the lands of the West, while behind them the black crows of the Death-goddess plucked the eyes from the severed head of Bresalek the Green Man and feathered their nests with his hair.

233

CHAPTER NINETEEN

At Kham-El-Ard, Fynavir felt full of unease. No word had come from Ardhu, not one message from the West. Traders from the Ridgeway spoke of the Chief Boar's rampages and how Ardhu's warband could not seem to catch up with it. "It is born of magic," they said, shaking their heads darkly. "A creature from the underworld. Maybe no man can ever harm it, and Ardhu will chase it till the day the Sun falls from the sky…"

Fynavir shivered, pulling her red fox-skin cloak tighter about her shoulders. She tried to set her mind to the stitching on a pair of shoes; her bone needle slipping in and out, in and out of the fine deer-hide, trailing a piece of dried gut thread. Outside, the wind was buffeting the Great Hall on its crooked hill, sighing in the eaves like a living thing. And perhaps it was a living thing of sorts, the breath of the world that could whisper the first hints of spring or scream like a foul and malevolent hag. It was screaming today, its sound an incessant torment.

"Ardhu, I pray you come back soon," Fynavir murmured to herself. The bone needle flashed in and out. In and out… "We need to set things right between us. A king should not be chasing across country on some fool's errand, even if a worthy one… He should be in his high seat, beside his queen. He wants an heir, I know he blames me that there is not one, but I will show him if only he will return to me. Prydn will have an heir!"

A sudden urgent rapping on the hall's broad door made Fynavir jump in fright. "Oh!" she exclaimed in alarm, as the bone needle pierced her finger. A drop of blood fell into her lap, soiling her tunic. "Who is there?"

The door creaked open. A dwarfish girl hopped in, dragging a clubfoot, and stood without fear or deference. Her forehead was abnormally broad and bulbous, and protruding eyes stared in different directions. Despite her unappealing visage, she had beautiful reddish-gold curls spiralling past her twisted hips. Fynavir recognised her as Brangyan, one of the Ladies of the Lake, her deformity marking her from birth as one touched by the world of spirits. And so it often was… children born with extra fingers, webbed toes, a squint, or a clubfoot were often taken in by the priests and priestesses of various orders, for it was clear the spirits or gods had marked them.

"Greetings, Brangyan of the Lake." Fynavir inclined her head politely. A

234

little knot of fear twisted in her belly — could this strange girl be bringing ill news? "What business have you in Kham-El-Ard this day?"

"I bear greetings from the Lady Mhor-gan, sister of Ardhu, sister of ravens, all-seeing lady of the funeral rite. She asks that you visit her in the lake valley where our Order dwells. She wishes to speak with you on a matter of import."

Fynavir's cheeks turned whiter than her hair. Ardhu. It had to be something to do with Ardhu. Maybe he was hurt...or worse. Or was it An'kelet? She wanted to grab Brangyan and shake her until she spewed the answer, but she knew that was not the way. "I will come at once," she said, scrambling for her thickest cloak against the biting wind. She could feel eyes of the women and men in the hall on her, inquisitive, concerned.

"Lady!" Her attendant, Khelynnen, a pretty maiden from Place of Light, tugged on her sleeve, trying to draw her back. "You can't go tramping in the marsh-lands dressed like that! You need felt boots, an otter skin! And if you must go, shouldn't you take one of the lads as a guard? The days still draw in early, and both strange men and spirits may fare abroad in the night-mists!"

Fynavir tore the girl's fingers from her sleeve. "Peace...I am called, I must go." Quickly, she went with Brangyan into the outer ward of Kham-El-Ard, and down the slope past the defensive ditches with their rows of glistening wooden spikes.

"Your servant-woman need not have feared." Brangyan brought from beneath her cloak a small bow made just for one of her height. "I am the best archer in my order, and my arrows are treated with poisons that will stop a man's heart within a beat."

Together they walked down the well-worn track to the old Henge, before turning upstream and crossing the main fords of Abona, where River Mother's consort Borvoh the Boiling churned in the weir, restless from the heavy winter rains.

After a short journey through a land of withies ands soggy pools, they began a slow descent into long valley enclosed on either side by steep banks, though the northern side was higher and steeper, a barricade that cut the valley off from the sacred landscape of Khor Ghor.

However, the vale-side was a sacred place in itself and had been for many lifetimes, ever since the first Merlin had floated the skystones on rafts down the shining coils of Mother Abona, from the Western mountain known as God-of-Bronze. Tumuli littered the high northern slopes, facing toward the Great Temple on the Plain beyond, while on the far side of the river, beyond stands of deciduous trees, new farming systems had sprung up and a great livestock enclosure ringed the brow of the Hill of Ogg the Eloquent, where it was said the sky first whispered words to men and gave them the art of speech.

Brangyan led Fynavir away from the trackway that split the valley's heart and toward another fording place in the river, which surged into two channels before forming a small, mirror-bright lake. A wooden causeway jutted into the waters, its edges fringed by sentinel reeds, and at the end stood a roundhouse with a sloped roof that touched the water.

The House of the Nine Ladies of the Lake.

Brangyan gestured for Fynavir to mount the causeway and enter the hut. Nervously she walked along the creaking planks, glancing back hopefully at her companion, but Brangyan remained behind in the faded afternoon light.

Fynavir entered the roundhouse and glanced around. A fire burned in a hearth of stone slabs, its smoke spiralling up through the smoke-hole in the ceiling. Fresh herbs and medicinal plants hung from the rafters. Offerings lay on a many-shelved shrine at the back — crow feathers, a broken archer's wristguard, a shard of the spiralled pottery used before the Tin-Men came and found scattered all over most sites of veneration. Mhor-gan, Ardhu's sister, was kneeling by the fire, tending the flames that must never be allowed to die. "I am glad you have come." She spoke without glancing up at Fynavir. "We must talk."

Fynavir felt her heart begin to thud. "Is it...news of Ardhu? Tell me, sister, I cannot bear it! Is he dead?"

"No, No!" Mhor-gan rose and steadied her with a comforting hand. "Calm yourself. The Ladies of the Lake have many eyes, and we can assure you that Ardhu is hale and well — although he has not yet found his quarry, for the one that trained the beast made sure her minions served her well. However, T'orc's reign of terror is nearing an end — winter is almost over, the skies are growing bright. Chief Boar's men are weary of flight and want to return to their own hearths, while T'orc snaps at his own handlers...he wants naught more than to eat acorns and rut with wild sows in the forest! Soon, the warband will catch them, and Ardhu will mete out the justice of the King of Prydn."

"Why have you called me here, if not for news of my husband?"

"It is of you I wish to speak, not my brother. Have you forgotten what night is coming up soon?"

"All days have become as one since the warband went seeking the dread boar. Enlighten me, sister."

"It is Y'melc, the feast of Lambing. The beginning of spring. The day is

236

ruled by Fiery Arrow, who breathes on the hearth-fire and wields both flame and lightning."

Fynavir nodded. "I know of Her. She has a sanctuary in the land of my birth, where the tallest stones in all Ibherna stand guard. I remember a little of her rites from my childhood, but I was sent to the northlands as a young maid and have dwelt in many foreign homes since then, and my memory does not serve me well. As a priestess, I beg you offer me guidance, that I may do the right thing on her Feast and give no offence to gods or men."

Mhor-gan smiled. "You must stand as Brygyndo that night, as queen of your people and the Fiery One's representative. You must pass from house to house and receive gifts, and in turn, confer luck and blessings on the people of Kham-El-Ard and Place-Of-Light. Then you will be put to bed with the bride-doll of the goddess lying beside you, and a magic wand hewn of an ash-limb; these shall be burned on a sacred bone-fire the next morning at Sunrise, and the ashes scattered over the fields to make them fruitful."

Fynavir's mouth worked; her eyes were bitter. "I am hardly a good choice if it is fruitfulness the people crave. So far, I am barren, and they all know my shame. The old women laugh behind their hands whenever I pass, or cluck with mock sorrow!"

Mhor-gan ran a practised hand over Fynavir's stomach, pressing, kneading, and eventually coming to rest near her hipbone. "When a new spirit is ready to go into the world, you will quicken. It is only a matter of time."

Fynavir hung her head; she could not look into the other woman's face beneath its loops of dark braids. "I am filled with doubt...I once heard a rumour among maidens that if ...if another is in your mind beside the one to whom you are vowed...that the spirits will send no child?"

Mhor-gan laughed out loud, her teeth flashing. "Ah Fynavir... Ardhu has no other woman, he is enamoured of you! He defied the Merlin to wed you — no mean feat! What you heard was the chatter of silly virgins... Children are born from love, from hate, from long-time lovers and those who seek merely to ease their flesh on a lonely night! It is all in the hands of the spirits how and when the gift of babies arrive."

Fynavir still did not raise her eyes; scarlet stained her cheeks. For all her learning, Mhor-gan did not realise that she spoke of herself, not of Ardhu!

"Thank you for your words of comfort," she finally managed. "I will prepare for the feast of Y'melc, as you have directed, even though I am not worthy to emulate such an esteemed One as High Brygyndo."

"You are worthy in the eyes of the tribes. People far and wide have heard that you are the daughter of Mevva the Intoxicator. They hear tell of how your flesh is white like the chalk that is the bones of the earth, white like Mother Moon who draws the shades of the dead to her. To them, you are a symbol of white-cliffed Albu itself, and only the king of that land may possess you." She poked at the fire, her eyes suddenly shadowed. "And that is another reason why I have summoned you here today. It is not Ardhu's safety that worries me, but yours. Art has many enemies among the chieftains of Prydn — violent, fractious men who cannot see the good he does. The eyes of Afallan see far, Fynavir, and our ears hear what others miss. Many have spoken treasonously, seeking their own power; they cannot draw the sword from beneath the stone, but they can still abduct the white Queen, the sovereignty of Prydn, and claim king-right through you."

"That is madness!" cried Fynavir. "I am no goddess, I am not my mother! I want no man fighting over me, or treating me like some lucky talisman! I would stain my white hair blue if I thought it would keep these beasts of men away!"

"I fear it would not," Mhor-gan sighed, "not now that they have scent of what they desire — a white Queen, a whole kingdom. So, I beg you, although you must continue in your daily duties, be on your guard till Ardhu returns from the Boar Hunt. Lady Nin-Aeifa and I have gazed into the sacred lake and seen many things; some we fear, some we do not understand — the omens of the Otherworld are often not clear to decipher. But there is sorrow and fear, and love and triumph, a setting Sun and a wan Moon that is yet to rise."

Fynavir returned to Kham-El-Ard, much troubled. But at least she knew that Ardhu and An'kelet were unharmed, which soothed the fears she found hardest to bear. In the days that followed, she tried to cast her worries aside and concentrate on preparing for Y'melc. With deft hands she created the Bride, the god-doll, from dried sheaves of wheat and early flowers. With Khelynnen and other women, she went to the herdsmen to ascertain there would be enough roundels of cheese and pitchers of milk to satisfy all the celebrants, while leaving some to be offered to the Fiery One herself and to any wandering spirits that might chance upon the Feast. Houses were swept out and domestic rubbish tossed into the middens; it was a time when all life would be refreshed and renewed.

The eve of Y'melc soon came, a clear night with a hard frost and many

238

stars. A full Moon, round and yellow as the cheeses that had been prepared for the occasion, hung over the heights of Kham-El-Ard and turned the sacred pool below into a silver mirror that reflected the faces of the nine Ladies of the Lake. The Ladies had gathered at Sundown and poured ewe's milk into the water before bathing in it, one by one. Now they all sat in a semi-circle, tallow cups burning in their hands, singing as they rocked rhythmically from side to side.

Fynavir let Khelynnen robe her in her finest kirtle, dyed red with the root of madder. The girl then combed down her wintry hair and circled her neck with seven rows of northern amber. Great crescent earrings from the mainland coast were placed upon her earlobes and ochre was rubbed on her cheeks. Ready to face her people, Fynavir lifted the Bride, the sacred image of Brygyndo, from its place beside the hearth and carried it into the courtyard, trailing grains of wheat and petals in its wake.

In the centre of the yard the priests of Khor Ghor had come to oversee the lighting of the Fire-Cross of Brygyndo. Although they celebrated the festival of the Ewe's milk, they played but a small part, for Brygyndo was not a spirit of stone or sky but of earth and childbed and hearth-fire. She was a patron of women, and women's lore and mysteries, though smiths revered her too, for her holy fire kept the forge hot and her breath hardened their metals.

Fynavir spotted the Merlin, hawk-faced beneath his hooded robe, and nodded politely in his direction. He frowned back at her, as always, distrust still evident in his black eyes, before turning away to kindle a torch with his strike-a-light. When the torch was ablaze, chasing shadows around the fort, he strode forth and touched the flame to the Cross-of-Brygyndo that the village folk had wrought from river-reeds. It burst into flame and the priests raised it on high and carried it Sun-wise around the enclosure, with its crooked, crazed arms shooting sparks into the darkness and threatening to ignite hair and thatch.

As the wood burned through and flaming fragments tumbled to the ground, the priests placed the Cross on a waiting, unlit pyre at the fortress gates. They blew upon it and chanted over it, and the eternal flame of Fiery-Arrow was kindled from it and roared up into the gloom, lighting the buttressed entranceway to Kham-El-Ard. The watchers roared in delight and ran forward with pieces of kindling, which they thrust into the hottest part of the conflagration. Within minutes, the night was alight with waving brands.

The procession moved down the great hill, following the course of Abona toward the Place-of-Light. Fynavir found herself scooped up with all gentleness by the mighty-armed smith, Ech-tor, the father of Ka'hai, and placed upon a wooden chair which two stout village youths hoisted onto their shoulders. "You are Blessed Brygyndo tonight," Ech-tor said. "Queen of them all. Therefore your feet must not touch the earth."

Laughing and singing, the party made its way through the marshy lands below the Place-of-Light, before winding its way up to the settlement on top of the escarpment. The whole village was ablaze with torches, and women singing and holding out bride-dolls and their own small children for blessing from the goddess.

Fynavir went amongst them in her chair, her own Bride effigy seated beside her, and bestowed on them gifts of grain and milk and cheese. In return they gave her draughts of fermented milk, sweetened with honey, which made her head spin; mostly, she was used to drinking watered-down beer, for the more potent mead was deemed a drink of men. Unless you were Mevva, her mother, whose very name signified the golden drink of the gods.

She shivered. She did not want to think of Mevva, red and carnal, heaping scorn on the children who could never match her. Tonight she would only be Fynavir... and the Bride.

The festivities went on long into the night. Great stars set, and the Moon sailed West and grew small to the eye. Fires burned down, and were relit again, mead and beer flowed free, and mutton was served sizzling on wooden trenchers. Men and women started to dance, weaving round the fires, before leaping across the flames and vanishing into their huts or the nearby bushes.

Fynavir sat in a place of honour outside the headman's dwelling. She was nodding off, her lids heavy from the fermented drink, the battered Bride-doll leaning drunkenly against her shoulder. Khelynnen was completely intoxicated, and lay slumped against her mistress with her mouth open and little ragged snores coming out.

"Khelynnen..." Fynavir dragged herself upright and shook the girl's shoulder. "It is time for us to go. Long past time, I fear."

Heavy-headed, Fynavir stumbled across the settlement, clutching the Bride-doll to her as if it was a child. Khelynnen lurched after her, the bone pin tearing loose from her hair and spilling long dark coils over her befuddled face.

One of the lads who had carried Fynavir's chair from Kham-El-Ard approached them, a well-built fellow with a shock of auburn hair. "I am Drem son of Khas. If it is your will, Lady Fynavir, I will escort you back to Kham-El-Ard."

Fynavir hesitated a moment. There was little to fear for two women walking the short miles between Place-of-Light and Kham-El-Ard. Wild boars and wolves never came so close to human habitations, unless the winter was so hard that they were unnaturally hungry. As for men with bright blades and sharpened arrows, it would take someone extremely brave or foolhardy to mount an attack right on the doorstep of Kham-El-Ard, even with the Bear away chasing the Boar.

And yet Mhor-gan had given her stern warning...

"Yes, we would appreciate your company, Drem, son of Khas," she said, a shiver running down her spine at the memory of the priestess's words. "I am sure you have a very stout arm to defend us from all manner of evil creatures... the hares and badgers, or perhaps old beaver-man in his dam on the river!"

"I will do my best, lady," Drem responded, his crooked teeth flashing in the dimness.

The three made their way down the escarpment, Drem leading, while Fynavir supported the stumbling and complaining Khelynnen with one arm while trying to carry the Bride-doll tucked under the other. She half-wished she had left the girl to sleep off the drink in some hut at Place-of-Light, but Khelynnen was a comely girl and might come to grief among all the high-spirited youths that dwelt there, training to become warriors for Ardhu's cause. Fynavir didn't want to have a serving-girl whose belly would grow big as the full Moon over the next nine months.

Once the little group was on level ground, they headed swiftly across the boggy fields toward the river. The Moon was lost behind the trees, and a sharp breeze, heralding the approach of dawn, blew out of the East and made Fynavir tremble like a leaf in a gale.

Soon they reached the banks of Abona. Fish jumped in the dark, while a night-prowling owl hooted in the distance. Wind hissed in the grass, while trees creaked and groaned, their branches clacking. All natural nightly sounds, noises Fynavir had heard a thousand times before. Why then these feelings of unease, of rising panic, that burned away the warm cloud of drunkenness and made her suddenly, frighteningly sober?

Suddenly she saw it...a metallic glint between the boles of two large oaks. Darkness swirled, and immediately the minute gleam vanished like a firefly snuffed out. But Fynavir sensed that something was out there, in the dark of the woods, and it was watching their progress with hot, intent eyes.

"Quickly, quickly!" She prodded Khelynnen, trying to force her to pick up her feet.

"Lady, I can't," the girl wailed. "So tired…"

Drem turned and glanced at Fynavir and saw the naked fear in her face, and his own big, raw visage whitened. "What is it, Lady Fynavir?" he whispered. "Why do you look so strange?"

She leaned over toward him and hissed in his ear: "There's a man in the bushes, maybe more than one. I can feel eyes watching us."

The youth began to sweat and his eyes widened with terror. He had not foreseen such a thing when he had offered to escort the Queen to Kham-El-Ard. The worst he had expected was to chase off a fox or a hare. Hand shaking, he reached towards the hilt of his dagger, given to him in his manhood rite just two weeks before.

Fynavir grabbed his wrist. "No," she said kindly, "you are too young. I will not have you give your life in a fight you cannot win."

"But Lady, I am sworn to protect you…" he began, but again she shook her head and pressed her finger to his lips.

"Drem, you are more use to me alive than dead. Don't be foolhardy. Do as I tell you, I beg you."

"Yes, Lady. What is your will?"

"We must keep walking, until I say otherwise. Maybe the stranger is just a passing traveller who is curious as to our doings. Maybe he will either come forth in friendship and all will be well, or maybe he will just journey on into the night."

At Fynavir's side, Khelynnen, sensing something was wrong, began to snivel. Fynavir tried vainly to hush her, while keeping attuned to the shadowed trees around her.

There… she heard it now… a heavy footfall to her right, followed by crackling of twigs and branches deeper in the woods. A frond swayed, and she caught a faint glimpse of figures moving, keeping pace with the two women and the lad as they hurried along the banks of the river.

Fynavir stared hard into the darkness that stretched ahead — miles ahead, it seemed. The hill-fort wasn't far away, but she knew these strangers would make their move long before she reached it. But perhaps…perhaps…

She tugged on Drem's sleeve, trying to seem commanding and reassuring at the same time. "They are all around us now. We must assume they are enemies. Drem, did I not hear that you ran straight and true, faster than the other village boys?"

"Anwas the Winged, who rides with noble Ardhu is my brother. He is the fastest runner in the entire West but I am catching up."

"Then go… use those fast feet to fly to Kham-El-Ard. Tell them we have been attacked and that they must bear word to the Merlin and to the Lord Ardhu, wherever he may be."

"Lady, I can't leave you at their mercy…"

"Do as I say — this is my command as your Queen. As Ardhu's woman I am the one most likely to be spared by them, the only one whose life may have value. Go. Go now and the gods give you speed!"

She gave him a hard shove in the back and he staggered out into the path. He cast her one pitying look and then bounded away into the darkness like a frightened deer.

As he broke for freedom, the woods sprang to life. Men jumped out of trees and from behind bushes. Arrows whirred and skittered on the path as they fired at Drem's retreating back. Khelynnen started to scream, till a tall man with stone bracers on either wrist stepped up to her and struck her across the face, knocking her to the ground. She fell instantly silent.

"Stop it! She is just a girl!" Fynavir flung her god-dolly to the ground and raced toward the man looming threateningly over her serving-woman. She noticed that, beside his high status bracers, he also wore a leather jerkin with a plate of gold sewn to the breast, similar to Ardhu's Breastplate of Heaven. However, it was a rectangle rather than a lozenge, and was quite battered.

The man turned to Fynavir and smirked. He was of great height and no longer in the first flush of youth, although there was still a ruined comeliness to his face. Ruined, because one side had been slashed by a dagger in some bygone battle, leaving a gouge from the corner of his eye down to the edge of his mouth. Greying dark hair hung round his shoulders, and his eyes were pale grey flecked with amber. Wolfish eyes, without pity.

"So, you must be the fabled Fynavir, queen to the boy-king Ardhu," he said, eyes raking over her appraisingly. "Many chiefs speak of you beyond Khor Ghor, of your beauty and your otherworldly whiteness, and how you are born of a goddess. How you are Sovereignty, the Land itself, and how any man that possesses you will be the King! "

"Maybe men should talk less of women they haven't met and deal with hardships within their own folds," she shot back icily.

"Although you are white as snow, fire burns within you," he said, nodding. "I like that. I am Melwas, King of the Summer Country, and I claim you here by warriors' right, and from this day forward you shall be as my wife and dwell with me in the Summerlands. Together we will rule

Prydn, and the fledgling boy you wed will fall, toppled like a stone raised in a bed that is too shallow. "

"You are mad!" she cried. "Ardhu will hunt you down and kill you!"

Melwas sneered. "He is far away; do not think rumours of his exploits haven't reached the Summer Country! Indeed, he seems more interested in chasing his wild Boar than he does you, my little snow-white one. Maybe it is animals that hold his fancy, or the pretty man from Ar-morah who they say always rides at his side. But fear not, I will attend to you every night, and soon we will have a whole hut full of sturdy, divine sons!"

She recoiled, though she knew it was useless to run. "You are Moon-mad if you think I'll willingly go with you!"

"You will come with me," he said, an edge of danger in his voice. "And without a fuss. Or... I kill this one, here and now." He grabbed Khelynnen's hair, dragging her to her knees and pressing the blade of his dagger against her throat. "And then I will take my men and burn down your fancy fort and the village on yonder downs. I'll kill the men and children but take the women as rewards for my men, and they will spit and curse you, for it will be your own selfish stubbornness that doomed their menfolk and made them slaves."

Fynavir stared at Khelynnen, who was paralysed with fear, her eyes pleading. She could not be responsible for her death, nor the deaths of any of the people who lived nearby.

"Very well... you have won," she said to Melwas. "I will go to the Summer Country with you. Just leave the innocent folk of Kham-El-Ard in peace."

Melwas let Khelynnen's head fall. She crouched on the ground, weeping. "A wise decision. I would not gladly kill the lowborn; there is no honour in that. Come, woman, I must bind your arms and feet...I will not chance you trying to escape along the road."

Resigned, she meekly extended her hands. Grinning, Melwas tied her wrists and ankles with gut ropes. Lifting her to his shoulder, he carried her into the woods, where she saw the rest of his band waiting, a rag-tag group of hard-faced men armed with bows and staves. They had a cart with them, drawn by a dispirited-looking ox and filled with war-equipment and food supplies. Melwas dumped Fynavir in the cart amidst the bows and baskets; an object for future use, just like the cart's contents, spoils from a bloodless war.

"Don't any of you bastards touch her," he warned the leering men. "Or I'll feed your ballocks to my hounds. You mind she's not damaged in any way on the journey home… she's not some slut; she's going to be my wife."

The warriors prodded the ox with long sticks, and slowly the cart lurched away through the woods. The men roared and jeered, filled with crude mirth. Fynavir lay staring at the lightening sky, trying to hold back tears of rage and fear. Why had she been so foolish, so careless, when she had been warned by Mor-ghan? She was a failure in all she did; it was as if the spirits conspired against her.

"Ardhu… An'kelet… you must find me!" she whispered desperately to the four winds.

Behind her, on the riverbank, the discarded Bride-doll broke apart in the breeze and its bright fragments dispersed upon the flowing water.

CHAPTER TWENTY

Hwalchmai and Rhagnell rode swiftly across country, seeking signs of Ardhu's men. Rhagnell had tracking skills, learned from years in the forest with Bresalek, and soon she picked up a trail, not of Ardhu, but of Rhyttah Chief Giant and his band of brigands.

"Pig-shite," she said, dismounting her steed and kneeling beside a pile of dung on the trampled earth. "With the marks of many footprints around it."

Hwalchmai grimaced in disgust. "Looks big enough to be horse-dung, but smells a hundred times fouler."

"That is because T'orc eats flesh, not grass," said Rhagnell solemnly.

They journeyed on, and began to find more evidence of the passage of T'orc and his guardians. A village lay burnt and devastated, and then another. Finally they found one settlement that still stood; it was large and had been hastily fortified by a ring of boulders and earth.

As they approached, a dozen archers leapt up onto the makeshift defensive wall and faced them with bows nocked. "What business do you have here?" called out an older man, who appeared to be a headman or minor chief; he had bronze threads sewn in his cloak and carried a black basalt axe.

"We seek the warband of Ardhu Pendraec," replied Hwalchmai. "We seek to help him defeat Rhyttah Chief Giant and the great boar T'orc."

The chief spat on the ground. "He is about, for all the good he's done. He's chased the Boar for days, going round and around like a puppy chasing its tail! Yet he can never catch it, and every day more innocents are killed. The very rivers of our land turn red, and the clouds are full of the ashes of the pyre."

"It shall not be so much longer," said Hwalchmai. "The time of this evil is at an end. Which way did Ardhu's warriors go?"

The petty chief pointed with the butt of his axe. "West."

###

Hwalchmai and his lady galloped on, passing into wilder lands filled with wind-blasted trees and scrubby heathland. Suddenly Rhagnell yanked on her

horse's reins, drawing it to an abrupt halt. "There is something in the wind…
someone comes. We must hide."

Hastily, they hunkered down amid a jumble of huge, irregular boulders
that lay is if they had been tossed from some giant's apron. They held tight
to their mounts' bridles of woven grass, willing them to be quiet and still.

Over the brow of the nearby hill marched a party of warriors, hard-faced
men clad in the skins of wolf, bear and deer, with the heads left on to serve
as head-dresses. Their leader was a massive one-eyed man, with arm-
muscles that rippled as he swung a flail toward the flank of a huge black
boar that had a heavy bronze chain attached to its hind leg. It squealed and
snorted, eyes glowing, and thrust honed tusks into the air. "Down you
beast!" the big man growled at it, yanking brutally on the chain. "I know
you'd love to gore me, but I am master here!"

"Chief Rhyttah, the animal grows wilder each day," said one of the
warriors, gazing uneasily at the champing boar. "Blood-lust and the evil
spirit inside it have made it mad. I fear even you will not be able to control it
ere long."

"Nonsense," said the big man, Rhyttah Chief Giant. "I will control T'orc
until the day he dines on the innards of Ardhu Pendraec. Then I will slay the
boar and eat its heart, and ingest both their strengths into myself."

"Why do we not turn and meet Ardhu in battle?" asked the other man.
"We traipse over the hills and dales like men Moonstruck!"

"You are no tactician, are you, Gronu." Rhyttah grinned, his upper lip
curling in derision. "I weaken him, tire him out. When at last I change course
and meet him head on, with T'orc charging before, he will not be expecting
the about face, and he will perish."

"May it be soon, Lord Rhyttah," grumbled the man Gronu.

"It will, Gronu, never fear."

In the clump of boulders, Hwalchmai drew his axe and would have
sprung out in a rage, but Rhagnell wrapped her strong arms around his waist
and pulled him back. "No, that is not the way! There are too many of them
for us to take on, to say nothing of the beast. We must find Ardhu, and tell
them what we have seen and heard."

"But they may well vanish into these harsh uplands again!" snarled
Hwalchmai.

"No… this time there will be no escape." Rhagnell took her short
woman's bow from her shoulder and raised it, putting an arrow to the string.
Carefully she aimed through a crack between the lichenous boulders, seeking
the flank or chest area of T'orc.

247

"No!" Hwalchmai grabbed her wrist; "you dare not shoot the beast. One arrow will not kill such a mighty one, but it could make him go mad. He might well kill Rhyttah and his men in his rage, but he would also turn on us, and we have no weapons to bring down such a powerful animal."

"I do not intend to kill him," said Rhagnell. "Just a little wound. A prick."

"Why?"

"You will see." Rhagnell shook free of her lover's restraining hand and aimed her bow again. "Trust me, Hwalchmai. I know what I must do."

This time, Hwalchmai allowed her to fire. The arrow skimmed through the grass, a low deadly shot. It grazed the hind leg of T'orc, tearing off a strip of flesh and bristle, then fell away into the moorland scrub. The giant boar squealed and danced about in anger, blood dripping from its wounded leg.

Unaware of the animal's wound, Rhyttah shouted an oath at the boar and hauled on its chain, waving his flail in a menacing way. "Move on, pig, or you'll have a taste of my wrath!"

"There," said Rhagnell smugly. "I have done what I intended. T'orc will lead Ardhu's warband to him by the trail of gore he leaves behind. A trail Rhyttah has not noticed. And I do not think he would dare touch the monster to bind the scrape, even if he did."

Hwalchmai hugged her. "You are as clever as you are good to look at. Now let us find my cousin and tell him our news!"

They came upon Ardhu's warband later in the day. The warriors were riding over a high ridge where bleak stone stretched to the sky and a cold wind was singing. Anwas the Winged, the tracker, knelt down on the damp earth, examining the ground, but his face was pinched and solemn; the soil was so deliberately churned by feet he could make no sense of what he examined.

Hwalchmai gave a joyous shout and spurred his steed ahead into the midst of the group. Laughing, he and Ardhu embraced. "So you still have your head, cousin!" said Ardhu, ruffling the other youth's hair.

"Aye, that I do. But Bresalek — the Green Rider — has lost his! And his life is not all I have taken... with me is his wife, Rhagnell, a woman of noble lineage, who is now to be mine."

Ardhu glanced at Rhagnell and then back to Hwalchmai. "You amaze me, kinsman. Adept in the warrior's art, adept with fair women!"

Rhagnell urged her mount forward. "Ardhu, lord of the West, I greet you, but Hwalchmai and I have more to tell than of our doings. We have spotted your quarry on the other side of yonder ridge. They are growing weary…"

"Are not we all?" grumbled Bohrs, from behind Ardhu.

Rhagnell ignored him. "And T'orc is injured…"

"What?" interrupted Ardhu, his eyes widening. "I had no knowledge of that!"

"Nor could you," said Rhagnell, "for it was I who wounded him with an arrow. Just a scratch, but enough to leave a trail of blood that should prove easy work for your tracker!"

Ardhu turned again to Hwalchmai. "It seems you have chosen well in a wife — artfulness as well as beauty! Let us go now, and put an end to these long days of wandering in the wilds, chasing what has oft-times seemed like mist and smoke!"

###

As Rhagnell had predicted, it did not take long to pick up the trail of T'orc. Little clots of gore clung to grass and tufts of heather; carrion birds swooped down and pecked at them, cawing, eager for the feast. They flapped back up into the air, wings beating madly as Ardhu's men cantered past.

The trail went over a hillock and into a wooded coomb where stunted oaks clumped together like sentinels, forming a gnarly barricade. A black mountain rose to the sky above the coomb, its peak scalped bald by wind and the slate skittering down its sides. A cairn rose on the crest, jagged with stones like pointed swords.

"What is this mountain called?" Ardhu asked, feeling ill at ease. "Do any among you know?"

Drust Mightyfist made a sound. "I hail from this area. It is called Mineth Beddun — the mountain of graves."

The company could see no sign of Rhyttah or the boar on mountainside or in valley, but suddenly An'kelet nodded and pointed with his spear-butt to a thin trickle of smoke that wafted up between the trees tucked in the back of the vale.

"Someone has pitched camp in there…and they are being none too careful."

The warband entered the forest cautiously, picking their way over moss-furred roots. Anwas was foremost, searching for blood spots on the forest-floor, or other signs of animal or human passage.

Suddenly Ardhu's mount Lamrai began to tremble. Her nostrils flared and she danced fearfully on her hooves, tossing her head and fighting against Ardhu's control. She wheeled around, trying to head back out of the shadowy grove.

"What is it?" Ardhu stroked her neck in an attempt to calm her. "Do not fail me now, my noble one…"

At the moment, a terrible crackling noise filled the forest. It was an awful sound that resembled a thousand breaking bones. It grew louder, and the earth began to tremble. Slender birch trees swayed and danced, and then suddenly split asunder, fragments of bark flying hither and thither like spears.

A terrible, high-pitched squealing filled the grove, and suddenly Anwas the Winged was flung up into the air. He screamed in agony as he hurtled into the branches of a tree and hung from a fork by his cloak, with blood pouring from a gouge in his side.

T'orc the Chief Boar stood below him, pawing and snorting, his great jaws working and gnashing. Redness dripped from his tusks.

Ardhu stared at the ravening animal, his adversary. Surely the beast was more than just some maltreated creature, goaded to madness by his malign sister; Morigau must have summoned some evil spirit to enter its skull. It was grotesque — fat and bulbous, its skin the colour of an old corpse and massed with fly-bites and scabs, its head ugly and squat with a great wide snout dripping snot and froth. The eyes under leathery folds gleamed red and tufts of coarse, upstanding bristles as sharp as knives sprang out all over its spine and brow. Twisted tusks dripped with Anwas' blood.

As if sensing Ardhu's repulsed gaze, T'orc slowly turned away from Anwas to face the young king mounted on the trembling Lamrai. One foreleg pawed the ground, puffs of noxious mist surrounded flaring nostrils as the beast breathed heavily in the cold air.

"Look out!" An'kelet was the first to move. "He is going to charge!" The Ar-morahan prince spurred his mare forward, aiming with his great long spear. He alone of the company had such a reaching weapon; for although the spear was popular upon the continent, the choice weapons for warriors of Prydn were still dagger, axe and bow.

With a cry, he launched the spear, seeking to smite a deathblow before T'orc could move. Unfortunately the horses of the warband, terrified and fighting against their riders' control, bashed into the flanks of his frightened mount and caused his thrust to go wide. Balugaisa with its many tines scraped along T'orc's flank and stuck shallowly into his hindquarters.

An'kelet leaned forward over his horse's neck, one-handed and grim-faced, trying to drive home the spear, to get the deadly barbs locked within the stinking, cadaverous flesh of the beast.

The boar released a deafening bellow and whirled in a circle, biting at the shaft sticking from its flank. Not expecting such a sudden, powerful move, An'kelet was jerked violently forward, over his steed's withers and onto the ground. Immediately, the warband closed ranks to protect him from the crazed animal that squealed and shrieked and stamped in pain.

Ardhu drew Caladvolc and pressed forward. At that moment he spied the shapes of men within the trees, with bows drawn. "Look out — they are firing on us!" he cried, and he flung up Wyngurthachar just as a score of arrows whirred between the trees. Several struck harmlessly against the Face of Evening and bounced aside; but out of the corner of his eye, he saw Per-Adur wince in pain and grab his shoulder. A black-feathered shaft stuck out of his flesh.

The attackers were surging forward, their voices raised in a horrible, ululating battle cry. They broke through the trees and flung themselves with abandon at Ardhu's warband, striking the horses' knees with great heavy stone war-hammers that crippled them instantly. Within minutes, many of Ardhu's men were on the ground, beside horses screaming and bucking in pain, while the great boar T'orc, crazed with its own injuries, stabbed at both beasts and men with its sword-sharp tusks.

Ardhu leaped from his saddle and slapped Lamrai's flank, sending her careering out of the wood, away from the battle scene. Here, in the green shadows, where roots reared like serpents and the air smelt of ancient death, was not a place where a mounted man could gain the advantage.

Caladvolc in one hand, shield upraised, he ploughed into the heaving mass of fighters, forcing his way through. A north-man screamed, pierced through the throat by Ardhu's blade, and fell away; T'orc's huge body crashed down on the flailing figure, and silenced his screams forever. Blood bubbled up in the churning mud, spattering Ardhu's shield and golden breastplate.

Art had now spotted Rhyttah, who was fighting hand to hand with Hwalchmai. He let his gaze fall over the huge figure, surely a giant's spawn by his great height, with a bald shining head tattooed with a black crescent Moon. Rhyttah grinned like a mad man, his teeth as uneven as flagstones, as he parried Hwalchmai's blows, and tried to get beneath his guard.

"Rhyttah Baddaden, Chief Giant!" shouted Ardhu. "You have claimed the beards of mighty kings to weave your cloak. Now at last I have hunted you down like the beast you are, and will have yours!"

Rhyttah brought his arm down with blinding force, shattering Hwalchmai's wrist in one violent motion and sending his dagger flying. Rhagnell grabbed her lover from behind and dragged him to safety, staggering in pain... but Rhyttah was no longer interested in him.

Instead the huge man lurched toward Ardhu, his shoulders bunched, his war-axe swinging menacingly. "So, I meet the boy-king of the West," he sneered. "I have heard all about you from your sister Morigau. All about you. She had many interesting tales to tell as we rolled together in King Loth's own bed!"

"I'm sure she did," retorted Ardhu. "But nothing truthful ever came from my sister's lips; her words are the hisses of snakes, filled with venom. She has used you. And now you will die."

"It is not I who will die!" shouted Rhyttah and he lunged at Ardhu, his axe upraised.

Ardhu stepped back, and slashed at the big man's brawny arm. The tip of Caladvolc dug into his bicep, drawing bright red blood. Rhyttah's axe-blow went wide, and Ardhu closed in so that they were almost torso to torso, fighting hand to hand. Art kept Rhyttah's arm pushed up, over his head, with the blood running down, unable to use his axe. The big man, more than a head taller than the slight youth, was fumbling at his belt for another weapon, a long knife that he carried in a leather sheath, while Ardhu sought to block him and draw his own dagger.

"Look out! Ardhu, beware!" An'kelet's voice came from behind the fighting warriors, full of fear and urgency.

Alarmed, Ardhu half-turned... and saw T'orc bearing down on him. The animal was squealing in high-pitched tones which sounded almost like human screams; its eyes rolled in its fearsome skull and drool sprayed from champing mandibles. Its back bristled with at least a dozen arrows, none of which had come even close to killing it. An'kelet's great spear was still embedded in its hindquarter, its haft smacking into trees and men as the animal charged.

Ardhu whirled around, letting Rhyttah's arm drop, and tried to leap away to safety, but T'orc thudded against his legs, throwing him across the forest as if he were as insubstantial as a feather. He struck the bole of a tree and slid to the ground, the breath driven from his lungs. The impact tore Caladvolc from his grip and it went spinning through the air, landing with a clatter a few feet away.

T'orc was on him almost instantly. The ground shuddered beneath his hooves; foul breath blasted over Ardhu, hot and rank with carrion-scent.

Death was in the creature's eyes, and pain and madness. With an enraged bellow he thrust forward with his tusks, catching the inside of Ardhu's leg and tearing a long gash. Blood spurted out, soaking both Ardhu and the boar's bristling pelt.

"Ardhu, use the razor — the hag's razor!" Through a darkening mist he could hear An'kelet yelling, saw him leap over a fallen tree trunk and come running towards him with his long, foreign blade in hand.

Fighting waves of pain and nausea, Ardhu grasped T'orc's head in an arm-lock and jabbed violently at the piggy eyes, attempting to blind or distract his adversary. His free hand scrabbled wildly at his belt, seeking the sacrificial razor he had taken from Ah-nis's cave, but his fingers were slick with blood, and the honed weapon slid between his fingers onto the grass.

In the distance he could hear Rhyttah laughing, his voice booming out like thunderclaps: "Ha ha HA!"

A bolt of anger ripped through him at the sound of that mocking mirth; surely the gods would not allow him to die in such away, mauled by some monster of his sister's making and jeered at by one of her twisted lovers. With a harsh cry, he punched T'orc straight on the nose with all the strength he had left. The boar squealed shrilly and backed up for an instant, before lunging forward again, slobbering and champing with renewed fury.

It was all the time Ardhu needed. Grabbing the hag's razor from the grass, he swung at the boar and slashed at its face. The razor's blade bit deep in the horny hide and blood spurted. T'orc bellowed again, but this time there was a note of fear in its cry. It began backing away from Ardhu, shaking its massive head in a spray of blood and mucus.

The hunter had become the hunter.

Adrenaline shot through Ardhu's body, blotting out the agony of his gashed leg. In a half crouch, he stalked T'orc as the boar retreated from him. He was like a beast himself at that moment, covered in both his own blood and the beast's, his face chalk-white and his lips drawn back in a feral snarl. "It is time for your spirit to pass, ugly one," he rasped. "Time to put an end to your terror."

The boar stopped abruptly, lungs pumping like bellows, its hindquarters trembling. It looked as though it might drop…but unexpectedly its eyes ignited, and uttering hideous grunts, it made one last assault on its enemy.

It did not get far. An'kelet rushed round to its right flank and grasped the still- swinging haft of his spear. With an effort, he managed to yank it free of the tough, leathery skin, and then plunged its barbed head in deeper, seeking the monster's vitals.

T'orc leapt in the air as Balugaisa dug deep. Ardhu was not its concern now; only the pain and the blood and the mindless terror as its tormented life neared its end. Ardhu staggered forward and threw himself on the beast's back, bringing the razor across T'orc's exposed throat and slashing wide the great vein of life. A huge jet of blood shot out, drenching the glade with stinking hot gore. The great beast slumped, with the young still King astride its twitching body.

"T'orc the Chief Boar is dead!" he cried, and he chopped the tuft of hard bristles from between the monster's ears and held it up as a trophy.

Across the clearing, Rhyttah cursed and turned to flee into the deeper parts of the forest. The men of Ardhu's warband immediately surrounded him with weapons drawn. They circled him like wolves, eager for vengeance for their own fallen, for their wounded king.

"Your followers are dead," said Ka'hai. "And now your demon-boar is dead too."

"I would shoot out his remaining eye!" cried Rhagnell fiercely, aiming at Rhyttah's face with her bow. "In returning for breaking Hwalchmai's wrist."

Hwalchmai cradled his wounded arm against his chest, face grim. "No, don't touch him, Rhagnell, Ka'hai, any of you. Ardhu is the slayer of the Boar... it is for him to decide the fate of this murderer, this slayer of innocent women and children!"

Ardhu clambered off the body of T'orc and limped towards his men. Blood was still running down his thigh; it was an evil wound, rough and jagged-edged, but at least it had missed the artery — he would not bleed to death. Face white, he approached Rhyttah and stood before him, the gore-smeared razor in his hand.

"You," he said in a voice deep and pitiless, "take off your cloak — the cloak wrought of the beards of slain chieftains. Now."

Rhyttah ripped out the pin at the neck of his cloak and let the mantle fall. Bohrs snatched it up, and examined it, frowning at such an unwholesome oddity.

"Burn it,"Ardhu ordered. "Let those dead chiefs' last remains go to join their spirits across the Great Plain."

Bohrs took out his strike a light and kindled a flame, and soon the woodland was full of the scent of burning hair.

"There... the cloak that symbolised your pride and your cruelty is no more," said Ardhu, still standing mere inches from his enemy. "Now... kneel. Kneel, I say!"

A mutinous gleam filled Rhyttah's single eye, but Bal-ahn and Ka'hai prodded him with their blades, forcing him to his knees before Ardhu.

Ardhu grabbed the long greasy black braid that grew at the nape of Rhyttah's neck and yanked his head backwards, exposing his throat. "I will shave you now, and shame you as you shamed and humiliated the unfortunate chieftains you slew." Raising the Hag Ah-nis's bronze razor, he roughly cut away the big man's beard and moustache, while the warriors of the warband laughed and jeered.

"Your braid must go too," he added, slashing through the coarse hair, then running the blade of the lice-caked scalp. "And the rest comes off too. A shaven head is the sign of a slave, and that is what you are, aren't you? A slave to Morigau!"

"She will ruin you yet…" Words burst from Rhyttah's bruised lips. "She has a weapon greater than any I could wield. She calls him…Mordraed!" He started to laugh harshly, almost maniacally. "Would your men like to know all about him, how he came to be?"

Ardhu went ashen. "Be silent, or your life will be forfeit this instant."

"Is it not already? Would you spare me, even after all the crimes of which you accuse me? I do not deny I did those things…and enjoyed doing them!"

"I might have a use for you. You know Morigau's…mind. I would not slay you purely for spite or for love of blood."

"Oh, the noble Lord Ardhu," sneered Rhyttah. "Spare me your mercy, boy. I will never help you or your precious, righteous cause. I spit on you and your mercy…" and he hawked at Ardhu, the spittle striking the centre of the young king's golden breastplate and running down in a yellow gobbet.

Ardhu's lips tightened. "So be it. No mercy shall be shown." Lashing out with the Black Witch's razor, he cut the Chief Giant's throat in one fluid motion. The huge man made a gurgling noise and crashed to the ground, his spirit leaving his body in a red tide.

An'kelet approached Ardhu, placing a hand on his shoulder. "It is done and over. Come, friend, we must attend to your wound. You are still bleeding."

Ardhu glanced down; he had almost forgotten his own pain, the ragged gouge marring his thigh. Looking at the oozing slash, a wave of light-headedness overcame him; his legs became as jelly and the world dipped and tilted alarmingly.

An'kelet's arms reached out to catch him as he fell. Ka'hai rushed over to grab his legs and help carry him away from the gore-soaked clearing to a sweeter-hued part of the forest. They laid him on the mossy greensward, using a cloak as a headrest, and Betu'or, who had some training as a healer, cut away the lacings on Ardhu's leather trews to examine the wound.

"It has missed the great life-river in his leg," Betu'or said, with some relief. "The bleeding looks bad, but properly packed, it will stop. The biggest fear I have is that the wound may get flesh-rot. None who get flesh rot live to see another year."

Rhagnell stepped forward, reaching to a bag that hung at her waist. "I too had some training in healing, while I lived in the wilds. I have dried Midsummer's plant — that is good to clean wounds, and comfrey also. Fresh would be better, but we must do with what is available. After, we can gather oak-sap from the trees and use that to staunch the blood flow and make a seal. How well the young King heals is then in the hands of the Great Spirits."

Bohrs' face creased up, red and frustrated between bristling tufts of his bushy beard and equally wild hair. "Gods, why did this happen, when the great victory of Mineth Beddan is upon him? What if he is maimed? By law, a man cannot rule if he has a physical blemish!"

Rhagnell shot the burly warrior a harsh look. "The quicker you and the men go out and get me some oak-sap, the less likely it is that Lord Ardhu will be blemished. Now go!"

Bohrs and half a dozen of the men scattered, while the rest remained, gazing solemnly at their fallen chief and talking in low whispers.

After a while, Ardhu's eyelids flickered and he sat up, pale and shivering. "The boar… Rhyttah…"

"Do you not remember, lord? Both are dead," said Rhagnell. "Your quest has been successful. Prydn is safe."

Ardhu tried to smile; it came out a grimace.. "Aye, I do remember. Ah…the pain…" He clutched his leg.

An'kelet knelt beside him, gave him a draught of strong beer from a handled beaker. "T'orc gored you with his tusk," he said. "It is a nasty wound. But I have seen worse. You are young. You will heal."

"Yes… yes." Ardhu lay back, his sweat-soaked hair a midnight stain across his white forehead. "I must get better. Morigau cannot be allowed to win."

At that moment Hlwch Windyhand the Archer made a hissing sound from between his clenched teeth. He whirled around, snatching his bow from his shoulder and setting an arrow to the string,

"What is it?" asked An'kelet, rising and reaching for his spear.

"I can feel thunder in the ground beneath my feet," said the archer. "One comes, seeking us, following the trail our horses have left."

"Who would seek us?" asked Ba-lin and Bal-ahn almost in unison, those two identical youths who, men said, had but one soul between them.

"It could be Morigau," muttered An'kelet. "Maybe she has been watching our battles from afar. Or maybe it is more men loyal to Rhyttah. Prepare yourselves, men of the Warband!"

The warriors grabbed their weapon and stood, grim and silent, poised for attack. There was great crackling of branches and twigs, and a youthful figure on a lathered, staggering horse burst into the clearing. He stared at the circle of armed men, his eyes big and round with terror.

"Drem!" Anwas the Winged, who was lying on the ground, being treated for his own tusk-wound by Ka'hai, lifted a shaking hand to his kinsman. "Leave your weapons, men, it is Drem, my sister's son! What brings you here?"

Drem slid from his horse's back; he tried to walk toward Anwas, but his knees gave way and he fell heavily. "I have been riding for days with scarce a stop, " he gasped. "I have been in strange lands under strange skies, menaced by boar and bear and wolf and cannibal-men! I come to bring word of a great evil, a terrible thing that has happened at Kham-El-Ard."

Ardhu staggered to his feet, grey-faced with pain and exhaustion, his eyes like shattered flints. "What evil? Speak, boy!"

Drem began to sob; great noisy ragged sobs. "The Queen... Lady Fynavir... she has been abducted."

A horrified murmur went through the warriors.

"By whom?" Ardhu demanded.

"By... by Melwas, King of the Summer Country."

Ardhu grabbed the lad's shoulder. "Do you know this for certain?"

Drem nodded. "I was with the Lady Fynavir when the evil bastards attacked. She told me to flee and raise the alarm, and so I did, but at one point I heard men near me so I hid in the bole of an old dead oak. While hiding, I heard them speak the name of Melwas."

"This is grave news indeed," groaned Ardhu, and he limped towards Lamrai, who was tethered to a tree. "Men, to your horses...we must ride for the Summer Country in all haste."

"Art...you cannot!" cried Ka'hai. "You will kill yourself!"

Ignoring his foster-brother, Ardhu tried to vault up onto Lamrai's back. The mare snorted and danced about, unnerved by the scent of blood and the boar on his clothes. Ardhu's strength failed, his arms giving way, and he sank back to earth, landing heavily on his wounded leg. His lips went white and he slumped on the ground in a half-faint, still clutching Lamrai's reins.

"Attend to the king, attend to the Pendraec!" Hwalchmai shouted, running forward. "Cousin, you mustn't be a fool! You cannot throw away your life, even for Fynavir! Women are sometimes stolen like cattle, that is how it has always been! What say you, An'kelet? Tell the fool to wait till he is well!"

An'kelet did not reply. He stood with night in his eyes, a great copper figure with the Balugaisa in his hand and his long Ar-morahan daggers gleaming at his belt. He was, as Ardhu has first seen him, the man of bronze, inscrutable, god-like. A muscle flickered in his jaw, and then he was running, moving swift as lightning, hurling himself atop his horse, which was tethered beside Lamrai. Snatching up the reins, he gave a great cry and drove his heels into the beast's flanks.

It reared, not used to such violent handling, and with a harsh whinny, it bolted through the forest, An'kelet bent low over its flowing mane.

Like a man possessed the Prince of Ar-morah rode out across the bleak moors and sheltering dells, the bald hills and the black hills, heading south at great speed toward the Land of the Summer Stars.

CHAPTER TWENTY ONE

Another day passed and night had fallen once more when the warriors of Melwas reached the Summer Country with their captive. Lying bound in the wagon, Fynavir could smell the scent of burning logs, animals, cooking. The skies above her blurred, the stars obscured by a haze of wood-smoke.

"Out you come." Melwas reached into the cart and dragged her out, cutting the bonds on ankles and wrists with his dagger. "Time to meet your new People."

Hand clamped on her shoulder, he pushed her toward a circle of mean-looking thatched huts. "People of the Summerlands, look what I have brought you!" He propelled her into a guttered street, a ring of flickering torchlight. "My new woman! Your new Queen!"

The folk of Melwas gathered around, staring at Fynavir — a dour, unsmiling crowd wearing tattoos of fabulous birds and beasts on their flesh and little else. Their woven skirts and trews looked crude, the cloth coarse, and their only jewellery was made of old cast-off bones — there was no gold or jet or other wealth. Their eyes hardened with suspicion as they gazed at the newcomer.

Watching those grimy, brooding faces, Fynavir remembered hearing that denizens of the Summer Country were a strange breed, ignoring the matters of the Five Cantrevs for nigh on a thousand years as they eked out a meagre existence in the shadow of the Great Tor. Perhaps, if they had no love of outsiders, she could play upon their fears and persuade them to ask Melwas to release her.

Taking a deep breath, she cried out, "People of the Summer Country, listen to me. Your lord, Melwas, has carried me here against my will. I am the wife of Ardhu the Terrible Head, anointed of Khor Ghor. I ask you to beg your lord to return me to my rightful home — death and destruction will befall you all if I am not brought to Ardhu's side!"

One solitary village laughed. The others' faces remained like masks, fierce, mud-smeared. Melwas stiffened at Fynavir's side, and suddenly his fist shot out, striking her to the ground.

As she lay stunned, head reeling from the blow, he grabbed her by the hair and yanked her to her feet. "You will never try that trick again, woman!" he snarled, spittle from his cut mouth striking her cheek. "My people listen to me and no one else — do you understand?"

An old crone hobbled forward, pointing at Fynavir with a finger bent with arthritis. "Master, why this one, of all the fine women you could have had from the Summer Lands. She is as white as dead bone... it is unnatural!"

An unhealthy gleam entered Melwas's eyes. "Her whiteness is a sign of holiness, hag. Her mother is the Peaked Red One of Ibherna. She is the White Phantom, the White Lady, protectress of Albu. Any man who takes her as his own has right to rule as King as long as she is by his side."

"But you are already King here in the Summerlands," someone in the back of the throng shouted.

Melwas grimaced. "Aye, but what have our people become these long years? Hermits, hiding from a changing world. Friends to no one, not even each other! Yet once, long ago, we were Chosen People! My mother-ancestor, Evaen, was bathing in the lake when a great crane wrapped its wings around her in lover's embrace. Nine Moons later she bore a son, Trigaran, founder of our people, who wrought a magic bag made of Crane-skin from which our luck flowed...till it was lost by unwise fathers before me! Now, by taking this white woman, this spirit-touched one, I will restore the glory that was ours, before we were pushed into this marsh-bound land. She is Sovereignty and I will be the Sovereign through her — we will leave this place and take the lands and glory that is due us!"

"These tales sound fine to naive and youthful ears," the crone shrilled, waving her raddled arms, "but what of Ardhu Pendraec? Surely he will come for her and bring ruin on us all just as the White One said!"

"He is a mere boy!" Melwas shouted. "Aided by the trickeries of the sorcerer, Merlin! He will not prevail against us. He cannot even put a brat into his wife's belly!"

There was a burst of raucous mirth from the crowd. Standing beside Melwas, Fynavir shuddered with embarrassment. Melwas caught her chin in his hand, and pulled her towards him. "I will put an end to your barrenness," he grunted, flashing a lascivious grin that made the torn flap of his lips gape like a horrible second mouth. "I will ride you like my prize bull rides my cows, giving them new calves every spring!"

Fynavir shrank away, revolted and angry. "How dare you compare me to a cow!"

He caught her round the waist. "I dare, because that is what you are to me — a thing that brings me wealth and power, and will breed me heirs... You must understand this, white woman: you will be treated with honour if you obey my wishes, but if you seek to deny me what is rightfully mine, you will suffer. We are a harsh people in the marshes of the Summer Country; we do not throw flowers before the feet of our women and bow to their every whim like your southern tribes do. I expect obedience and compliance in all things." His hands wandered up from her waist, groping, seeking.

"Don't touch me!" she gasped. "Ardhu will kill you, you ill-visaged pig!"

"You need a lesson in humility, woman," he sneered, and with a vicious movement he suddenly ripped her dress from neck to hem. Bone toggles showered. She tried to cover herself with her veil-like hair, but he grabbed her arms and roughly pinioned them behind her back. As she started to sob in shame and fear, he smirkingly dragged her around the encampment like a prize beast. His men laughed, leered and made crude gestures, begging Melwas to throw her to them. After what seemed eternity the marsh-king lost interest in the sport and pushed her down onto her knees in the churned mud in the centre of village. The mob sneered and hooted as she cowered; the women looked contemptuous and the men were still hot-eyed and foul-tongued with lust.

"This will be your Queen!" Melwas shouted again, prodding her roughly in the back of the leg with the toe of his leather shoe. "See how fair she is, how perfect, as befits a goddess? But she is also a woman, born of earth — she does not float in the sky with Sun and Moon..." He laughed lustfully, hauling Fynavir to her feet and yanking back her hair to expose her breasts. "Her paps are not made of gold, as you can see, and the Sun does not shine from her thighs! She is still a woman like any other woman, and will obey the lord who won her by right of capture!"

Hatred in her eyes, Fynavir stared up into his pitiless face. She knew her fate was sealed, that she could neither soften this warlord's will nor appeal to his followers for help. She'd seen many men try to abduct Mevva and force themselves upon her, but her mother was a warrior as well as queen, and she had beaten every one of them in single combat and painted her flesh with their blood. Fynavir had no such strength of arms, all she had left to her was her defiance. "Right of capture!" she spat. "You fought no battle with my husband for me! You crept through the woods like a thief in the night, choosing a time when you knew Ardhu would be away! Not one blade was drawn, nor any arrow fired! You are a coward, a brute...and you will die for your dishonour of me!"

"You tongue is too free, woman," he snarled back. "Put it to better use." He grabbed her shoulders and bent her backwards, forcing his broken mouth over hers, his hands rough and proprietary on her naked flesh.

"If you touch me again," she spat, when she was able to tear her mouth away, "I will curse you so that you are unmanned, and can never lay with a woman again! As the daughter of a goddess, you should fear my curses!"

Melwas made a sign of protection with his hand and spat. "You have said enough," he growled, his tone threatening. "More talk of curses and I will cut out your tongue!"

Roughly, he bundled her toward the largest hut in the village and shoved her unceremoniously through the door, while the villagers laughed nervously, ill at ease with the stranger-woman's talk of curses. Inside the hut was a low hearth filled with sputtering embers, an array of weaponry, drinking vessels, and a bed-place topped by many skins. Melwas tossed Fynavir on to the pallet and flung himself on top of her, filled with both anger and lust, trying to jam his knee between her legs and push them apart. She screamed and bit him; she didn't care what punishment he gave, she would not let him defile her without a fight, poor as her effort might be. Her slapped her face once, then yet again, and grabbed her flailing arms and pinned them at her sides. "The more you fight me, the more I want you," he snarled, panting, his eyes fixated on her naked flesh as she writhed beneath him, trying to shove him away.

Suddenly the door of the hut banged open. An old man entered; he wore a floor-length robe and his hair was cut bluntly at brow and mid-back, making him appear to wear a shining helmet of silver. He had a narrow, imperious face, the face of a man who was used to respect. Three serpents were tattooed on one cheek, and a grid pattern on the other. Fynavir guessed that he must be the tribe's shaman.

Scowling, Melwas swung round. "Why do you bother me, old one? Can't you see what I am doing?"

The old man looked sourly at him. "If you truly wish to marry this woman, certain procedures must be followed. You have stolen the White Phantom from the bed of another man, and if you take her to your own bed so soon, and she then grows great with child, there will be rumours that the child is Pendraec's, not yours. This could cause division amongst our people. It is my counsel that you do not lie with her for one passage of the Moon, until we know that she has no child in her."

"And if she does? I will not wait for her for nine months, Kanhastyr!" shouted Melwas.

"It will be dealt with," said the shaman Kanhastyr. "There are many ways to expel an unwanted child."

Melwas snatched a ragged skin from the floor and flung it at Fynavir who wrapped it around her nakedness. "So... you have a reprieve, then, bitch. One turn of the Moon. But I shall be watching you; you'll still be here with me every moment."

Grabbing her arms, he bound the wrists together with hemp rope and dragged her from the bed. He flung the end of the rope over one of the roof's supporting beams and, pulling down on the rope, hauled Fynavir almost onto the tips of her toes, her arms painfully extended above her head. He then secured the twine to an opposing beam. "I won't make it comfortable for you, I can assure you," he snarled in her ear. "You may regret you did not choose to willingly lie in my bed. And you'll end up there anyway."

He turned to Kanhastyr and beckoned him to go outside. "If I must cool my head and my loins, Kanhastyr, then give me one of your potions to quell my ardour!"

The men exited the hut, leaving Fynavir to weep bitter tears of despair and pull upon the ropes that bound her until blood ran freely from her wrists.

An'kelet rode across the wilds of Albu like a man possessed. His horse stumbled with weariness, sweat lathered on its neck; he cursed it and shouted in frustrated temper, then cursed himself for his own impatience and begged the animal for its forgiveness. After all, if the mare had not bent its neck to him and allowed him to ride upon her back, his journey would be much longer.

Too long.

He tried to focus on facing Melwas and not to think of Fynavir in the hands of the dour chieftain who lived in the Summerlands. He did not know the man or what his intentions might be...Melwas might kill Fynavir to spite Ardhu and draw him into conflict; or sacrifice her for luck to the strange water-gods that lived in the bogs of his homeland. He might keep her as slave or concubine, or give her to his men as a diversion if she displeased him.

Terrible images flashed through his mind of her white, broken body sinking into the mud of the marshlands, her eyes staring blankly at the fading sky, her spirit lost forever to men. He fought to banish the images, to force them away, for he knew that such hideous fancies would weaken him, tying his belly into knots of anguish and making his spear-hand shake with rage and fear.

No. He had to collect himself, empty his mind of fearsome thoughts. He must be more than warrior now.

He must be a killer, with no thoughts of honour.

A killer, and a hunter.

A hunter whose quarry was the King of the Summer Country.

He reached the marshlands surrounding the Tor of Hwynn son of Nud shortly after Sunset. Clouds turned to flame in the West; weird night-birds trilled and called. Marsh-mist coiled from the saturated ground and fey lights flitted over the bog — the spirits of lost men trapped between the Underworld and Otherworld. An'kelet turned his gaze from their tricksy light; they were dangerous, for they could maze a man and lead him to his death in deep water.

The marsh was not a safe place to wander after nightfall, so An'kelet halted his weary horse and set up camp, resting in the shelter of an upended willow that lay half-splayed in the green-dark bog-water, roots spiralling down into the murk. He tried to keep wakeful, but as the stars and Moon westered, and the chirping and croaking of bog-dwelling beasts dwindled into silence, he slipped into a deep, restless sleep.

He woke in the morning with the pallid winter Sun beating into his face. He groaned and quickly sat upright, ashamed that he had allowed his bodily exhaustion to overcome him.

His shame was promptly replaced by alarm. He could hear voices nearby, coming closer. Cursing, he snatched the haft of his spear and crouched down behind the trunk of the willow, hoping he would not be spotted

"A rare find, Gam-el. I wonder where it came from." He could now tell that one of the speakers was a woman.

"From some fool who dared to walk uninvited in Melwas's lands!" the woman's companion replied. This voice was deep, a male's "He must have drowned in the bog. A bit of good luck for us — but not such good luck for him!"

The couple laughed raucously, and An'kelet suddenly realised the 'find' they were talking about was his horse. He had tethered the animal to a bush last night, but the mare must have broken free while he slept and wandered away.

Carefully, An'kelet shifted his position so that he could view the newcomers. They were standing a few feet away, an older man with a balding head and red beard and a woman whose face had a soft, sucked-in look from a lack of teeth. Both wore crude outfits of tanned hides, old and stained, and smelled very foul indeed. The man held An'kelet's horse by the rein.

"What should we do with the beast?" the woman eyed the black mare.

"Eat it?"

"Well, it's big and fat — tempting, I admit. But she ain't ours; she's on Melwas's land, so she belongs to the chief."

The woman sniffed and stared downheartedly at her grubby bare feet. "Not fair."

"It might be all right, O-on! Our chief is getting married in one moon, remember? He'll no doubt have the beast cooked up and we'll all get a bite anyway! Grand, it'll be! He might even look on us with favour because we found the animal!"

The woman rubbed her thin arms. "Maybe. But I don't like that idea of this marriage. It'll bring bad luck; I feel it in my bones. Why is Melwas so set on that strange whey-faced one? The woman is too white... it ain't natural."

"She has fine tits and a royal mother!" retorted the man. "That's good enough for him. It's not for us to question!"

The woman screeched and hit out at the man. "You weren't supposed to be lookin' at her..." They stumbled away, dragging An'kelet's mount behind them, the man laughing as the woman batted at him in mock anger.

An'kelet felt his pulse quicken. What was nearly a disaster might prove advantageous in the end. Despite his immediate urge to confront the couple and force them to take him to Melwas, he kept silent and let them go unmolested. Once the sound of their cackles and shrieks had vanished in the distance, he emerged from behind the fallen willow and followed the trail they had made through the reeds across the foetid marsh.

After several miles An'kelet noticed the ground beneath his feet growing more solid. Up ahead, he could see a tract of dry grass-land bordering a clear blue lake. Round houses clustered on the shore, while rows of tethered coracles bobbed in the shallows — the main occupation of the villagers was fishing, since neither farming nor animal husbandry fared well in such watery environs. A protective wall of sharpened stakes surrounded the houses, but there were no other signs of defence; bog and lake made impassable walls against incursions from the outside world.

An'kelet shouldered his spear and hurried toward Melwas's domain. The retaining wall, which had been left unguarded, shielded him against any spying eyes. Bent almost double, he inched his way along its length down to the lakeshore.

By now the light was failing; the Sun still in winter's grip, the days still brutally short. Nightjars screamed as they dipped and dived over the water, and the Moon's ghost appeared, half full. The Western horizon spouted blood as the Sun fell away towards the lands of the Dead.

No one was about, so An'kelet silently slipped thigh-deep into the freezing water and thrust his spear through the bottoms of all the coracles except the largest and most sturdy one. The other craft sank soundlessly, trailing bubbles.

He then turned his attention to the settlement. Only a few hundred yards away women swished by in their long skin skirts, bringing in their weaving looms and drying racks for the night, while husbandmen penned the few scraggly cattle they owned and called in their roving dogs. Warriors staggered toward their hearths, already deep in their cups, unbuckling their dagger-belts and stone wrist-guards in preparation for drunken slumber. "Selgi! Selgi! Where is that brat of mine?" he heard a woman cry, her voice mixed with annoyance and worry.

The night drew colder and teardrops of ice appeared on the grass where An'kelet crouched. He watched the Moon sail overhead and the stars dance in their nightly procession.

Soon… soon…

A night-guard emerged from one of the huts and squatted beside a guttering fire between the dwellings. He carried an axe but after toying with it for a while, dropped it in exchange for the delights of his drinking beaker. Sighing, he stretched out his stubby legs toward the fading warmth of the fire-pit.

It was the last warmth he ever felt.

Swift as a striking snake, An'kelet leapt from his hiding place and flung himself at the man's back. Arondyt tore into the sentry's ribcage and pierced his heart, and he died with not so much as a cry.

An'kelet rose from beside the corpse, his hands and blade bloody. Battle-madness washed over him in dark waves, different from anything he had ever before experienced. His prowess in warfare had come from skill and his measured, thoughtful nature, not from the crazed rage that possessed many others. Yet now he was changing, his body tingling with adrenaline, his very features warped and twisted by the power of his wrath and his desire for the blood of his enemies. He had entered the state the priests called the hero's warp-spasm; half in the world of men, he was also half in the domain of the gods, his strength greater than ten, his aspect terrible and inhuman — a Sun with blazing eyes and pitiless death-rictus grin, and wild burning hair that blew out in the strengthening breeze.

Throwing back his head, he howled like some fell beast at the ascending Moon.

His cry brought Melwas's warriors running from their huts. Laughing like a madman, An'kelet charged towards them, slashing with Arondyt, severing arms and piercing legs and unguarded torsos. Screams rang out in the gloom as bodies toppled to the earth and blood fountained. One man leapt on An'kelet's back, and tried to drive a dagger into his throat; with a cry of amusement, An'kelet grabbed his assailant's arms and tossed him straight over his head into the fire-pit. The man's fur cloak touched the glowing embers and he ignited like a torch, and ran shrieking in agony throughout the village, a hideous fireball that eventually collapsed in a heap beside the lake.

"What do you want, bloody-handed stranger?" one of the men cried, trying to set arrow to his bow with trembling fingers. "We do not know you...we have no quarrel with you!"

"Oh, but you do!" shouted An'kelet. "Call Melwas to me and maybe some of you shall see the dawn!"

"I come!" a voice snarled behind An'kelet. Whirling, he saw the door of a large hut bang open, and a naked warrior step forward with a lethal-looking rapier in his hand. His hair coiled like a wild snake around his face, and his mouth was marred by raised scars the colour of raw liver. Yellow wolf-eyes blazed from under scowling brows.

"Are you Melwas, King of the Summer Country?" asked An'kelet brusquely. He shoved his daggers into his belt, and reached to touch the haft of the Balugaisa where it hung in its sling across his back. It seemed to call to him, his favourite weapon, tempered in the poisoned blood of the monster Kon-Khenn.

"I am," replied Melwas. "Who are you, who attacks my people and disturbs my sleep?"

"Where is the woman...where is Queen Fynavir, wife of the Pendraec?"

Melwas flung his head back and laughed. "So that's what this is about, is it? The white bitch! But you, with your bright Sun-hair and foreign voice, are not her husband, Ardhu the so-called high king!"

"No, I am not. I am his right-hand man, An'kelet son of Bhan and the Lake Priestess Eilahn, greatest warrior of the Western world, wielder of the long spear, Arondyt, sword of Light, and Fragarak the Answerer. Now tell, me, I will not ask again — where is Queen Fynavir?"

"Where do you think the slut is?" snarled Melwas. "In my hut, where else?"

The implications of Melwas's words, in addition to his nakedness, made An'kelet's growing madness spiral to even greater heights. A red haze clouded his vision; his lips drew back in a dangerous, animalistic grin. He said no more to his adversary, who stood, hands on hips, waiting for some type of formal challenge, a request for hand to hand combat for the possession of the woman.

Instead, in a vicious, purposeful motion, he yanked out the Balugaisa, took three long strides toward Melwas and thrust the spear straight into his belly with all his might. The king of the Summer Country uttered a strangled sound and clutched vainly at the spear. An'kelet continued to push forward, driving the barbs through flesh and bone, till the deadly head tore out of Melwas's back. An'kelet was almost breast to breast with his adversary, his eyes blazing with the changeling light of the warp-spasm, burning into his enemy's dying gaze. "When you touched the Lady Fynavir, most perfect of women," he said, "your life from that moment was forfeit to me. For the evil and dishonour that you have done her, may your spirit be trapped forever in these bogs and never go to the house of your Fathers!"

Melwas tried to speak, but his mouth was gushing blood. An'kelet yanked back the spear-head with its fearsome barbs, and Melwas collapsed, his innards torn to ribbons by the brutal passage of the spear. An'kelet grabbed his opponent's hair and hauled up the body, slashing the face with Arondyt, before stabbing the blade repeatedly into the dead man's groin. "There!" he cried, tossing the mutilated corpse at the feet of Melwas's oncoming men, who stopped abruptly in their tracks, fearful of this man of bronze with his mad eyes and death-wielding arm. "Melwas has no face and he is no longer a man... his spirit will not go into the Otherworld but will stay here unto eternity to pay for the sins of his days! Attend to him and do not raise your hand to me, least you meet the same doom as your accursed master!"

The villagers started to shriek and wail, even the warriors hesitating to come forward against this wild-visaged foe with his terrible weapons. An'kelet lifted the bleeding corpse of Melwas and as one last indignity to the slain chief hurled the body at his followers. It crashed into them heavily, sending them reeling back, while An'kelet resheathed the Balugaisa and shoved his way into Melwas's hut. He paused, his throat tightening, as he saw Fynavir dangling from the crossbeam of the roof, her wrists black with caked blood, her only clothing a scrap of skin. Dark bruises marred her skin...cruel finger marks. Her head hung down, hair tangling over a face too thin, too pale, with huge circles underscoring the closed eyes. As he approached, she stirred, her head slowly lifting and her eyes flickering open.

"An'kelet..." her voice was a rasp in her throat. "Where is Ardhu?"

"Not here..." An'kelet could say no more, emotion rising in him.

"But you... you have come for me..." She tried to smile, her dry lips tremulous.

"I would never leave you to such as Melwas." He strode to her side and slashed through the ropes that bound her wrists.

Her arms fell to her sides and she stumbled forward, weak and fainting. He caught her as she fell, lifting her off the ground in his arms.

"Melwas... he is dead, isn't he?" she whispered

"Yes."

"Good!" she said, with uncharacteristic viciousness. "But his men... they will kill you... us. I cannot flee with you as I am. You must leave me and save yourself."

"If I were to live and let you die, my own life would be worth nothing!" he said fiercely, brushing her knotted hair away from her bloodless face. "Either we both die here together... or we both live, to whatever end!"

Heading to the back wall of the hut, An'kelet gently set Fynavir down on the ground, where she rubbed her wrists and legs, trying to restore some circulation. While she did this, he cut a large gap in the wall with Arondyt and kicked out the wattle with several sharp blows. "Come, Fynavir," he said. "Throw your arms around my neck and climb onto my back. Hold on as tight as you can. That way, my arms will be free to fight off Melwas's men if need be."

Fynavir staggered up, clasping her shaking arms around him and folding her legs around his middle. With his two Ar-morahan daggers in hand, Arondyt in the right and Fragarak in his left, he pushed through the gap in the hut wall and raced out into the night.

The village was a scene of tumult and panic. Women were screaming and keening over the bodies of the dead, while dogs raced around, maddened by the blood-scent and the commotion. Warriors loomed up out of the smoke and the reek, faces grim, leading ordinary farming folk armed with sickles and clubs studded with deadly flint spikes.

"There he is!" one screamed, and An'kelet felt the air ripple as an arrow whirred past his head. "The bastard who killed chief Melwas! He has taken the stranger woman, the white one of ill-luck!"

"Get them!" another voice howled, full of bloodlust and rage. "Sacrifice them both in the lake!"

An'kelet started to run. Fynavir was no great weight, but he was terrified an arrow or other missile might strike her exposed back. He had an awful vision of both of them impaled by a flying spear, bound together like lovers, flesh joined to flesh in the eternity of death. 'Please, great Ancestors, let her live. Goddess, if she is really a scion of your flesh, protect her now, I beg you... I beg you!'

As they reached the edge of the village, a roaring tribesman suddenly jumped out from behind a hut, brandishing one of the lethal clubs An'kelet had spotted earlier. He swung it wildly at the Ar-morahan prince, and one of its spines ripped into the muscle of An'kelet's left arm, drawing a gush of bright blood that drenched his sleeve. An'kelet leaped back, narrowly avoiding another blow from the club, and flung Frag-arak at his adversary using his left hand, a move his enemy did not expect, for his gaze was fixed on the longer and more noticeable Arondyt. The blade somersaulted through the air, a spinning wheel of bronze fire, and struck the man firmly in the gut. He shrieked in shocked pain and crumpled to his knees, and An'kelet snatched the man's own weapon and hastily sent him to whatever gods or spirits he was vowed to.

Retrieving Frag-arak, An'kelet began to run with all speed towards the lake. On his back, Fynavir glanced over her shoulder; through the shadows she could see gesticulating figures silhouetted against new-kindled fires and the glint of flame on unsheathed metal. "They are coming! They will not give up until we are dead!"

"They may have no choice," said An'kelet, panting as he forced his legs to move even more quickly. He was now mere feet from the lakeshore, his keen eyes searching for the single coracle he had left afloat. And there it was, in the reeds, bumping gently against the half-submerged ruins of the coracles he had sabotaged.

An'kelet gestured to Fynavir and she released her hold of his neck. He lifted her into the coracle, and climbed in after her; it was a small craft, intended for only one sailor and their bodies were pressed together, his larger frame covering hers protectively. Pulling the Balugaisa from its sling, he put it to new use and pushed the craft away from the shore with a great thrust, shoving it out toward the centre of the night-shrouded lake.

"Look, they are getting away!" Torch-bearing figures were converging on the shore, running up and down as war-drums began to beat and horns blared in the shadows. Several more arrows whined in the air like angry bees and skittered across the surface of the water. "After them, in the boats... Melwas must be avenged!"

The angry villagers plunged knee-deep into the water, seeking the boats that they used everyday for fishing, the craft they knew they could manage like no others in all Albu. Their hands flapped about, groping and grasping in the cold waters…and then they found the Sunken coracles, some upended, others sinking into the mud, all damaged beyond repair.

Angry shrieks went up, rising in intensity until all voices blended into one single voice trembled and ululated, then fell in a series of wails and shrieks that sounded barely human. It was a dreadful sound and Fynavir covered her ears with her hands, even though she recognised that it was a cry of despair.

A cry of defeat.

The coracle sailed out into the lake, skimming across the wide waters under the Moon

An'kelet and Fynavir had escaped. The gods, it seemed, had smiled on them.

CHAPTER TWENTY TWO

Once An'kelet and Fynavir reached the far side of the lake, they beached the coracle and began to hastily make their way toward the South, using the conical bulk of Hwynn's Tor, black against the star-speckled mantle of the sky, as a way-marker. Fynavir was weak; her legs threatening to give way with every step, so An'kelet carried her at intervals. His own wounded arm was painful and still bleeding, a slow, dark trickle that soaked his tunic through. It was not a serious wound, but he knew it needed to be washed and bound to avoid an infection that could prove lethal.

But there was no time to attend to such matters; they had to keep moving... The lands around were still hostile territory, and the news of Melwas's death would spread swiftly as fire, as such news always did. They had to reach the lands of the Dwri to be assured of safe passage to Kham-El-Ard.

"Do you know where we are?" asked Fynavir against his shoulder, her numb, bruised feet dangling over his arm. "How long do you think it will take us to reach home?"

"Two days or slightly more if we were both fit youths blessed with fleetness of foot." An'kelet smiled grimly. "But neither of us are fit, lady."

"I know..." She touched his wet sleeve, noting how he flinched. Her fingertips came away stained dark "We need to stop... there must be a safe place where we can make camp for the night."

"I believe we are travelling near the banks of the River Brui," said An'kelet. "Another few miles and we should be out of the Summer Lands, and into friendlier places. We must not become too over-confident and let our guard down, however. Enemies and desperate men are everywhere."

"An'kelet..." She had not asked it yet, but now, glancing down, he saw her eyes troubled, tearful. "Where is my husband? Why did he not come?"

"Ardhu is wounded — he couldn't ride, Fynavir. He took a deep injury to the leg while fighting T'orc. But do not fear, his wound should heal in time."

Fynavir was silent for a while, contemplative. "He couldn't come for me... but you did."

An'kelet glanced down at her. "I could no more leave you with that bastard Melwas, than cut out my own heart with my dagger. I swore an oath to protect you... and all that is in Ardhu's kingdom."

"So that is why you rescued me? Because you swore to guard Ardhu's chattels?" Her voice was slightly bitter, disappointed.

"No, not exactly." He gave her a crooked smile nearly as bitter as the tone of her voice.

She stared up into his face and suddenly the darkness and sorrow in her eyes lifted, as night lifts before the day.

They soon found the banks of swift-flowing Brui and followed it southwards. Eventually, they reached a spot where the river curved out and was fringed by a stand of weeping willows. Within this clump of tangled foliage, they found an old midden, heaped with shells, and the charcoal from a long-dead fire. An'kelet examined the burnt remains and deduced that they were old, their makers long gone from that place.

"We will stop here for the rest of the night," he said, setting Fynavir down on the dewy grass. "I will make fire." He went to the site of the old burning, and used his strike-a-light to ignite a small heap of dried moss, leaves and bits of wood. The ignited flame was feeble, but cast some slight warmth in that wintry world.

"Let me tend to your wound," Fynavir said, when he was done "It cannot be allowed to fester. You could lose the arm — or worse."

They walked to the edge of the water and An'kelet knelt while Fynavir peeled away the shreds of his torn and bloodied sleeve, and laved the gouge in his upper arm with river-water until it was clean. An'kelet endured her ministrations in silence; not because of pain from the injury, which was slight, because he dared not speak, dared not move. Her close proximity, the touch of her hands on his skin, the glimpses of her body as she bent in the flimsy strip of skin she wore... he could scarcely endure it.

"I am no healer," she said. "But that will do until we can get you to see the Merlin. Now I must wash myself, the stink of Melwas's hut is still upon me and the stain of his hands..."

An'kelet caught her fingers, cold and white. "Fynavir, did he...hurt you?"

"If you are asking if he used me...no. But he was not...kind."

Turning her back to him, she let the filthy skin fall and waded out into the swell of the river. He could see bruises and wheals dappling her back and buttocks, and his heart twisted with anguish and rage. How could Melwas have done such a thing!

"Fynavir, be wary, the tow of the river may be too strong!" An'kelet shouted, as she swam out too far for safety, too far from his grasp. Even battered and bruised, she was beautiful and he would not be surprised if some river-spirit leapt from the depths to try and steal her away.

She returned immediately, swimming into the shallows. "What's wrong? Your face, you are white as a bone!"

Words fell from his lips, unwise words, and unguarded, but exhaustion and emotion drove him. "I could not bear to lose you again. When word came that Melwas had abducted you, it was as if I had been pierced by a thousand spears."

"And you came for me. Alone, risking all, you came for me... I owe you so much. If there is a way to repay you..."

Heat jolted through him from face to groin, despite the chill of the winter's night. "I ask for nothing, but I also would refuse nothing that you willingly gave me."

She stood up in the river, water pouring in runnels off her bare flesh, and waded towards him. He sat on the bank, transfixed, unable to tear his gaze away from the sway of her full breasts, and from her rounded hips, the soft gold at their join filled with promise and desire.

His own desire rose up in him, and he reached to her, pulling her into his arms, his mouth hungrily seeking hers. Together they fell into the shallows, water surging about them. She tugged at his tunic, yanking it over his head, and at the lacings of his deerskin trousers. Her lips and fingers ran over his taut muscles, the Sun-bronzed flesh of chest and shoulders, teasing him, maddening him, making him ache with need.

Vaguely, through a haze of desire, he was aware he was making the most momentous and terrible decision of his life. He was about to betray the vows he made to his priestess-mother, that had made him the best and most noble warrior in the world.

Worse still, he was about to betray his friend.

His king.

But he could no more stop himself now than he could stop the turning of the seasons, the rising of the Sun. It was as if both he and Fynavir had been caught in some primordial spell that bound them together and dismissed all other loyalties, giving no heed to the fate that would befall them should their tryst ever be discovered.

The icy water splashing over their flesh did not quell their ardour; but instead heightened the sensations as they lay with the weeds twined around them, caressing their skin just as they caressed each other. It was as if the Brui cleansed them, washing away the past, moulding them anew, making them, for the first time in their lives, truly whole in their union with each other.

An'kelet gazed down at Fynavir, her head thrown back, eyes closed and her lips parted. Water swelled between her breasts, glittering. "Fynavir, Fynavir…" he chanted her name like a prayer, though he knew of no gods or spirits that would bless this union.

The union of traitors. A union that could bring down a kingdom.

She opened her eyes. He saw his own image mirrored in them, his spirit trapped in their depths in all willingness.

Nothing then mattered, not Ardhu, not his mother the Priestess, not his prowess as a warrior. The only thing that mattered was this night, and the heat of his heart, and the desire of the flesh.

Dawn came too swiftly, bringing reality with its blood-red light. An'kelet woke, shivering, and glanced down. Fynavir lay asleep, half under him, wrapped in his cloak. The little fire was cold embers near her head. He shook his head, fearful and wondering and glad all at once, captivated by her beauty, her fragility, yet terrified at what he had done.

His need of her had changed him; he could not deny the unsavoury truth. The pure, almost holy quality that his mother Eilahn had conferred upon him was gone, dead, charred like the ashes of the fire. It had died in Fynavir's arms. He was forsworn to both Ardhu and the Priestess Eilahn of the Lake of Maidens. He would never be the same again.

Thinking of the night's passion, he shook his head in dismay. They had rutted like beasts out in the open, where any passer-by might have spotted them. And in the river, no less…the icy river! At the last, he had realised how cold he was, how Fynavir trembled against him like a leaf and seemed near to falling into a faint, and he knew that their actions put them both in danger of freezing to death. By the spirits, it was only just past Y'melc, too early for frolicking naked under the stars! He had carried Fynavir to shore and stoked up the fire he had kindled earlier, then bundled her under his cloak and warmed her limbs with mouth and hands. Eventually, they had both slept, growing warm by the crackling flames.

As he lay there, propping himself upright on one elbow, grief and consternation mingled on his face, Fynavir began to stir. She rolled over and gazed up into his eyes. She too looked troubled. Reaching up, she touched his arm. "An'kelet, what have we done? What are we to do now?"

He stared at the ground, unable to meet her anxious gaze. "Maybe... maybe we should head for the coast and take a boat to Ar-morah. My kin might give us shelter."

Fynavir shook her head. "No, no, that won't work. Ardhu would hunt us — he would have no choice, even if he had no stomach for it. The chiefs of Albu would demand that he take revenge, or else they would depose him as weak and unmanly. No, he would have to hunt us until one of us was dead. And if he were to bring his warband to Ar-morah, Albu would be open to sea-pirates, evil men and schemers like Morigau. They would pounce like a wildcat upon its prey, and the Isle of Prydn would burn."

"What would you have me do, then, lady?" His voice was strained. He knew what she was to say next...knew, because it was the only option.

"We must go back to Kham-El-Ard." Fynavir's voice wavered as she strove not to weep. "It is the only way. The only honourable way. We must pretend as if nothing has happened between us, that your loyalty to me is only through the friendship between you and my husband."

An'kelet pressed his hands to his forehead in frustration. "Ah, you cannot ask me to do this; it is beyond my endurance to see you at his side, in his bed, while I cannot even touch you..."

She took his hand, kissed the long, strong, golden fingers. "I will find a way...I will ask to go riding with you as my guard, and we can find some private place, some hollow... A stolen moment is better than none...Ardhu would never suspect! He loves you as his brother!"

An'kelet groaned at her last words, self-loathing washing over him in a black tide. "That he does is the worst of it, Fynavir. For I am traitor to him, and unworthy to stand as a warrior of the Circle of Khor Ghor."

She pulled away, staring at the ground, embarrassed by his obvious distress. She had never seen him so distraught, so unsure — he who was so bright and strong and certain, the rising Sun at Midsummer. "It is the only way, An'kelet. I can think of no other, unless you leave me forever from this day onwards and make your own way to your people across the sea, or to Ibherna, or even to the dark forests of the middle-lands, where men are fierce and would welcome warrior-skills such as yours. I could tell Ardhu a tale to cover your tracks — I could say you took a wound while fighting Melwas and died from fever, and that friendly locals made your pyre and I scattered your ashes into the river at dawn."

"Hush! All this talk of death!" He placed his fingers to her mouth, and then replaced them with his lips, in a kiss so deep, so powerful she felt as if he were trying to possess her spirit, to draw it from her body and bring it into him to join with his own spirit. When he finally released her, he pulled her tight against his chest and said, "I won't leave Prydn, my fair one... I will never leave you. For all the trials I may face, none could be worse that never seeing your face again. I will return to Kham-El-Ard with you, and play my part."

"It will be all right...you will see," she cried, heart leaping at the thought that he would be near her at Kham-El-Ard, and that she could somehow steal away with him. Ardhu would never find out; she'd be careful and clever.

An'kelet looked at her sadly; his smile was thin and weak. "My love...it will never be 'all right'. Never again."

Fynavir and An'kelet stood at the gates of Kham-El-Ard, gazing out across the fields toward the ancient track called the Harrow or Temple Way, which came from the West to join the centre of all things at Khor Ghor. The Merlin stood beside them, brooding and silent; his raven-sharp eyes darting first to An'kelet then to Fynavir, searching, weighing each one up. They both stood straight as spears, neither looking at the other.

"My lord Ardhu is coming," said Fynavir. "My lord, the victor over the Chief Boar, will soon be home."

Messengers had come the day before; Ba-lin and Bal-ahn and the faithful young Drem. Fynavir had rewarded them with golden mead poured by her own hand, and with ingots of bronze, and amber amulets from the cold dark sea in the north where her long-dead sire had hailed from.

And now the great aurochs-horns were blowing, their voices deep on the wind, and the men of the warband and their banners were visible on the horizon, marching steadfastly for home. At their head was Lamrai, her grey mane tossing on the morning breeze, with Ardhu seated on her back, and the wan Sun glinted off his breastplate of gold and golden belt buckle and the polished surface of the Face of Evening. The people of Kham-El-Ard cheered as he rode toward them, their young king, the victor over many foes.

But Ardhu had no eyes for any of his people, as he spurred Lamrai into a sudden gallop, and charged up the crooked hill on which his fortress stood. His eyes were only for Fynavir, standing in her gold-beaded cape, with a headdress of swan's feathers upon her hair.

"My lady, it is good to see you unharmed!" He swung from his horse's back and tossed the reins to Ka'hai. "When news of Melwas's treachery came to me, I did not think there would be a happy outcome. Praise to the spirits that you are whole and well."

He walked towards her, and she could see that he had a slight limp, and winced slightly when too much pressure was placed on his left leg. She took his hands in hers, gently, and kissed his cheeks in greeting, and the people of Kham-El-Ard cheered even louder. Drums began to beat and a reed pipe wailed out; there would be much celebrating in Ardhu's great hall for the next three days till the new Moon.

Ardhu turned to An'kelet, who stood in silence, his arms folded and his head bowed. The young chieftain's eyes were full of gratitude. He clapped the taller man on the shoulder. "My friend, how can I ever repay you? I am eternally in your debt for returning Fynavir safely to me."

"It was my duty," An'kelet murmured. "I could do naught else."

"And you killed Melwas single-handedly, saving me the trouble!"

"He is dead indeed, and cursed beyond the grave."

"Then we shall all feast tonight, in my high hall, and the men-of-words shall tell tales not only of how Ardhu the Bear felled the Chief Giant and the Chief Boar, but how the brave An'kelet, Man-of-Many-Arts, saved Fynavir White Phantom, queen of her people, from the grasp of Melwas, king of the Summer Lands!"

The crowd roared their approval, and pressed forward eagerly, sweeping all into a vast celebration that lasted from dusk to dawn every day until the Moon was new.

It was the Time of the Bhel-fires, one of the most joyous festivals in all the year for the people of Prydn. A time to worship both Father Sun and Old Earth Woman, and invoke the Ancestors that they might confer continued fecundity on man and beast.

In the circle of Khor Ghor Ardhu stood with An'kelet on his right side and Fynavir on his left, and the Merlin before all three in his robe of many teeth and claws. Above them towered the immense Door into Winter, Portal of Ghosts; while from the other massive trilithons fell shadows that slunk and stretched and veered with the movement of the Sun. The gold dagger and inlaid axes on the Gate of Kings had been unveiled and glittered warmly in the rich, dying light; symbols of Ardhu's continuing power, the greatest reign of any in Prydn since the time of Samothos, who came to Prydn nigh on five hundred years ago, following the Westward paths of the sea.

Ardhu lifted his arms toward the scarlet West, his eyes dark with emotion. "Bhel-Sunface, to whom the pyres burn this eve, I offer you my thanks for the great blessings you have conferred upon me — the defeat of T'orc, and the fall of Melwas and return of Fynavir, my wife... My wife, who is now with child and will give my kingdom an heir to take on my mantle when I am gone!"

The Merlin gestured to a priest-acolyte and a calf was led forward on a rope. Ardhu drew Carnwennan, and with a swift, brutal motion cut the animal's throat. It collapsed in a heap before the Altar Stone, blood pumping from the severed neck-vein and feeding the thirsty earth at the foot of the stone. Ardhu, without flinching, promptly slashed the palm of his own hand, letting red droplets fall to mingle with the calf's blood, signifying his own bond with the earth, with the stones of which he was earthly lord. Turning from the sacrifice, he took more blood from his hand and painted his face, and daubed it onto Fynavir's brow in the prescribed patterns of life and death and binding. Finishing, he turned to the silent An'kelet and used the last of the blood to draw similar marks on his cheeks and forehead.

"For you are as my family," Ardhu told his friend, his first warrior, acclaimed above all others in Kham-El-Ard. "So you shall share in this blessing. If not for your valour in the slaying of Melwas, this occasion would be one of sorrow and not joy."

An'kelet could find no words to say, but clasped Ardhu's hand in a tight grip.

The young chief did not see the shame and sadness in his eyes.

Instead he turned back towards the Great Trilithon, its gigantic stones blood-hued in the Sunset, and spoke to the Merlin, a sombre figure reading omens from the death-throes of the calf that Ardhu had slain. "And what does the mighty Merlin, lord of seers, have to say upon this day? What words of advice have the spirits of this holy place whispered in your ear?"

Merlin sighed; he was getting old, and felt the pains of age more strongly every passing day. He wondered if Morigau had cursed him in some way. The thought made him cantankerous, and more afraid than ever that soon he would not be able to guide and watch over Ardhu and the Five Cantrevs of the West.

"They say only that when the enemies outside the fold are vanquished, the wise ruler will look for greater enemies within," he said sourly.

Ardhu shook his head, his eyes burning with the force of his belief. "I do not have that fear, Merlin. My warriors shall forever form a stalwart circle

279

around me, even as the Stones of Khor Ghor stand in their unbroken circle for eternity."

He turned to Fynavir, smiled. "Are you ready?"

"I am, lord." She bowed her head, the blood on her face blazing like the sky.

"And An'kelet, my friend, my brother?"

The Man of Bronze raised his spear Balugaisa in salute to the stones, to the spirits, to his King…and to his Queen. "I am ready, lord!"

"Then let us go forth and feast, and jump the Bhel-fires on Kham-El-Ard!"

Taking the White Phantom's hand in his own, the Stone Lord of Prydn passed under the colossal arch of Winter's Door and strode across the Great Plain towards the setting Sun.

STONE LORD: HISTORICAL NOTES

First and foremost I must thank all those who supported me in writing this novel, especially the Stonehenge team, my partner Dan Rendell (who created the blog and did lots of PR) and artist Frances Quinn, who painted the cover. For more of Frances' work, see http://echdhu.deviantart.com/

Stone Lord is a historical novel, perhaps even more properly a historical *fantasy* novel, due to its use of Arthurian themes and the remoteness of the time period in which it is set. It is NOT proposing a new theory on Stonehenge or King Arthur. It came about simply because there appears to be older, mythic substrata in the Arthurian mythos — hence among other things, anachronistic mentions of Stonehenge (eerily accurate in some respects: the bluestones did come from the west, and it is a burial ground.) The idea of hurling swords into lakes and the sword in the stone could also easily be prehistoric; water deposition is well known and Stonehenge itself has a 'sword in the stone' — the famous dagger carving on one of the inner trilithons.

Most of the places in STONE LORD are real and can be visited today — Stonehenge, Durrington Walls, Woodhenge, Marden henge, Avebury, Silbury, West Kennet barrow and the Sanctuary. Others exist but are on private land — the site for Kham-el-Ard, the sacred pool and the 'Old Henge' by the river, while others existed but are now gone... the settlement called Place-of-Light is Boscombe Down, where the rich Amesbury Archer burial was found. A sculpture near the housing development commemorates him today.

In regards to dating, I have deliberately not given STONE LORD an exact date. It takes place after the main phases of Stonehenge are complete, but as the beaker culture is waning, so approximately the time of 'Wessex I'--the Bush Barrow 'king' of 1900 BC wears similar gold ornaments to Ardhu. However, I have kept some of the earlier 'beaker' traditions in the story.

Durrington Walls plays a large part in several scenes involving the winter solstice; however, in reality this huge settlement had fallen out of use by the time of Wessex I. Using it is deliberate artistic license on my part! I have mentioned that burial mounds were encroaching on the site, which is what did happen during the Bronze Age.

For naming characters I decided to modify the familiar Arthurian names to give them a more 'archaic' flavour, something that sounded 'proto-Celtic' (since many now believe some form of the Celtic languages were in Britain by 2500 BC, brought via trade with Europe's Atlantic.) Some are based on the names of mythic characters that do in fact seem to be earlier prototypes for the Arthurian characters... Excalibur derives from Caladbolg, sword of an Irish hero, while Guinevere's name is cognate in meaning with Findabhair, daughter of the ancient Irish Queen Medbh.

Rituals are of necessity my own creation, but I have based them on cultures at a similar developmental stage, and also what we do know — that there was an emphasis on sun, moon, and death at most stone circles. This was not so much an era of gods and goddesses but of powerful spirits... it was later in the Bronze Age that the deities took on human faces.

As for the antagonists, this was difficult. Obviously they couldn't be Saxons, as in the original Arthurian legends. So I was a bit 'creative' and loosely based them on the Sea Peoples who harried lands around the Mediterranean later in the Bronze Age, and on the Phoenicians who supposedly sailed to Britain to purchase tin (although no Phoenician artefacts have been found in Britain.)

For anyone desiring to learn more about ancient Britain, both the monuments and possible beliefs, I recommend the following books:

STONEHENGE by Mike Parker Pearson
RITES OF THE GODS, STONE CIRCLES OF THE BRITISH ISLES, and PREHISTORIC AVEBURY by Aubrey Burl
BRITAIN 3000 BC by Rodney Castleden
WARFARE IN PREHISTORIC BRITAIN by Julian Heath
PREHISTORIC SHAMANISM by Mike Williams

You can also visit the STONE LORD blog at — http://stone-lord.blogspot.com for more discussions on prehistory and various aspects of the book.

Lightning Source UK Ltd.
Milton Keynes UK
UKOW032031221112

202638UK00001B/280/P